EXONERATED

◆ ◆ ◆

A Mystery

◆ ◆ ◆

S.A. DYMOND

Published by Chunky Pops Publishing, LLC

Cover Art by Darcie Saleh.

Library of Congress Catalog-in-Publication Data:
Dymond, S.A.
Exonerated/ S.A. Dymond
pages; cm. - (Exonerated)
TXu001806569 / 2012-04-15
ISBN 978-0-9969677-2-3 (hardcover)
ISBN 978-0-9969677-0-9 (eBook)
ISBN 978-0-9969677-1-6 (eBook)

STEP 1: The Premeditated Act

The mangled piece of flesh plopped into the jar's tinted liquid. It swayed unevenly as it slowly sank, leaving a trail of liquid crimson tentacles that faded to pink before dissolving. When the flesh came to rest on the bottom, he tightened the lid and put the jar aside, turning back to her. With a long breath, he took her in from toes to head, relishing, almost giddy. The contorted look of pain that was frozen on her face twisted his lips into a devilish grin. He felt the urge to contemplate the meaning of her final expression, but he had little time. He couldn't dally. He still had work to do.

Carefully removing his leather gloves and replacing them with heavy rubber ones pulled from his duffle bag, he grabbed her limp, blood-smeared hand and dipped her fingertips into the small bucket, making sure each digit was at least halfway submerged. After a full minute, he removed her fingers and examined the tips. Frowning beneath his mask, he picked up the small metal bristle pad, isolated her index finger over the bucket's rim, and went to work scrubbing vigorously underneath her fingernail until the nail was thinned and her finger pad was nonexistent. He repeated the process on each finger, then moved on to her other hand and started with the acid again. Once satisfied with her fingernails, he meticulously checked the rest of her body for any substance holding his genetic code. He went so far as to sweep the body with a blue light.

He found nothing, but still he checked a second time.

Only when he was certain that no one else would find anything, he slung the duffle over his shoulder, grabbed his memento of preserved flesh and the bucket of acid, and slipped out the back door.

◆ ◆ ◆

FIVE DAYS LATER

With eyes squinted and coffee in hand, Ed Roletti exited the convenience store and strode to his cruiser. He pulled out the sunglasses from his shirt pocket and threw them on. The rays from the midday sun struck the bald spot on the back of his head, heating his exposed scalp. He found it annoyingly uncomfortable—not so much because of the heat, but because, despite only being in his late twenties, he was losing his hair. Soon enough, he conceded grudgingly, he'd have to apply sun block to his bald spot.

Sighing, he leaned against his cruiser and took a sip of coffee. Glancing around the parking lot, his mind wandered off. He recalled a time when his father had taken him to this very convenience store to get a slushie. He'd guzzled it down so fast that he got brain freeze before his father had paid for the thing. Smiling at the memory, he took another sip of coffee. The police radio in his cruiser broke his reverie.

"All units. All units," the female operator's voice called out. "One—eight—seven. Repeat. One eighty seven. Address: 54 Oakmont Drive. One female. Over."

Gravity took hold of the cup of coffee released from Ed's hand. It crashed to the asphalt, popping the lid off. Hot coffee splattered, striking Ed's slacks. *What?! It can't be!* He took a deep breath and brought the microphone to his mouth. "What's that address again?" he asked with a quivering voice, gripping the CB tighter to control the shake of his hand.

"Five four Oakmont. Over."

He threw the door to his cruiser open and frantically jumped in, starting it up and switching on the sirens simultaneously.

The operator was saying something but her voice barely registered in his mind as he slammed the cruiser in reverse, the screeching tires momentarily overpowering the siren's song. He jammed the gear in drive and peeled out of the parking lot, heading straight for 54 Oakmont, knowing the route all too well. He moved down Laggertown Road recklessly, kicking up dirt, gravel and grass as he shot around a pick-up truck too slow to heed his siren's call on the two-laned thoroughfare. She must've been incorrect, he thought. The operator must've misstated the address. It couldn't be 54 Oakmont, he tried to convince himself. It just couldn't.

But as he turned onto Oakmont and cut around the bend, he knew. A perimeter of police cruisers had been set up around the small, white house, blue and red lights flashing in a deluge that he observed through bleary eyes. He blinked, setting free his tears, his throat tightening. *No! No! It can't be! It can't be her!* His head shook in defiance of reality. He slammed on the brakes just behind a squad car and clawed at the door, exiting in a sprint, head down. He had to reach to her! He knew he could save her if he just got to her in time.

He looked up to find yellow tape but its significance failed to register. He dodged around a cruiser and split two of his colleagues, bumping into both men in his effort to get by.

"What the -," Officer Ray Lucen yelled out at his back. Ed barely heard him. Then, louder, "Stop him!"

All heads on the porch turned at the commotion, eyes finding Ed.

"Stop him!" Ray hollered again. "Don't let him in! Ed! Don't go in! Ed!"

Still, the shouts didn't fully register in Ed's mind. He needed to get inside his childhood home. He needed to help his little sister. He could save her if he only got to her in time! When he reached the porch stairs, he looked up to find Chief Byron Stadmore coming toward him quickly. He tried to dodge left but the Chief, despite his age, agilely compensated, embracing Ed in a bear hug. Ed flailed and yelled but the Chief held tight. He bobbed his head around the Chief and noticed that a gaggle of officers had formed up ranks, blocking his path. *Why won't they let me save her?!*

The Chief, still holding tight, spoke soothingly in Ed's ear. "You can't go in there, son."

"Mary!" Ed bellowed, reality dawning. He began to bawl as the fight in him ebbed, his grief taking hold. But he battled it, renewing his efforts, trying desperately to break free of the Chief's grip. "No! Mary!" At that moment, he hated the Chief and the other officers in his path. *Why won't they let me help my sister?!*

The Chief's grip constricted around Ed's torso. "She's gone, Ed," he said softly, his face close enough that his breath gusted against Ed's ear.

Ed continued to fight. "My sister!" he wailed, twisting. He couldn't give up. "My little sister!"

Strong hands gripped the sides of Ed's face. "She's gone, Ed," the Chief said sternly, eye to eye, hands squeezing firmly. "You hear me? She's gone."

Shocked back into the moment, Ed's eyes widened, his lower lip quivered, and his chest shuddered with sobs.

"There's nothing in there you want to see," the Chief declared firmly, his bushy, grayed mustache quivering. "You understand me?"

After a moment staring into the Chief's eyes, Ed dropped his head and sobbed.

Some time later, after Ed's tear ducts had run dry, the Chief whispered to the side, "take him back to the station."

Ed looked up as Ray's hands grabbed at his torso. "Ed," Ray said consolingly, "let's go to the station, buddy." He pried Ed's grip loose from the Chief's uniform. "Come on," his friend coaxed. Ed had no fight left. He let Ray all but carry him away.

They got to the cruiser and Ray placed Ed in the passenger's seat.

Ed was numb, his face bloated and tear-strewn, eyes red-rimmed, gaze blank, mind distant. Then, a solitary, momentous question popped into his mind. "Why her?" he asked just before Ray shut the door, the question escaping his lips on its on volition. "Why?" he asked, looking up into Ray's face.

Ray's lips pursed, his head shaking briefly before he looked away.

Ed needed an answer, he needed a justification, something to explain it, to make it seem bearable. His gaze held on Ray, waiting for some sense of reassurance, however slight.

It was a long moment before Ray answered. "God only knows, Ed. God only knows."

STEP 2: The Investigation

Step 2.1

After Ed was taken away, Chief Byron Stadmore returned to the porch. Robby exited the house, his navy blue windbreaker flapping in the light summer breeze, his forensics kit in his left hand. “What do you got?” Byron asked.

The head forensics investigator shook his rotund head, his helmet of thick chocolate hair billowing gently in the light summer breeze. “It’s a grisly one, Chief. Got strangulation marks around the neck, and multiple stab wounds to the vitals.” He scratched at his tightly trimmed goatee with broad, pudgy fingers. “The Examiner will have to tell us cause of death.”

Byron cogitated on that for a few seconds while he dabbed his brow with a handkerchief to mop up the beads of sweat. “What else?”

Robby exhaled audibly. “She’s been cut up good, sir. Mutilated almost beyond recognition. Slashes all over her face, her tits half cut off, arms and hands slashed up…which is consistent with a defensive posture, but the rest…”

The rest, Byron knew, didn’t need to be said. He shook his head. “At least we know she fought back.” *Hopefully the mutilation took place post-mortem…*

Robby nodded hesitantly.

“What about rape?”

“Strangely enough, she’s still got her panties on.” He shook his head, a befuddled look on his face. “We’ll have to leave it to the Examiner.” He shook his head again before adding, “my guess is the answer will be ‘yes.’”

Bryon pursed his lips, thinking back on his time as a cop. “I’ve been in this Department for 34 years, Robby, and been Chief for eight, and I’ve never heard of nothing like this happening in this town.” He turned his gaze to the front door of the house. “I suppose I'll go and take a look." He patted Robby on the shoulder and moved to enter the house.

"Mind where you walk," Robby called after him. "There might be some rooks puking on the floor in there."

Byron raised his hand in acknowledgement of the inapt comment before somberly lifting the yellow tape and scooting under it.

The tiny house was abuzz, cops of different ranks scouring the place. Rookies were searching the living room, flipping the cushions on the dingy, mauve-colored couch that looked old enough to be original to the house. Crime scene technicians had their dusters and kits out and were closely examining the television, the walls, the carpet, and the remotes. Byron moved into the kitchen, where the murder took place. Mary's body—or what must have been Mary's body—was sprawled out on the linoleum floor, cut up worse than Robby had described, in Bryon's opinion. He threw his handkerchief over his mouth to stifle the reek of dead flesh sweltered by the summer heat. The flash from Detective Suarez's camera went off in an erratic pattern, briefly highlighting portions of Mary's body that were otherwise cast in shadow by the semi-opaque curtains.

Unbecoming of a veteran, Byron gaped. Mary's brown, shoulder-length hair was matted with dried blood that clumped together, forming a handful of burgundy locks, which, along with the pallid, bluish complexion of death, gave her the semblance of a nightmarish medusa. Checkerboard slashes covered Mary's face. One gash on her cheek was so deep and so wide that Byron was able to see her teeth. He had seen many deaths in his days, many homicides, many putrid, fetid bodies, but the sight of a row of teeth through opened flesh made him cringe, and he jerked his head away. Pretending to be surveying the room, he glanced around furtively to see if any of his men had noticed. He couldn't look soft in front of his men, he reminded himself, and he vowed not to turn away before he saw the extent of it. Besides, he had held this girl on his lap as a child. She demanded his respect. And so did her brother.

He gave Officer Nuck a perfunctory nod and turned back to what used to be Mary, resuming his examination where he'd left off. Her breasts were mutilated, just as Robby had said—chopped to the point where one had been entirely removed, leaving raw, red flesh exposed in chunks. The knifework, Byron concluded summarily, was anything but precise. Only a dull blade could have done that. He prayed that it was performed after her death. His eyes moved down to her distended midriff, which was smeared in swirls of multi-shaded blood that darkened near the epicenter of each stab wound. Thank God she had her panties on, because Byron didn't what to know what the killer had done down there. He'd leave that one to the Medical Examiner. It was enough that he'd have to read the report.

His gaze darted back to Mary's face. Her eyes were closed, and he wondered transiently if the first man on sight closed them or if Mary had managed to do it herself. In either case, he had no desire to see the pain and torment permanently marked in those lifeless orbs.

"I can't believe it's Ed's sis, Chief," Jim said, stepping up next to Byron and peering down at the body. The captain and head of Byron's Homicide Unit stood with his hands on his hips, his lower lip fat with tobacco, his beer gut displacing his tie slightly off-center. He sucked on the wad of chew in his mouth and yanked up his pants with a wiggle.

"Me neither, Jimbo." Byron looked her up and down again. "I knew her as a child. Served with her father. Such a sweet girl."

Jim curled his lip, extracting tobacco juice. "Yeah, well, someone's going to pay for this. We'll get him," he said confidently. He headed for the back door, threw it open and spat a glob of brown liquid on the ground, then wiped the back of his hand across his mouth.

Byron quickly surveyed the kitchen. Bloodstains covered the old, yellowed stove in abstract patterns, as if a live chicken had been butchered directly on it in preparation for dinner; and sitting next to the stove in an orderly fashion were three knives of various sizes—two bloody and the other, strangely, perfectly clean. Detective Watkins was dusting the knife handles. The icebox stood ajar, its only contents a handful of condiments and a milk carton turned on its side, slowly dripping white liquid onto the shelf below where it pooled and congealed. A box of cheerios lay on the counter next to the icebox, small circular pieces of cereal strewn about the counter and floor, some crushed to pulp, others intact, some painted red.

He'd seen enough. Byron left the house and headed for the station. He turned his thoughts to his junior officer, wondering what he'd say to Ed.

◆ ◆ ◆

"There's got to be DNA from the killer in this house somewhere," Captain Jim Pollack barked at the detectives and officers in the room, his speech taking on a slight drawl due to the wad of chew wedged between his lip and lower gums. "The way this went down…looks like she put up a fight." He glanced around. "Find me something to work with, damn it. Prints, blood, hair, spit, cum…"

Officer Smith walked by, her lithe hips swaying hypnotically under the tightness of her police belt.

After managing to pull his attention away from her ass, Jim said, "Sorry 'bout that, Tammy," with little actual remorse.

"Go fuck your balls, Jimbo," she sassed him.

He smiled widely, shifting the chew to his right lower lip. Feeling the need to justify himself, he called after her, "You're the only female officer in my unit."

She flicked him the bird over her shoulder as she exited the front door of the house.

"My kind of girl," he muttered, placing his hands back on his hips. "Right," he yelled at everyone, "like I was saying. Prints, blood, hair, spit, cum. Find me some. The killer left something here." He watched his men work for a moment before heading to the back door to spit. He narrowly missed Officer Royce with a stream of brown juice, then headed back inside, but not before apologizing to Royce for the near mishap, of course. He still retained some of the manners his mother had taught him.

Officer Nuck approached him at the door. "Found these two, Captain," Nuck said, holding up two bags of evidence.

Jim squinted, reaching out to bring the left bag closer. He released it and examined the right bag. "Two killers?" he questioned the officer.

Nuck glanced at the blonde strand, then at the black strand. He shrugged. "Could be."

"Please tell me you found one of them on the body," he said expectantly. "Or both."

Nuck shook is head. "Living room, sir."

Jim worked his chew for a second, marginally disappointed. “It’s a start, I suppose. Mark them and get them to the lab.”

“Will do, Cap.” Nuck strode off.

Jim stepped up to the body and crouched down while examining the victim’s feet. Finding nothing out of the ordinary—other than black, sparkly nail polish on her toenails—Jim looked over at Robby, who was on his knees meticulously combing the body with a magnifying glass. Every few seconds Robby prodded flesh or dried blood with tweezers or a swab. “Got anything, Robby?” Jim asked as he rose to his feet, grunting, his girth making it a bit of a struggle. He was left a little winded. *Fucking A, I got to get to the gym one of these days.*

Robby didn’t answer, and Jim saw fit not to interrupt the head forensics investigator. So he waited, idly pulling on the chew in his lip.

Finally, after muttering a curse under his breath, Robby looked up. “She looks to be clean,” he noted, sounding incredulous. “I searched her twice. Nothing. The lab might be able to tell us if we got two types of blood here, but I don’t see any other possible anomalies.” He met Jim’s eyes. “Best we could hope for is semen inside her…and you almost hope not to find that.”

Jim exhaled. “Unless it’s all we got.”

“Unless it’s all we got,” Robby echoed dolefully. “Whoever did this cleaned up his tracks but good.” He eyed Jim, a befuddled look on his face. “And where’s the rest of her tit?”

Jim raised his brow in response. It was a good question that had, unfortunately, too many potential answers. Of course the sickest one popped into Jim’s head. He pictured a guy hunched over the body, gorging on flesh. He shook himself. “We’ll get him.”

“How do you know it was a ‘he’ that killed her, cocksuckers?” Tammy asked wryly as she walked by, that droll smile dotting her pretty face.

Jim smiled fondly.

Step 2.2

Doctor Harold Costello lifted his wizened face from the body lying before him and slowly straightened his frail, old frame. "Get back there and put a mask on," he growled, his shaky voice holding tones of anger, his gloved finger extended menacingly, albeit shakily.

Jim threw his hands up in the air, and with an expression of feigned penitence, wheeled and headed for the supply shelf next to the entrance. He grabbed a paper mask from the box and strapped it on his face.

"And gloves too," the Doc yelled over his shoulder, returning to the body.

Sighing through a paper barrier, Jim grabbed two latex gloves and snapped them on. He approached Mary's body and the Chief Medical Examiner.

The Doc dropped his scalpel on the metal tray, rattling the other utensils. "Couldn't you wait for my report?" he asked Jim, clearly annoyed. "I'm only halfway finished."

"Couldn't wait on this one, Doc," Jim responded earnestly, his mask muffling his voice.

The wrinkly folds on the periphery of the Doc's mask vibrated. "You young pups are always so eager," he commented grumpily.

Jim chuckled under is breath. Having turned 52 last month, he was far from a young pup. But in comparison to the Doc, who must have been close to 80, he supposed he would always be a youngster.

The Doc grabbed a lancet from the tray and made an incision above Mary's heart, then grabbed forceps and spread the flesh open. Mary's skin and meat—and presumably rib bones—made a crinkling noise as they parted.

Jim flinched at that sound and the callous manner in which the Doc made it.

"What is it you want to know, Detective?" the Doc asked, seemingly resigned to Jim's presence.

"It's captain, not detective."

The Doc's eyes flickered callously.

"For starters," Jim said, "did you find any DNA of my killer?"

The Doc glanced at his notepad and shook his bald, vein-covered head. "Nothing worth testing located on the exterior of the integumentary system." He shoved his hand between the opened forceps down to his wrist and began twisting it, the visible portions of his face scrunching in exertion. The sound emitted from Mary's chest cavity was a squishy one.

Jim turned away and fought back a gag. *Why the hell did I come down here?* "In English please, Doc."

His response was brusque. "Nothing on the exterior of the skin, in the hair, or under the fingernails. In fact, the fingernails were doused with a highly potent cleaner—possibly an acid—and scrubbed to the point of severe abrasion. She no longer has fingerprints. The only thing you'll find under the fingernails is bone." He held up Mary's hand demonstratively with his free hand while twisting his other hand some more.

The flesh underneath Mary's fingernails was gone, all right, and the cream of her bones stuck out like lollypops partially peeled away from their wrappers. It was odd that Jim hadn't noticed that at the crime scene.

"A relative will have to confirm her identity." The Doc looked as if he was trying to yank Mary's heart out.

Jim cringed, thinking of Ed having to look upon his sister in this condition.

"I have yet to check the orifices, of course. So the possibility of finding something to send to the lab remains open."

Jim kept his gaze on Mary's feet, once again noticing the black nail polish. Ignoring the squishy sound and the Doc's horse grunts, he asked, "Any signs of rape?"

The Doc eyed his notepad. "A cursory review suggests signs of penetration and trauma consistent with significant force."

"So that's a yes?" he asked facetiously.

In response, the Doc yanked his hand free of Mary's chest cavity amid a popping sound, as if he had just opened a jar of pickles. He peeled off his gloves and turned to his notepad. He made notations while maundering to himself, then picked up his handheld recorder and maundered some medical jargon into the machine. When he finally stopped talking, he glanced up at the large clock on the wall. "Ah," he said, whipping off his smock and tossing it into a receptacle. "Time for lunch." He shuffled to the door.

Jim shook his head as he followed in the Medical Examiner's wake. He supposed he would get some lunch. Maybe vegetarian today.

◆ ◆ ◆

Criminal investigations needed to be thorough. Otherwise, what was the point? The crime went unsolved, the victim's family and friends were denied proper closure, or even worse, the perp walked, his or her criminal actions effectively sanctioned by the government. It was surprising, then, how many investigations failed to be comprehensive, failed to uncover sufficient evidence to hold up in court. Whether due to illegal procedure, incompetence, lack of a cohesive front, an overloaded caseload, or mere shoddy police work, this failing happened to the best police units from time to time. Captain Jim Pollack liked to think that his small Homicide Unit was immune to such problems, but the truth was, it had fallen victim to one or all of these bases at one time or another during his tenure at its head.

Moving down the wide corridor in the police station, Jim strengthened his resolve, vowing not to let anything fall through the cracks on this investigation. He vowed to push his detectives and officers until they gave all they could...and then gave some more. This homicide affected one of their own, after all, which meant it affected them. Anything but a thorough and complete investigation would be a personal affront to Jim, and a personal failure. He wouldn't let Ed fall victim to shoddy police work. That would be too cruel and twisted a fate. And how would it make Ed feel about his colleagues, about his profession? Yes, Jim's resolve was strengthened.

He gritted his teeth as he entered the small briefing room, making his way down the narrow center aisle, glancing left and right at the detectives and officers comprising his team for this investigation. The chatter died down and officers made for their seats.

"All right," Jim said loudly, placing his file on the front desk and wheeling at the whiteboard. "Let's get started." He tapped the black marker in his hand.

"*The Albany Times-Union* has reported on this case on the front page of today's newspaper," Detective Watkins cut in, his tone informative and flat, today's paper held above his tapered head. The man's head looked like an upside-down squash. His beady eyes, which were magnified by thick, oversized glasses, inspected Jim in an emotionless, automated manner. For some reason, despite having worked together for a number of years, the look of his head still made Jim shiver. A good detective, thorough and efficient, but socially awkward, formalistic in his police work, rigid in his personal routines.

"Made *The Post* and *The Daily News*, also," Officer Royce added from the back.

Jim nodded grimly, scrunching his three chins. He didn't need to explain the gravity of their investigation but he saw fit to drive the point home nonetheless. "Yep, it's a big one, all right. More so because it affects our family than because of its newsworthiness. But that's just another reason to get this one right. We're under the spotlight." He flipped open his file and perused it. "Suarez, did you get in touch with the neighbor yet?"

"I did," the newly-minted detective responded, glancing down at his notepad, his brown wavy hair dropping to cover his swarthy face. Jim swore the man got darker everyday. It made Jim wonder whether the detective was working or sunbathing. Ernie brushed the strands away before speaking. "Gretchen Holland. Lives at 133 Oakmont. Said that normally when she drove home from work each evening, Mary would be working in the garden on the side of the house. On May 25th, Mary wasn't outside and she noticed that no lights were on in the house, so she assumed Mary was out for the evening. The next night, she saw the same thing. Said she thought that maybe Mary was out of town. On the 27th, she passed the house around noon and noticed that Mary's front door was ajar. That's when she called it in." He flipped the page of his notepad. "Didn't recall any suspicious vehicles or people, or anything else of note."

"How far away's her house?" Jim asked.

"Pretty far. Must be eight or nine acres separating the two."

"Too far away to hear any screams, then."

Suarez nodded.

"All right. Who searched the area surrounding the house?"

"That'd be me and Parker and Legs," Officer Royce responded, his eagerness evident in his tone.

"Legs?" Jim exclaimed. "Who the hell is Legs?"

"That's me, Captain," Officer Eng said, his eyes downcast in embarrassment.

"Do I want to know where that nickname came from?" Jim asked Eng dryly. "No wait!" He put the back of his hand to his forehead and closed his eyes in feigned pensiveness. "Let me guess. You…cross-dress on the weekends. Your tranny name is Beatrice."

The room laughed. Eng reddened.

"So what is it then?"

"I shave my legs."

"Mmhmm," Jim murmured, quizzical. Did he really want to know why? *Hell yeah.*

Legs glanced at his neighbor's cockled face and did a double-take. He looked back at Jim. "There's other reasons to shave your legs," he defended.

Jim stared at the rookie with narrowed eyes, waiting for Eng to continue before he had to prod him. He didn't like where this was going.

"I'm a swimmer!" Legs exclaimed defensively, throwing his palms up. "Makes me more aerodynamic."

Jim shrugged, satisfied. "All right, Legs. You find anything?"

"Nothing out of the ordinary. We found some rabbit traps set near the wood line and an axe, but nothing bloody -"

"The garden," Parker threw in.

This was what Jim loved about young officers—they were so eager to say something that they often said the most idiotic things. It gave Jim plenty of material to work with… "Well, I'll be damned," he cried out, pacing rigidly, one hand on his belt to hold up his pants. "A garden! Did you inventory the vegetables, Parker? Let's see…we got tomatoes, cucumbers, squash, maybe some herbs—cilantro, basil." He stepped over and leaned down into Parker's face. "I sure hope you confiscated it all so we can make a salad for lunch." He stood up. "Smith!" he called to the female officer while keeping his eyes on Parker the entire time. "How about you go get us some salad dressing."

Parker recoiled, looking dejected.

"Vinaigrette or ranch, boss?" Tammy retorted.

The officers laughed raucously. Detective Suarez snorted coffee out his nose. "Shit," Suarez sputtered, reaching for a napkin.

Detective Watkin's face was blank, his eyes mechanical.

Weirdo. Jim smiled, his breathing heavy from his rant. He needed to lose weight, he conceded. The alternative was to forego taunting his officers, which, he quickly decided, was no option at all. Ribbing the young bucks was too much fun. Turning back to business, he asked, "No footprints in the garden, Parker?"

The rookie shook his head.

"Forensics," Jim prompted.

"We got nothing right now," Robby responded. "Examiner's not done with the autopsy. We pulled a handful of prints from the house, and we got two different strands of hair, but the lab work hasn't come back."

Jim huffed, causing his gut to bounce. "Am I going to get to write anything on this whiteboard? You all know you love my handwriting. Don't you want to see my handwriting? All you got to do is give me a reason to write." He paused to let that seep in. "Anybody, now. Does anybody have anything?"

Officer Smith raised her hand.

"Ah. Tammy. Listen up boys to what a real officer has to say."

"No signs of forced entry."

"You hear that boys? You know what that means?"

"It suggests that the victim knew the killer," Detective Watkins ventured tonelessly.

"No," Jim yelled. "Means I get to write on this here whiteboard with this here marker." He yanked off the marker top and began writing, the squeak of the marker the only sound in the room. "And yes," he yelled, swiveling round and stepping to the side to reveal the word *ASSOCIATION* on the whiteboard. "Bill is correct. Chances are, Mary knew the killer." Jim resumed his pacing. "What's the next move?"

"Speak to the family members about Mary's associations," Detective Watkins answered.

"Bill!" Jim exclaimed, upset, but thinking he should've known that Bill would've answered. "Stop answering for the rooks. They'll never learn if you keep giving them the answers."

"They may not learn anyway, Captain," Bill retorted mechanically, not a hint of sarcasm in his tone.

"You hear that. You going to let that affront go unanswered? Parker, who should we speak to?"

Parker's expression was one of serious cogitation. "How about Ed?"

"Holy shit!" Jim said exaggeratedly. "The boy has a brain after all." He scanned the room and stopped at Officer Lucen. "Ray. You think you can speak to Ed?"

Ray nodded hesitantly. "He's in bad shape, Cap, but I'll see what I can get."

"Be discreet. We don't want him thinking about the investigation too deeply, or worse, going vigilante on some past boyfriend."

Ray nodded again.

"Suarez," Jim followed up, "speak to Ed's mother. See if you can get the names of Mary's boyfriends and friends. Where'd Mary work?"

"Star Diner," Ray responded.

"Bill, you speak to her work colleagues."

Detective Watkins nodded.

"Rooks—I want you out on State Street, speaking to the business owners and employees, seeing if they noticed anything or anyone suspicious in the area. Time for you rooks to get some hair on your chest…even you, Legs."

The room cackled, including Legs.

Jim held up his hand to quiet them. "All right. Let's find this guy and put him where he belongs. No mistakes. No holes. Let's show the nation what Schenectady County PD can do."

Step 2.3

He knocked on the door lightly, but no one answered. Grimacing, he knocked louder. Still no answer. He reached for the door handle and gave it a gentle twist. Finding it unlocked, he cracked open the door and slowly popped in. Despite his slim build, the weathered floors creaked under him. “Ed?” Ray called. “You home?”

No answer.

“Ed,” he said louder.

No answer.

The small house was dark and musty. Perhaps Ed was visiting his mother at the Rockwall Old Age Home. Recognizing the worst possibility but remaining optimistic, Ray decided to investigate. He shut the door behind him. “Ed,” he called upstairs. “Hello!”

No answer.

As he headed for the stairs, he caught movement out of the corner of his eye. He flinched, fixing his gaze through the kitchen to the back porch. After a second of squinting, he recognized the movement. Framed by the kitchen window, the very top of a rocking chair’s backrest swayed, its even motion giving it a rhythmic quality despite the utter lack of sound. From this distance, no head was visible in the chair. Although he knew in the back of his mind that it was Ed in the rocking chair, Ray moved through the kitchen cautiously, unable to fight his police instincts in the dimly lit house. The hinges on the screen door protested as he pushed it open, then sprung into action as he released it. The door slammed into the frame, bouncing in waning, concussive impacts. Ed, rocking in an oversized red chair with a small doll in his lap, didn’t even twitch. *Not good.*

Ray studied his friend, thinking back to when they met on the first day of their police training. Ed had been vivacious then. All he’d talked about was being able to start his career as a cop, about being able to follow in his father’s footsteps. Now, he was a shell of that eager man. It was difficult to tell in the small, screened porch, with the sun below the vista of forest, but Ed’s face seemed thin, his cheeks hollow, and his hair disheveled despite its cropped length. He had stubble on his drawn face—likely two days worth—and his mouth sat slightly ajar. His red-rimmed eyes gazed off into the distant woods.

Ray gazed into those eyes, examining, expecting to find pain. Instead, he found what seemed to be a depthless well of hate, a raw emotion that supplanted any possible sorrow. Ray's eyes widened frighteningly. He knew that look—the look of a man that would stop at nothing to get vengeance, the look of a killer. Ray swallowed hard. Bolstering that queasy feeling was Ed's grip on a small doll, which gave the impression that he was attempting to strangle it. The notion of a voodoo trick brushed Ray's thoughts before he pushed it aside. Ed was not the type, Ray judged. Besides, didn't you need to know the exact person you wanted to injure to perform voodoo, and wouldn't you use a male doll to hurt a man? Finding his train of thought preposterous, Ray shook himself. "Ed. Hey buddy," he said softly while sitting in a chair facing his friend.

Ed's face slowly turned and his rocking slowed, its rhythm broken by the intrusion. He exhaled loudly through his nose.

"You need anything, Ed?"

Ed's eyes returned to the forest behind his small house. "No," he answered in a resigned tone.

Ray took a deep breath. "Everyone at the station sends their deepest condolences, Ed." He paused, groping for the right words. Not finding them, he said, "I know it's difficult, Ed, this whole ordeal, but I need to get some information from you."

Ray presumed that Ed's silence was acquiescence. "Was Mary in a relationship?"

Ed rolled his neck and stared at the doll, turning it in his hands. "Nothing serious."

"Was she dating anyone in particular that you know of?"

"She dated a lot of guys," he answered, his eyes still fixed on the doll. "I couldn't keep track of them all."

Frowning discreetly, Ray asked, "What about ex-boyfriends? Did she recently break up with anyone?"

Ed perked up at the question and the blaze behind his eyes flared, as if things had come together in an acute moment of understanding. "Dennis," Ed grated. "They dated for six months or so and Mary called it off months ago." He looked down at the doll again before turning to regard Ray, his lucidity seemingly returned. "There was something off about that guy, Ray. I never liked him." His face pinched in anger.

Ray fretted, wondering what his friend would do, contemplating if he knew Ed as well as he thought he did. "You know his last name?" Ray pulled out his pocket notepad.

"Kerisol. Dennis Kerisol."

Ray jotted the name down. "Anyone else?"

"Before that…John something…can't remember his last name. That lasted only a few weeks. Guy before that was Chucky. Chucky Dericardo."

Ray wrote the names down. "What about her friends? Anything unusual you recall? Any fights or arguments?"

After a moment Ed said, "No. But Jenny was her best friend. She may know something. Jenny Johansson."

Ray nodded. He thought he had enough to go on for now. "You need anything, Ed? You want me to stay here with you?"

Ed shook his head, his gaze honing in on the woods again.

Ray rose and stood awkwardly, contemplating what to say. "You let me know if you need anything, or even if you just want someone to talk to. Give me a call, night or day. All right, buddy?" He patted Ed on the shoulder.

"We have to find him," Ed muttered, his tone icy. He looked up at Ray, his eyes piercing. "*I* have to find him."

"We will, Ed. We will," was the only response Ray could think of. As he walked back through the house, his concern for Ed and what his friend might do almost overwhelmed him. *Don't go vigilante, Ed. Don't do it…*

Detective Ernesto Suarez was a first generation American, his parents having emigrated from Honduras. His family settled in Schenectady, New York merely because his father had a friend there. Growing up poor, with uneducated parents who each worked two jobs just so he and his four siblings could eat dinner each night, it was a miracle that Ernie managed to make it to college. The fact that he was now a detective in the Schenectady County PD Homicide Unit—a title he held for only 19 days now (yes, he was counting)—was astonishing even to him. He only wished his parents would've been alive to see the chevrons put on his uniform.

He turned into the parking lot, passing the large brick sign reading *The Rockwall Home*. Glancing at the squat building, he ventured that if his parents had been alive, at their age, they could've been living in a place like this. Exiting his unmarked car, he scanned the facade of the old age home. It was as bland as could be, and it looked…old. Fitting, he thought.

As he passed through the automated sliding doors, the smell of something akin to watered down formaldehyde mixed with soiled diapers hit him. No, he concluded emphatically, he wouldn't have stuck his parents in a place like this no matter their condition. And the things he heard about how some residents were treated in old age homes. Well, he made a mental note to make sure his Living Will, when he got around to getting one drafted, contained a clause that he should under no circumstances be placed in such a facility. Better to rot away in his little sister's unfinished basement, he judged.

Wrinkling his nose, he approached the front desk and flashed his badge. "Detective Suarez, Schenectady County Police Department," he informed the attendant, who looked like she could've been a resident of the Home rather than an employee.

"What can I do you for, Detective?" the attendant asked gruffly. A heavy smoker, he surmised.

"Need to speak to Elizabeth Roletti."

She nodded. "Heard about Beth's daughter. Horrible thing, that. But Beth probably doesn't know the difference."

"She's that bad?"

"Alzheimer's does that…" Watching her computer screen, she clicked her mouse a few times. "But in the moments when she's with it, she sure is a chatter box. Likes to sit on the bench out front and watch people come in and out." She clicked her mouse a final time. "Room 356, third floor. Take the elevator over there," she said, pointing. "And go to the nurse's station first when you get to the third floor, on the left of the elevator. A nurse might be able to help you with Beth."

Nodding his thanks, Ernie took the elevator to the third floor and approached the nurse's station. "Hello," he said to the two women behind the desk. "I would like to speak to Elizabeth Roletti."

"Not visiting hours yet. You family?" one nurse asked without even looking up from her paperwork.

"No, sorry. Detective Suarez, Schenectady County PD." He flashed his badge.

She looked up, studied him skeptically, then said, "I'll have Tracy help you with Beth." She grabbed the phone and hit a few buttons. "Tracy to the nurse's station," she said over the intercom. "Tracy to the nurse's station."

Moment's later, a nurse approached, her dark hair pulled back into a ponytail, her pink scrubs hanging loosely on her skinny frame. The fact that she was slightly taller than him, even in flats, niggled at Ernie. True, he'd always been the short guy, but still…

"This Detective here wants to speak to Beth," the station nurse informed Tracy.

Tracy eyed Ernie, then gestured for him to follow. "She had a pretty good morning," she advised conversationally, glancing over her shoulder while moving down the hall, "but who knows how she is now. It might be a waste of your time, Detective. She's in Stage 4 Alzheimer's."

Having no idea what the stages meant, he said, "Well, let's give it a shot."

Tracy brought Ernie into a small room that smelled of moth-balls. The room's lone window was cracked, causing the sheer drapes to flutter gently. An old lady was asleep, the back of the bed slightly inclined, a lunch tray suspended over the bed by an arm-stand, a plastic cup of fruit sitting precariously on the tray's edge. Ed's mother slept fitfully, her head making minute jerks, white strands of hair crisscrossing her face, her wizened mouth moving as if in a trance.

Tracy moved to the bed and softly shook Beth awake. Ed's mother roused slowly and glanced around the room with shifty eyes, as if she had no idea where she was or how she got there.

Ernie was immediately discouraged, guessing that Stage 4 Alzheimer's was close to the end, if not *the* end. *This will likely be a waste of time.* Of course, he thought—the new detective always gets the shit work. Sighing, he stepped up to the bed, figuring that he might as well ask some questions since he came all the way down here.

Beth fixed her gaze on him. She didn't blink, but her pupils dilated and contracted, and her lids moved like a broken automated sliding door. "Ed, is that you?"

After glancing at Tracy, Ernie cleared his throat. "No, ma'am," he said, raising his voice and leaning in. "My name is Ernesto. Not Ed. Er-nest-o. Ed is your son, ma'am."

Beth dismissed him with an angry wave and a huff. Noticing her tray, her eyes widened. "What happened to my chicken?"

Tracy smiled knowingly, as if expecting the question. "You had chicken yesterday for lunch, Beth," she replied, bending over and rubbing Beth's back. "Do you remember? Today was eggs for breakfast, and you ate it all."

Pure confusion was plastered on Beth's face. She looked up at Tracy. "What's your name?"

"Tracy. I'm Tracy, Beth. I'm your nurse. This here," she gestured to Ernie, "is a detective from the police department."

Beth glanced at Ernie anew, as if he'd just entered the room. He wondered briefly if the Captain was fucking with him by giving him this assignment. The new detectives always seemed to get pranked, or so he imagined. If it was a prank, it was a damned good one, he admitted.

"Are you my son?" Beth asked, grabbing for his hand.

He smiled uncomfortably, jerking his hand away, unsure how to respond. Luckily, Tracy intervened. "Beth, this is a detective," she said, deliberately mouthing each word. "He's not your son. Your son's name is Edward. This is Detective -" she looked at Ernie.

"Suarez," he filled in.

Beth studied him, but it seemed like there was little contemplation behind that expression.

Having Beth's attention, he figured he would see if he could get some answers from her. If Captain Pollack was fucking with him, and he still got some leads, he would show the Cap where to stick it. And maybe, just maybe, the shit work would be pushed on to someone else. It was optimistic, he knew, but it gave him some renewed energy for the interview. *Now if I can only find some damn patience…* "Ms. Roletti, I want to ask you about Mary."

"Mary?" Beth queried quizzically.

"Uh, your daughter. Mary Roletti."

Beth fixed her empty eyes on his face and nodded once. "My daughter's name is Mary." Ernie was unsure whether that was recognition, recollection, or simply imitation.

"That's right," Tracy chimed in, looking like a proud teacher commending a student who got the answer correct.

Ernie forged ahead. "Did Mary have any boyfriends that you remember?"

Beth glanced at her tray.

Please don't ask about your fucking chicken.

"I remember she dated Sid," Beth said.

Pleasantly surprised, Ernie took out his notepad and pen. "Do you remember Sid's last name?"

"Sid?" She chewed on her lip for a few seconds. "You mean Sid Manfield?"

Ernie wrote the name down. Oh yeah, he was going to stick it to the Captain.

Beth continued as if she was regaling them with a glorious story. "Sid took Jill to the World's Fair down in Queens, I remember. She raved about it. I was so jealous."

"Jill? Who's Jill?" Brow furrowed, Ernie's gaze oscillated between Beth and Tracy.

Tracy leaned closer to Beth. "Beth, the Detective is asking about Mary, not Jill. Mary!" She turned to Ernie and whispered, "Jill is her sister. Talks about her all the time, but usually in the present tense, as if Jill was here right now."

As if on cue, Beth asked, "Is Jill home yet? She said she would bring me a caramel."

Tracy gave Ernie a knowing look, then turned back to Beth. "Jill is dead, Beth. She's not here. She died a long time ago."

Ernie had had enough. He put away his notepad and pen and pulled out his business card. "Goodbye, Ms. Roletti." He motioned for Tracy to following him out of the room.

"Can you go pick up some milk?" Ed's mother called after him.

Once outside the room, he handed his card to Tracy. "Give me a call if she has a lucid moment that you think will last for an hour…or even if she mentions to you the names of any of Mary's past boyfriends."

Tracy nodded, shoving the card in the shirt pocket of her scrubs. "I can't believe she's gone."

"You knew her?"

Tracy shrugged. "Just from high school. We weren't friends or anything."

Ernie moved away. *No sticking it to Captain Pollack this time.* As he exited the old age home, he thought of a new clause for his Living Will. A clause that said if he ever reached the point of being in Ms. Roletti's state, he should be smothered to death.

◆ ◆ ◆

With two manila folders in hand, Sergeant Robby Burns strode into the room in the police station housing the Homicide Unit. "Autopsy and lab report, boys," he said excitedly, slapping the folders on his hand. These were the things he loved about his job. What would the autopsy report say? Would it confirm his predictions or reveal something altogether surprising?

He sat at an empty desk and flipped open the autopsy report. Detective Suarez stood up from his desk and moved to look over Robby's shoulder, his coffee mug held close to his face. Robby ignored the new detective despite his closeness. "Cause of death—multiple stab and incised wounds to the torso causing severe hemorrhaging."

He dropped the autopsy report and clapped his hands cheerily, raising his voice. "Dave owes me 50 bucks on that one." He looked up at Suarez, his teeth bared in a wide smile. "He bet it would be asphyxiation." He wondered why a new tech would even attempt to challenge him. "As if a few marks on the neck are determinative. Ha! That boy's got a lot to learn. It's all in the details." There was nothing better than winning a bet, he noted to himself for the umpteenth time,…except maybe proving your opponent dead wrong. He held up the report and began pointing out areas in a photograph to Suarez. "You see, the way this went down I had to assume that the killer was just getting off on strangling her. Having a bit of fun."

"What, are you the station criminologist now, too?" Suarez asked.

Robby waved the comment away dismissively. Who was a new detective to question him anyway, even if it was made in jest? *Was it made in jest?* His gaze flicked to Suarez for a second, measuring. Definitely made in jest, he concluded after reading the man's expression. But this only fueled his need to school the young detective in the art of crime tech. If there was one thing he was good at—other than horse handicapping—it was accurately predicting a cause of death. "I bet the killer strangled her early on in the whole event, too. Maybe even during the rape. Was there rape?" He scrunched his face and skimmed the page, mumbling aloud rapidly. "Stab wounds of varying depths and lengths…punctured internal organs…blah blah blah…more than…" He flipped the page. "Hmm," he grunted interestingly, momentarily distracted from his goal. Raising his voice, he said, "Upward trajectory."

"What's that mean?" Officer Nuck asked, resting his arms on the top of the cubicle.

Robby looked over at the young officer, almost eager to depart his knowledge. "Knife—or actually knives, since there were two different knives used—entered the body from below. Means the killer was stabbing underhanded instead of overhanded." He demonstrated a few underhanded thrusts. It reminded him of the handful of blood spatter simulations he'd been involved in.

Nuck gave a sustained nod.

Returning to the report, Robby scanned the next page silently. Not much of interest, really, until he reached the bottom. "Forced penetration," he said aloud, his demeanor changing. "She was raped." *As I assumed, of course.* He shook his head at the tragedy of it. These were the assumptions he almost wanted to get wrong. Having been in forensics for more than 14 years, his assumptions of this nature had been confirmed the vast majority of the time. He was rarely wrong, in fact. He was even at the point where he could correctly identify the cause of death within two minutes of starting his examination. Not only did it help move the investigation along quicker, it made taking money from the newer crime scene investigators like hitting the exacta at the horse track—easy as pie with the right betting strategy. It was somewhat callous, he knew, considering the criminal acts involved, but it was part of his job, so he embraced it. He read on out loud. "Time of death: approximately 2:30 AM, Sunday, May 22."

"Any DNA? Any semen?" Suarez asked.

"Let's see," Robby voiced aloud, grabbing the lab report in the next folder.

A few more officers huddled around Robby's desk. After a moment, he huffed, displeased. "Nope. No semen, no blood, no saliva. Nothing found on the body." He looked up at the small crowd. "Whoever did this was smart enough to cover all his tracks," he said disbelievingly. "This case should've been open/shut with the autopsy and lab reports." He scratched his head and leaned back in his chair, trying to think of something he missed, some new twist. "Maybe this guy's in law enforcement. Or a private investigator. Or a former cop."

Suarez rolled his eyes. "That's taking it a little too far. You think a cop could butcher like that?"

Robby shrugged listlessly, now starting to get irritated with Ernie's banter. "Wouldn't be the first time," he pointed out while pulling the lab report up to his face, playing it cool. "I'd put money down on that…"

"What about those fingerprints we lifted?" Officer Royce asked. "All four turn up with matches?"

Robby pursed his lips optimistically. It was a good question. He scanned down the page. "Three in the system, one unknown." He kept reading. "I'll be damned. Two sets match the strands of hair at the scene, including the set found in the kitchen." He looked up with a smile, finally uncovering a break in the case. "Looks like we got us some suspects, boys."

The officers in the room perked.

"All right," Suarez said to all. "Let's get to work."

Robby picked up the phone and dialed Jim's extension. "We got suspects, boss," he declared while handing the lab report to Suarez.

As Robby hung up the phone, the officers edged closer to Suarez as the new detective flipped the folder open.

Smiling, Robby dug into his pocket. "I got 20 on contestant number one," he announced with a hoot, pulling out a 20-dollar bill. "Who wants some action?"

After questioning a few of Mary's coworkers at the Star Diner, Detective Bill Watkins called in to the station to get the info on the one lead he managed to get. He figured he would make the house call since his visit to the Star Diner was shorter than expected; and it turned out that it was only a short drive to the trailer park where the lead lived.

He approached the mobile home and gave the door his customary knock—three raps, with each one evenly spaced and of the same dynamic. Waiting for the resident to open the door—which should not have taken so long, he concluded suspiciously—he cocked his head and began speculating about what the person who opened the door would look like. The property was registered to Jennifer Johansson, so he presumed it would be a woman that opened the door. Yet Jennifer could have a boyfriend, or a brother, or an old father that lived with her, so there was some chance that a man would open the door. It was equally possible that Jennifer could have children. That added another variable, but since the State records indicated that Jennifer was in her mid-twenties, he thought it statistically improbable that her child, if she had one, would be old enough to answer the door. Knocking again, he quickly settled on a woman. Now he had to determine what she looked like. Would she be skinny or obese? Perhaps merely shapely. Blonde, brunette, redhead? Short or tall? There were so many choices—18 to be exact, with an approximately six percent chance of choosing accurately amongst those characteristics, excluding gender.

He glanced at the mobile home and the surroundings. The smell of cigarette smoke emanated from the home, which suggested ‘skinny’ to Bill. Maybe it was just his twisted sense of reality, but most people that smoked cigarettes were skinny. He further guessed blonde, but admittedly had nothing to support such an assertion except the fact that she lived in a trailer park, which really was no basis at all. Just a hunch, then, but it would suffice. He was capable of having such things, he reminded himself. So there he had it—skinny, blonde female. It was a true detective’s game, which Bill believed helped to build and hone his investigative prowess. Since he began tallying his guesses, he was batting .716. Fairly impressive statistics, he liked to think.

The sound of a muffled bolt being released from behind the door tugged him from his musings. The thin door to the mobile home was yanked open by a young woman who looked to be a complete wreck. Her long dirty blonde hair was frayed and disheveled, with dark roots sprouting out half an inch from her scalp, suggesting she had neither the time nor the money to maintain the dyed color. How would Bill score this? She was technically a brunette, but masqueraded as a blonde. He pondered for a moment before ultimately deciding that natural brunettes still counted as blondes if they dyed their hair. The critical factor was the outward manifestation rather than the genetic trait. Her driver’s license likely identified her as a blonde, he predicted, which he used to bolster his point.

He added this one to his mental statistics before examining her other features. Her eyes seemed to be too wide for her thin face, and, consistent with prolonged crying, they were puffy and blood-shot. Her nose reddened at the nostrils, and her bony neck ended at a visible collarbone halfway hidden behind a frail, faded, powder blue T-shirt. As she stood with one hand leaning on the door and a cigarette between the sinewy fingers of her other, she openly measured Bill. She took a drag from her cigarette before asking, "Yeah?"

"Jennifer Johansson," Bill asked, reading from his notepad.

The woman took another drag, her hand visibly shaking. "That's me."

Was she just extremely overwrought, Bill wondered, or was something else at play? "I am Detective Watkins with the Schenectady County Police Department. May I come in, miss? I would like to ask you some questions about Mary Roletti." His head bobbed over Jenny's shoulder, catching glimpses of the fridge and a counter in the tiny kitchen. "Is this not a good time, miss? I could come back, or you could come down to the station some time today or tomorrow."

She took another drag, then reached over to a small table next to the door and ashed her cigarette in a dented soup can. "Now's fine. Come on in." She sniffled loudly.

Bill nodded his thanks and entered as Jenny shut the door behind him. He surveyed the tiny home. It looked barely livable. Clothes were strewn about the small living area, half-eaten food sat on the counter, dishes were piled in the sink, and the entire place reeked of cigarettes. The lack of order horrified him, and he tightened up, trying to maintain a semblance of order within the tiny atmosphere he occupied. He made sure not to touch anything. He might as well have been smoking, he decided, for all the secondhand smoke he was inhaling. He tried to breathe as little as possible.

Jenny moved around Bill and leaned against the island counter, wrapping her free arm around her waist and using it as a prop for the elbow of her other arm. The position permitted her to rest her cigarette at mouth level, where the simple twist of her wrist brought the tobacco stick to her lips. She waited with eyes fixed on the brown carpet, her head somewhat downcast. *As if there is guilt behind her eyes that she does not want me to see.*

He delved into his first question. "So, how did you know Mary?"

Her lower lip quivered as she regarded him. "She was my best friend," she said shakily amidst the exhalation of smoke.

Bill nearly coughed. His mind told him to flee, to run to his car where there was structure, where he was in control of his environment, but the detective in him fought back, sending a new thought to his brain. *She seems very nervous*. "How long did you know her?"

"We was best friends since the beginning of high school." Her eyes rolled to the ceiling in rudimentary calculation. "Probably 10 years." She put the butt of her cigarette out in a tray before crossing her arms.

"And how often did you see her?"

"Oh, once or twice a week. Mostly on the weekends when we would go out." Her mouth curled downward and she wiped her eyes. "But we spoke almost every day," she added through a restrained sob.

"Let me ask you about the weekend of May 21. Was there anything unusual that happened to Mary that you know of?" He came close to touching the island and flinched away, shuffling two small steps sideways, placing himself equal-distant between the door and the island.

She shook her head. "I wasn't with her Friday night cause I had a date. But we went to Warren's on Saturday night. Had some drinks, did some dancing, and then I dropped her at home." She turned and glanced around the kitchen, then snatched up a pack of cigarettes, removed one, and lit it up.

Bill took a minor step backwards to remove himself from the zone of smoke, making sure to maintain his distance from certain fixtures. "So Saturday night she went home alone?"

Jenny nodded.

"What time was that?"

Jenny exhaled. "I'd say it was about 12:30. Maybe 1:00."

"Did anything happen at the bar? Did any guys hit on her or anything like that?"

Jenny snickered, then pouted. "Guys always hit on Mary. Lord, she got hit on regularly at the gas station."

"Did that make you jealous?"

She glared at him with revulsion in her eyes. "Am I a suspect?" she asked, sounding offended.

"Not at the moment," Bill responded matter-of-factly.

Jenny began sobbing. "We was like sisters. I'd never hurt her."

He tried to interpret her tone, looking for flaws, but failed. He changed the focus of his interview. "Were there any creepy guys that particular Saturday night that you recall?"

Apparently assuaged, Jenny pursed her lips in thought. "No. But John happened to be there that night."

"John?"

"Oh, sorry. John and Mary used to date a few years ago."

"Do you know his last name?"

"Yeah, it's Wakefielder. He lives up in Gloversville. At least he used to when they dated."

Bill wrote the name down. "Did they have words that night?"

Jenny shook her head. "They just said 'hi' and that was it."

"What about other boyfriends? Any bad relationships or bad breakups?"

"Well, there was Dennis Kerisol, who was the most recent fling. John was before that. And then Chucky before that. There was a whole host of others in between that was short-lived. Nine times out of ten, it was Mary that did the breaking up. She got bored pretty quickly."

"Do you know Chucky's last name?"

"It's Dericardo. He lives over off of 67, past the airport."

"Do you know if Dennis or Chucky or John ever got physical with Mary?"

She took a drag. "Mary never confirmed it, but I think Dennis hit her once. I know they used to fight like cats and dogs." She exhaled smoke. "I know he did time in juvy for robbery."

Bill jotted it all down. "Anything else you can think of?"

She shook her head.

Bill placed his notepad and pen away and pulled out a business card. "If anything comes to mind, please give me a call. The more we know, the faster we can catch the killer."

She nodded.

As he left, he took a deep breath of fresh air, quickly moving to his car—a familiar place, things in perfect order, structure. He squeezed a glob of sanitizer into his hands and rubbed vigorously, then sniffed at the bottle to help remove the scent of smoke from his nostrils. The comforting smell relaxed him. After a moment, he turned his thoughts to Jenny. He had the inkling that she was hiding something. He would get to the bottom of it, but first he had to calculate his new batting average. Blonde, skinny female. The numbers flowing through his head produced the answer within seconds.

Step 2.4

"We are following all leads," Captain Jim Pollack said into the gaggle of microphones and digital recorders shoved into his face. "The investigation is moving along rapidly."

Officer Ray Lucen weaved around the reporters blocking the sidewalk, trying to be inconspicuous.

"Can you give us any names?" a reporter in the back yelled out.

"We cannot disclose the names of any potential suspects or persons of interest at this time since the investigation is ongoing."

Ray entered the station as the Captain said, "That is all I have for now." Ray nodded to the station officer at the front desk and pushed open the door leading to the back offices.

"Ray," the Captain called out from behind. "Hold up."

Ray turned and waited, the door held ajar.

"How's our boy?" the Captain asked when he reached Ray's side, keeping his voice down as they moved through the building.

Ray cringed, torn between protecting his friend and revealing to the Captain his fear that Ed was on the verge of going on a vindictive manhunt; yet it was merely a suspicion, and Ray knew such unsubstantiated notions were to be taken with a grain of salt. Besides, nothing Ray knew about Ed's character suggested that Ed would go off and start putting holes in Mary's past boyfriends. Yet if Ray didn't say something and Ed wound up snapping, the weight on Ray's shoulders for those deaths would be too much to bear. He was also cognizant that if he said something that was inaccurate, something that overstated the danger, it could destroy Ed's career—assuming his friend still wanted to continue on the Force. That was something he hadn't previously considered.

Ultimately, he decided it was too soon to convey his fears.

Realizing he had not answered the Captain, he said, "seems to be hanging in there. But he's all alone, Cap. I wish his mother had her wits about her. At least they could have shared each other's grief."

As they moved past the interview rooms, the Captain nodded grimly. "You think we should send someone over? For his own protection?"

"Don't think that's necessary. I'm going to try to spend some time with him every night."

The Captain nodded again, shuffling alongside Ray. As they made the turn down the corridor leading to the Homicide Unit, he asked, “Did Ed give you anything useful?”

“Two names and one partial. All past boyfriends.”

The Captain nodded perceptively. “This has scorned lover written all over it, if you ask me.”

Ray’s first response was a sigh. Then he said, “looks to be shaping up that way, Cap. If not, then we may have a cold case on our hands.”

The Captain’s frown quickly transformed into an expression of rigid determination, as if the mere mention of a cold case was an anathema to his very being.

Ray wondered if he went too far with that comment. He cleared his throat to ease the tension in his bones.

They walked in silence another ten paces before entering the room housing the Homicide Unit.

“All right. Ed’s got us some names,” the Captain announced, looking to Ray.

Ray whipped out his notepad. “Dennis Kerisol.”

“He is out,” Detective Watkins cut in levelly, swiveling in his chair. “The best friend gave me his name. We just ran him. He has a solid alibi. He is currently incarcerated at Hale Creek for grand larceny second degree. Serving six years.”

“What about Chucky Dericardo?” Ray asked.

“I obtained his name as well. Officer Eng is running him right now.” Detective Watkins looked to the corner. “Officer Eng, do you have anything on Dericardo yet?”

Legs popped his head out from a cubicle shoved into the back corner of the room. “Just got it.” He withdrew his head and began reading, his voice projecting. “Charles Dericardo, a/k/a Chucky Dericardo. 26 years of age. Johnstown address. Social Security records show he’s currently employed at Universal Electric. One prior. Petit larceny in 1998. Served 15 days in juvy detention.”

“Damn, Ed’s sister had a penchant for bad boys, it seems,” Robby commented with a smirk. “You’d think she would’ve shied away seeing as how she came from a family of cops.”

The fact that it seemed to amuse the head of forensics galled Ray. But, of course, being Robby’s inferior, he held his tongue.

"Good news is," Robby continued as if his previous comment wasn't made, "we got a positive match on Dericardo's hair and fingerprints at the scene."

"Let's bring him in," the Captain directed. "Suarez, you pick him up. Take Nuck with you."

Suarez nodded. Officer Nuck perked with apparent excitement, then his expression loosened, suggesting he was trying to play it cool. Ray recalled being like that in the not too distant past when he was a young, green officer. The thought brought him round to Ed, who had been at his side throughout his career. "I also got a partial," he said. "John. Past boyfriend."

"I obtained that one, too," Bill said, awkwardly clasping his hands behind his head and reclining in his chair. "Wakefielder is his last name." His tone, although far from smug, annoyed Ray. He supposed it was as close to smug as Detective Watkins could get. It seemed like everyone was out to one-up Ray today.

"You run him yet, Legs?" the Captain asked.

"Doing it right now, Captain," came Leg's voice from the corner.

"Any other persons of interest?" the Captain asked as they waited for Legs.

"The best friend," Bill said. "Jenny Johansson."

The Captain chewed on that, shifting his weight and crossing his arms. "What's your basis? Any motive?"

Bill shrugged stiffly. "Just a hunch, right now. I ran her. She is clean, but there might be something there."

"Let me guess," Ray threw at Bill, playing to the crowd. "She's 6'3" and 225 pounds of pure muscle." *Let him chew on that...*

Suarez cackled. The officers in the room stifled their laughs, likely on account that Bill outranked them. But at the moment, Ray didn't care about that.

Bill cocked his head and threw his hands up nonchalantly, his expression stagnant.

Ray didn't know what to make of it, but he assumed it was Bill's form of arrogance. "So you think the best friend raped Mary? What, does she have a cock or something?" Let him try to answer that without sounding a fool, Ray thought.

"It could have been a job for hire," Bill answered tonelessly, his head cocked awkwardly.

Fucking asshole. Ray's eyes narrowed as he moved to sit at an unmanned desk.

"Got him," Officer Eng announced, breaking the friction in the room. "John Wakefielder. 33 years of age. Gloversville address. Unemployed." He paused while presumably reading. "This guy's got a shitload of priors. And violent ones, too. Menacing in the third degree in 1997. Sentenced to one year probation as a juvy. Forcible touching, 2000. Served 60 days in juvy detention. Assault second degree and attempted robbery third degree in 2006. Served five years."

"The best friend also informed me that Mary saw him on the night in issue," Bill added.

"Looks like our number one suspect, boys," the Captain said.

"Got no prints or hair on him at the scene, though," Robby commented.

The Captain raised his eyebrows. "Well, let's bring him in and see what he has to say. Bill, you pick him up." He glanced at the officers in the room. "And take Parker."

"Really?" Parker asked, clearly astounded.

Bill huffed. "Jim?" he pleaded, albeit rigidly.

The Captain waved him away, causing Bill to mutter, although his expression remained flat. "You rooks learn anything on State Street?" he asked Parker.

"Only thing we got was a couple that skipped out on their bill at Sweet's Motel. Hotel clerk didn't remember faces or the make and model of the vehicle."

"What other forensic ID do we got at the scene, by the way?" the Cap asked Robby.

"Well, the two strands of hair were Dericardo and Kerisol. Both also had prints match up. The third prints happen to be Ed's."

The room went suddenly quiet, cops looking at the walls or the floor or their own laps. And Ray knew instantly what consumed everyone's mind, because it was precisely what he himself thought. Could Ed have offed his sister? It was natural for cops to consider and investigate all possible leads, and Ed certainly couldn't be ruled out, but the mood in the room suggested that each man was doing his best to disregard the thought—or at least push it to the back of the mind. Ray convinced himself that the answer was 'no,' but he knew that at least a few cops in the room would pursue the possibility.

The Captain cleared his throat, causing most in the room to start. "Bill, you want to bring in the best friend for questioning?"

"It would be provident."

The Captain nodded. "Ray," he tapped Ray on the chest lightly, "take Smith and bring her in. She might not put up a fight if a policewoman is at your side."

Officer Smith rolled her eyes.

Ray turned to Bill. "You got that address?"

Bill methodically tore a page from his small notepad, then handed it to Ray. The handwriting looked almost like typeface. *Damn freak...*

"All right," the Captain said with a loud clap. "Go get us some suspects."

He had spoken to Parker only once before. His hypothesis as a result of that initial encounter was that Officer Gill Parker was an idiot. The conversation that just ensued about holsters—if it could actually be classified as a conversation—supported his hypothesis. Still, Bill conceded, more information was required to confirm his hypothesis.

As he turned his unmarked vehicle down the narrow, gravel road, Detective Bill Watkins sought to obtain that information. "How did you pass the officer's entrance exam?" he asked Parker.

"What do you mean?"

The boy's face looked outright confused. It was one expression Bill easily recognized, as people always tended to display it around him. Other emotions were not so simple to decipher. "Am I correct in asserting that you cheated?" It was the only plausible conclusion Bill could reach based on the information at hand. He slowed the car as the road became bumpy.

"Studied for three weeks," Parker said pleasantly. "Passed on my first try."

Bill cogitated. *There is one other possible conclusion.* It must have been some sort of fluke, as there was no way Parker was smart enough to have passed the officer's exam. He shook his head, thinking that with officers like Parker entering the ranks, the police department would be dysfunctional by the time he retired. To maintain a competent department, Bill would be compelled to continue to operate in the field even after making captain—or even chief, perhaps. It was difficult to imagine Parker as a detective, but with sufficient time on the Force, the boy would make detective irrespective of his grave mental deficiencies. My, how things would slip through the cracks on cases where Parker was lead detective. Bill calculated the number of cases annually he would need to personally handle to pick up the slack. He factored in the approximate number of witnesses he would need to question, suspects he would need to interrogate, reports he would need to file, and so on.

The bang and dip of the car from a large pothole brought his mind back to the road. A small shack was visible around the bend through the thicket of skinny trees. Bill ducked his head to get a better glimpse. The shack looked to be almost in disrepair, with its gutters hanging loose, gray paint flaking off the wood of its façade, and two of four ground-level windows boarded up as if in preparation for an oncoming hurricane. As they rounded the bend, Bill got a better look at the small house. Under the carport sat a beat-up muscle car that looked to be nonoperational, with its hood propped up, a transmission sitting beside a front tire and brake discs lying near the rear. A dinted, red F-150 sat next to the carport in the grass—a routinely used parking space, Bill surmised, from the ruts carved out of the ground. Stopping his car as quietly as possible behind the muscle car, Bill noticed a jug sitting on the porch truss. Its shape and size were consistent with the type used to make moonshine. Off to the side of the yard sat a metal bar that was either for doing pull ups or for hanging laundry. *Or hanging people...*

"All right, listen up," Bill said to Parker, giving the young officer a stern expression, or at least what he thought was a stern expression. He had never been good at conveying his emotions. "This suspect is likely dangerous, possibly armed." He glanced at the home again. "I am fairly certain he has tattoos all over his body."

"How do you know that?"

"Deduction," he said flatly. These things could easily be deduced. The suspect was a prior criminal, not married, a high school drop-out, and a part-time construction worker—at least according to his rap sheet in the system. It was simple deduction that he would possess a weapon and that he would have tattoos. Bill squinted at the porch, looking for signs of life.

Parker squinted as well. "Should we call for backup?"

Bill regarded Parker. New information often changed a conclusion, Bill acknowledged. *Perhaps Parker is smart enough to have passed the entrance exam.* "We should not," he answered. "It would be precipitous at this juncture."

Parker displayed the smile of a simpleton and nodded.

Retraction. He probably cheated. "Let's go. Be on your toes," Bill advised.

They exited the car and gently shut the doors. Approaching the porch, Bill glanced in the small window on the far end of the house. All he could make out in the darkened corner was a rickety armoire. The porch steps protested as they put their weight on the old, semi-rotted boards. If the suspect did not know they were there before, he surely did now.

Bill moved across the small porch briskly, leaving Parker two steps behind. He did not want to give Parker the opportunity to knock first. No, he wanted to give the shack his customary knock of three raps. He should have mentioned that to Parker in the car, come to think of it, but no matter, since he managed to get to the door first. Why such a thing was so important to him, he was unsure. It was simply something the tick in his brain compelled him to do.

He knocked. "John Wakefielder," he called out. He waited for the door to open or for a response, but neither came. He glanced at Parker, who threw him the same inane smile. That simply confused Bill. He knocked again, slightly louder this time. "John Wakefielder," he called out. "This is the police."

The faint sound of what he thought was shuffling boots brushed his hearing and he suspiciously moved down the porch to a window. He cupped his hands on the glass and glared inside, making sure to keep his body away from view—a bullet in the gut would do him no good. The front room was half basked in rays of light from the untreated windows, highlighting furniture that was only fit for a junkyard, in Bill's opinion. The movement of a shadow in the kitchen toward the back of the house caught his eye briefly before it was gone. It could have been a figment of his imagination, he conceded, it could have been the movement of a tree, but there was no breeze, and he had an awkward feeling about the whole situation. Atypically, he started to worry, the tick in his brain lying dormant.

"Should I knock aga -"

Bill shushed the young officer, holding up his finger.

Parker craned his neck and raised his eyebrows, leaning ear first into the door.

Bill heard something but it took a moment before he put it together. It was the slow screech of a screen door. Someone was trying to sneak out the back. "He is going for the back," he shouted to Parker, already moving to the porch stairs.

Parker's eyes widened as Bill passed him. Bill removed the gun from his holster as he rounded the corner of the house. Within two strides, Parker was past him, sprinting with the speed of a thoroughbred. Parker angled to the left, disappearing behind the house, and then, "Police! Stop!"

Bill picked up his pace. Despite his leanness, he was out of shape, and when he made it to the back of the house, Parker was already breaching the line of trees fifty yards away, the officer's youthful body maneuvering at ease around the wooden obstacles. Bill followed, losing ground by the second. He caught a faint glimpse of a man in the woods ahead of Parker, and he noted surprisingly that Parker was gaining on the man rapidly.

"Stop or I'll shoot!" Parker yelled.

Such things were only said in the movies, Bill noted. *He could not have passed the exam.* Bill pondered this new information despite his lungs' demand for satiation, attempting to decide whether he had sufficient information to substantiate his hypothesis that Parker was an idiot.

When he made it to the woods, he heard a wordless yell from Parker, followed by an angry grunt. By the time Bill approached, Parker had the man in handcuffs. Bill pulled up awkwardly, braced his back against a tree and sucked in air, unable to speak.

The suspect, his hands cuffed behind his back, his face in the underbrush, writhed amid the forest floor.

Parker stood up, barely winded, a triumphant grin painted on his face.

"Parker," Bill said between breaths, "you are remarkably fast. Did you run track?" *Perhaps not mentally capable, but certainly physically so...*

Parker shook his head. "Played cornerback in high school."

Regaining his wind, Bill turned back to the business at hand. He walked over to the man in cuffs. "John Wakefielder?" he asked.

"Go fuck yourself," the man spat.

"You are coming down to the station. But you also just gave us cause to search your house. Thank you."

The man growled, then muttered, "fucking pig," or something to that effect.

"You were right," Parker said to Bill.

Bill cocked his head, unsure to what Parker's statement was directed.

Parker pointed down to the suspect. "He's covered in tattoos."

Bill studied the tattoos on the man's arms and neck, displayed in contrast to his off-white wifebeater. *Simple deduction.*

He instructed Parker to haul the suspect back to the car. Then, he calculated his new batting average. *Tattoos.*

Step 2.5

Detective Ernie Suarez entered the viewing room annexed to the small interview room. He looked through the two-way mirror at the suspect. Leaning into the Captain, he whispered, "Look at this guy. What the fuck was a girl like Mary doing dating him? He looks like Jed from *The Beverly Hillbillies*."

Jim chortled. "You old enough to have watched that show?"

"I've seen the re-runs," Ernie retorted.

"Taste in men is a funny thing, Ernie. I never did understand it myself. Any trouble bringing him in?"

Ernie shook his head. "We caught him coming home from work. Came along easily, as if he was expecting us." He shot the Captain a meaningful look.

The Captain returned it. "Why don't you get in there and see what he has to say."

This was his chance, Ernie thought, his chance to show the Captain just how good of a detective he was, how good of a detective he could be. It was very likely that this would be the biggest case he ever worked on. It could make or break his career. There was no room for error.

Ernie grabbed the file and perused it briefly, acting as if he was learning the suspect's information for the first time. In truth, he had spent the last two hours studying everything there was to know in the system about Chucky Dericardo. He had it all memorized, but if he learned one thing in his years as an officer, it was that perception was everything, so the faster he was perceived to pick things up, the more trust his superiors would give him. He closed the file demonstratively, hopefully displaying to the Captain that he didn't need it as a crutch. Before opening the door, he motioned to the video operator, who switched on the recorder.

Ernie opened the door casually and entered the room. Chucky Dericardo sat at the small table, his hands clasped before him, his mouth ajar, revealing a few severely crooked teeth. His light blonde hair extended down his neck into a small mullet, and his upper lip was covered in peach fuzz that was only visible when it was struck by rays of light at the right angle. He was skeletal in his thinness, borderline emaciated. Ernie's first thought was that this guy didn't look strong enough to have committed the crime—or smart enough, for that matter. And Chucky's file confirmed the latter impression, establishing that he worked a blue-collar job at the Universal Electric turbine factory, and that he dropped out of high school before gaining a degree. Chucky didn't seem like he had the wherewithal to have committed the crime so cleanly. Still, Ernie knew that background information and first impressions could be deceiving, so he went into the interrogation determined to either confirm or rule out this guy as a suspect.

"You dated Mary Roletti," he said flatly to Chucky, more so as a statement than a question. Ernie fixed his hard gaze on those beady eyes and gave the young man an expression suggesting that he knew everything there was to know, and that Chucky better fess up.

Chucky nodded uneasily while unclasping his hands and leaning back.

There's something there. He's nervous. The fact that Chucky was distancing himself was a telltale sign that he had something to hide. Obviously, different detectives had different styles when it came to interrogations. Usually Ernie thought it beneficial to ease into the questioning before putting weight on the suspect. He often started with an innocuous question. He found that building a friendly rapport typically loosened the suspect up, and more often than not that permitted Ernie to get the information he sought. Here, however, Chucky's manifestations suggested to Ernie that he could lay into the man right away. So he did. "She dumped your ass."

Chucky remained silent but began fidgeting, his feet tapping in arrhythmic beats.

He wants to confess. Ernie stood and raised his voice, shoving his finger in Chucky's face. "And so you wanted revenge. She was the best thing you ever had, the best girl you'd ever get. You couldn't stand to see her with anyone else. You couldn't stand to lose her. It was you or nobody."

Chucky leaned farther back, away from Ernie's finger. "It wasn't like that, I tell ya," he stammered, his voice soft.

Ernie moved behind Chucky, leaned down toward the man's ear and lowered his voice. "You were pissed off last weekend. You were bitter. You were embarrassed. You probably got drunk and decided to do something about it. You went to her house and butchered the shit out of her. But not before you raped her."

Chucky's head shook in denial, his mouth moving wordlessly.

Ernie opened the file and tossed the crime scene photographs on the table before Chucky. "Take a second look at your handiwork."

Chucky looked uncomfortable as his eyes shot down to the photos. He slowly moved his hand to the table and began sorting through the photos, blinking incessantly.

Ernie watched Chucky intently. There was no horror or queasiness in the guy's expression as he perused the photos. It was an abnormal reaction. One that suggested Chucky had seen these portraits before. A normal person would have vomited on the desk after being show pictures like this for the first time. Fairly certain now that Chucky was the killer, Ernie slammed his palms on the desk.

"Why'd you do it?" he scolded. When Chucky failed to answer, Ernie changed his tone and said, "If you don't work with me, you're going away for life. You know that, don't you? I can help you. I can speak to the District Attorney and put a good word in, but you have to help me out. Maybe you'll get a good plea. But you got to tell me what happened, and why. That's the trade off."

Chucky rubbed his hand down his face, hesitating, before he said, "Was angry about being dumped, that's true…but I didn't kill her."

Ernie laughed haughtily. "You think I'm a fucking idiot? You think you'd be in here without us having the shit on you?" Now fully immersed in the act, he got into Chucky's face. "I got your DNA and prints all over the fucking body and the house. Got a witness who ID'd your pickup truck at the house. A jury will take one look at the evidence and put you away for life. You're done! You're going to rot in jail until your bones are frail and your asshole is worn thin." He stood up and paced the room. "But I'm giving you this one opportunity to admit it. Once I walk out of this room, that chance is gone. It's now or never." He let Chucky mull those false facts over as he glared at the two-way mirror.

Chucky remained silent.

Undeterred, Ernie delved into the specifics. "Where were you Saturday night last weekend?"

"Saturday? At home."

"Alone?"

Chucky swallowed hard before nodding.

Officer Nuck cracked open the door to the interview room. "You got a call, Detective. Seems to be urgent."

Ernie nodded, knowing that it was just an indication that the Captain wanted to speak to him. He moved to exit but stopped in the doorframe and swiveled his head. "This is it, Chucky. I shut this door, you lose my help for good. What'll it be?"

Chucky regarded him for a moment. "I want a lawyer." He sat back and stared at the wall, his arms crossed.

Damn! Although surprised, Ernie recovered quickly. "If that's your choice, then good luck." He shut the door behind him and gestured a 'how'd I do?' to the Captain.

"We got a statement. We got a motive. And no alibi. Body mannerisms suggest he's guilty. He didn't even flinch when you showed him the crime scene photos."

Ernie shook his head disconcertedly. "I thought I'd be able to get more. Didn't think he'd be savvy enough to request counsel."

"You never know with these types—what they see on TV or in the movies." He patted Ernie on the shoulder. "You did good, Ernie. You did good. Let's hold him until we see what the other suspects have to say. In the meantime, get started on a search warrant for his house." With that, the Captain exited the viewing room.

Ernie stood and glared at the suspect through the two-way mirror, thinking that he could've done more, that he should've gotten more. Despite the praise from the Captain, he wondered pessimistically if he'd get another opportunity like this.

◆ ◆ ◆

"He is a freak," Detective Bill Watkins said while standing in the viewing room attached to the small interrogation room, his tone filled with astonishment. At least he felt like he instilled his tone with astonishment. He was never really sure. He had been told in the past, on numerous occasions in fact, that his speech was devoid of emotion, that his voice lacked any inflection, that his face was always flat. He found such comments odd. Internally, he felt as if his emotions were sufficiently conveyed. He eyed the junior officers beside him, trying to discern a reaction that would confirm or deny whether his astonishment had been conveyed. He squeezed his facial muscles harder, trying to hold his eyebrows in a high arc.

"Are you serious?" Officer Eng asked with a laugh. "Parker?"

Officer Royce added his own deep chuckle.

Satisfactorily manifested, it seems. "You should have observed him," he continued, trying again to inflect his voice. He almost forgot to maintain his face. He forced his eyebrows up again. "It was extremely fast for a human. Perhaps 24 or 25 miles per hour. I estimate that Officer Parker covered 200 meters in approximately 26 seconds, and he did so while laden with his utility belt." Now came the difficult part—adding hand gestures to his facial expression and tone. It was tantamount to juggling, Bill thought. He threw out a, "Zzzzzzz," accompanied by a darting gesture. "Officer Parker had the suspect collared before I was even in eyesight." *There, I did it.* Bill's hands dropped to his side, his face reverting to neutral.

"I went through basic with Parker, Detective, but I don't recall him being fast," Royce commented.

Bill threw his hands up, wondering if it looked forced. "If I did not see it myself..." A strange thought came to Bill. It was a conversational thought, colloquial, something in the nature of idle chatter. It was not the type of thing that usually popped into Bill's head. He was excited to voice it. "We should send Officer Parker over to Saratoga to run against the ponies. Robby would love that action." He smiled, impressed with his quip—particularly with his use of the word 'ponies' instead of 'thoroughbreds.' He glanced at the junior officers to gauge their reaction.

Just then, an officer brought the suspect into the interview room and uncuffed the man. Despite its novelty, Bill's comment was quickly disregarded. Business beckoned.

John Wakefielder was in his mid-thirties, with tattoos all over his neck and arms, and bronze hair hanging over his cobalt eyes. His broad facial features and coffee-colored skin suggested that he had a bit of Native American in him. John looked to be an unsavory character. Just the type to have committed the crime, Bill thought. Wasting little time, he entered the interview room and sat down. "Why did you run?" He did not attempt to alter his tone or his face. This was business.

John ran his hand through his hair, removing strands from his face. "You got a cigarette?" he asked coolly.

"If you answer my question, I do," Bill replied flatly. The first few exchanges of an interrogation were the most telling ones, Bill reminded himself. Since John just deflected Bill's question with a question of his own, it was clear to Bill that John was not the type to simply confess. Nor would trickery likely work. John's composure indicated that he had experience dealing with cops, which was also plain from his criminal history. This interrogation, therefore, required a more subtle approach, which involved playing off the suspect's own personality. But rest assured, Bill would get the information he sought.

John glared at Bill, apparently disgusted. It was an expression that Bill recognized. "This ain't my first time being asked questions by a fuckin' pig. I don't got to tell you shit," he spat.

Calm and collected, Bill opened John's file. "Correct," he said, his eyes on the file, "this is not your first time, is it? Menacing, forcible touching, assault, attempted robbery—you must be going for the cycle? Trying to commit every crime in the book. You probably have spent more time in this interview room than I have." He craned his neck toward the door. "Is your name on a plaque outside?" Bill was again surprised at his own colloquialism.

John seemed almost proud.

Inwardly, Bill was annoyed, but he did not let it show—although he supposed he was incapable of doing so even if he tried. In any event, he did not want to give the suspect the upper hand.

His rational mind continued down the path he had chosen. "I do not, however, see any white collar crimes. No fraud, forgery, bribery. Nothing to indicate that you have a brain. Nothing to indicate that you are capable of anything more than unadulterated violence." He chuckled mechanically. "But that is perfect, is it not? A jury would have a field day with your criminal history. I will wager that you get convicted of murder in the first with less than half an hour of deliberation."

John's eyes widened and his brow scrunched minutely for the briefest of moments before the man regained his composure. That expression gave Bill pause, as it implied that John did not expect to be questioned about a murder. *He is guilty of a crime. The only question is whether that crime is murder. Or perhaps he is better than I anticipated...* Unsure as to the correct supposition, Bill decided to press John to see if he could break the man down. The longer he kept the guy talking, the more likely he would be able to break through the guy's defenses. The best thing to do in situations like this was to state the facts plainly, without voicing assumptions or surmise or conclusions, and then see how the suspect reacted. If the suspect altered or questioned a fact as stated, it likely meant he was the killer, since only someone with intimate knowledge of the facts could correct an inaccurate statement. If he said nothing or defended himself, well, he still could be the killer, it just took longer to figure it out. "You dated Mary Roletti. She broke up with you. It just so happened that you saw her Saturday night, the same night she ended up cut to pieces and raped. Can you put two and two together?"

John's mind was churning, Bill deduced, as evinced by those shifting blue eyes. Perhaps he was trying to think of some way out, or maybe he was simply recalling the events of that night. Memory recall caused such a physical reaction, Bill conceded. *But so does the creative portion of the brain when improvisation is required.*

"Mary's dead?"

Although he decided not to adjust his facial expression, Bill huffed. "That is what the papers and television stations around the nation are saying? You have not heard?"

John propped his elbows on the table and clasped his hands before his mouth. A faint grin was visible behind the misshaped sphere his hands formed.

He is tickled pink. He wanted her dead.

"I saw her at Warren's last weekend," John said.

Bill waited, but John added nothing. "Then what?"

John seemed deep in thought, and there was a significant pause before he spoke. "She got killed Saturday night, right?" John asked.

"You tell me."

John leaned back in the chair, his grin widening. "Someone finally axed that bitch." He chuckled maliciously.

"Your sentiments are touching. Did you know that statement can be used against you in court?"

"Problem you got, pig, is that you're not charging me with that crime. I was at Erica's house all Saturday night after Warren's. Got me some ass. You ain't pinning me with no murder." His tone became brazen and he pointed to the door. "Now how's about you go get me a fucking cigarette—seeing as how you brought me all the way down here for nothing."

Bill studied the man, wondering if it was just bravado. John had given him a clear motive, but the manner in which the man spoke suggested certain innocence. Bill pressed on, looking for a crack in John's armor. "Who is Erica?"

"Erica Rosedale. Lives over in the Brandshire Houses. Apartment 7F. Met her a few times before Warren's." With poise, he crossed his arms, displaying his forearm tattoos prominently.

Bill leaned forward, hopeful that he was displaying cold anger. "If this does not check out," he whispered, "you are going away for life."

"Check away, then."

Bill rose and entered the viewing room where Officers Eng and Royce had been watching through the two-way mirror. "Go check it out," he instructed Royce.

Royce nodded and exited.

"Check for surveillance tapes also," he yelled after Royce.

"You want me to keep rolling tape?" the video operator asked.

"No," Bill answered. "We may be waiting for a while." He turned to Officer Eng. "Get him food if he asks, or let him use the restroom. Otherwise, he sits in that room until Royce gets back."

"Got it," Officer Eng said.

"And no matter what, do not give him a cigarette." He moved to exit but stopped at the door and wheeled, another quip popping into his head. "Actually," he said to Officer Eng, pulling his mouth up into a smirk, "give him a cigarette…just do not give him a light."

Multiple witticisms in one day. I am on a roll.

◆ ◆ ◆

"What the hell? Is she making a get-away or something?" Officer Tammy Smith queried glibly.

"What?" Officer Ray Lucen asked.

"'You got a damn smoke screen in there," Tammy said, pointing to the interview room.

Ray glanced through the two-way mirror. Cigarette smoke hung thick in the air, giving the room a creamy, hazy quality. "Damn old ventilation system," he muttered. Turning to Tammy, he asked, "You get the bank records?"

Tammy handed the records over. "How long's she been in there?" she asked, her brow scrunched.

Ray snatched the pages. “Only about twenty minutes, I think,” he said, preoccupied with the records.

“She must be plowing through cigarettes. What do you think, she smokes three packs a day, maybe more?”

Ray gave a noncommittal grunt as a response.

Tammy sat down, crossed her legs and waited, examining the ends of her black hair.

After a few minutes of reading, Ray looked up. “There’s nothing on this girl but Bill’s twisted intuition. All we got here is a $1,000 withdrawal a week before the murder. What’s your take?”

Tammy shrugged. “We know she didn’t do it herself. She clearly couldn’t have raped the victim. Could be she was in there with a dildo…but I doubt it.”

“Nice take.”

She shrugged again. “Just thinking it through.” She glanced at the suspect. “Could be she had help. Or maybe she hired someone. Is $1,000 enough? Could be for the right person. Had to be a sick fuck, though, right? But what’s her motive?”

“Other than jealousy, I don’t know.” Ray glanced at the suspect and watched her take drag after drag for a few moments. *She looks nervous. Or is that simply grief? Or stress?* Ray decided to play it straight with this suspect, feeling in his gut that she had no part in it. He nodded to Tammy and entered the viewing room. The acrid smell of smoke struck him immediately. *Awck.* He pushed through it. “Hi,” he said to the suspect, sitting across from her. “I’m Officer Lucen. I know Detective Watkins asked you some questions this morning, but I just want to follow up and get some more information. Okay?”

Jenny Johansson nodded while bringing a cigarette to her lips.

Through the fog of smoke Ray noticed that Jenny’s eyes were blood-shot and framed underneath by dark, baggy circles. Thoughts of Ed surfaced and momentarily distracted him. He pictured Ed’s blood-shot eyes amid a lifeless countenance. He ventured that if Jenny was truly Mary’s best friend, she probably felt just as Ed did—except she was being treated like a potential criminal on top of her emotional turmoil. Sympathy overwhelmed him as he wondered what this girl must’ve been going through. He cleared his throat to rid himself of the feeling so as not to taint the interrogation. He tasted cigarettes in the back of his throat. “Mary was your best friend?”

She nodded.

Ray thought he observed tears welling up in her eyes, but it could've just been the haze of smoke. "Did you and Mary ever date the same guy?"

Jenny sniffled. "Once in high school. But it was two years apart."

That qualification suggested that she knew what Ray's line of questioning would be. If they dated the same guy within a short time period, it could've suggested that one was dumped for the other, thereby evoking jealousy, which in turn could've been a motive to kill. Yet two years apart strongly indicated that jealousy was not a factor with respect to that particular guy. And besides, it was six to eight years ago—too far removed, too remote in time, he thought. *She didn't have any part in this murder. But let's go through the motions so Bill won't get his panties in a bunch.* His questioning became somewhat perfunctory. "Did that make you angry, to have your best friend dating your ex?"

"I dated him after she did, actually." She added heatedly, "And it was high school for God's sake."

"And there was no guy you were chasing that she stole or dated?"

She exhaled smoke toward the ceiling. "She liked the bad-boy type. I don't."

Seems true. He quickly changed the subject. "I got your bank records right here, Jenny. Looks like you withdrew $1000 from your savings account 11 days ago."

"You pulled my bank records?" she asked with a consternate tone before adding her cigarette butt to the crowd already present in the ashtray. "Don't you need a warrant or something to do that?"

Ray ignored the accurate question. He had his sources. "What'd you use that grand for? Doesn't look like a typical withdrawal for you. I mean your paycheck is only about $600 every two weeks. A grand is a lot to withdraw."

She lit up another cigarette. Her face was austere, her shaking hands visible even through the haze. "It ain't a lot to pay someone to kill, though, is it Officer?"

She's a sharp one. "That depends."

She shook her head and sighed. "I gave that money to my mother. I help her out from time to time. She needed rent money.

Ain't the first time neither. Go ask my mother if you want. Or check my bank records further back in time."

"Did your mother deposit that money into an account?"

"Doubt it. But go ask her landlord if she made rent this month and if she just paid last month's rent too. She ain't got no income, Officer…so you tell me where that two-month's rent money came from."

"I'll be back in a minute," Ray said, exiting into the viewing room. He shut the door and addressed Tammy. "You got anything else?"

"Nope. She seems sincere to me. Story seems plausible."

Ray nodded. "Well, just in case, you better go check out the mother and the landlord—if only to keep Bill off our backs."

"Gotcha." Tammy rose. "You going to hold her until I get back?"

He glanced at Jenny. "Nah. I don't see any reason to. She looks like she needs some rest."

"That and some nicotine gum," Tammy said over her shoulder as she exited into the hallway.

Ray nodded his agreement. He popped his head into the interview room. "Ms. Johansson. You're free to go." As he shut the door, he internally wished her a swift and easy grieving process. "Cut her loose," he directed the Officer waiting in the hallway.

With grieving on his mind, Ray moved down the hallway with the intention of spending the evening with Ed. That is, should his friend want company.

"What did you see after that?" Bill asked the witness on the phone. He had her pegged. She either did not fully witness the gang-related stabbing, she was too scared to talk, or she was partial to the assailants. As she fumbled through an answer of fragmented sentences and non-sequitors, Officer Royce approached. Bill threw his finger in the air to inform Royce to wait while he got off the phone. "I apologize, miss," he said into the phone, "but I will have to continue this conversation another time. Is tomorrow at noon okay?" When she assented, he said, "I will give you a call then," before hanging up. "What did you learn, Officer?" he asked Royce.

Royce shook his head. "It's a solid alibi, sir. I spoke to Erica Rosedale. Said they hooked up Saturday night and John spent the night. The building has surveillance. The super and I reviewed the tapes." Royce glanced down at his notepad. "We got John and Erica coming in around 1:53 Sunday early morning...and John leaving alone around 8:30 AM."

Bill considered this information, looking for holes. Wakefielder's guilt felt proper to Bill. "You can make out his face on the tapes?"

"Yep."

"It is clearly him?"

"Seems pretty clear to me."

Disappointed, Bill cringed, although he was certain that it was only internally, as he did not attempt to display it. Still, his mind continued down logical investigative tracks. "What was Mary's time of death?"

"Autopsy says 2:30 AM Sunday."

Bill thought for a moment. "Do you think he could have exited the building, killed Mary in such a manner, then reentered Erica's apartment in that time frame?" His mind quickly calculated, and he voiced his thoughts. "37 minutes, including travel time. A very small window considering the extensive nature of the crime and the distance—approximately 18 miles, I would estimate, and only a portion of which is highway."

Royce threw his palms up, shaking his head. "There's no way. He would've been on the surveillance cameras."

Something in Bill could not let this go. The most credible information led to Wakefielder. Everything in the picture fit except Wakefielder's alibi. "What if he got out another way?"

Royce's face changed. Bill was unsure how to interpret it. "They got cameras in the lobby, elevators, and both stairwells. Erica lives on the seventh floor, so he couldn't have crawled out the window, and there's no outside fire escape. It's a solid alibi, Bill. This guy's clean."

Reluctantly, Bill pulled his thoughts away...but not too far away. *He is clean of this murder, maybe, but he is certainly not clean.* Bill rose and grabbed his suit jacket from his chair back. "Did you confiscate the tapes?"

Royce nodded.

"Let's have you and the other rookies review them just to make sure there is nothing suspicious going on. He could have put a wig on and walked out a minute after he arrived."

"All right," Royce said before moving away.

Bill threw his jacket on as he moved down the hall to the interview room. Just before he opened the door to the viewing room, a call from down the hall brought his head around.

"Detective," Officer Parker yelled, jogging toward Bill.

Bill had almost forgotten that a search warrant had been executed at Wakefielder's house. That was uncharacteristic. He made a mental note to call his physician, then his mind returned to its investigative work. "Did you find anything I can use, Officer Parker?"

"Nothing about the murder, sir," Parker responded, pulling up in front of Bill.

Bill frowned. It took a second, but he noticed that his frown had not been a conscious action. *Hmm.* He was intrigued that such news could foster that type of reaction. He would have to explore it further, analyze it.

"But we got a brick of marijuana weighing 1.4 pounds."

Bill looked at Officer Parker's wide smile and fabricated one of his own. Although it was not any help with the murder investigation, his suspicions about John having committed a recent crime were borne out. Bill knew this guy had something on him. He was vindicated. "It does not help us with the murder, but it does explain why he ran. Excellent work today, Officer Parker." He clapped Parker on the shoulder and entered the viewing room without waiting for a response, then moved straight into the interview room without breaking stride. He shut the door behind him and sat across from John. "Would you like a light for that?" he asked, flicking his head to the cigarette wedged behind John's ear.

"Hell yeah," John said.

"Then let us talk about marijuana." Bill forged another wide smile, feeling genuinely happy to shove it down this smug asshole's throat.

John's face darkened, then paled.

"Let me ask you this: Do you know the weight at which a misdemeanor for marijuana possession becomes a felony intent to distribute?" Bill let his amusement shine, using as many physical manifestations as he could muster, his hands seemingly gesturing autonomously.

John paled further.

“No? Do you know what the word ‘recidivism’ means, and how it comes into play during sentencing?”

John cursed under his breath.

Bill turned and glared into the two-way mirror. Addressing his colleagues on the other side, he said, “Someone get Mr. Wakefielder a light.”

Oh, I am certainly on a roll today.

Step 2.6

"You think she's cute?" Captain Jim Pollack asked, swiveling in the chair behind his desk in his small office.

"Who's this now?" Detective Ernie Suarez asked while scratching his nose.

"No. Not in particular," Bill responded matter-of-factly, his face deadpan.

Jim waved Bill's lack of taste away. He turned to Ernie, hoping to sway the man to his side. "That new assistant district attorney. You know, blonde, curly hair. Freckles. Dimples. You know."

Ernie stroked his chin for a moment. "She's okay."

Jim shook his head. "You guys are crazy. I may have to find some new detectives that actually have an interest in women."

Bill remained expressionless, but at least Ernie sought to defend himself. He brought his hands to his chest. "I have a bias for brunettes. You know, being Latino and everything."

"And I got a bias for women," Jim retorted smartly. "Period." Another quip popped into his head. "Bill, here, apparently prefers his pistol hand. That, or he's asexual."

Ernie snorted. Jim slammed his palm on the desk, baring his teeth in a guffaw. *What would this office be without me? Lifeless and drab is what.*

Bill blinked hard. "I have been married for 14 years."

"That's exactly why you prefer your pistol hand." Jim laughed harder. It was really too easy.

Ernie covered his mouth and turned his head, fighting to keep from bursting.

Bill threw his hands in the air, looking as exacerbated as he possibly could, which was only mildly. "Can we get back on the subject?"

Jim's laugh waned. "All right, all right." He cleared his throat. "We got a solid suspect, so what's the problem?"

"The problem is we have not explored all avenues," Bill answered mechanically. Sometimes Jim thought his underling had a mild form of autism. Bill had to do everything by the book, in proper order. While it made Bill a strong detective, at times like this it was a seriously annoying character trait. "There is one suspect we have yet to even question," Bill continued.

I'm not caving on this one, Bill, no matter how obsessive-compulsive you are.

Ernie nodded flimsily, looking uneasy to be supporting Bill's position.

Until recently, Ernie had been a straight up 'yes' man, doing what he was told, when he was told. Now, having been raised to detective, he seemed to be coming into his own, more confident to voice his opinion and stand behind it. Jim supposed he didn't begrudge the young detective for that, as Jim had been the same way. *And it got me to Captain.* Jim chewed on his lip as he regarded his two detectives. "Don't even fucking say it."

Bill stood calmly. "How can he not be a suspect, Jim? We have his DNA in the house."

"He's Mary's fucking brother, for God's sake! Of course his DNA's in the house. He grew up in that house. His DNA's probably on the shitter upstairs." Now worked up, Jim yanked open his desk drawer and removed his pouch of chewing tobacco. He pinched a wad and shoved it into his mouth. The hit of nicotine relaxed him as he corralled his lip muscles around the chew.

Ernie seemed to muster his courage. "All we're asking is to question him, Cap. We're not going to throw him into an interview room and go at him."

Jim inclined his head in irritation. "What's the point of that?"

"To get the truth," Bill answered flatly. "We cannot simply rule him out on account that he is one of our own."

"And if Ed's innocent," Jim retorted, "you'll wind up fucking him up more than he already is." Jim shook his head to reinforce his argument in his own head. "Imagine what he'll do if he believes the whole Force thinks he butchered his own sister. We'll probably find him hanging from a rope in his bathroom."

"What if he killed her?" Ernie asked, his voice lowered. He glanced over his shoulder at the open door—probably, Jim suspected, to see if anyone was in earshot. He swiveled his head back to Jim, looking relieved.

Jim grabbed an empty paper cup and spit tobacco juice into it. He looked out the window at the parking lot, perusing the vehicles for no apparent reason. "How long have you known Ed? You know that the Chief was like an uncle to him. I don't see it in Ed at all." Bill started to protest, but Jim cut him off with a stern finger in the air. "Unless the Chief tells me otherwise, Ed's not a suspect," he said in a tone he hoped left nothing more to be discussed on the matter. He waited for Bill or Ernie to continue arguing, but neither did. He stood up. "So Dericardo is our number one guy?"

"Other than Ed, there are no other suspects or interested persons," Bill commented.

Jim shot Bill an agitated glare and rolled his eyes. Breaking his own moratorium, he asked, "You seriously think Ed did it?"

"Not really," Ernie responded first, "I just wasn't prepared to rule him out yet. Looks like Dericardo is our guy, but we don't exactly have a strong case against him."

Bill shrugged noncommittally.

Jim knew it was not necessarily about the results with Bill, but more about the process. *By the book.* He sighed grudgingly, then stuck his head out of his office. "Ray," he called.

"Yeah," Ray answered from across the room.

"Get in here."

Jim moved back to his desk and propped himself on an empty corner.

"What's up, Cap?" Ray said as he entered the office, glancing at Bill and Ernie.

"How many times have you seen Ed since the murder?"

"Three."

"Does he look like he's faking? Like he's not really grieving or upset?"

Ray flinched, his expression transitioning from bemused to offended. He glared at Bill contemptuously for a moment before answering. "He's not faking. I've known him for seven years."

"He is not a detective, Jim," Bill commented bluntly, throwing his hand toward Ray.

"I have a fucking degree in psychology," Ray retorted angrily, moving to get in Bill's face. "Who the fuck are you?"

Bill held his ground and regarded Ray with his chin raised. "For one, I am a detective…"

"I got more experience with -"

"All right, all right," Ernie said, barring each man with an arm. "We're on the same side."

"Enough," Jim said loudly.

"You don't know what a killer looks li -"

"Enough!" he yelled again. Bill and Ray quieted, Ray's face still displaying anger and Bill's face still neutral. Jim spat into his cup. "Ed's not a suspect. He's off the table. Ray, go back to your desk."

Ray stormed out of the room, muttering.

Bill's mouth opened.

"That's it!" Jim cut him off sternly. "I don't want to hear about it anymore. Dericardo is our guy. We got a motive, we got his prints in the kitchen, his hair in the living room, and we got him unaccounted for on the night of the murder."

Ernie nodded, apparently knowing the limits of his newfound voice. Bill huffed, still unaware of those limits or simply unable to control himself.

"I'm going to go let the Chief know," Jim said. "Go get the warrant and see what we can find in Dericardo's house." He ushered them out of his office. Removing the wad of chew, he tossed the cup in the trash and moved down the hall to the Chief's office.

He approached the Chief's secretary. "Hey, Sandra. Is he available?"

Sandra glanced at the phone. "He's still on the phone with the Mayor. Do you want to wait?"

"I'll wait." Jim moved to the couch.

"Oh," Sandra said just as Jim sat, "he just got off." She picked up the phone and hit a few buttons. "Chief, Jim is here to see you." After a brief pause, she turned to Jim. "Go on in."

"Thanks." Jim opened the door and entered the Chief's office. It was what one expected a Chief's office to be. Large and spacious, dark wood paneling on the walls, one wall filled with certificates and honors and the other with one, large painting. Chief Byron Stadmore sat in his cushiony chair, behind his wide mahogany desk, a strained look on his face as he combed his mustache with his fingertips. He swiveled to face Jim. "Mayor's on my ass, Jim. I was just going to come see you. He wants a defendant badly."

"We got one, Chief." Jim sat, a smile on his face.

Byron looked surprised. "Which one?"

"Dericardo. The other two have solid alibis."

Byron nodded coldly. He sat in thought for a moment. "You think we got enough? No DNA on the body, no witnesses, no violent priors, only a fingerprint on the toaster and a strand of hair in the living room. He was an ex-boyfriend, so it's explainable that he was in the house. *And* more than two years have passed since they broke up. Crimes of passion usually take place sooner, with no time to cool off."

Jim eyed the Chief apprehensively. "You keeping tabs on me, Chief? I didn't realize you knew so much about the suspects."

Byron shrugged. "It's my ass on the line, Jim. The Mayor calls me every damn day on this. I have to make it my business to know."

Jim nodded and reclined in the chair. "He's the only one we got, Chief. Nothing else adds up. The best friend dropped her off from the bar that night, so she didn't go home with some stranger. She wasn't dating anyone at the time, and her last boyfriend has a solid alibi. If it wasn't Dericardo, then we got nothing, no leads, no suspects. Nothing to give Ed some closure."

The Chief exhaled resignedly. "You think Dericardo did it, though?"

Jim nodded, but it was equivocal. His decision was due more to process of elimination than to concrete evidence. But that's how it worked sometimes in this business. Smoking guns were far and few between.

Byron picked up a pen and fingered it restlessly. "You think Ed had a reason to kill his sister?"

Not this again. Jim glared, feeling uptight, wanting to take the same tone with the Chief that he did with Bill and Ernie, but knowing that he couldn't. He didn't answer right away.

"I'm just thinking out loud," the Chief said defensively. "That's how we were taught to think. Remember?"

Although he was determined to stick to his guns, Jim nodded reluctantly. "Ed didn't do it. There's no motive. No family money to inherit. No indication of a feud or hatred. No mental issues. And look how he's been the last week. A killer that commits a murder in this fashion is cold as ice. That's not Ed."

"All right. I suppose I just needed to hear it voiced out loud." He dropped the pen on his desk. "Dericardo's our guy, then."

"I'll let the DA know," Jim said, rising and moving to the door.

As he headed back to his office, a doubt took root in the back of his mind. *Is it a mistake not to question Ed?* When he reached his office he shut the door and ruminated, running the arguments for and against his decision through his mind over and over. Yet even after an hour, he was no closer to an answer. He yanked open his desk drawer, reaching for his chew.

STEP 3: The Accusatory Instrument

A knock came at the door. “Yeah,” Franklin Dorey yelled out, his head still buried in trial transcripts.

His assistant, Janette, cracked open the door. “Jim Pollack’s here to see you.”

He looked up. “Tell him to hold on one sec.”

She nodded and shut the door.

Franklin gave his attention back to the transcripts, exhaling his annoyance once he flipped the page. *This is a royal screw up. Who doesn’t ask about the signature in a forgery case?* Still, he would break it to the young assistant district attorney softly—for the kid was a newly admitted attorney. “Here’s where you went wrong,” he said to the ADA in the chair on the other side of his desk. “You never crossed him on whether this was his handwriting.”

The ADA looked perplexed. “What if he would’ve said ‘no’? I thought it was a big risk.”

“Then you have another document with his signature on it—a check or a lease or something—and you shove it down his throat. Boom—he’s instantaneously discredited. So basically there’s little risk and a lot of reward. It’s a rarity that a defendant takes the stand in his own defense. You have to be prepared to take advantage.”

The ADA nodded, jotting notes down.

“All right,” Franklin said, tossing the transcripts across his desk gently before adjusting his gold cufflinks. He squinted at them for a fleeting second, wondering if they needed polishing again. No, he concluded, not until next week.

The ADA stood. “Thanks, Mr. Dorey,” he said with a smile of both appreciation and reverence—or at least Franklin assumed it was reverence.

What else should an ADA in his first year think of The District Attorney? "Any time." He liked being a mentor. He liked seeing young ADAs blossom into top-notch prosecutors. True, it was time consuming, and sometimes it was futile since the ADA was not likely to learn anything, but it was well worth the effort; mainly because the more prepared his ADAs were, the more convictions they would get and the better Franklin's record would look. That was somewhat of an ulterior motive, he admitted, and perhaps it was his main motive for mentoring to the extent that he did, but the higher his conviction rate, the more likely that it would advance his political career. At a minimum, it ensured that he would be reelected District Attorney each term.

Yet he didn't want to spend the rest of his career prosecuting criminals. He had greater ambitions, and he thought that, while his prosecutorial skills were refined and probably stronger than any other prosecutor in the county, he had other talents that could take him far in the political realm. So mentoring was important, as it indirectly affected his career.

A light knock came from the door. A second later it swung open and Jim entered. The hefty police captain shut the door and waddled to the chair opposite Franklin. The police Captain seemed to gain weight each week, Franklin observed. *Too many donuts.* "Look what we got here," Franklin said jovially. "Homicide actually decides to pay me a visit. Is today my birthday?"

Jim plopped into the chair and chuckled deeply. "I thought this was Wendy's office. Damn, the layout of this floor is confusing." He glanced around the room. "I should've known, though, that this wasn't Wendy's when I noticed how small this office is."

Franklin scratched his chin. "I thought Wendy got a restraining order against you. Didn't I prosecute that myself?" To drive his joke home, he held up a sheet of paper as if it was the restraining order.

"Ha! That expired yesterday, actually, so I'm good. No stalking charges for me."

Franklin laughed, shaking his head. "What do you got?"

Jim leaned in, his grin splitting his plump face. "The big one," he mouthed.

"No shit!" Franklin exclaimed. "Already?"

Jim displayed feigned modesty. "When you got someone like me heading homicide..." He shrugged. "These things happen."

We're peas in a pod, you and me, Jim.

"I just need you to tell me we have enough for a criminal complaint," Jim appended more seriously.

"Give it to me." *Please let it be a slam dunk.*

Jim opened the file in his hands. "Charles Dericardo," he stated deliberately before looking up to meet Franklin's gaze, as if the name in and of itself meant something of import to Franklin.

The name meant nothing, but Franklin repeated it aloud. As Jim gave him the details, the pieces began to come together in Franklin's mind. No, it wasn't a slam dunk with direct evidence, but there was damaging evidence that the defense would be hard-pressed to explain or counter. He decided quite quickly that no plea would be offered. This case needed to be tried and he needed to get a conviction for murder in the first and rape in the first—nothing less would do.

"So you think we got enough?"

Franklin sat back and smiled. "More than enough."

Jim returned the grin.

He eyed Jim confidently. "And I'm prosecuting this one myself. I don't trust it to anyone else," he confided in a partial truth. *And winning a conviction under the national spotlight could do wonders for my career.* He was almost salivating. "We'll get the complaint drawn up. Is he in holding?"

Jim nodded. "We're still searching his house."

"Is he represented?"

Jim pursed his lips in annoyance. "Asked for a lawyer pretty quickly."

Franklin perked. "By name?"

"Nah. Got a public defender."

Relieved, Franklin reclined. That would simply make his job all the more easier, depending on which public defender it was, of course. There were only two attorneys in the public defender's officer that had any wits about them, so he wasn't too worried. "All right. Let's wait until the search is done to see if we got anything else to add to the complaint, then we'll make the arrest." He swiveled his chair to face his computer.

"I'll let you know," Jim said while exiting the office.

Franklin opened a blank document and stared at it for a time. Then he began typing. *Mayor Franklin Dorey. Attorney General Franklin Dorey. Senator Franklin Dorey. Congressman Franklin*

Dorey. They all looked good on paper. Perhaps he should say them out loud to see how they sounded. Before he did, he glanced at the door of his office to make sure it was completely shut.

◆ ◆ ◆

Detective Ernie Suarez pulled up to the tiny shack that was Chucky Dericardo's home and parked behind a squad car. He exited his vehicle and put his hands on his hips, glancing around and examining the surroundings. The houses in this community, although single family, were packed together, leaving what looked like only enough space between them for a thin person to squeeze through moving sideways. *The Captain would probably get stuck.* Ernie laughed at the thought of Jim Pollack stuck between two houses while pursuing a suspect. *Would probably need grease to squeeze him out.*

A few neighbors were outside for the show. Some sat on stoops, smoking cigarettes solemnly, eyeing Ernie with knowing countenances, while others gathered at the street and whispered to each other in between glances at Dericardo's house. Ernie rolled his neck before turning his attention to the house. It was tiny. Very tiny, like a split-level without the split. It was only marginally larger than a trailer home, in fact, and it probably had only one bedroom. Similar in size to the house that Ernie was raised in, except Ernie's childhood home was packed with six other bodies. He sighed as a flood of memories crashed into his skull.

The outside of Dericardo's house was painted a dirty canary yellow, or it was painted yellow and simply dirty. Probably the latter, Ernie surmised. The color didn't seem to suit the suspect at all, but then again, Ernie supposed that Chucky Dericardo was just a renter. He assumed Dericardo couldn't afford to buy a home working on the assembly line at Universal Electric, even a home like this, so he guessed that this home had been painted long ago by the owner.

A beat up, faded black truck that looked to have been in numerous fender benders without being fixed sat on the gravel driveway, the front bumper hanging precariously low to the ground despite behind held up by a fraying green-colored rope of twine. Ernie shook his head at the ineptitude of the bumper fix. His eyes narrowed in contemplation. The pieces didn't seem to fit together. A guy who could plan and execute a murder so competently couldn't think of anything better than twine to fix his fender—and a guy that worked on an assembly line putting together turbines, no less. Chucky probably used a blowtorch daily, Ernie thought, welding metal pieces together, but he couldn't figure out how to fix a loose fender. It didn't make sense. But, then again, little in life did, and particularly so when it came to crime. The smartest people could commit the stupidest crimes and vice versa. He shrugged as he moved to the front door.

He entered the small living room to find beat cops searching the home at the direction of Officer Nuck. Nuck looked content wielding authority, which brought a smile to Ernie's face despite the strong smell of stale beer and cat feces in the room. He recalled the first time he was put in charge of a search. It had only fueled his drive to move up in the ranks.

Officer Nuck turned at the sound of Ernie shutting the front door. Irritation flashed on Nuck's face before he gained his composure. Ernie understood. No one wanted power and control taken away. Being a newly anointed detective, Ernie was cognizant of that and how it affected the psyche of a young officer. It had happened to him on a few occasions and he hadn't liked it one bit. *Don't worry Nuck, I'm not here to usurp your authority.* He smiled as Nuck approached.

"Detective," Nuck said, almost in a tone asking "what the fuck are you doing here taking away my control of this search?"

"Steve," Ernie responded with a smile. "Find anything so far?"

Nuck glanced around the tiny space and shook his head. "Nothing. And we've been through the whole place three times."

Ernie nodded, almost expecting as much. "Well I'll just take a quick look myself." He patted Nuck on the shoulder.

Nuck shot him a respectful yet agitated look. "Be my guest," he said, stepping to the side.

Ernie didn't blame him for being pissed off. He knew exactly what Nuck was thinking—that Ernie was questioning Nuck's capabilities. He wasn't at all. It was more so a question of the capabilities of the beat cops working under Nuck. They could miss something an experienced eye would catch. Besides, the place was small enough that it would only take Ernie 15 minutes to look around. Once past Nuck, Ernie turned slightly to catch a glimpse of Nuck's face. *Yep, there it is.* Ernie returned his head forward so

Nuck couldn't see the smile on his face. He knew what was going through the officer's head. Nuck realized that if Ernie found something, it would confirm that Nuck had done a poor job of searching the house. It was one thing to have a superior think you may be incompetent. It was an entirely different thing to have a superior confirm you were incompetent.

"All right, boys. Let's look for loose floorboards or hidden compartments," Nuck directed the beat cops. "Pay attention to the details."

Ernie's smile widened. He went about his business, staying out of everyone else's way, searching the living room, the kitchen, the bedroom, and the bathroom. It took all of 15 minutes, and he found nothing. He approached Officer Nuck. "Let's wrap it up pretty soon and report back. The DA needs to get the criminal complaint filed ASAP."

Officer Nuck nodded, looking relieved. "Got it."

Ernie exited the house and glanced around. He noticed a woman on a stoop of the house directly across from Dericardo's and decided to speak to her. He crossed the street and said, "Hi, miss."

She nodded, a cigarette held to her lips. She was lean, but not a healthy looking lean, her graying hair was wiry and unkempt, her face was elongated and her skin seemed to droop, betraying her age. Ernie guessed she was in her seventies, but heavy smoking seemed to age the face prematurely, so she could've been in her sixties.

"I'm with the police department."

"Hello, policeman," she said, her voice raspy.

Ernie bit his lip but remained calm. "Do you know your neighbor across the street?"

She blew out smoke. "Yes."

"Did you happen to see him this past weekend, on Saturday night? Do you know if he was at home?"

"I don't know."

It was clear he was going to learn nothing from this woman, so he glanced around to see if other neighbors were still outside. They all apparently had gone back to their own homes. "Good day, miss." He turned.

"But he rarely goes out," she yelled after him.

Ernie stopped in the middle of the street.

She took a drag. "That truck of his is always in that driveway, and he doesn't have another car." She flicked her cigarette, grabbed a piece of knit-work sitting next to her and began manipulating the needles.

Ernie glanced at the truck and nodded his thanks to the woman. He returned to his vehicle and made for the station. His feeling that the pieces were not adding up returned and niggled at him.

Maybe he should've been more adamant with the Captain that Ed be questioned.

◆ ◆ ◆

"You ready?" Jim asked as he approached Ray's desk.

Ray nodded.

The room was silent, all eyes cast upon the Captain. "Let's go then." He glanced at his watch. "I hate to rush this but I've got a press conference scheduled in ten minutes."

Ray rose, displaying a resolute expression. Jim guessed it was because Ray wanted to give Ed some closure, and putting the killer behind bars was the only way to do it. Jim also thought he saw a hint of sorrow in Ray's eyes, although he was not normally attuned to such features, especially in men. He patted Ray on the back as they exited the room and gave his officer a sharp nod of support.

Ray returned it, looking reassured.

"Captain," a shout came from behind as they turned down the hallway leading to the holding cells.

Jim and Ray paused and turned. Detective Suarez came into the hallway and stopped before them.

"Cap," Ernie said before pausing, concern etching wrinkles on the skin around his mouth. As his lips moved in apparent conflict, Jim's eyes narrowed, wondering what was up.

"Spit it out," Jim finally directed in annoyance, his arms crossed.

Ernie scratched his head. "Uh…mind if I follow along."

Jim shook his head incredulously. "Let's go," he said, waving Ernie along as he turned and set off. *What was that about?* There was something strange going on in his unit recently. Maybe it was the high-profile nature of this case. He personally had been more anxious than normal on account of being hounded by the media and, of course, simply trying to bring this case to a swift and proper resolution. Perhaps it was merely the heinous nature of this crime that had everyone on edge. Or concern for Ed's well being. Maybe all of the above. Whatever it was, he hoped it would go away once they turned this case over to the DA—which would be happening once he reached the end of this hallway, thankfully. "Public Defender still in with him?" he asked Ray.

"As far as I know."

Jim shrugged. After being buzzed through to the holding cells, they stopped in front of the cell housing Chucky Dericardo. "You ready?" he asked Ray.

Ray took a deep breath before nodding firmly.

"All right. Let's close this one up."

Ray pulled the cuffs off of his belt, opened the door and entered, Jim and Ernie following behind him. The public defender immediately rose. He was a sinewy man, with disheveled black hair, thick-framed brown glasses, a dingy navy suit, and a faded tie with an abstract pattern that dated it to the 1970s. His crooked mouth was moving, as if he was attempting to object to something, but no words came out. Jim almost laughed, as much as at the public defender's appearance as at the look on Ray's face. A second later, Ray recovered himself.

"Charles Dericardo," Ray said in a stern voice. "You're under arrest for the rape and murder of Mary Roletti." Ray moved around the table behind Chucky and handcuffed the suspect. He read Chucky the *Miranda* rights.

The Public Defender turned to Chucky. "Don't say anything. Now or later. Don't talk about the case to cellmates. Don't talk on the phone in earshot of any cops. Okay? Just keep your mouth shut unless I'm with you. Okay?"

Chucky just stared at the attorney blankly. Jim studied Chucky's face, trying to decipher whether it registered shock, fright, relief, or absolutely nothing. It was difficult to tell. The man seemed reserved, almost like he didn't have it in him to have killed Mary in such a way. Then again, Jim had seen more than a few soft-spoken, mild-mannered, model citizens go ballistic during his years as a cop. Who knew why people snapped? He and Ernie pulled out of the room as Ray led the suspect out.

Ray moved down the hall with Chucky. Jim watched him trail away for a moment, took a deep breath, then turned, ready to confront the media.

"Captain," Ernie said next to him.

"Yeah," Jim responded, swiveling his head.

Ernie again looked conflicted. After a brief pause, he said, "never mind," before rapidly fleeing the other direction.

What is with that boy?

Yes, he would be glad when this case was behind them.

"No, sir, I don't. I don't think it will be much trouble at all," District Attorney Franklin Dorey said into the phone resting on his shoulder. He reclined in his chair, listening to the Mayor go on and on about the Roletti case. Exasperated, he reached for his forehead and squeezed his eyes shut. There were so many idiots in politics. He often wondered how they got elected. *By a bigger bunch of idiots. That's how.* The wholesale incompetence in government at all levels amazed him. Franklin hoped to change that—at least in his small town and county, or maybe even in the State. That thought was an injection of confidence that gave him the go-ahead to interrupt the Mayor. "Sir…sir, I have it under control. Besides, he's represented by a public defender. And not a very good one, either. A conviction shouldn't be a problem."

Then the Mayor asked him if he thought the defendant would try to change venue to another county for the trial. Franklin snorted petulantly. He hated when laymen wanted to discuss legal strategy. Ninety nine percent of the time they had no idea what they were talking about, like now for instance. And if Franklin capitulated, he'd have to start from the beginning and explain every single legal concept before making his point. Then the Mayor would only be emboldened to ask another legal question or make a legal comment. It would be an endless cycle. "Why don't you leave that to me…sir. I've got it under control," he answered brusquely, hoping his tone conveyed his dislike of the topic.

Just then, a knock came at his door and it instantly cracked open before he could give an acknowledgment. Wendy Carter popped her head in, her silky, black hair hanging straight down in the door's gap. His ADA in charge of homicides pushed her black-framed glasses—which always reminded Franklin of a secretary in a porno—up her petite nose and moved to pull away upon noticing Franklin on the phone. He waved her in. She slipped in, shut the door lightly behind her, sat in the chair opposite Franklin, and crossed her legs, glancing around the room in search of momentary entertainment. She held a piece of paper in her hand tightly, almost crushing it.

Franklin examined her, his mind willingly distracted from the phone conversation. In addition to being attractive, she was a competent ADA. Wendy had been the ADA overseeing homicides for nine years now, and Franklin didn't think he could've functioned without her. She would be second-chairing the trial, of course, so they would be spending a lot of time together in the upcoming months. "Uh huh," he said listlessly into the phone. "Uh huh."

Wendy flashed him a troubled smile, then fidgeted anxiously, looking like she had something important to discuss. It was as good a reason as any to end his conversation with the Mayor—if it could even be called a conversation. "Mr. Mayor, I hear you. I hear you. But listen, something just came up in the office so we'll have to end this discussion. I'll keep you apprised." The Mayor kept talking. *Why?* "Uh huh. Yep. Certainly. Uh huh. Okay. Bye-bye now." He hung up the phone and rubbed his eyes. "That man makes me crazy. He thinks he's a damn attorney. Maybe we should let him prosecute the case."

"That would be a horrible idea," Wendy said.

"It was a joke."

"No. Franklin, you don't understand. We're going to have our hands full."

Bewildered, his back went rigid in alarm. The concern in Wendy's voice tingled down his spine. "What do you mean?"

She gulped. "Don't ask me how, but Dericardo got John Upton."

"What?!"

Wendy held up a letter from John Upton's office and passed it across the desk. Franklin grabbed it and read. It was only two sentences, but those two sentences were cause for concern, informing his office of Upton's representation of Dericardo. His first thought was 'how the hell did a poor, uneducated, lowlife like Charles Dericardo come to be represented by the best criminal defense attorney in upstate New York?' His second thought was, 'oh yes, he had his work cut out for him.' After that, his thoughts were totally overwhelmed by fright. He wasn't scared of facing John Upton, per se, but he quickly realized the potential implications of doing so in such a high-profile case. If he got a conviction, he could probably have his choice of office in the next elections. Hell, he would even have a possibility at Attorney General. If he lost, however, his political ambitions would be quashed, and he would be stuck prosecuting crimes the rest of his life or trying to grind out a living with a small law practice. This trial was all or nothing, then, and that scared the shit out of him.

"We're going to need some more ADAs on this case," Wendy said, as if in validation of Franklin's internal fears.

Franklin nodded, his heart thumping. A lot more ADAs, he judged.

STEP 4:
The Hearing

He walked down the hallway with his police hat tucked underneath his arm, head straight but eyes fractionally lowered so as to avoid eye contact. His face felt strange, almost adolescent. This morning was the first time he'd shaved in three weeks, so naturally it would feel different, but there seemed to be something more to it. He fought to keep his hand from his chin, realizing in that instant what was affecting him; that the smooth, oily quality of his face transported him back to his childhood, back to good times, back to when his sister was alive. He sniffled softly. Needing to focus on something else, he honed in on the clank of his shoes on the marble floor of the wide hallway. It did nothing but remind him of a death march. From his peripheral vision, he noticed eyes on him, and he thought a few camera flashes went off. He steeled himself to keep any emotion from his face. It was difficult, but he knew that doing so now would be infinitely easier than when he entered the courtroom. If he couldn't do so now, then he probably shouldn't even go in, he decided. Finally, he reached the courtroom doors and grabbed the large, bronze-plated handle.

A hand landed on his chest, halting him. "Are you sure about this?" Ray asked, his face uncomfortably close.

Ed took a deep breath before nodding firmly.

Ray looked like he wanted to say more but held his tongue and nodded back.

Ed opened the door and stepped inside the courtroom. He was immediately overwhelmed. The courtroom was packed. A quick survey of the room revealed everyone from media, to fellow policemen, to public officials, to the homeless guy who hung out on the courthouse steps. His face paled slightly as he wondered if he'd made the right choice in coming. Could he control his emotions, his rage, his sorrow, during the trial with so many faces trained on him. He knew that while everyone would be watching the trial, his presence would invite frequent glances as the facts of the murder came to light. As Ray's hand came to rest on his back, Ed realized he was still standing in the courtroom's entrance, and that he had caused murmurs to spring up throughout the room. He tried to wick the embarrassment from his face.

Ray leaned into his ear. "How about the very back?" he said, pointing to the pews at the back corner of the room.

It was a good idea, and in response Ed cleared his throat, moved into the pew and sat, straightening his uniform. He glanced around and acknowledged a few officers looking his way, but made an effort not to seek anyone out. A few moments later, the Captain and the Chief entered the courtroom. They moved in to sit next to Ray. The Chief bent across Ray and patted Ed on the knee, like a father would a child. Ed closed his eyes briefly and sighed. He quickly realized that he would be sighing a great deal throughout this trial—that is, if he wasn't crying or seething.

Three loud knocks came from the door behind the bench.

"All rise," the bailiff called out. "The Honorable Kenneth Talini presiding."

"Be seated, be seated," the Judge yelled before the room was fully standing and before he was even visible. He stepped up to the bench and sat in unison with the gallery. He was a short man, semi-stocky, with a bald pate and an austere face boasting wide nostrils and drooping jowls. Ed recalled the one time he had testified in a case presided over by Judge Talini. It was a grand larceny case, and Ed was the arresting officer. His one hour of testimony was not enough to allow him to form an opinion of the Judge, but from what he'd heard, Judge Talini was a fair judge who was all business. Many judges leaned toward the prosecution, but not Judge Talini, Ed had heard. The man was square in the middle. That didn't bode well for his sister's trial, yet the law was so prosecution-oriented that it probably wouldn't matter—at least Ed persuaded himself it was so.

The Judge glanced down at the desk before him, shuffled some papers around, then lifted his head to regard the gallery. His eyes narrowed transiently before he glanced at the court reporter. Once he received a nod from the court reporter, he turned to his Part Clerk.

"People of the State of New York versus Charles Dericardo," the Part Clerk announced. A side door near the bench opened and Chucky was ushered into the room by two court officers. Every neck in the gallery craned to get a glimpse of the defendant, and a few flash bulbs went off. Chucky wore the customary orange jumper, with his hands and feet shackled together, causing him to shuffle along with his hands held before his waist. His blonde hair was disheveled, his eyes reddened, and his marginally bucked—and crooked—teeth protruded from his lips ever so slightly. He kept his head pointed forward without glancing at the gallery. He made it to the defense table and settled in next to his attorney.

John Upton, Esquire. The fucking bastard! Ed had the nerve to catch the man outside after the hearing and beat him senseless. He trained his eyes on Upton's back. Ed could tell, even from this distance, that the man's navy pinstriped suit was of the finest quality. His pristine walnut brown hair was gelled into a standard part that annoyingly reminded Ed of Clark Kent. The likeness was somewhat of a bad omen, Ed thought. Upton put his arm around Chucky and whispered into his client's ear. The man had an air about him, a flavor—one that turned Ed's stomach sour. What on earth could possess a man to help criminals get away with murder? And why this case in particular? Why Mary? Ed knew that Chucky was destitute, that he couldn't afford a lawyer, let alone the biggest defense attorney north of Manhattan. So why…and how? It didn't make sense.

Ed glanced at the District Attorney for reassurance. Franklin Dorey was smiling as he discussed something with ADA Carter. The DA looked confident and poised, which permitted Ed to relax.

"All right," Judge Talini said, "we have a few motions to deal with and a suppression hearing. Is that correct, Mr. Upton?"

John Upton stood, buttoned the top two buttons of his three-button suit, and clasped his hands behind his back. He was a tall man when upright. Towering but somehow not imposing. He briefly turned to regard his client, permitting Ed a view of his face. Except for a chiseled chin, Upton's face was kind. His silver cufflinks sparkled from the light off the large chandelier overhead. "That is correct, Your Honor. We have three motions and we also seek to suppress a purported statement made by Mr. Dericardo while in police custody."

The Judge shuffled through the papers on his desk. "Ah," he said, apparently locating the motion. "Please continue."

Upton resumed fluidly. "The first motion, Your Honor, is to close the courtroom to all media. As you are aware, Your Honor, this is a case that has attracted national media attention, and we submit that it is extremely prejudicial to Mr. Dericardo to have the media taking pictures, shooting video, blogging, rifling through their bags and so forth, during the pendency of the trial." He sat, signaling that he'd made his point.

The Judge's expression didn't chance. He swiveled his head to the DA. "Counselor?"

"Well, Your Honor," the DA began, rising slowly from his chair. "The courtroom is inherently a public forum, and criminal cases are generally open to the public. And the public includes the media. The defendant has failed to present a sufficient basis to disturb that policy. The fact that this is a high-profile case, standing alone, is not grounds to deny the media their constitutionally-guaranteed coverage."

The Judge turned back to Mr. Upton.

"Your Honor, as you know, this is a small town, and a scarcely populated county, so the more media there is the more potential that coverage, which undoubtedly will be rampant, will permeate and influence the jury members, whether they attempt to avoid it or not. At a minimum, Judge, the Court should restrict the number of media in the courtroom and the methods of reporting."

"May I respond to that, Your Honor?" the DA asked.

The Judge waved him off, apparently having heard enough. Yes, Ed thought, this Judge was certainly all business...and curt at that. "It is certainly true that this is an open forum, but in my time on this bench I have learned that media attention can potentially alter the course of a trial, particularly with the onset of the internet and mobile devices that provide for instantaneous news publication. However, I do not believe there is sufficient justification in this case for a wholesale preclusion of the media." He looked to the gallery. "All of you reporters in the room, listen up. In fact, please stand."

The reporters glanced around nervously, concern on their faces.

"Come on, now. Stand up," the Judge directed.

Nearly half the room rose cautiously, heads swiveling to find companions, a few probably wondering if they'd be jailed for some reason or if their press credentials would be stripped.

Judge Talini surveyed the room with pursed lips. "There will be no video recording of this trial, no audio recording, no photography of any kind. No iPhones, blackberries, smartphones. No blogging, Facebooking, YouTubing, Tweeting, or Instragramming during the trial. I probably missed a few, but I'm sure that most of you are already impressed that a man of my age is aware of these things."

The room laughed. Even Ed found himself cracking a smile for a brief moment.

"And I assure you," the Judge continued more sternly, "I am able to use all of these things and will be periodically checking them for violations of my directive. If you so chose, you may report the old-fashioned way. That is, with pen and paper. But be mindful that this is a serious trial. A man's liberty is on the line, so do not be disruptive." He paused. "You all may sit. What's next, Mr. Upton?"

"Thank you, Your Honor. Our next motion is to fix bail. There is nothing to demonstrate that Mr. Dericardo is a flight risk. He has lived and worked in Schenectady his entire life, he has no passport and has never been outside the country. Moreover, the alleged case against Mr. Dericardo is entirely circumstantial. There is no DNA or fingerprint evidence on the victim's body. As such, we ask that bail be set at $15,000."

"Mr. Dorey, a response."

"Yes, Your Honor," the DA responded. "This is a most heinous crime, some of the details of which I'm sure you are already aware of." The Judge shrugged noncommittally as the DA continued. "Mr. Dericardo is a grave threat to society, and to women in particular. The seriousness of the crime is cause to deny bail outright. Furthermore, Mr. Dericardo has a prior conviction. Based on that, we contend that bail should be denied."

The Judge wrinkled his nose before ruling. "In felony cases, the Legislature provides that bail is in the discretion of the Court except in rare circumstances that are not present here. I am in receipt of a fingerprint report establishing that Mr. Dericardo has previously been convicted of a misdemeanor as a juvenile. I am not accustomed to denying defendants bail, and I will not do so in this case. However, the circumstances warrant that bail be fixed at an amount commensurate with the depravity of the alleged crime and the potential threat to the public. Bail is set at $1,000,000. Next motion."

Ed smiled, happy with the ruling.

"Yes, Your Honor," Upton responded, as if losing the prior motion meant nothing to him. "I had the opportunity this morning to review the People's witness list, which includes at least one relative and one close friend of the victim. It is likely that these witnesses will be in the gallery during part or all of the trial. As a result, we submit that all witnesses should be sequestered, or more aptly, barred from the courtroom until they testify. There is significant prejudice to Mr. Dericardo that could result if the People's witnesses were privy to each others testimony."

"Any response, Counselor?" the Judge asked the DA.

Ed's anger flared. He waited for the DA to defend him.

Mr. Dorey leaned into ADA Carter and the two had a brief conversation under their breaths. Then he rose. "Uh, no Your Honor, as long as it is applied to both sides."

"We don't object to that," Mr. Upton said, "of course, excluding Mr. Dericardo himself."

The Judge nodded his agreement. "That motion is granted. All witnesses will be sequestered until after they testify, at which time they can sit in the gallery if they so chose." He turned to the court reporter. "Off the record."

The court reporter removed her fingers from her stenotype machine.

Ed clenched his jaw in anger, grinded his teeth, and slammed his fist into his leg. That fucking defense lawyer just got him banned from his own sister's murder trial. *That fucking bastard! I'll fucking kill him!*

Ray tried to give him a consoling elbow, but Ed ignored it, his eyes fixed on that smug asshole at the defense table.

Judge Talini placed his forearms on the bench and leaned on them. "Since we are about to start the hearing, at this time I will ask all witnesses to please leave the courtroom. Counselors, do we have any witnesses present other than Mr. Dorey's first witness for the hearing?"

Both attorneys turned and surveyed the gallery.

"None on my side, Judge," Mr. Upton answered.

"I believe I have a few, Your Honor," the DA said before turning again and looking straight at Ed. "Officer Edward Roletti, in the back, Your Honor, and Sergeant Robby Burns, here toward the front."

"Gentlemen, I apologize but I will have to ask you to leave the courtroom. The DA will notify you of the date of your testimony. On that particular day, you should wait outside the courtroom until you are called. Do not enter the courtroom, as other witnesses may be testifying at that time."

Ed felt his face flush with fury. With all eyes fixed on him, he stood. He narrowed his eyes, trying to pierce John Upton with his gaze alone. The man's mouth puckered into a smirk. On the verge of doing something stupid, Ed stormed from the courtroom, slamming open the double doors.

"Ed, I'll come with you. Wait up, buddy." Ray's voice was barely perceptible in the distance behind him. Muttering angrily, Ed burst through the front doors of the building and sped down the long stone staircase, thinking of ways to kill John Upton and Chucky Dericardo…and how to get away with it.

◆ ◆ ◆

Captain Jim Pollack sat in the back of the courtroom, listening to his detective testify at the hearing. Ernie was coming into his own, Jim admitted. He was becoming a competent policeman, a competent detective. Testifying was, by far, the most difficult part of being a cop, in Jim's opinion. It took practice, discipline, study, and basic trial and error to be good at it. The truth could be bent somewhat, but there was a line that couldn't be crossed, and the story had to be believable at all times. The moment something was said that was borderline unbelievable, it could shatter the officer's credibility and effectively destroy the case. It had been mostly trial and error that taught Jim these lessons. But Ernie was doing a good job, even under cross examination by John Upton. It spoke well for Ernie's future in the Force.

Jim's thoughts turned to Ed. He felt a pang of remorse for the kid, mixed in with a bit of anger. The boy hardened himself enough to come and watch the trial, only to be kicked out by the Judge. He'd have to check in on Ed and make sure the kid was hanging in there.

"No further questions," Upton said before sitting.

Ernie stepped down from the witness stand.

"Mr. Upton," the Judge said, "do you have any witnesses?"

"No, Your Honor."

The Judge, who looked to have been taking meticulous notes during Ernie's testimony, glanced down at his notepad. There was a long pause while he studied his notes. "This was a hearing pursuant to the precedent of *People versus Huntley* to suppress statements made by the defendant to police at the Schenectady County Police Station. Having received the testimony of Detective Ernesto Suarez, I make the following findings of facts:

"Charles Dericardo was asked at his home if he would be willing to come to the station to answer some questions. He willingly accompanied the officers to the station and was placed in an interview room. He was not given *Miranda* rights and was not placed under arrest, nor handcuffed or otherwise restrained. He was free to leave at any time and was informed of the same. He sat in the interview room for approximately ten minutes prior to Detective Suarez entering the room. He was questioned for approximately 15 minutes and voluntarily answered each question. In particular, he was asked why he committed the crime. In response, he answered that he was, quote, 'angry about being dumped,' end-quote. It was not until after he made this statement that he requested an attorney. All questions ceased at that point."

The Judge shifted in his chair and took a sip of water. "I find Detective Suarez's testimony to be credible. Consequently, I make the following conclusions: Mr. Dericardo voluntarily came to the station and answered questions. He was not in custody. The length of time in the interview room and the brevity of the questioning establish that he was not in police custody at the time the statement was made. His right to counsel was not triggered until he expressly requested an attorney, which was after the statement at issue was made. At that time, the questioning ceased in accord with proper procedure and constitutional mandates."

The Judge paused and glanced at both attorneys' tables. "I find that Mr. Dericardo's statement at issue was knowingly, willingly, and voluntarily made. Accordingly, Defendant's motion to suppress is hereby denied. The statement that he was, quote, 'angry about being dumped,' end-quote, is admissible at trial." He turned to his Part Clerk. "Did I block this in for Monday?"

As the Part Clerk pulled up the calendar on the computer, Jim sighed in relief, smiling. He knew that the incriminating statement was the most damaging piece of evidence against Chucky, and without it there likely would be no conviction—particularly without DNA evidence on Mary's body.

"Yes, Judge," the Part Clerk answered.

"Jury selection will commence Monday," Judge Talini announced before banging his gavel on the bench. He promptly rose to exit.

"All rise," the bailiff yelled as the Judge made his way out of the courtroom.

The Chief clapped Jim on the back as they rose. Smiling wider, Jim shook the Chief's hand, delighted at how the case had started.

◆ ◆ ◆

As Ray turned the corner, the house came into view. Just then, Ed exited the front door and made for his police cruiser in the gravel driveway, his rapid pace bespeaking his determination and single-mindedness, his face dark and dangerous.

Shit! Ray slammed on the gas pedal and screeched into the driveway behind Ed's cruiser, angling his own car to block Ed's exit route. Ray hopped out of his car and moved to the driver's side window of Ed's cruiser. "Ed. It's Ray, buddy," he called out, making sure that Ed knew it was him. He slowed as he approached the car window. Ed sat rigidly in the car, both hands locked in a death grip on the steering wheel, his gaze lowered, brow furled, lips scrunched in rage. Not wanting to provoke his friend, Ray stopped a full yard from the car. Unable to keep the nervous quiver from his voice, he asked, "Where you headed, Ed?"

Ed didn't move. There was a long pause during which Ed seemed to be deciding whether to answer at all. "Move your car," he demanded in a disturbing tone.

Ray took a gulp, unsure what to do or say. He'd never before seen his friend this crazed, this possessed, and he wondered exactly what Ed intended. He unconsciously took a small step backward. He glanced around Ed to the passenger seat. *No. Come on!* He had no idea how to handle this now, so he decided to be direct, ignoring the bout of fear that threatened to topple his legs like an avalanche. "Where are you headed with that shotgun?"

Ed exhaled audibly through his nose, his knuckles blanching on the steering wheel. Still his gaze didn't rise to meet Ray's own.

Ray waited for an answer, but none came. *What has this turned you into, Ed?* "There's no good that can come from this, Ed. You won't even be able to get to Chucky. It's insane."

Ed laughed maliciously. "Not him," he said under his breath.

What?! If Ed wasn't going for Chucky, then who? After a few seconds, it dawned on Ray. "Killing Upton won't bring your sister back, and it won't help you. All it will do is prolong the trial so Chucky can get another lawyer, and it will put you behind bars." He wasn't the best at being persuasive, and he didn't know if he was getting through to Ed, but the longer he kept talking, the longer Ed stayed put; and the longer they stayed in the driveway, the greater the possibility Ed would cool down. So Ray went on, almost stream of conscious. "Hell, you're a police officer, Ed. Do you know what they do to cops in prison? Let the justice system sort it out, like you do every day in your job. It's no different, even if it's your family involved. John Upton's just doing his job. There's no saying that Chucky will be acquitted just because he has Upton as his lawyer." Ray wasn't so sure of that last statement, but he voiced it nonetheless. "It's not worth it, Ed. It won't satisfy you. You still have your life, buddy. I know it's hard, I know you want revenge, but don't throw it all away like this."

"They took her from me," Ed whispered menacingly. Then, he turned and made eye contact, his gaze piercing.

Disquieted, Ray held that gaze for only a fraction of a second. He swayed lightly on his feet as he glanced at the empty street for no other reason than to avoid that gaze. The start of Ed's engine brought his head round.

"Now move your car," Ed demanded loudly over the rumble of the engine, his gaze returned forward, undeterred.

Throughout his life, Ray had been the nice guy, the compassionate guy, the level-headed guy. Never the assertive guy, the bullish guy, the commanding guy. His demeanor permitted him to get pushed around a bit. Oh, it was a bit ironic, he knew, that he was now a cop, but the Force needed cops with skills other than simple brawn, and that was partly why he joined up. Now, Ray had two choices: walk meekly to his car, move it, and let Ed go do the unthinkable, which would be right in line with Ray's character, or stand his ground and force Ed's hand.

Ray gritted his teeth and took a deep breath. If there was any time in his life to put his foot down, it was now. He stepped forward, stuck his hand through the window and clawed his fingers around Ed's forearm.

Ed looked first to his own forearm, then tracked up Ray's arm until their gazes locked. Ray thought he saw a little awe and esteem mixed in with the rage boiling behind Ed's eyes. It was just enough to compel Ray forward. "The only way you're doing this is if you shoot me dead first," he said through a clamped mouth, his gaze holding fast, his heart pumping hard.

Ed pursed his lips contemplatively. The fact that Ed was contemplating at all scared the shit out of Ray, but he didn't let anything show on his exterior. He waited for Ed's arm to move for the shotgun. Almost expected it.

Ed twitched. Ray gasped.

Another few heartbeats passed. Then, Ed shut the car off.

Ray sighed internally, his hands shaking. As he opened the car door to let Ed out, his friend began to bawl uncontrollably, Ed's head falling forward to rest on the steering wheel.

Compassionate Ray returned in a flash.

STEP 5:
The Trial

Step 5.1

The courtroom was abuzz with chatter, raising the hair on the back of his neck. He hadn't tried a case in some time, and never had he done so with a full gallery behind him. Ignoring the butterflies in his gut, he turned to Wendy. "What do you think of them?" Franklin asked. He pulled a stack of manila folders out of his trial bag and placed them on the prosecution table before him.

His ADA bent down, grabbed her own trial bag and yanked it up to the table with a grunt. "They look pretty good to me," Wendy responded. "The only one that scares me is juror number ten." She pulled a yellow notepad from her bag and perused it. "He donated money to a few candidates on the way left."

Franklin nodded his agreement. Number ten also scared him. Democrats were a rarity in Schenectady County. "Let's hope he gets sick or has an emergency so we can replace him. I like both alternates."

"Me too," Wendy replied, flipping the pages of her notepad before scanning a page.

The other jurors seemed to already be in hand, Franklin thought ephemerally. But he knew better than to assume such a thing. Jury selection was 99 percent a guessing game and one percent an art. When Franklin started his career as a young, inexperienced prosecutor fresh out of law school, the DA at the time told him that a win at trial came down to one thing: what type of jury panel you had. And you really had no idea what type of panel you had until they rendered their verdict. Franklin had seen a panel of staunch republicans acquit a man of performing illegal abortions. He'd seen a panel consisting of mostly college students send a man to jail for life based solely on circumstantial evidence. He'd seen white collar defendants bring in multiple jury consultants to psychoanalyze the prospective jurors, only to have the jury deliberate for 20 minutes before convicting. Some jurors have their minds made up from the start, while others are fickle and capricious, unable to make up their minds at all. And delving into a prospective juror's background didn't necessarily tell you which category he or she fit. That's why finding the right jurors—the ones who Franklin knew couldn't be swayed by the other side—was the determining factor in a trial. That's why most trials began and ended with jury selection. For this trial, he was confident he had struck the right prospective jurors from the panel using his peremptory challenges. But not overly confident. With twelve jurors, all it took was one holdout to get a hung jury.

Franklin glanced over at the defense table. John Upton wore a charcoal suit with a baby blue shirt and solid red tie. He didn't wear his cufflinks or rings. His outfit played to the masses, Franklin thought. A little left, a little right, not too flashy or flamboyant. Upton's nonchalant manner and relaxed facial features, however, were cause for concern. Franklin wondered what Upton thought of the jury panel.

He shifted his eyes to Chucky, who sat next to Upton. The defendant was hunched toward the table and staring blankly at the mahogany wood comprising the front side of the Judge's bench. Dericardo's suit was faded, and it looked snug to the point of restricting movement. Franklin glanced down at Chucky's pant legs under the table. *Yep*, Franklin quipped internally. Chucky's bare legs were visible above his socks, evincing that his pant legs were way too short. Franklin surmised that it was the only suit Chucky owned, and that it probably was old. Maybe it was from high school. Maybe it was the suit Chucky wore to the prom or something. Franklin laughed under his breath as he turned back to his legal pad. His comfort level rose as he reviewed his notes for his opening statement.

"All rise," the bailiff announced a few minutes later. Franklin and Wendy rose along with everyone else. Franklin clasped his hands before him.

"Sit, sit," Judge Talini said as he gained the bench. He moved his black robe out of the way and sat. "Are we ready?" he asked the Part Clerk and the court reporter.

They both nodded.

"Okay, let's go on the record." He paused to get the go-ahead from the court reporter. "This is the trial of the People of the State of New York versus Charles Dericardo. Please state your appearances."

Franklin rose. "Franklin Dorey, District Attorney of the County of Schenectady, for the People."

"John Upton, Law Offices of John Upton, on behalf of the defendant Charles Dericardo."

"Twelve jurors and two alternates have been impaneled. Is the jury satisfactory to you, Counselors?"

"Yes," Franklin responded.

"Yes," Upton echoed.

The Judge made some notations. "Mr. Dorey, are you ready to proceed with your opening?"

"Yes, Your Honor."

"Any outstanding issues that we need to deal with prior to bringing the jury in?"

"None from the defendant, Your Honor."

"Nor from the People."

"Okay. Let's bring in the jury." Judge Talini nodded to the court officer.

"All rise, jury entering," the bailiff announced. The door next to the jury box opened and the jury members filtered in single file, taking their seats in order.

"Good morning members of the jury," Judge Talini said, his voice carrying in the courtroom. "It is my job to explain a few things to you about how this trial will proceed and to give you some preliminary instructions. I will also be giving you instructions in more detail at the end of the trial, but for now I will only cover the basics so you know what will happen."

As the Judge gave his preliminary instructions, Franklin surveyed the jury members anew. Juror number one was a portly woman with a furled brow and two chins. She was the office manager of an orthodontic office, meaning that she worked with many children and teenagers. A good juror.

Despite being on welfare a number of times, juror number two was registered as a republican. She was a single mother of two, each child having a different father. Her stringy, strawberry-colored hair was pulled into a ponytail and her mouth hung to the side, giving her an expression of perpetual distaste. She looked at Chucky with disdain, although it could've just been her crooked face, Franklin admitted. Still, a good juror.

In his early fifties, juror number three was a retired firefighter. He was tall, had a chiseled chin, the physique of a twenty-year-old, and the haircut of a teenager. He had served 25 years with the fire department before retiring with a full pension. Now he played golf four times a week. He probably had his share of women in his days, Franklin surmised from the look of him, but he didn't seem to be the kind of guy that was a dog about it. Franklin got the feeling that this guy treated women with respect. Questionable, but he'd do.

Juror number four was a petite black woman in her forties. She was a divorcee not once, but twice, and her first husband had cheated on her. She probably despised men, which made her a perfect juror for this case. Franklin smiled at the recent memory of Upton's face during voir dire when the Judge asked if Upton wanted to use his peremptory challenge on her.

Juror number five was an attractive college student at Syracuse who was home for the summer. She seemed ditsy. A typical blonde, Franklin thought, as he watched the girl twirl her long hair around her finger. He pegged her as a follower—doing what others did because she was unable to understand her duties and perform them. Applying the facts to the law was beyond her. Whatever the more bullish and outspoken jurors decided, she would go along. That benefited Franklin.

Juror number six was a man so old he probably couldn't even hear. He slouched in his chair, his chest rising every now and then in labored breaths. Hell, maybe he was actually asleep. If not now, then he certainly would be snoozing during the trial, Franklin guessed. That didn't concern him at all. In fact, he liked the idea, as the man would probably just go along with the consensus for fear of being in the minority without a basis to support his position. Old men didn't like people thinking they were old.

Juror number seven was a middle-aged Asian man who ran a dry cleaners in town. Franklin was sure he didn't understand English, and during questioning Franklin couldn't understand a word the guy said. Upton tried to challenge him for cause, but Judge Talini denied it, apparently having no problem understanding the man's broken English. Still, that boded well for Franklin. All this juror had to do was say something, anything, and it would likely be construed as "guilty" or "yes." Lucky number seven.

Juror number eight actually worked for Universal Electric, the same company that the defendant worked for. She was in the purchasing department and performed administrative tasks. She was never on the factory floor and claimed to have never seen Chucky before. It was somewhat suspect to Franklin, but Universal Electric was a huge company with a huge factory in the area. There were over 5,500 employees in this factory alone, so he supposed it was possible that they never ran into each other. Franklin was unsuccessful in challenging her for cause, but he now viewed it as a blessing. He ultimately decided she would be a good juror since she grew up in a broken home.

Juror number nine was the suit. A CPA that seemed unable to dress down, even after being told that he should dress comfortably. Franklin suspected that nothing short of a double-breasted suit with suspenders was comfortable to this guy. Not a great character trait for a juror, but the fact that he was a steadfast republican spoke volumes of his ideologies. The finance guys were all republicans.

Juror number ten was the problem child, the chink in the armor. The man was thin with a narrow head that tapered at the chin. Just the look of him made Franklin squirm. He worked for a local not-for-profit that helped feed the homeless and the poor. Righteousness was not a good quality for a juror as far as the prosecution was concerned, especially when the juror was a registered democrat. He was the wild card. Franklin quietly sighed.

Juror number eleven was barely visible despite her elevated seat in the back row of the jury box. Sitting behind the firefighter, the frail old lady wore white glasses, a lavender dress from the 1950s and a latticed, white headscarf. She looked innocent, with the corners of her mouth curled up, but her answers given during jury selection quickly belied that perception. She was a shark, with strong opinions dating back to before Franklin was born. That was a time of men opening doors for women, men using their coats to cover puddles, a time of proper bows, hand kissing and the like. She was an ideal juror—stuck in a time period when women were treated like women, and too close-minded to even entertain an adverse opinion.

Juror number twelve was a doctoral student studying psychology at Binghamton. His eyes were fixed on Chucky, his mouth moving as if whispering to himself. Franklin assumed he was attempting to get inside Chucky's head, trying to figure out what made Chucky do it, what made Chucky tick. Franklin loved this guy. He would probably treat the trial as a case study rather than an actual criminal trial, spending more time psychoanalyzing Chucky instead of weighing the evidence. With this guy the question wouldn't be if Chucky did it, but why.

The two alternates—a female high school teacher and a worker at a deli—sat in limbo in the back row of the jury box, not jurors…but not not jurors either. They were torn between obsolescence and influence. Franklin always wondered how being an alternate affected a juror's ability to be attentive, to stay focused, to contemplate the evidence, and to assess witnesses' credibility during the trial. He wondered how outcomes were affected when a juror was replaced by an alternate.

Leaving such musings for another time, he focused on the now. By and large, it was a good jury. He caught a glimpse of Upton's face out of the corner of his eye. The man looked tickled. It rattled Franklin at bit, and once again he realized just what this trial would mean for his career. It was the penultimate crossroads that would lead him on to greater political power or leave him behind, forever to consort with those of little or no influence. His knees began to shake, and he fought his nerves to control them, focusing his thoughts on something pleasant. *Wendy orgasming, Wendy moaning...*

"Now we will have the opening statement from the District Attorney," the Judge announced after concluding his preliminary instructions.

His mouth suddenly dry, Franklin took a sip of water from his plastic cup, making sure to move slowly so the shake of his hand was not visible. He mustered his confidence, recovering quickly as was befitting a prosecutor of 26 years. "Thank you, Your Honor," he projected with a bright smile. "Ladies and gentlemen of the jury…"

◆ ◆ ◆

"Over the course of this trial, you're going to hear many things," Franklin said to the jury, his gold-lined pen lodged between the fingers of his right hand. "You're going to hear about a bright, young lady named Mary Roletti. She had her whole future ahead of her. She grew up here in Schenectady, and came from good stock. Her father, John Roletti, was a police officer. Sadly, he passed away from a heart attack a number of years ago, but he served this town and served it well. Mary's brother, Ed, is now a police officer, and he follows in his father's footsteps. Mary's mother suffers from Alzheimer's and lives at the old age home, but she was a loving and caring mother. So you see, there's nothing untoward about this family. Mary, in fact, worked at the Star Diner as a waitress while she took classes at night. She dreamed of becoming a beautician, and was taking steps to make that happen. All in all, she was on the right path, trying to make something of herself without the support of her parents, who were unable to help her in any way.

"She was an attractive girl. You'll see the pictures. She had the eye of many men, and it's not going to be a secret that she dated quite regularly. But I want you to remember, throughout this trial, that dating is no crime. Dating many men is no crime. Choosing who you date and when is no crime." Franklin edged closer to the jury box and slowly swiveled his head as he spoke to make eye contact with each juror. "You're going to hear that Mary dated the defendant, Chucky Dericardo." He turned and pointed to the defense table.

The jurors' eyes followed.

That would be the one and only time he would use Chucky's name during this trial. He preferred to refer to a defendant as "the defendant," while repeatedly using the victim's name. He found that such devices humanized the victim and desensitized the jury to the defendant. "You're going to hear that Mary broke up with the defendant after a few months of dating. Remember that: Mary ended the relationship." He emphasized this phrase by softly pounding his fist into his open palm. "It is vital to this trial. Why? Because, as you'll see, it gives the defendant a motive. What's a motive? I'm certain you've heard the word on TV before. A motive is simply a reason. The defendant had a reason to hate the victim. He had a reason to kill the victim. And you'll also hear that not only did Mary break up with the defendant, she quickly began dating someone else." He took a small step back. "Please, keep that in the back of your mind during this trial. Think about that when you hear the defendant try to explain certain things away."

Franklin quickly moved to the prosecution table and took a small sip of water. "Now, you're also going to hear about the manner in which this heinous crime was committed. You'll see pictures as well. I warn you now, it will be difficult, it will be gruesome, it will be trying, but you must look at how the crime was committed, you must see the manner in which Mary was tortured before she was killed. You're going to hear testimony from a medical expert about that. He will tell you she was beaten, strangled, mutilated, raped, stabbed and sliced with multiple knives. Words cannot describe it. Even the word 'heinous' cannot do it justice. Can you imagine these things happening to you or someone you love?"

"Objection," Upton yelled, shooting to his feet.

"Sustained," Judge Talini said quickly. "You are to disregard that last statement. You are not to compare or visualize this happening to you or someone you know in any fashion during this trial." The Judge gave Franklin an admonishing glare.

Franklin knew certain things were improper, that objections would be lodged and that the Judge would sustain those objections, but small things, standing alone, would not be cause for a mistrial or overturning a conviction on appeal. So Franklin knew he could get away with certain things. And, of course, once the jury heard something, it was almost impossible to cleanse it from their minds. The Judge's curative efforts would be ineffective in that respect.

"You'll see," Franklin continued, "the brutality and utter disregard for humanity involved in this crime. You'll also hear from the Detective who questioned the defendant at the police station. His name is Ernesto Suarez. You'll hear from Detective Suarez what the defendant said. This is one of the most important things you will hear during this trial, because it came directly from the defendant's mouth." He turned again and regarded Chucky, knowing without seeing that the jurors followed his gaze. "This is what the defendant said." He paused for emphasis.

"I was angry about being dumped," Franklin declared in a measured fashion. "Let me repeat that. He said, 'I was angry about being dumped.'" He paused again to let that sink in, turning back to the jury. "Remember earlier we talked about motive. Well, there you have it, from the defendant's own mouth. The defendant was angry with Mary for dumping him. He couldn't stand to see Mary with another man. So he did something about it. Something horrific."

Franklin clasped his hands together and slowly paced before the jury box. "Now, you'll also hear from a forensic expert who is from the police department. You're going to hear that the defendant's fingerprints were in the house. And not only that. His fingerprints were found in the kitchen—the exact place where the murder took place. You're going to hear that the defendant's hair was also found in the house. So you see, he was there."

"Objection," Upton drawled.

Judge Talini paused before ruling. "Overruled. I'll allow it." He turned to the jurors. "You will recall my preliminary instructions. Opening statements are not evidence. This is only what the parties intend to prove to you." He nodded for Franklin to continue.

"Now," Franklin said smartly, bolstered by the ruling in his favor, "I'm going to ask you to consider all the evidence you're going to hear as a whole. That means you should look at the totality of all the evidence. I want you to do this because I am going to prove to you that there is no other possible person that could have committed this crime. Mary's other past boyfriends are not around. The defendant is the only one with a motive that is not accounted for on the night of the murder."

Franklin threw his finger into the air. "Oh, and one other thing. You're going to hear that the defendant has a criminal record, that he is familiar with breaking the law."

Franklin stepped up to the jury box and smiled. "I'm going to have a chance to address you again at the end of the trial. I will do my best to put the pieces together for you then, but I think you all will be able to do it on your own fairly easily." He rested his hands on the railing of the jury box and leaned in, lowering his voice marginally and speaking evenly. "At the end of the trial, I'm going to ask you to render a verdict of guilty of murder in the first degree, and rape in the first degree." He took a brief pause while he studied the faces before him, the faces of those 12 members of society that held his political career in their hands. "Thank you all for your time. Our legal system would not function without your assistance. We'll speak soon."

Wendy gave him an approving nod as he sat.

"And now, ladies and gentleman," Judge Talini said, "we will have the opening statement on behalf of the defendant."

◆ ◆ ◆

Chief Byron Stadmore snuck into the back of the courtroom and took the first open seat he saw. He sat for a time watching but not really listening to the DA's opening statement, his eyes glassy in deep thought. His mind flashed over the moments that comprised his 34-year career as a police officer. There were many moments, some more vivid than others, some fresher, some better left in the deep annals of his mind. As was consistent with his current state of mind, he unconsciously honed in on the moments where he could have, should have, acted differently, those few moments where his errors botched things up. He realized that mistakes were inevitable in a career that spanned as long as his had, but still, that didn't stop his mind from looking back in hindsight, from playing out the various scenarios that could have eliminated or remedied his failures. And it didn't stop the guilt from resurfacing with a power that gave each memory a contemporaneous feel.

He dropped his head for a moment and sighed inwardly. This case, this trial, it would be the end, Byron decided. It was time to step down, time to turn over the reins. He understood that the outcome of this case would define his career, for better or worse, but such things were out of his control. He had served to the best of his ability. Let the public think what they will. He was tired…and old. Self-conscious pretenses meant little to old men—or so he tried to convince himself.

Perhaps he should have hung them up a few years ago, he considered. His full pension had been vested for some time now. He wondered why he found it so difficult. Maybe he was afraid of being obsolete, of having no purpose. He supposed he would find out soon enough.

He pushed such thoughts away as John Upton rose to speak, the man's lanky frame slowly but smoothly unfolding into an upright position. "Good morning, ladies and gentleman," the defense attorney said with a mild manner and refined smile, his hands unassumingly pushed into his pants pockets. "As you know, I represent Mr. Dericardo. We met briefly during jury selection. It's good to see you all again."

The man had a way about him, Byron conceded, with his relaxed manner and smooth speech pattern. He was soft-spoken, warm, immediately likable, and he didn't speak down to the jurors. He was southern debonair without the southern. He broke a number of stereotypes about lawyers—defense lawyers in particular. He didn't come across as conceited or brazen or commanding. He simply spoke as if he was one of the jurors. A regular joe. Byron quickly realized how jurors could become enamored with Upton, he saw how jurors could easily believe what Upton told them. He glanced at Franklin to gauge his long-time friend's assessment of Upton's opening. Unfortunately, the back of his friend's head provided no answer.

"I'm sure what I tell you right now is going to surprise you, but I want you to be prepared." Upton paused, turning to Franklin. "I agree with most of what the District Attorney just said to you." A quiet murmur sprang up in the courtroom. Byron was surprised to find his own voice added to the chorus. He surveyed the jurors, finding shock and uncertainty written on their faces, their eyes shifty.

Upton smiled knowingly for a moment. "I agree that Mr. Dericardo dated the victim. There's no dispute about that. I don't even dispute that Mr. Dericardo was upset about being dumped. No one likes to be dumped. But," he punctuated the word with a finger in the air, "that relationship ended more than *two years* before the victim was murdered." He held up two fingers, parading his long digits to the jury. "Two years. I'm going to show you that crimes of passion do not take place after two years. When a person is angry about being dumped and is compelled to kill or hurt someone, he or she takes action immediately. Why? Because emotions thin and wane with time. When people act out of passion or emotion, they do so immediately. That's the way it works. So you'll see, two years is too long a wait to be a crime of passion. I'm going to ask you to remember that time period every time the District Attorney brings up the word motive or talks about Mr. Dericardo's so-called confession, because it doesn't make sense in this case.

"Two years," Upton said more strongly. Nodding, he stepped closer to the jurors, resuming his nonchalant manner, this time with one hand in his pocket and the other flourishing tiny circles in the air. "I also agree with the District Attorney that Mr. Dericardo's hair and fingerprints were found in the house. That won't be in dispute." He threw his arms wide, laughing incredulously. "But you just heard repeatedly from the DA that Mr. Dericardo dated the victim. Wouldn't you expect his fingerprints and hair to be in the house? What's more, you're going to hear about where the fingerprints and hair were found. The hair was found in the living room, which is not where the crime took place. The fingerprints were found on the toaster, which showed no signs of being involved in the crime. In fact, the toaster was the one thing in the kitchen that did not show signs of being involved in the crime. Everything else in the kitchen, it was all affected by this crime. But not the toaster. I tell you, when you see how this crime happened, how there was a serious struggle that went on, you'll realize that Mr. Dericardo's hair and fingerprints would have been all over the victim or the kitchen floor had he committed this crime."

"Objection," Franklin said.

"Sustained," Judge Talini responded quickly, his face austere. "Mr. Upton, closing statements are the time for argument, not openings."

"The last thing I'm going to show you," Upton said, almost as if ignoring the Judge's admonishment, "is that on the night of the crime, Mr. Dericardo was at home. How do I know this? Because he was on the phone at the time. That's how. So this will be simple. Charles Dericardo could not have committed this crime."

Byron was mesmerized. When he shook himself free from Upton's spellbound tone, he realized that everyone else in the room was just as enchanted with the defense attorney.

Following the DA's lead, Upton stepped up to the jury box and rested his hands on the railing. "The judge is going to instruct you on the law, but it's no secret that the standard you must employ in this case is one of beyond a reasonable doubt. You've probably heard it on TV before. In order to convict Mr. Dericardo, you must find him guilty *beyond* a reasonable doubt. That means if you hold a reasonable doubt…that is, *any* reasonable doubt, you must find him not guilty." Upton stood for a second longer with a smile before pushing off the rail and returning to his seat.

"All right," Judge Talini announced, "let's take our lunch break."

"All rise, jury exiting," the bailiff called out.

Yes, Byron thought as he prodded his old bones to stand, this case would mark the end of his career. And from the look of the jurors and everyone else in the courtroom, some of whom were still staring at Upton with enchantment in their eyes, Byron did not think history would regard his legacy kindly.

Step 5.2

"The People call Jennifer Johansson," the DA announced.

Detective Bill Watkins eyed Jenny as she brushed past the DA and made her way to the witness stand. She wore black, pleated pants and a lavender sweater vest covering a white button-down shirt, the collar pulled out over the vest. The back of her sweater collar poked out from underneath her shirt collar, which simply annoyed Bill. Dishevelment was repulsive. He almost shouted out a comment, but caught himself at the last second. Good thing she turned around to approach the witness stand, because it hid the imperfection. Her hair was straightened, running just past her shoulders, and her face bore touches of makeup—a hint of mascara, rose on her gaunt cheeks, and a nude-colored, glossy lipstick. It was the polar opposite to how she had looked when Bill first met her in the trailer park. Bill was immediately suspicious, even considering that this was court and people were supposed to look presentable.

Jenny stepped up to the stand and swiped her strawberry bangs from her face. She looked…emotionless. An expression he knew well. Or so he'd been told by a sufficient number of people for him to accurately postulate that his expression lacked emotion. He knew he was calculated and analytical, so such comments did not surprise him. Staring at Jenny, he ran the calculations in his mind as to the possible reasons for her expression. She was numb from the loss of her friend, she was naturally stone-faced, she was scared, she played a part in the crime, or perhaps Bill was simply misinterpreting her expression. He considered each option and various permutations as the Part Clerk swore Jenny in, her right hand raised in the air. *Is her hand shaking?*

Yes. Yes it was. Interesting, Bill thought.

She sat and brushed her bangs again.

No, Bill concluded, he had not misjudged Jenny's expression. Something was off, and despite that the investigation was over, he still intended to find out what that was. His intuition was rarely wrong. Bill cocked his head, regarding her from a different angle.

"May I inquire, Your Honor?" Franklin asked the Judge.

Judge Talini nodded. "Proceed."

"Good morning, Ms. Johansson." The DA stepped to the lectern.

"Morning," she responded timidly.

"Ms. Johansson," Judge Talini said, leaning over the bench toward the witness stand, "please keep your voice up. Sound seems to drown out in this large room."

She nodded, her bangs jerking.

"Do you know Mary Roletti?" the DA asked.

She nodded.

"You must provide verbal responses," Judge Talini instructed.

"Okay. Yes."

She's nervous. Too nervous.

"And how do you know Mary?" the DA asked.

"We were best friends."

"How long did you know her?"

"Um, we met in high school. During freshman year."

She still looked emotionless, Bill noted. Blank. Eyes glossy. He assumed that the mention of her so-called best friend would evoke a reaction of some sort. Apparently not. It was quite unusual.

"So you have known each other for about 10 years now?"

She nodded again before hastily answering, "yes."

"How often did you see her since high school?"

"We, uh, saw each other a few times a week, and we spoke on the phone almost every day." She rubbed her nose. It was a telltale sign she was hiding something.

"Are you familiar with the boys she dated in the last few years?"

"Yes."

The DA flipped his notepad resting on the lectern. "Do you see anyone in the courtroom that Mary dated?"

Her gaze moved to the defense table. "Yes," she said firmly, her expression hardening.

Finally, a normal response. Was it feigned? After a brief contemplation, Bill suspected that it was.

"Can you point to him, please."

She pointed directly at Dericardo, her eyes narrowing.

"Let the record reflect that the witness has identified the defendant, Mr. Dericardo," the Judge stated.

"And can you tell us when they dated and for how long?"

"It was about two or three months that they dated. Maybe a couple of years ago."

The DA left the lectern and paced before the witness stand, his hand propped under his chin. "And who ended the relationship?" The DA's face scrunched, almost as if he was in acute pain. Bill wondered if the DA had enough fiber in diet. Fiber was essential to a balanced diet. Bill's diet was regulated and regimented.

"Mary ended the relationship," Jenny responded, resuming her blank stare, her gaze pointed toward the floor.

"So she dumped him?"

"Objection," John Upton called out.

"Sustained," the Judge said without explanation.

The DA smirked. "How did Chucky take it?"

"Objection, Your Honor," Upton said more calmly.

Judge Talini inched toward the witness stand. "Ms. Johansson, were you present when Ms. Roletti ended the relationship?"

"No," she said timidly.

"And," the Judge continued, the DA standing by silently, "did you speak to Mr. Dericardo afterwards about his mental state?"

"No."

"That objection is sustained, she has no first-hand knowledge of Mr. Dericardo's mental state."

The DA resumed his pacing. "Let's move on to May 21st of this year. Were you with Mary that day?"

"Yes."

"Can you please tell us what happened that day?"

Jenny nodded before speaking. Her hand rose above the box, gesturing as she spoke. "We decided to go out. I picked her up at around seven."

"You picked her up at her home?"

"Yes."

"Please continue."

"We went over to Warren's Bar & Grille. We did some dancing and some drinking. Had a good time." She sniffled. It looked forced to Bill.

"What time did you leave?"

She cast her eyes to the ceiling. "Oh, about 12:30 a.m."

That—eyeing the ceiling—was often done when someone was nervous or was going to lie. It permitted the brain to process a fib. Bill attempted to decipher exactly what the lie was. Maybe they left later than 12:30. If so, how did that impact Jenny's role?

The DA exhaled. "Did you and Mary leave with anyone else?"

"No."

"And you dropped her off back at her house?"

"Yes."

"You saw her enter her house?"

"Yes. I waited in the car until she went in the front door."

"Did anything look suspicious at that time within or around the house?"

"No."

The DA moved back to the lectern and glanced at his notepad. "A few more questions, Ms. Johansson. Between the time Mary dated the defendant and now, do you know the boys she dated?"

"Yes."

"Can you tell the jury who they are and what they are doing now, if you know?"

She nodded. "There was Dennis Kerisol. He's in jail. And there was John Wakefielder. He was at the bar that night, but left with another girl."

"That's all the questions I have. Thank you." He sat.

John Upton stood calmly and buttoned his suit jacket. Despite his height, he glided to the lectern and placed his hands on the sides, his arms bent. "Hello, Ms. Johansson," he said with a kind smile.

Upton's demeanor was relaxing, Bill found. He studied the defense attorney briefly before turning back to his ongoing examination of Jenny.

"Did you ever see Mr. Dericardo and Mary fight?"

She frowned, shaking her head. "No."

"Ever see Mr. Dericardo angry or violent?"

"No," she said timidly, glancing at the DA, as if seeking help. That was an interesting turn of events, Bill noted. It seemed that, all of sudden, she looked concerned that she would say the wrong thing.

"And am I correct that more than two years have passed since they dated?"

She nodded.

"That's a 'yes'?" Upton asked with another smile, his tone devoid of patronization.

"Yes."

"And another of Mary's past boyfriends, John was his name, was at the bar the night of her murder; isn't that correct?" His voice remained calm, without sounding accusatory.

"Yes…but…he left with another girl."

My, Bill thought, the defense attorney knew his business. He was able to get Jenny to sound defensive, thereby putting the DA's back against the wall instead of Dericardo's back. Bill knew the truth about Wakefielder's whereabouts, but the jury did not. This was how a defense worked, but Upton seemed to take it to another level.

"Did Mary and John talk that night?"

Jenny's mouth twitched. "They might have said, 'hi.'" She glanced at the back of the courtroom. Bill turned in his seat and followed her quick glance. He did not see anyone of note, but memorized a few unknown faces that looked suspicious.

"And John dated Mary after Chucky, right?"

She nodded slowly. "Yes."

"Let me ask you this," Upton said before pausing to eye the jurors. He turned back to Jenny. "Did Mary dump John?"

"Objection," the DA said, half standing.

"If you know," Upton appended.

"Overruled," the Judge said.

"Yes, she dumped him."

"And that was recently?"

"Well, yes…but…he was with another girl."

"I'll move to strike that portion of the answer that was not responsive to the question, Your Honor," Upton said to the Judge, smiling softly while moving back toward his seat.

"So stricken," the Judge said. "Members of the jury, you are to disregard that portion of the witness's answer that was not responsive to the question. Strike it from your mind."

"No further questions," Upton said, sitting.

Extremely tactful and effective, Bill thought. *It will be difficult to get a conviction.*

"Redirect?" the Judge asked the DA.

"Yes, Your Honor," the DA said, rising. "Did you ever see Mary and John fight?" he asked Jenny before moving away from his table.

"No," she said, shaking her head emphatically.

"Did you ever observe John become angry or violent?"

"No." Her head lifted in confidence.

Not a bad tactic, Bill ventured, using the defense attorney's own questioning against him.

"And John left the bar with the other woman that night before you and Mary left, right?"

"Yes."

"Did you see John or his car anywhere near Mary's house when you dropped her off that night?"

"No."

"Nothing further, Judge." The DA sat.

Upton stood. "No further questions."

"Okay," Judge Talini said. "You may step down, Ms. Johansson."

She nodded, rose, and stepped off the witness stand. Bill watched closely as Jenny sighed in relief. He focused on her chest, watching to see if her breathing was erratic or shallow. Yes, she was hiding something, he concluded again, this time with renewed zeal.

"Your next witness, Mr. Dorey," the Judge prodded as Bill stood to follow after Jenny, his mind compelling him to investigate. He could read the trial transcript later. Now, he required answers.

I should have fucking killed him! Seething, Ed stepped up to the witness stand and raised his right hand when prompted, forcibly pushing John Upton from his mind. He took a deep breath to control his anger before swearing his oaths. He sat, lips pursed, then consciously relaxed his face. He needed to face reality. If he was going to play his part in sending his sister's killer to jail, he needed to remain calm on the witness stand. No outbursts, no yelling, no refusing to answer questions, no jumping out of the box and strangling the life from the defense attorney. He kept his gaze from going to the defense table for fear of losing control, but he still managed to see the blurry forms of Chucky and Upton in his periphery. He shifted his gaze to the floor.

The DA stood and gave a slight head nod, jumping right into it. "Officer Roletti, who is your employer?"

"The Schenectady County Police Department," he answered with more of a bark than intended. The DA was on his side, he chided himself. *Relax, Ed.* He drew in another deep breath.

The DA, apparently hearing the tension or anger in Ed's voice, took a short pause before asking his next question. "And what is your rank or title?"

"Both my rank and title is Police Officer."

"How long have you been with the police department?"

"It will be six years this fall."

"And who is Mary Roletti?"

Not expecting such a blunt transition, he choked on his words, then gulped. A flood of emotions struck him. He wanted to say 'she *is* my sister.' But Mary was gone. Dead. He could no longer refer to her in the present tense. "She was my sister," he finally answered, his eyes watery, his throat tight. He felt a hundred eyes on him.

The DA gave him a sympathetic frown. "Was she older or younger?"

"She was my little sister, five years younger." *And she was my only sister. Now I'm alone.* He sniffled, his lower lip starting to quiver. He fought his emotions. He couldn't cry on the stand before this crowd. He wouldn't. He let his anger brew, hoping to supplant his deep sorrow.

"Were you two close?"

He nodded. "Very close." Gulping, he added, "We spoke all the time and lived close to each other. I checked in on her all the time."

"And the house that she lived in, located at 54 Oakmont Drive, did you also live in that house at some point?"

"Yes. That was our family house. Mary and I grew up in that house, and then when my dad passed away and my mother got Alzheimer's and went to live at the Rockwell Home, I moved out and Mary stayed in the house. But we both lived there most of our lives." He didn't know if he could continue. He almost stood and ran. *Be strong.*

"You mentioned your father. What was his occupation?"

"He was also a police officer. He served probably 25 years and died of a heart attack about ten years ago."

"Let me change topics. Do you know the defendant in this case?"

Ed's anger surfaced, flashing on his face. He slowly looked at the defense table. Chucky didn't meet his gaze. "I know him," he ground out.

"Can you identify him please?"

"That's him," Ed said, pointing to Chucky. "Chucky Dericardo."

"And how do you know him?"

"He dated my sister a few years back." He had to grind his teeth to keep from barking.

"And did you and Mary talk about that relationship ever?" the DA asked, raising his voice.

Ed took another breath and nodded, ripping his gaze from Chucky and focusing on the DA. "We talked about all of her relationships."

"Do you know if she broke up with Chucky?"

"Yes. She broke up with him." *And I would kill him if he wasn't already going to jail.*

"Objection," Upton called out.

"What's the objection?" Judge Talini asked.

"May we approach, Your Honor?" Upton asked.

Judge Talini waved the attorneys up, looking reluctant. Ed eyed Upton as the defense attorney approached the bench, noticing how he stood a full head above the DA. Upton leaned down toward the Judge. Ed could only make out whispers between the attorneys and the Judge, so he quickly lost interest. His gaze caught Chucky again. This time, Chucky returned the stare. Ed's eyes narrowed in hate, but the return of the attorneys to their respective tables broke his focus.

"That's all I have for you," the DA said. "Thank you, Officer Roletti."

"Cross, Mr. Upton?" Judge Talini asked.

Now was the time Ed really had to control his emotions. He couldn't let Upton goad him into saying something that would hurt the case. He couldn't snap at the defense attorney or worse, jump out of the box and attack Upton. Control, he reminded himself. *Control.*

Upton stood nonchalantly, his lanky frame slowly straightening. "No questions, Your Honor."

That surprised Ed. He glanced at the DA, who was frowning slightly, eyes shifting in suspicion. The DA leaned over to his ADA and began whispering. Upton sat down with a minor smirk.

Ed's hate for Upton redoubled. He briefly forgot his place. Gripping the witness box tightly, he glared at Upton and Chucky.

"You may step down, Mr. Roletti," Judge Talini said.

Ed blinked in surprise, turning to look up at the Judge.

"You are excused," the Judge said.

Ed stepped down from the witness stand.

"And you may also sit in the gallery to watch the rest of the trial, if you so choose, Mr. Roletti," the Judge added. "Having testified, you are no longer under sequestration."

Despite open seats in the front row behind the defense table, Ed moved to the gallery and sat near the front behind the DA. He held on to his anger like a life preserver, but he still had enough fortitude to forego the temptation to sit behind Chucky. Leaping over the courtroom fence and attacking Chucky or Upton would only land him in jail. No, he decided, he wasn't going to miss any more of this trial.

Step 5.3

Where is she going now?

After leaving the grocery store, Bill assumed Jenny would head home, but she passed the turn she needed to take to get to the trailer park. It was suspicious, and Bill felt a renewed sense of confidence in his instincts. Now he wondered not just where she was going, but what she purchased at the grocery store. There were many dangerous things that could be found at a grocery store. If it came down to it, he could obtain the receipt from the store. But that would take a few weeks at minimum, assuming a Judge signed the subpoena. He would need hard evidence before that happened…and if he had hard evidence, he likely would not need to see the grocery receipt. He would obtain it nonetheless, he decided, if it came down to it. Protocol demanded it.

His stomach growled, likely on account of his grocery store thoughts. He checked his watch. 12:49. 11 minutes until lunch. Today is Tuesday. Following Jenny as she turned left onto a wooded road, Bill glanced at his packed lunch sitting in its brown bag on the passenger seat, the top of the paper bag perfectly flattened and folded over. Bill knew exactly what was inside—a turkey sandwich. Tuesday was turkey sandwich day. It had taken Ellen a few months, he recalled, before she was able to get his sandwiches right. Monday was a muenster cheese sandwich with lettuce on whole wheat. He liked muenster cheese. Tuesday was a turkey sandwich with mayo, lettuce and tomato on whole wheat. Wednesday was white bread—anything in between was okay. It was his one day where he let loose. Thursday was tuna salad on whole wheat. And Friday was fried fish—that, of course, Ellen did not make. Friday was Bill's day to eat out, and the fried fish stand was close to the station. Yes, he recalled with a shiver, those first few months before his wife learned his system were troubling. He glanced at the paper bag, a cold sweat brewing at the thought of not finding turkey inside.

He turned his attention back to the road, which was windy and slightly inclined. He removed his foot from the pedal, decelerating to put more space between Jenny and himself. There was nothing worse than having a tail get blown. He followed at a slower speed, making sure to speed up slightly around the bends.

After about two miles, Jenny turned left, entering a neighborhood of small houses. Bill followed, but he waited to turn until he was certain Jenny wouldn't spot him. He glanced at his watch again, waiting patiently for 1:00. Only three minutes away.

Jenny's car slowed, her brake lights engaged. Bill quickly pulled over, stopping his car in front of a pale green house with a dilapidated metal fence enclosing the front yard. He craned his neck over the car parked in front of him, then quickly glanced at his watch again. Two minutes.

Jenny pulled over and parked in front of a white cottage. Bill could not make out any of the details, like the address, but he would get that in due time. Jenny exited her car with grocery bags in hand. She pulled the screen door open and entered the house. Apparently, the door was unlocked. Very unusual these days, Bill thought, especially in a neighborhood such as this. He looked around at the small houses. None were more than one story, and most looked to have frontage of only 17 feet.

He glanced at his watch. *And...now.* With an eye on the house, he grabbed the paper bag and placed it on his lap. Slowly, he unfolded the flap and spread the edges open. Glancing in first to make sure everything was copacetic, he reached in and removed his turkey sandwich. Relieved, he began to unwrap the plastic layer by layer with his thumb and index finger, occasionally lifting his head to keep an eye on the house. A suspect could slip right under your nose on a stake out, he reminded himself. It had never happened to Bill, of course, but he had heard stories from other officers. Bill had to be diligent, even during lunchtime. Protocol demanded it.

Briefly glancing down at his unwrapped sandwich, he brought it to his mouth, biting one corner. He eyed the bite mark as he chewed. His next three bites would have to be to the remaining corners, of course. He glanced at the house again. When he was finished with his lunch, he would give the house his full attention—assuming Jenny did not exit first. Protocol.

◆ ◆ ◆

Detective Ernie Suarez strode to the witness stand. He had on his best suit, his dark hair was slicked back, and his shoes were shined. It did little to mask the nerves coursing through his veins. He'd prepped with the DA last night for his testimony, and he'd previously spoken to the Captain at length about proper etiquette. Sit upright, but not too rigid. Maintain eye contact with the questioning attorney. Do not become agitated or angry at the defense attorney's questions, as he will most surely be trying to trip you up, and do not let emotions show generally. Do not mince words. Do not expand on questions, only answer the question posed to you. Do not speak with an overly animated voice. He wasn't sure if he remembered all of the rules. His mind was a little fuzzy with the immensity of the stage he stood on, but this conviction and his career rested largely on the next few hours. In preparing, he had read and reread the transcript of his testimony from the suppression hearing. His testimony today would be very similar, if not virtually identical, and since he'd been informed that the defense would be looking for discrepancies to use against him, he needed to have down cold what he said at the hearing. The entire case, after all, likely rested on his shoulders, as he'd be testifying to Dericardo's confession—arguably the most important piece of evidence in the case. He had to be sharp.

As the Part Clerk swore him in, Ernie pushed the haze from his thoughts, focusing solely on his task. "I do," he answered the Part Clerk, his voice shaky. The mere act of speaking, however, quelled some of his nerves.

The DA jumped right in just as Ernie sat. "Detective Suarez, were you involved in the investigation of the murder of Mary Roletti?"

"Yes," he responded, leaning over into the microphone, his hands clasped before him so as not to fidget.

"In what capacity were you involved?"

He brought his fist to his mouth and cleared his throat. "Well, a number, actually. I was on the scene after the 9-1-1 call. Not as lead detective, but as one of three detectives on scene. I interviewed the neighbor who had called 9-1-1." He thought for a moment. "I spoke to Mary's mother, and I was the person who questioned Mr. Dericardo about the crime." He felt that his answer was a little too long, and he unconsciously began to slouch, almost as if shying away with embarrassment. Catching himself, he corrected his posture.

"And do you see Mr. Dericardo in the room today?"

"Yes, that is him there," he answered, pointing to Chucky.

"Let the record reflect that he has identified Mr. Dericardo," the Judge said.

"Can you tell the jury what Mary Roletti's neighbor said?"

He nodded. "The neighbor's name is Gretchen Holland. lives at -", he glanced at his notepad, "133 Oakmont Street."

"I'm going to object, Your Honor," John Upton announced. "The witness seems to be reading from something instead of testifying from memory."

"What are you reading from, Detective?" the Judge asked him.

Ernie swallowed hard, wondering if he'd already fucked up. "Well, this is my notepad from the investigation, Your Honor," he answered meekly.

The Judge nodded. "He can use it to refresh his recollection." He turned to Ernie. "You may not read from it directly. You can refer to it before answering."

Ernie nodded.

"So," the DA continued, "what was it that Ms. Holland told you?"

"She told me that she usually saw Mary working in the garden each evening on the way home from work, and that on -" he paused as he glanced at his notepad, "May 23, she didn't see Mary. She didn't think much of it, but the next evening was the same thing. So she figured Mary was on vacation. But she said that on May 27, she drove by and noticed that the front door was ajar. That's when she called 9-1-1."

"And you responded to the dispatch call?"

"Yes. I was one of many officers who responded."

"What did you see at the crime scene?"

"I observed a female, D.O.A., lying on the kitchen floor."

"Could you elaborate briefly on what the scene looked like?"

He gulped. "Uh, there was a large puddle of blood on the floor, the victim's body was mutilated in multiple places, she had stab wounds, and -"

"Objection," Upton yelled out. "The witness is not qualified to discuss the type of wounds."

"Sustained. He's not a medical doctor." Judge Talini began writing something. It made Ernie nervous. He wondered again if he fucked up.

"What else did you see?" the DA prompted.

Don't start stuttering. The patch above his upper lip began to form beads of sweat. He took a deep breath to compose himself. "Well, the kitchen was a mess. There were bloody knives on the counter. Two knives, I believe, of different sizes. The fridge door was open wide, with milk spilled over and cereal all over the floor. Blood stains throughout the kitchen." He shrugged, not recalling any other details, his thoughts starting to cloud.

"May I approach the witness, Your Honor?" the DA asked the Judge.

"You may."

The DA approached him, gave his a sharp nod, and handed him a handful of pictures. "Do you recognize these, Detective?"

Reassured, Ernie focused again. He flipped through the photographs. "Yes," he answered more confidently. "These are the pictures from the crime scene."

"Did you take these photographs?"

Ernie quickly flipped through them again. "I took all of them except these two." He held them out to the DA.

"Do you know who took those photos?"

"Detective Watkins took those."

"I'll move these pictures into evidence, Your Honor," the DA said to the Judge.

"Mr. Upton?" the Judge asked.

"No objection, Your Honor."

The DA moved to a projector and hit a few buttons. A picture popped up on the large screen on the opposite side of the room from the jury box. It was the one Ernie had taken of the victim. A full length shot of the body sprawled on the kitchen floor.

Jurors gasped. Murmurs sprang up in the courtroom.

"Let's have order," Judge Talini yelled out, a hint of annoyance in his voice. He gave his gavel a halfhearted bang on the bench. Ernie was surprised that the Judge had a gavel. He thought such things were only used in movies and TV.

"Is this an accurate picture of the victim at the crime scene?" the DA asked Ernie while standing next to the projector and pointing at the screen.

Ernie leaned into the microphone. "Yes, it is."

"What about this one?" the DA asked matter-of-factly, hitting a button on the projector to change the picture.

This picture was a close up of Mary's face, revealing the checkerboard slashes and gaping wound in her cheek. Ernie glanced at the jury. The young woman in the front looked pale as a ghost. The old woman in the back had her hand over her mouth. The other jurors sat with their eyes wide or rapidly blinking, the latter as if the photographs couldn't be real and would go away if they blinked enough. The realization that the jurors were uncomfortable gave Ernie more confidence. "Yes, that is the victim," he answered, turning back to the DA.

"And this one?"

"Uh huh."

"And this one?"

"Yes."

The DA took Ernie through the remaining photographs.

"And did you determine who the victim was?" the DA asked as he shut the projector off and returned to the lectern.

"Yes, we determined that it was Mary Roletti."

"Was the victim's name of any significance to you?"

He took a breath. "Oh, absolutely," he said sheepishly, finding his own answer a little awkward. "She is officer Ed Roletti's sister."

"Now," the DA began, returning to his table. He grabbed a clear plastic bag. "Do you recognize these?" He handed the bag to Ernie.

Ernie flattened the wrinkles from the bag, making a crinkling sound in the quiet courtroom. "Yes, I do. These are the knives that were found in the kitchen next to the stove."

"How were they found?" the DA probed while focusing his gaze on the jurors.

"Well," Ernie said, "there was blood all over them."

The DA paused for a moment. "Let me ask you about the investigation after that. How did you participate in the investigation?"

"I interviewed the victim's mother and I conducted the questioning of the suspect." He knew the important part was coming up. He clenched his hands together tighter in an effort to control his nervous energy.

"By 'suspect' you mean Mr. Dericardo?" The DA placed his finger on his chin, tapping.

"Yes." He glanced at Chucky, who was staring at the Judge's bench, his gaze blank.

"What did you learn from Ms. Roletti's mother?"

"Nothing. She has Alzheimer's and couldn't answer any questions." Boy, was his mouth getting dry. He wanted to squirm but settled on licking his lips.

"And how did you come about questioning Mr. Dericardo?" the DA asked as he began pacing in front of the witness box.

"Well, we determined that he dated the victim and that he was unaccounted for on the night of the crime, so we asked him to come down to the station to answer some questions." He had been prepped to say "question" rather than "interrogate." Interrogation implied that it was involuntary, and although it could be argued that Chucky's questioning was an interrogation, admitting as much would jeopardize the strength of the confession. So "questioning" Dericardo is what he did.

"And what does 'unaccounted for' mean?" the DA asked while pausing and making eye contact with Ernie.

Ernie leaned into the microphone. "He had no alibi."

"Okay. Did Chucky agree to come down to the station to answer questions?"

"Yes. He came down voluntarily and I asked him a few questions."

"What did you ask him?"

"Well, I confirmed that he dated the victim and that she dumped him. Then I asked him why he did it, why he committed the crime."

The DA turned and regarded the jury. "And what was his response?"

This was it. The big moment. "He said he was angry about being dumped."

"He was angry about being dumped," the DA repeated loudly, the corners of his mouth curled up.

"Objection," Upton said.

"That's sustained, there was no question asked." Judge Talini became stern. "Mr. Dorey, I have already instructed Mr. Upton, and now I will instruct you: save the argument for your closing statement."

"No more questions, Your Honor," the DA responded, returning to his seat.

"Your witness, Mr. Upton," the Judge said.

Ernie made eye contact with the defense attorney. Nervous again, he shifted in his seat, trying to find a comfortable position. He seriously needed to wet his mouth.

"Detective," Upton began, towering over the lectern, "in your investigation, did you learn of John Wakefielder?"

"Yes," he croaked.

"And you learned that he dated the victim, correct?"

"Yes."

"In fact, he dated the victim *after* Chucky. Isn't that correct?"

"Yes."

"And the victim dumped John? *She* ended the relationship?"

"That's what we learned." Ernie was beginning to get agitated. He glanced at the DA, who was frowning. It was enough to remind him that he needed to keep his cool. He tried to take a deep breath without it being noticeable.

"And," Upton said, hanging on the word, "John was at the bar the night the victim was murdered. Isn't that correct?"

But he has an alibi, Ernie thought, still slightly perturbed. *Just answer the question that is posed*, he reminded himself. "Yes."

Upton reviewed his notepad silently. Ernie shifted in his seat, regaining his composure.

"You were the detective that questioned Mr. Dericardo?"

"That's correct."

"Was he a suspect at that time?"

"Well, he was more a person of interest."

"Uh huh. How long did you keep him in the interrogation room before you began questioning him?"

"He was in there maybe 15 minutes," Ernie replied, before hastily adding, "but he was free to leave at any time."

"Did you tell him he was free to leave at any time?" Upton asked, smirking pleasantly.

"I did, during the ride to the station."

Upton nodded with his eyebrow's raised. "And you just testified that you asked him why he committed the crime?"

"That's correct."

Upton looked pensive, with his brow furled and his eyes narrowed in deep thought. He placed his right hand in his pants pocket and took small steps toward the witness stand. It unnerved Ernie—partly because it reminded Ernie of a lion stalking his prey, and partly because Ernie thought he knew what the next question would be, which made him uncomfortable.

"When Mr. Dericardo answered you that he was angry about being dumped, did he say anything directly after that?" Upton stood right in front of the witness box, a mere few feet from Ernie.

The question was as Ernie suspected. He'd spoken at length with the Captain and the DA about this question and the answer that he'd give. Did Chucky say something after his damaging statement? Yes, he did. He said, '*but I didn't kill her.*' As far as this trial was concerned, that statement worried Ernie. The DA had explained that the only person that could or would contradict Ernie was the defendant himself, who was the only person present in the room—besides other officers, of course, but they weren't testifying. The DA had explained that if Ernie testified that Chucky only said the first part of the statement, Chucky would have to testify to contradict Ernie's account. And Chucky wouldn't testify, as it would open him up to a lot of questions he didn't want to answer. Upton would never allow it, the DA had informed him. Besides, even if Chucky testified to the contrary, it was Chucky's word against Ernie's. Given the choice between the credibility of a police officer and of a defendant, a jury will believe the police officer 99 times out of 100, the DA had said. So there was no risk in stating that Chucky made no statement other than the damaging one. The fact that Ernie was lying while under oath initially bothered him, but the Captain convinced him that a little bending of the truth was often necessary to ensure convictions. If we all knew a man was guilty, the Captain told him, we had to do all we could to get a conviction; that included while giving testimony in court. So for this question, Ernie was prepared to answer.

"No," Ernie said, shaking he head. "That's all he said."

Upton's head rose, as if he had an "ah ha" moment.

Ernie panicked.

"You're sure. Mr. Dericardo didn't say anything else to qualify that statement?"

Fuck, Ernie thought vexingly. Upton knew something, or had something and was going to destroy Ernie with it. For a split second, Ernie thought his career was over. He thought he'd be convicted of perjury. Before he repeated his answer, the DA jumped up.

"Objection, Your Honor," the DA said. "Asked and answered."

"Sustained," the Judge agreed.

Ernie was relieved but tried not to let it show. He had ephemerally considered caving in.

"That's all I have for this witness, Your Honor," Upton said to the Judge. Then he turned back to Ernie. "Thank you, Detective," he said with a cheery smile and a half wink hidden from the jury.

Fretting, Ernie feigned a cough to the side to hide his unease.

"Just a brief redirect, Judge," the DA said.

Judge Talini nodded his assent.

"Detective, why did you rule out John Wakefielder as a suspect?"

"He had a solid alibi. He went home with a girl that night that lives at -" he glanced at his notes and flipped a few pages, "the Brandshire Houses. Her name is Erica Rosedale. We reviewed the surveillance tape. John and Erica entered the building at 1:53 a.m., and John didn't leave until the next morning."

"Could John have snuck out another exit?"

"Nope. Erica lives on the seventh floor and there is no exterior fire escape. So basically he had to use the elevator or stairwell to exit, and there are cameras in those areas."

"Nothing further."

"Recross?" the Judge asked.

"No, Your Honor," Upton replied, standing in a semi-bow.

"You may step down, Detective," the Judge said.

As Ernie made his way off the witness stand, he felt relief mixed with anxiousness. His testimony was done, and he did what he had to do. But the thought of Upton proving that Ernie had perjured himself kept his stomach in knots.

Step 5.4

He hadn't seen her since the funeral. He wondered if she understood. It was a difficult question to answer. What if she knew that her only daughter was dead during lucidity, only to have that knowledge slip away each time the Alzheimer's hit, like a light in the distance on a mountain road, appearing and disappearing with the curve of the road. One moment she would know unfettered sorrow, the next she wouldn't know her first name. What if the knowledge was a constant in the back of her mind, but she simply couldn't grasp a hold of it during her bad moments, like a demon dancing in the background, elusive, terrifying. Ed didn't know which would be worse. He supposed he never would. *Unless Alzheimer's is genetic.*

He paused before entering his mother's room at the old age home. He took a breath and steeled himself, not knowing what type of emotions would flare up upon seeing her. He entered the room.

She was sitting upright in her bed, eating a fruit cup, the signs of childhood pleasure plastered on her face. She was humming her contentment softly. Ed smiled genuinely. It was the first time since his sister's murder that he did so, he realized. All of a sudden, his shoulders dropped, his muscles relaxed, and the tension that had felt symbiotic of late released its latch on his body. "Hi, Mom," he announced.

His mother looked up from her fruit cup, clearly unsure whether the interruption was welcome. Then her expression changed. Her brow moved up and down, as if she was attempting to grasp a thought taken by the wind. "Are you my Edward?"

He laughed joyfully. "That's me, Mom. Your Edward." He moved to her with his teeth bared in a grin. She extended her arms, the fruit cup still gripped in one hand.

They embraced. Tears welled up in his eyes. He was home. He'd been away so long, he realized sorrowfully. He hugged tighter.

When they released, his mother noticed the fruit cup in her hand anew. Her eyes widened in excitement and she scooped up a full spoonful. Ed simply watched, his lips still parted in a smile.

After his mother swallowed, she looked up, meeting his eyes, her face racked with confusion. "Who are you?"

He took a deep breath, his anxiety returning. "It's Ed, Mom. Your son. Edward." He spoke softly, but a touch of agitation worked its way in. He sat on the bed while his mother eyed him suspiciously. He tried to ignore it. "So how have you been, Mom?"

"This fruit cup is lovely. I like fruit cups." She put another spoonful in her mouth. "Tell Ed to come inside, would you. It's time for dinner. He's probably out playing in the woods." She never looked up from her fruit cup.

"Mom," Ed said sternly. "*I'm* Ed. I'm grown up now."

She put the empty fruit cup down on her nightstand.

"Mom, have you heard what is happening with Mary's trial?" He didn't wait for an answer. "The prosecution is putting on their case. That means the trial should be over soon, and Mary's killer will be in jail." *At least he better be, or I'll kill him myself...and his lawyer too.*

She licked her lips as she regarded Ed, looking as if she was trying to make sense of his words but not wanting to let on that she had no idea what he was talking about.

"Mary?" she asked, scratching her cheek.

"Mary, Mom. Your daughter. My sister." He grabbed her hand and gave it a light squeeze, attempting to reassure her.

She glanced down at her hand, studied it, then looked back up at Ed. "Who are you?"

Ed sighed. It was hopeless…and frustrating. Seeing his mother in this state hurt him. And add that to the loss of his sister, well, he was on the verge of a nervous breakdown. The only thing that seemed to keep him sane and focused was his anger, his need for justice, his need for retribution, in some form or another. "It's just you and me, ma," he whispered, his eyes brimmed with tears. "Just you and me."

But his mother he couldn't help. "Okay, Mom. I'll come back and visit shortly. Love you." He bent over and gave her a kiss on the forehead.

She smiled at him. It warmed his heart, bringing back memories of his childhood. "Would you be so kind as to get me a fruit cup?" she asked, tilting her head in plea.

He nodded and exited the room, passing his mother's request along to the nurse. On his drive home, the realization hit that he would be all alone soon. The last remaining Roletti. It didn't make him sad, surprisingly. Rather, it fueled his anger. His father had been taken from him, his sister had been taken from him, and his mother had all but been taken from him. He could do nothing for his mother, but he vowed that he would find closure one way or another for Mary's murder. His mind raced as he contemplated the possibilities. Before he knew it, he was pulling into his driveway, his thoughts yanked back from the distance, like the recoil from a bow once the arrow is shot.

The figure on his front porch sat with elbows on knees, concern etched on his face. "Ray," Ed acknowledged as he approached the front door to his house.

Ray stood. "Hey, buddy. How's it going? Interested in any company?"

Ed nodded reluctantly. *As long as you don't quell my anger, Ray. It's all I have left.*

Ray followed him inside.

"Who is your current employer, Dr. Costello?" Franklin asked the Chief Medical Examiner. The old man sat hunched on the witness stand, almost as if he was trying to hide. The few strands of white hair that remained attached to his scalp were disheveled, reaching outward in no apparent pattern. His face was scrunched and wizened, his suit worn, his tie from a previous era. He epitomized the term "grumpy old man," Franklin thought. Despite that, Franklin knew that Doctor Harold Costello would give him what he wanted. The Doc had been the Chief Medical Examiner of Schenectady County longer than Franklin had been practicing law. The Doc knew his way around both a dead body and a courtroom. Upton would be hard-pressed to get anything of use out of the Doc on cross examination. As a result, this part of his direct case was less stressful than others. He didn't have to worry about the Doc damaging the case by saying something stupid.

"I am employed by the County of Schenectady," the Doc responded, his voice raspy and curt, his bushy eyebrows furled grumpily.

"In what capacity are you employed by the County?"

"I am the Chief Medical Examiner." He answered with no pomp. This was, in part, what made him a compelling witness.

"What are your duties as Chief Medical Examiner?" He had asked the Doc this line of questioning in two dozen other trials—albeit years ago.

The Doc scratched his cheek with a shaky hand before answering. "I have two roles, really. First, the Office of the Medical Examiner is charged with investigating cases of persons who die in Schenectady County in a suspicious or unusual fashion." He coughed loudly, his tiny frame shaking, but he quickly continued as if nothing was amiss. "This typically involves autopsies to determine cause of death. Second, as the Chief Medical Examiner, I have administrative duties."

"And how many people do you oversee?" Franklin knew all of these questions were dull background material, but the jury needed to know that the Doc was a well-credentialed physician who had been doing this for longer than some jurors had been alive.

"Three other medical examiners and 11 support staff."

"How long have you been the Chief Medical Examiner?"

"39 years," the Doc responded promptly.

Franklin glanced at the jurors and noticed that a few perked up in surprise. Good, he thought. "Are you board certified in any area of medicine?"

"I am. I hold an American Board Certification in forensic pathology, and I was previously certified in internal medicine, but that has lapsed."

"Okay. Let's turn to this particular case." Now it would get juicy. Franklin glanced at the jury to make sure he had their full attention. "Did you have cause to examine or perform an autopsy on the body of Mary Roletti?"

"I did."

"Why did you do so?"

"Well, as I mentioned before, if there is a death in this county and there is suspicion of criminal violence, the Medical Examiner is required by law to examine the body."

"And you personally examined Mary Roletti's body, correct?"

"That is correct."

"And did you issue a report as to the cause of death?"

"I did."

"What is your opinion as to the cause of death?"

The Doc glanced at the folder in front of him and opened it up. "The cause of death was multiple stab and incised wounds to the torso causing severe hemorrhaging and perforation of internal organs."

"Can you tell the jury what an incised wound is?"

"It is a cut where the length is greater than the depth." He cleared his throat with a loud "achem."

Old men always seemed to do that, Franklin thought transiently.

"In layman's terms," the Doc continued, "it can be referred to as a slash."

"Can you elaborate on the wounds and what you believe caused them?"

"Certainly." He glanced at his folder and moved down the open page with a shaky finger extended. Then he looked up. "There were multiple stab wounds of varying depths and lengths, suggesting the use of two different knives. One was consistent with a large butchering knife and the other a small paring knife. Approximately seven of those stab wounds punctured internal organs. The stab wound that perforated the liver was, by itself, sufficient to cause death, depending of course on when it was inflicted, whether before or after certain other wounds." He gestured to his own chest. "The stab wound that severed the inferior venae cava was also, by itself, sufficient to cause death, since it prevented blood flow to the heart." He glanced down and perused his notes briefly. "Now, the trajectory of each knife thrust was upward, suggesting that the victim was standing, facing the killer, and the killer was thrusting from an underhanded position."

Franklin lowered his voice to emphasis his next question. Sometimes, soft words created more of an emphasis than loud ones. The answer to this question was one he wanted the jury to lean in for. "Doctor, how many wounds did Mary's body have?"

He cleared his throat again, startling a few of the jurors. "Between stab wounds, incised wounds, and abrasions, I identified more than 100 on the body."

Franklin pretended to be looking at his notes while he let that answer marinate with the jury. "And based on the trajectory of the stab wounds, do you have an opinion as to the height of the killer?"

"Objection," Upton said, rising slowly.

"I'll allow it," Judge Talini responded after a moment of surveying the courtroom ceiling in thought.

"Between 5'7" and 5'10"," Dr. Costello answered.

"Did you find evidence of any other injuries?"

"Yes," the Doc answered, flipping through a few pages in his folder.

"What were they?"

"The body showed signs of forced penetration. There were abrasions on the vaginal walls suggesting the use of significant force, and trauma to the perineum, which suggests that the victim struggled mightily."

"After examining the body, did you reach a conclusion as to whether Mary Roletti's death was the result of a criminal act?"

"Yes."

"What is that opinion?"

"This was a homicide."

"Nothing further, Your Honor." *Nice and quick, right to the point.* All witnesses should be so easy, Franklin thought, sitting at his table and leaning back in his chair. He was completely unconcerned with what the Doc would say on cross.

"Your witness, Mr. Upton," Judge Talini said.

Upton strode to the lectern in two long, smooth steps. "Thank you, Your Honor. Good morning, Dr. Costello," he said pleasantly, wearing his insouciant smile.

"Good morning," the Doc responded cordially.

"Doctor, you just talked about the height of the killer, and you said you believed him to be between 5'7" and 5'10"?"

"Yes."

"And that was based on the location and trajectory of the stab wounds, correct?"

"Yes, in part."

"If the killer was hunched over when stabbing the victim, would that change your opinion as to his height?" The question was polite, as if Upton was inquiring about the weather.

"Possibly."

"What about if the killer was jumping, would that also change your opinion as to his height?"

"It could."

Upton slid his hands into his pockets. That habit was starting to annoy Franklin. The man was just so nonchalant, even during tense moments. Maybe Upton kept his hand near his dick. That was something a cocky, arrogant, son of a bitch would do.

"Can you tell the jury what Wood's lamp is?" Upton asked.

The Doc's eyes narrowed. "It is an ultraviolet light shone on the skin to detect various things not visible in normal light." His tone was somewhat biting.

But the Doc's gruffness was not agitation or anger, Franklin knew. It was simply the grumblings of an old man. Franklin glanced at the jury and saw that they thought nothing of the Doc's tone. *Upton probably thinks he is getting to the Doc.* Franklin lowered his head so as to hide the curl of his lips from the jury.

"And that includes blood?" Upton asked.

"Yes."

"Semen?"

"Yes."

"What about foreign hair?"

The Doc paused. "It could be used for that, but hair is easily detectible with a magnifying glass."

"Did you use Wood's lamp on Mary's body?"

"Yes."

"What did you find?"

"Nothing remarkable."

"Did you find anything on the body at all that contained DNA from anyone other than Mary?"

"No."

"So no semen was found, despite that there were signs of rape and a serious struggle?"

"Objection," Franklin called out.

"Overruled," the Judge responded quickly.

The Doc sniffed hard. "No semen," he grumbled.

"Let's be clear about this. No bodily fluid from Mr. Dericardo was found anywhere on the body?"

'No." The man's jowls shook.

Upton crossed his arms. "Doctor, how old are you?"

The Doc hesitated, likely on account of the non-sequitor. "83."

"When's the last time you visited a doctor to check your faculties?"

"Objection, Judge," Franklin yelled.

"Sustained," Judge Talini said with a frown.

“Nothing further.”

Franklin stood to correct a few points, his face still pinched from Upton’s last question. “Just a handful of questions, Your Honor.”

Judge Talini nodded.

“Is there any indication that the killer was hunching over or jumping when he was stabbing Mary?”

“No, sir.”

“Doctor, you just testified that you found no evidence of foreign DNA on Mary’s body.”

“Yes.”

“Do you have an opinion as to why that was?”

“Objection,” Upton said. “Speculative.”

“That’s overruled. If he has a sufficient basis, he can render his opinion.”

“Please, Doctor,” Franklin prompted, knowing this answer would render Upton’s cross examination a nullity.

“This killer was very meticulous. He went out of his way to make sure the body was cleaned of foreign substances. The victim’s fingertips were scrubbed with a highly potent cleanser, which I suspect was because the victim had managed to scratch the killer and could have had skin or blood underneath her fingernails. It was rather sophisticated and well thought out.”

“That’s all I have,” Franklin said confidently.

Upton rose. “Just one question, Doctor.” He pointed to his client. His words were measured. “Does Chucky Dericardo look like he is meticulous and sophisticated?”

“Objection,” Franklin yelled, trying to stem the damage. It was an excellent question, Franklin conceded. And although he knew it would be stricken by Judge Talini, the mere fact that it was voiced tainted the jury. It was Franklin’s own tactic used against him. Admittedly, it was a tactic of all good trial lawyers, so he supposed Upton would employ it. Right about now, the jurors were deciding just how sophisticated they thought Chucky was. It was cause for concern. From the look of Chucky, he supposed that sophisticated was the farthest thing from the jurors’ minds. *Fuck.*

“Sustained, sustained,” the Judge said with another frown. He glared at Upton but said nothing further.

“That’s all, Judge,” Upton said, his customary insouciant smile back on display.

"Doctor, you may step down," the Judge said.

Hopefully, Upton's improper question didn't stick. If Franklin had to show the jury that Chucky was smart enough to have committed the crime, the case was lost…along with his career.

◆ ◆ ◆

'Who is your current employer?' was a typical, boilerplate question that a prosecuting attorney asked during a trial. Franklin did so now, once again.

"The Schenectady County Police Department," Officer Eng answered, looking a little pale. Franklin hoped the young cop wouldn't faint on the stand. The examination was going to be brief, but Officer Eng looked like he'd had enough after only two questions. Franklin pressed on, trying to get through it quickly. "Other than general duties, do you have specific responsibilities regarding the police database?" It was a leading question, which was not permitted of a witness on direct examination, but hopefully Upton didn't object. Otherwise, he didn't think Officer Eng was going to make it.

Eng gulped audibly, his eyes showing his discomfort. After a long moment where Franklin held his breath, Eng answered. "Yes, I am the policeman responsible for searching data in the law enforcement computer system."

At least there was no objection. "Did you perform a search in this case?"

"Yes."

"And what did you discover?"

"I determined that Mr. Dericardo had a prior conviction." Eng was starting to look more comfortable. Maybe it was just the initial jitters. Franklin hoped so.

"Can you tell us about that conviction?"

"Uh, when he was a juvy he was convicted of petit larceny."

The use of slang terms on the witness stand was common among young officers, so Franklin was used to correcting them. "By juvy, do you mean juvenile?"

Eng flushed, realizing his error. "Yes."

Have to move quicker. Franklin picked up the pace of his questions. "And what about Dennis Kerisol, did you perform a search on him in this case?"

"Yes."

"What were the results?"

"It came back that he was convicted of grand larceny in the second degree and was sentenced to six years imprisonment."

Maybe it was the pace, but Eng didn't seem to be thinking about the answers. He just answered, which was good. Franklin pressed on at the same pace. "When did his incarceration begin?"

"Approximately five months ago at the Hale Creek facility."

"Has he been paroled since his incarceration?"

"No. He is not up for parole for another two years."

Franklin smiled. *Finally.* "Nothing further."

"Your witness, Mr. Upton," Judge Talini said.

"No questions, Judge," Upton responded.

Things were moving along well, Franklin thought. He would likely rest his case before the week was through. Then, the real test would come when Upton put his case on. Reminding himself that his political prosperity was on the line, Franklin started to worry just thinking about what tricks Upton had up his sleeve.

It was getting late, Robby Burns thought. He kept glancing at his watch, horses running through his head. *Good races today.* But the track wouldn't wait for him, and all he seemed to be doing was waiting to testify. *What's taking so long, damn it!* He eyed the backs of the attorneys as they conferred with the Judge at the bench, Upton wearing a brown pin-stripped suit and Dorey a light gray plaid. It reminded Robby of jockey silks. He glanced at his watch again. The races started at 11:30. He wasn't sure he'd make it to Saratoga in time for the first race, but at least, he told himself consolingly, he'd make it in time to play the pick-6. He snatched up the *Daily Racing Form* on the bench next to him and flipped through it for probably the fifth time this morning. It was dangerous, he knew, looking at it this many times. He could easily second-guess his handicapping. But what else was there to do except wring his hands.

Finally, the attorneys broke up, Upton returning to his seat with a half smile and the DA moving to the lectern. Robby put *The Form* down and glanced at his watch. *Still might make it.*

He took the stand, swore his oaths, and stated his name. The DA then asked him about his employment. "I am the lead forensics technician for the Schenectady County Police Department." He needed to get through this quickly if he was going to get his bets in.

"Did you personally work on this case?" the DA asked. The large class ring on his finger banged against the wooden lectern as he brought his hand down.

It reminded Robby of the sound the gates made when sprung open at the start of a race. "Yes. I supervised the technicians at the crime scene and I examined the victim's body myself. I took samples from the crime scene."

"What type of samples?"

"Well, there was blood, saliva, and hair follicles."

"What did you do with these samples?"

"Tested them." *So far so good.* He was tempted to look down at his watch, but he had enough forbearance not to. He glanced at the jury, reminding himself that he was being judged on his actions as well as his testimony.

"And you don't test the samples yourself, do you?" the DA asked, his ring knocking wood again.

And they're off! "No, no. It is standard operating procedure to send this over to the police lab where there are people specifically trained to test this material. They send me a report."

"Okay. What were the results of the lab tests?"

The report sat in front of him, but he didn't need it. Between forensics and horse statistics, he was used to memorizing results. "The blood and saliva turned out to be the victim's. The two hair follicles, however, came back with matches. One was brown in color, the other blonde. The brown hair belonged to Dennis Kerisol. The blonde hair belonged to Charles Dericardo."

Robby saw the jury glance over at Chucky, most paying particular attention to his blonde mullet. Robby smirked. *Ten bucks says you're going down...*

"Does the lab need to have hair or DNA samples in the system to accurately match a sample taken from a crime scene to a particular person?"

"Objection to form," Upton said, rising.

"I'll rephrase, Judge," the DA said quickly before the Judge could rule on the objection. The judge gave a half nod. Upton sat down.

"How is it that the lab is able to match these hair follicles to specific people?"

"Well, the lab will only be able to match a sample if that person's DNA—whether that be from blood, saliva, hair, or otherwise—is already logged in the system."

"Under what circumstances would a person's DNA be in the system?"

Robby shrugged. "If they were a prior criminal, their DNA would be in the system."

"Any other way?"

"Well, I suppose government employees would be in the system, but wait…that would only be for fingerprints," he said, thinking out loud. "So no, I guess the answer is, no. For DNA, only prior criminals are in the system."

The DA raised his hands above the lectern. "Let me be clear, because I don't want the jury to misunderstand -"

"Objection to the speech, Your Honor," Upton interrupted.

"Sustained," Judge Talini answered testily. "Leave the colloquy for another time, will you, Mr. Dorey."

"Certainly, Judge," the DA responded. He quickly turned back to Robby. "These two hair follicle samples, where were they found?"

"Both were found in the living room of the victim's house."

"And the living room is right next to the kitchen, correct?"

"That's correct."

"Okay. Let's move on." The DA briefly paused while he flipped pages on his notepad.

Come on, come on. Robby started to wring his hands in his lap.

"Did you perform any other forensic tests?" the DA finally asked.

Robby felt like he knew the answers before the questions were even asked. He answered hurriedly. "Yes, I performed a dactyloscopy." *What's a dactyloscopy?*

"What is a dactyloscopy?"

"It's just a fancy name for testing fingerprints by comparison."

"And you performed this test yourself?"

"Yes, I performed it."

The DA left the lectern and slowly paced, his hands behind his back. "How many prints did you test?"

Robby thought about conferring with the report before he answered, then thought better of it. "We were able to pull four different prints from the kitchen that were not the victims." He was pretty sure that was accurate.

"And the kitchen is where the murder took place, correct?"

"Yes."

"Okay. Where precisely in the kitchen did you find fingerprints?"

Damn it. For this, he had to open the report. It took him only a few seconds to locate the information. "On the counter, on the front door knob, on the refrigerator, and on the toaster."

The DA returned to the lectern. "And in performing a fingerprint comparison, were you able to match the fingerprints to specific persons?"

"For three out of four, yes."

"What were the results of that testing?"

"One fingerprint was matched to Dennis Kerisol. One fingerprint was matched to Ed Roletti. One fingerprint was matched to Charles Dericardo."

"So the defendant's fingerprint was found in the kitchen, where the murder took place?"

"Objection, asked and answered," Upton yelled out, albeit warmly.

The Judge's lips curled in thought. "I'll allow it."

"That's correct," Robby answered.

"Where exactly was his fingerprint found?"

He glanced at the report. "On the toaster."

"So you located the defendant's hair *and* fingerprints in the victim's house?"

"Objection, asked and answered," Upton said again.

"Sustained." The Judge's lips thinned.

"Oh, by the way, are you familiar with the current whereabouts of Dennis Kerisol?"

"He is currently incarcerated."

"Objection, Judge," Upton said, his tone hardening. "This witness clearly has no personal knowledge on this issue. His testimony is rank hearsay."

Judge Talini leaned into Robby. "What is your basis, sir, for testifying as to Mr. Kerisol's whereabouts?"

"My colleague told me after he performed a search of our system." *It's hearsay.* Robby knew it was hearsay. He took a class with the other officers about what was and wasn't hearsay. But that's how he found out, so that's what he said. He noticed a few officers in the back of the room, including the Chief, shaking their heads. *Whatever.*

"That objection is sustained," Judge Talini announced, leaning back. "Your next question, Mr. Dorey."

"That's all, Judge."

"Your witness, Mr. Upton," Judge Talini instructed.

At least someone is moving this along.

"Thank you, Your Honor." Upton slowly buttoned his suit jacket. He smiled pleasantly before he spoke. "Sergeant, was the hair sample the only DNA you found belonging to Mr. Dericardo?"

"Yes." That smile really annoyed Robby. He wondered if Upton was a gambler. *I guess you have to be to be a defense lawyer.*

"Are you aware that Mr. Dericardo dated Mary Roletti?"

"Objection," the DA said.

"I'll allow it if he knows," the Judge responded.

"I learned that, yeah."

"Would you expect a man to be present in the house of his girlfriend at some time?"

"Objection, Judge," the DA yelled spiritedly.

Jumping slightly, Robby almost forgot about the horses. Almost.

"Sustained," the Judge said tersely. "Move along, Mr. Upton."

Upton smiled again, one hand in his pocket. "You also located Mr. Dericardo's fingerprint on the toaster, is that correct?"

"Yes."

"Was the toaster close to the victim's body?"

"Uh…I'd say about six feet away on the counter."

"No fingerprints on the body?"

"No."

"What about around the body…on the floor or a chair or the kitchen table?"

"No."

"What about semen? Any semen on the body, or in the body?"

"No." *Now we're moving.*

"What about blood? Any blood other than the victim's found?"

"No."

"What about the bloody knives found on the counter…any fingerprints on the knives?"

"No."

"You also testified, Sergeant Burns, that you found a fourth fingerprint?"

"Yes."

"Who does that print belong to?"

Robby glanced at the report, then flipped the page. "Unknown."

"Unknown, huh." Upton turned around and moved back toward the lectern. He glanced at the DA and then looked behind the DA to the gallery.

Oh, he's a gambler. Robby found himself respecting the man more.

"You also found the victim's brother's fingerprints in the house, correct?"

Robby hesitated before answering, and his gaze flicked to Ed sitting behind the DA. His fellow officer was seething, his face beet red, his jaw clenched so tight that Robby thought he almost heard Ed's teeth grinding. Robby gulped, the gravity of the circumstances hitting him like a massive bet placed on an odds-on favorite that breaks his leg and is euthanized on the track. "Correct," he croaked.

"Nothing more," Upton said, still smiling.

Robby took a deep breath, keeping his eyes away from Ed's general direction.

"Just one question," the DA began, his index finger in the air. "Would you expect fingerprints from the victim's brother to be located in the victim's house, and more importantly, the house that the victim's brother grew up in?"

"I'll object, Judge," Upton said nonchalantly, "based on your prior ruling."

"Sustained."

"No more redirect, Judge," the DA said.

"You may step down, Sergeant," the Judge instructed.

Shaken a little, but now focused on the races, Robby stepped down. Once he was in the gallery, the Judge asked, "Anything else, Mr. Dorey?"

Robby continued down the aisle, finally getting the opportunity to check his watch. *Still got time!*

"At this time, Your Honor," the DA said behind him, the prosecutor's voice echoing in the large room, "the People rest their case."

Robby exited the courtroom visualizing races in his head, his blood starting to stir.

Step 5.5

"Thank you," Franklin said to the waiter as the iced tea was placed before him. He turned back to Wendy on the other side of the bistro lunch table. "I just don't get it," he said, somewhat exacerbated. He grabbed a packet of artificial sweetener, shook it, tore it open, and dumped it into his tea. "I mean, what are we missing?" The spoon clanked against the glass as he stirred.

Wendy brought her glass of water down from her lips. "I don't see anything. What's his expert psychologist going to say?" She shrugged. "That it wasn't a crime of passion. That's about it. He doesn't have anything else."

Franklin sipped his iced tea before shaking his head, not believing what was in front of him. "We're missing something, I tell you. This is John Upton we're talking about. He's got something up his sleeve. We can't be caught off guard." He curled his lips inward as he speculated wildly about the evidence or testimony Upton would present that would turn this case. A surprise eyewitness, maybe DNA evidence. Hell, knowing Upton's reputation, Franklin wouldn't necessarily be surprised if Mary Roletti walked into the room herself, took the stand, and testified that Chucky didn't kill her. He shook the ridiculousness from his bones. After a few moments of silence, he still had nothing.

"What about the cousin, this guy Barry Higgins?" Wendy asked, breaking off a piece of bread from the basket just placed on the table. "Maybe he will testify about an alibi." She sounded halfhearted. Rightly so.

Franklin scrunched his face incredulously. "I don't think so. It's got to be something nonobvious. We got to think outside the box." He snatched a piece of bread and began buttering it.

The table fell silent again. Franklin focused on his bread, taking a bite.

"How could he possibly rule out Chucky?" Wendy asked, clearly rhetorical. "No DNA, so that's not it. Chucky is unaccounted for at the time of the crime." Her face looked confused. "What else is there?"

"I don't know," Franklin said, his mouth full. "I don't know," he repeated, this time more downhearted. But if he wanted a conviction, he sure as hell would have to figure it out.

◆ ◆ ◆

"Your direct case, Mr. Upton," Judge Talini said after entering the room and taking the bench.

"Thank you, Your Honor."

Bill wondered how many suits Upton owned. Bill had only been present for six days of trial, but each day Upton had donned a different suit. Today was a solid dark gray, light blue shirt, and dark blue tie. Clearly, Upton had a least one suit for each day of the week, but Bill suspected he owned more. Many more. He decided to keep tabs, although he realized he'd already been doing so unconsciously.

"The defendant calls Barry Higgins," Upton said, his voice projecting.

Captain Pollack leaned over as the witness strolled down the aisle. "Where'd they find this guy?" he whispered in Bill's ear. "1982?"

Bill studied the witness with a keen interest. Barry Higgins looked skeletal, with a little pinhead, oversized square glasses, and a boxed crew cut of dusty blonde hair. The haircut made him look like an army recruit, although the thick glasses contrasted that assessment. The witness wore an inane smile and a thin wisp of a mustache that was barely filled in. Bill supposed that with the haircut and those dated glasses, the witness did indeed look like he was from the 1980s. 1986, perhaps. Certainly not 1982. His mouth twitched as he glanced at the Captain. In any event, Barry Higgins looked like anything but an intellect. He would offer nothing of import, Bill surmised before turning his thoughts to his own tie. He began counting the polka dots, mouthing the numbers under his breath.

Jim grunted next to him.

"Good morning, Mr. Higgins," John Upton said.

"Hi," the witness answered, sounding strangely chipper.

Not expecting such a tone, Bill brought his head up. He halted his counting at 17 polka dots and held it in abeyance.

"Where do you currently reside?"

"Port Saint Lucie, Florida," the witness responded with a bright smile before readjusting his glasses. The cadence of his speech rang strangely in Bill's ear, as if the man was a circus ringmaster announcing the high wire act.

"Where did you reside before that?"

"Right here in good old Schenectady, New York." The man's teeth were bared in what now appeared to be a perpetual grin, his mouth slightly ajar.

Judge Talini almost rolled his eyes.

Compelled to put his hand under the witness's chin and close the man's mouth, Bill started to stand. He caught himself and sat back down. A quick glance to his left revealed a furrow-browed Jim. Bill turned back to the witness with only a blink, unsure as to the impetus of Jim's expression.

"When did you move to Florida?" Upton asked.

"Oh…I'd say about four years ago, give or take a few days." He flourished a hand in what Bill assumed was uncertainty. Bill was seriously starting to dislike this man. Such…imprecision.

"Do you know Chucky Dericardo?" Upton continued.

"I sure do."

"How do you know him?"

"He's my cousin."

"And how precisely are you related?"

"Well…," the witness smacked his lips. "My mother and his mother were sisters."

"So you are first cousins?" Upton coaxed.

"That's right," the witness said cheerily. "First cousins."

The cadence of the witness's speech was now irregular, lacking rhythm, with unusual emphases. Bill preferred measured speech. It was more pleasing to the ear. But with his investigation of Jenny still ongoing, he attempted to listen to what the witness said, not how the man said it. It was a daunting task.

"Is that the extent of your relationship?" Upton asked, his right hand going to his pocket.

"Hmm. I suppose it's not." Mr. Higgins scrunched his face pensively, then sighed. "We were more like brothers growing up."

How is Jenny involved in this? The link had to be here somewhere. Whether gleaned through this witness or another, or even from another source, he would find it.

"Could you expand on that please?" Upton asked.

Mr. Higgins smiled brightly. His eyes reverted to the ceiling as he spoke. "Why certainly. Let me see. My dad died in jail when I was a little boy. Maybe three years old. So it was just me and my mom. Then my mom died when I was six. It just so happened that the previous year, Chucky's mom had died. Maybe my mom was so grief-stricken from her only sister's death that she couldn't go on. I'm really not certain. Anywho, I was gonna be sent to foster care, but Chucky's dad said he would take me in. So that's how me and Chucky became brothers."

Usually, eyeing the ceiling was a tell-tale sign of a fabrication, but Bill suspected that with this witness, it was merely unintelligence.

"Okay. So you grew up with Chucky?"

"That's right."

"And do you still have a close relationship with Chucky?"

"I certainly do. We speak once or twice a week and we see each other maybe twice a year."

Upton paused.

Where is this going?

"Let me ask you about May 21 of this year. Where were you?"

Mr. Higgins cocked his head to the side in a lopsided motion. "Well, I believe I was home that day in Port Saint Lucie."

"Did you speak to Chucky that day?"

"I recollect that I did."

"What did you speak about?"

"Oh, I don't know. Chitchat. This and that. You know, the usual."

Such vagueness and imprecision sent a shiver down Bill's spine. How could any person be so inarticulate? It made little sense.

Upton shifted on his feet. "Do you recall what time that telephone conversation began?"

"Hmm. I'd say it was about 10 O'clock p.m. We usually speak to each other at night. It's just how our timing seems to work out. Maybe we're nocturnal. I don't know."

"And how long did that conversation last?"

That was an interesting question. Bill anticipated the answer. *Hours, likely, as it establishes a viable alibi.*

"Maybe half-an-hour. I can't say for certain. Half-an-hour sounds good."

"Mr. Higgins," Judge Talini said, looking down at the witness. "You are not permitted to guess or assume. You may estimate, but you cannot guess. What is your recollection as to the length of the conversation?"

The witness brought his hand to his forehead, his fingertips pressed on the front of his skull. “Half-an-hour, I’d say.”

Bill blinked in confusion. He was unsure as to the defense’s strategy. He did not like being unsure.

“Nothing further, Judge,” Upton said, unbuttoning his suit coat and sitting quickly, as if unnerved.

For once, Bill thought, John Upton looked off kilter. *You did not expect it to go like this, did you?* Bill surmised that Upton did not elicit the testimony he wanted to, or thought he was going to. He wondered how Upton would adapt, how the defense attorney would recover or compensate.

“Mr. Dorey?” Judge Talini prompted.

The DA stepped to the court reporter. “I’d like to mark this as the People’s Exhibit number 14.”

“So marked,” the Judge announced.

“May I approach, Your Honor?” the DA asked, holding the paper toward the witness.

“You may,” the Judge answered.

The DA moved to the witness and placed the paper before him. “Can you tell me what this document is, Mr. Higgins?”

The witness adjusted his glasses and his smile faded as he concentrated on the document. Bill thought he saw perspiration bead on the witness’s forehead. The man certainly looked like he was straining.

“Looks to be phone records,” the witness proffered.

The DA turned toward the jury box, asking his next question without looking at the witness. “And whose phone records are these?”

“Looks to be Chucky’s phone records. His name is right here at the top. It says ‘Charles Dericardo.’”

The DA smirked. “And to your knowledge, is the address listed on those phone records the address where Chucky resides?”

“Well, I’ll be damned. I believe it is.”

“And what about the phone number. Is the phone number on those records Chucky’s phone number?”

“Right again,” Mr. Higgins said, smiling at the seemingly ingenuity of the DA’s questions.

Bill frowned internally, confused about the witness’s reaction.

“I’d like to move these phone records into evidence.”

“No Objection,” Upton seemed to growl.

Uncharacteristic. It seemed Upton was flappable after all.

"The People's 14 is now in evidence," the court reporter stated.

The DA pulled his gaze from Upton and cleared his throat. "Mr. Higgins, are these the records for a particular time period?"

The witness perused the document, adjusting his glasses multiple times. "I believe they are. Seems to be from May 21 to May 22 of this year."

"Okay, and do you see the highlighted outgoing call placed on the first sheet there?"

The witness squinted, despite his glasses. "I certainly do. It's highlighted in bright yellow. It certainly stands out." He held up the document and showed it to the jury, a smile plastered on his face.

The gallery and many jurors snorted or chuckled softly.

Bill failed to see the humor. He contemplated for a moment, but was unable to grasp it.

The witness's smile widened at the attention.

This is turning into an extremely strange trial.

"What number did Chucky call in the highlighted portion?" the DA asked.

The witness readjusted his glasses. His eyes widened, smile fading. "That's my number in Port Saint Lucie."

"So Chucky did call you on Saturday, May 21, correct?"

"Yes he did."

"Now, I want you to look at the column indicating when the calls were placed. What time did Chucky make that call to you on Saturday, May 21."

"This says it was at 9:04 p.m."

"And what time did the call end?"

"This says it ended at 9:27."

"So your phone conversation that night lasted only 23 minutes, correct?"

Mr. Higgins's eyes narrowed as the calculations—or whatever it was that was going on inside his head—took shape. "Why, yes. That's correct. 23 minutes."

The man must have a mental disorder, Bill thought. The calculation had run in Bill's head instantaneously.

The DA paused for a moment. "Are you aware that the victim's time of death in this case was 2:30 a.m. on Sunday, May 22?"

"Objection," Upton said.

"I'll withdraw the question, Judge," the DA said, returning to his seat. "No more questions."

"No redirect, Your Honor." Upton sounded slightly dour. *Yes, dour.* Bill decided he had interpreted the emotion accurately.

"Mr. Higgins, you may step down," the Judge said.

Mr. Higgins looked up at the Judge. "Thank you. I appreciate it." He moved to stand, paused, then leaned back into the microphone. "You all have a good day."

Judge Talini shook his head.

Jim snorted wetly.

Bill had already turned back to the polka dots on his tie. *22, 23, 24…*

◆ ◆ ◆

"I am a pathologist." Dr. Judy Stolin said, answering Upton's question.

She was a semi-attractive women, Franklin thought, with auburn hair, straight bangs hanging slightly over the rim of her black-framed glasses, thick pink lips, and prominent cheekbones. Age had just begun to produce faint lines on the pale skin of her face. It was apparent to Franklin that she had work done, so perhaps she was older than she looked. Cheekbones didn't look like that on their own…and her lips looked a little too thick to be natural.

Franklin had been waiting for this witness, his youthful enthusiasm returning. It was a rarity in criminal cases for a defendant to put an expert on the witness stand, and especially so in Schenectady County. As a result, Franklin had very little experience cross-examining experts. It presented a challenge…a real challenge. Experts were, well, experts in their field. That meant it was difficult to trip them up on substance. Unlike a standard fact witness, experts also had experience testifying. That meant they could pick apart questions, rendering them irrelevant, impotent, or worse, damaging to the People's case. There was nothing like a question turned on its head. With good expert witnesses, phraseology of a question was extremely important.

Franklin had never cross-examined Dr. Stolin, but ironically, Wendy had presented Dr. Stolin as a People's witness in a handful of murder cases. Dr. Stolin used to work at the Chief Medical Examiner's Officer under Dr. Costello. She used to testify for the

People. That meant she knew her shit. She knew not only what was needed to raise a doubt in the jury's collective mind to benefit the defense, but what was needed for the prosecution to establish guilt beyond a reasonable doubt. An expert witness that knew what was needed on both sides, and who could alter her testimony accordingly, was a dangerous witness indeed.

This was a challenge that Franklin relished. Good thing he wore his lucky cufflinks today. He glanced down at the gold sparkle poking out from under his suit sleeves.

Upton slipped his left hand into his pocket. "The jury has already heard testimony from the Schenectady County Chief Medical Examiner," he began, "but can you tell us what the field of pathology is?"

Dr. Stolin straightened her posture and turned to the jury. "Certainly. Pathology, which is a very small field in the world of medicine, is the study of injury and disease through the examination of bodily fluid or tissue. This can be done by touch or sight, including the use of a microscope, or it can be done in a laboratory testing specimens such as blood, urine, tumor tissue, and so on. There are various subspecialties within the umbrella of pathology. I am a general pathologist, meaning I test tissue and other specimen removed typically during surgical procedures."

She spoke slowly, was articulate and concise, and addressed the jury directly. That was an important tactic that was rarely employed. Most witnesses didn't know to speak directly to the jury, and most lawyers didn't have the foresight to instruct their witnesses to do so. But the jurors were the only people in the courtroom that mattered, and the questions were asked for their benefit. They liked to know that a witness was addressing them directly. The tactic instantaneously made a witness more personable. At a minimum, jurors paid closer attention. Franklin watched as the jurors perked. Yes, he had a challenge ahead of him.

"How long have you been practicing as a general pathologist?" Upton asked.

"Four years."

"And are you in private practice?"

"Yes, I have my own practice."

"Are you board certified?"

"Yes, I am currently board certified in general pathology and forensic pathology."

Upton removed his big paw of a hand from his pocket for a second, only to slip it back in. “Just to remind everyone, what is forensic pathology?”

Dr. Stolin leaned into the jurors, as if instructing students…and, technically, she was in a manner. “Forensic pathology is a subspecialty of pathology concerned with determining cause of death by a physical examination of a body. This procedure is often referred to as an autopsy.”

“If your practice is general pathology, why are you board certified in forensic pathology?”

“Prior to going into private practice, I worked as a Deputy Medical Examiner for Schenectady County.”

Upton smiled. “So that means you worked under Harold Costello, who is Schenectady County’s Chief Medical Examiner?”

“Objection, leading,” Franklin said, rising.

“I’ll allow it,” Judge Talini responded, his mouth twitching minutely, as if to say “not a big deal.”

“Yes,” Dr. Stolin answered. “He was my boss.”

Leading questions were impermissible on direct examination, but judges often gave lawyers leeway if the question and answer were not material and if the leading nature of the question was just employed to move things along quicker. Franklin had to be careful not to object too much, particularly if there was a possibility that the objection would be overruled. He didn’t want the jury to think he was hiding something or worried about this witness.

Upton continued with background questions. “How long did you work as a medical examiner?”

“Seven years.”

“Did you perform autopsies during that time?”

“Yes. Many.”

“Did you perform autopsies in cases involving stabbings?”

“Yes.”

Upton paused, removing his hand from his pocket and placing it on the lectern. His arm, due to its length, was bent awkwardly, like the lame leg of a flamingo. “Did you review Dr. Costello’s report in this case?”

Now, Franklin thought, came the meat of the testimony. *Let’s see what she has to say.* Maybe this was Upton’s surprise tactic. Maybe Dr. Stolin had a theory that could rule Chucky out.

“Yes, I did,” Dr. Stolin answered, eyeing the jurors.

Upton looked to the jurors, waiting briefly to emphasis something. "Do you agree with his findings?"

"Largely, yes."

Upton smiled.

That was a good tactic, Franklin admitted. If Dr. Stolin would've said she completely disagreed with all of Dr. Costello's findings, then her testimony could've been seen as highly suspect by the jurors. It was always better to concede minor or immaterial points. It provided credibility, so that when the one or two purportedly major errors were pointed out, they would be more believable.

"What is it that you disagree with in Dr. Costello's report?" Upton asked.

"Well, it's not so much that I disagree, but I believe he has omitted certain opinions that should have been included."

"What specifically did he omit?"

She shifted her entire body to the jury. "That the killer was left-handed."

That was interesting, Franklin thought. Anticipating the defense strategy, he realized that Upton still had to prove that Chucky was right-handed for this testimony to mean anything. *How will he do that? He certainly won't call Chucky to the stand, and he didn't ask the cousin about it.* Franklin started to worry a bit, thinking this must be the key to the defense. *But why didn't he ask the cousin?*

"Could you explain how you reached that opinion?" Upton asked.

"I conducted a reconstruction of the stab wounds?"

"And what does that mean, a reconstruction?"

"I conducted an experiment to see if I could reproduce some of the larger stab wounds inflicted on the victim's body, those wounds that would have been fatal if they, individually, were the only wound the victim received. This reconstruction involved creating a doll—I suppose we can call it a doll—of the size and approximate weight of the victim, and stabbing the doll in various ways using a knife of the size and shape found to be used in this case, and then measuring these wounds."

Ha! Reconstructions were riddled with flaws. Rarely did they sufficiently reconstruct the actual occurrence of the crime to provide any meaningful comparisons or conclusions. Normally he would object and ask for voir dire, so he could question the witness on her methodology in an effort to preclude the reconstruction testimony, but he had an inkling that it would do more damage than good in this case. Indeed, Upton eyed him briefly, apparently waiting for a challenge. Now Franklin was certain he wouldn't do so. *Perhaps my cross will be easier than anticipated.* He was both relieved and disappointed.

"What is the purpose of conducting a reconstruction?" Upton asked after a minor pause.

Franklin smiled internally. *Not going to play into your game, John.*

"The wound patterns may provide us information about the killer or the manner in which the murder took place?"

"What information did you glean from your reconstruction?"

"I stabbed the doll multiple times, underhanded, using both of my hands, and doing so with a slightly upward trajectory as was the case here."

"And just so this is clear, the Chief Medical Examiner agrees that the stab wounds were inflicted underhanded, correct?"

"That's correct. His report indicates that the knife thrusts were made underhanded."

"So based on your reconstruction, you determined that the killer was left-handed?" Upton held up his left paw.

The first thought in Franklin's mind was that those hands would be perfect for strangling. He had too many crimes swimming in his head.

"Yes," Dr. Stolin answered.

"Nothing further."

That's it?! Franklin expected more. Much more. There was, in fact, very little to do on cross. He again wondered if he was missing something. Maybe this dominant hand business was just a distraction to mask Upton's real surprise. *There has to be something else...or he would've asked the cousin about which was Chucky's dominant hand.*

"Your witness, Mr. Dorey," the Judge said.

In any event, Franklin had to deal with this witness first. He moved to the lectern and flashed his own carefree smile. "Thank you, Judge. You left the Medical Examiner's Officer more than four years ago, correct?" His tone was cordial. He found that it was much more effective to be cordial with defense witnesses—especially expert witnesses—rather than hostile or demeaning. If you showed the jury that you could be civil with a witness on the other side, it often diminished the influence of that witness. Franklin had no idea why. It just did.

"Yes," Dr. Stolin answered.

"So you haven't practiced forensic pathology, or conducted an autopsy, in more than four years?"

"That's true."

"How long has Dr. Costello been doing this?"

She laughed. "A long time."

"And, now, as a general pathologist, you often work with lawyers, analyzing specimens; isn't that correct?" Cross examination was the one time when you could ask leading questions. Franklin often employed it to pigeonhole witnesses into saying what he wanted them to say. Good witnesses were insusceptible to the tactic, however.

"That's true. My work in the legal field is almost exclusively in the civil realm, involving cancer or other diseases. But my legal work is only about 25 percent of my business. I also do work for the government and for other physicians who send me samples."

"Now, let me ask you about your opinion in this case. Your opinion is that the killer is left-handed; is that correct?"

"Yes."

Franklin displayed a pensive look to the jury, then spoke slowly. "Let me clarify this. Is it your opinion that the killer was predominantly left-handed, or that he simply used his left hand to stab the victim?"

She thought about the question for a moment. "Left-hand dominant."

Franklin smiled. "Are you left-handed?"

"No, sir."

"And yet you conducted a reconstruction using your left hand, so I'm at a loss. How is it that you can say that the killer was left-hand dominant based on your reconstruction, using your own non-dominant hand?"

"Well, my opinion is not based solely on my reconstruction. My reconstruction showed that the trajectory, size, and shape of the stab wounds were consistent with left-handed stabs where the killer is facing the victim and stabbing underhanded. What led me to believe that the killer was left-hand dominant was my personal experience dealing with stab and gun cases where the assailant virtually always holds the weapon in his…or her, dominant hand."

To her credit, Dr. Stolin's answer didn't sound defensive. Yet neither was it helpful to the defense. *Got ya!* This was too easy, Franklin thought. "So, in other words, there is nothing in this case in particular that leads you to believe that the killer is left-handed? Nothing that points directly in this case to a left-handed person? It's only your own personal experience in a handful of other cases from a number of years ago that leads you to this conclusion? Am I right?"

"Objection, Judge," Upton called out. "Compound question. And argumentative."

"Sustained. Please rephrase, Mr. Dorey."

Now for the real question. "What in *this* case, other than the reconstruction you did, leads you to believe that the killer was left-hand *dominant*?"

"Well…it's the fact that the stab wounds were inflicted using a left hand coupled with my personal experience in this field."

"Okay," he said, smiling incredulously. *Now to poke a few more holes.* "One of the things you just mentioned was that you assumed the killer was facing the victim. What if the killer was behind the victim and stabbing inward?"

"That's not possible from the wounds inflicted here. Even Dr. Costello would agree with that assessment."

"I'll move to strike the portion of the answer that was nonresponsive," Franklin said, facing the Judge. That answer was improper because Dr. Stolin couldn't testify to what another person would have done or thought. She likely said it on purpose, though, knowing it would increase her credibility with the jury. *Clever.*

"It's so stricken," Judge Talini said. "Jurors, you are to disregard that portion of the answer that did not respond to the question. Wipe it from your mind."

Two can play this game. "So, essentially," Franklin advanced, "you agree with Dr. Costello's assessment of this murder, but the only thing you would add is that the killer was left-handed; is that correct?"

"Yes."

"Can you tell the jury which is the defendant's dominant hand, left or right?" It was a risky question, particularly if Chucky was right-handed and she knew it, but Franklin took the risk.

"I don't know, that's not my expertise. I can only say how the victim died and what the assailant did. I presume there is other evidence that will show which is his dominant hand."

Franklin frowned at the last comment, as it was what he'd been thinking throughout his cross examination, but he decided not to move to strike it. He'd already put away this witness. "One last question: what if the killer was ambidextrous? Would that affect your opinion?"

"Well, despite the rarity of that, I suppose it would."

"That's all, Judge." *Not much of a challenge at all.* Looking at the big picture, Franklin supposed it was better this way. His political ambitions were hanging in the balance. He'd rather have a smooth ride than a bumpy one.

"Any redirect?" Judge Talini asked Upton.

Upton stood, nodding. "Doctor, if you observed Mr. Dericardo writing, would you be able to tell which hand was his dominant hand?"

"Objection," Franklin yelled. That was simply going too far. "Judge, may we approach?"

Judge Talini waved them up. "Where are you going with this, Mr. Upton?" he asked heatedly when Franklin and Upton stepped up.

Franklin looked up to Upton's face as the man answered. "Your Honor, Mr. Dericardo has been writing periodically during the trial - "

"No, no, no," Judge Talini interrupted. "That line of questioning and trial practice is improper and highly prejudicial. I won't allow it. If you want to get it in that the defendant is right-handed, you will have to present competent evidence, admissible-in-form. Having your expert pathologist watch the defendant write, in the presence of the jury, is not the manner to do that." He waved them away, sounding annoyed and confounded.

Franklin himself was confounded at Upton's tactic. *Then again, Upton knows this didn't go his way. Maybe he's desperate.*

"No more questions, Your Honor," Upton said, sounding slightly agitated for now the second time this trial.

Franklin smiled behind his hand. The focus of his thoughts shifted. He thought he had it narrowed down to two positions: attorney general and state senator. Maybe he would have it down to one by the end of the next witness.

◆ ◆ ◆

He hadn't slept in days. He knew his career was over, that Upton would come up with something to prove that he had manipulated the truth on the stand, that he had lied when he testified that Dericardo made no further statement after saying "I was angry about being dumped." Ernie just knew it. A disciplinary hearing would ensue, of course. Then he would be let go from the Force…and maybe even prosecuted for perjury. No jail time, thankfully, but a hefty fine and parole. He thought about what he would do, where he would work. He had no skills other than as a detective. Sighing, he found a seat.

Ernie had sat in the courtroom every day of trial, waiting, fretting, hanging on every word from every witness. So far, nothing to blow him up, but today, Ernie knew his day would come. *The beginning of the end for Detective Suarez,* he thought despondently.

As the witness was being sworn in, John Upton—Ernie's executioner—moved to the lectern, a thousand dollar suit hugging his spindly frame and an immutable smile branding his face. Ernie knew that Upton was laughing at him on the inside. Yet he couldn't muster any anger at the man for doing so—it was Ernie's own fault that he was in this position.

"Dr. Watt," Upton began when the Part Clerk was finished with the oaths, "what is your profession?"

"I am a clinical psychologist," Dr. George Watt said, scratching his trimmed beard. He was on the younger side, probably in his late 30s, with buzzed jet-black hair contrasted by pale, almost bleached skin.

Ernie took a deep breath, only nominally relieved that his fib wasn't called out on the first question. *One question down, who knows how many left…*

"Are you a doctor?" Upton asked.

"I have a Ph.D. I am not a medical doctor." Dr. Watt spoke slowly, articulating each word, emphasizing none. It was a manner of speaking that proclaimed him an elitist, or so it sounded to

Ernie. What's worse, it felt protracted, which was torturous for Ernie. He bit his lower lip in annoyance. A part of him wanted it to be over already, for Upton to play the trump card. That way, at least Ernie wouldn't have had to wait around, almost shitting himself from severe angst. Unconsciously, he began to bite his nails.

"How long have you been practicing clinical psychology?"

"14 years."

"And who is your employer?"

"I work for a private company called New York Clinical Assessments, Inc., but we do a lot of contracting with New York State."

"Do you have any particular focus?"

"For the past six months I have been working on a project with New York State assessing prisoners at Rikers Island."

Jim plopped down next to Ernie. "Anything happen yet?" Jim whispered.

Ernie shook his head sharply, giving Jim only a brief glance. He needed to focus on the testimony. Luckily, Jim said nothing further.

Upton pulled his hand from his pocket. "Have you worked with criminals before?"

"Occasionally," Dr. Watt answered. "Not criminals as a particular group, but I have assessed various patients who had criminal backgrounds."

"So for your current work with the State, you have been dealing with convicted prisoners exclusively?"

"Yes. I have assessed approximately 12 prisoners in that time, and it is an ongoing basis."

"And in that work, have you had experience with persons convicted of a crime of perjury?"

What?! This was it—the end. Ernie paled, shifting uneasily, his breath momentarily lost only to return in a torrent of gasps. He shook himself. *I didn't hear that right, did I? No, no! He said crimes of* "passion," *not "perjury."* His anxiety level dropped. Ernie had been hearing the word "perjury" all over the place. At the supermarket, on the phone, in his dreams, in the shower, on the radio, at work. He needed to stay focused. He'd almost just stood up and bolted. He rubbed his eyes vigorously.

"Yes," Dr. Watt answered, "a few of the Rikers prisoners I am currently working with were convicted of crimes of passion. I also have dealt with such crimes a few times in the past with other patients, and of course, I studied it while obtaining my Ph.D."

"All right. Can you please tell the jury what a crime of passion is?"

Dr. Watt nodded, clearly waiting for this question. "A crime of passion is a crime that is precipitated by a strong emotional reaction. Typically that emotion is jealousy, but a few other emotions as well. It often involves circumstances where the person committing the crime discovers certain behavior on the part of his significant other. The textbook example is the man who walks in on his wife in bed with another man. The husband goes into a rage and kills his wife and the other man."

Upton held his hands in the air before him. "In your experience, are crimes of passion committed two years after experiencing a precipitating event?"

"Good luck with this strategy," Jim whispered in Ernie's ear, leaning over, arms crossed and resting on his rotund belly.

Ernie gave him a dismissive nod, then turned back to the witness. He couldn't afford to miss anything, even if it meant snubbing his superior.

Dr. Watt looked thoughtful, his finger going to his lip for a moment. "I've never heard of such a situation…and it really defies the definition of a crime of passion. Immediacy is an important factor when dealing with crimes of passion. For a person to be under such an extreme emotional state to commit a criminal act in a rage, he or she must, in virtually every instance, experience the precipitating event contemporaneously with the crime. In other words, very little time must elapse between the precipitating event and the criminal act. The act must be an impulse. Two years is too long a period to constitute a crime of passion. Two months is too long. Two days, even, is most likely too long. It is seconds or minutes…or possibly hours."

Upton nodded. "Nothing further," he said, still smiling.

Holy shit! The tightness in Ernie's muscles immediately dissipated, his tension replaced with exhaustion. The anticipation, the anxiety, and the mental focus were certainly not easy things to control or maintain. This witness was probably not the one that Upton would use to call Ernie out. He eased back on the bench and reclined, yet he instinctively started fretting about other unknown witnesses.

"Your witness, Mr. Dorey," the Judge said.

"Not much there, right?" Jim said to Ernie, his soft voice confident.

Ernie finally gave his superior his full attention. "Not that I saw." *In more ways than one, Cap!*

"Doctor," the DA began, his tone cordial, "can what you would refer to as a 'precipitating event' be a motive to kill, although the criminal act may not happen immediately?"

Dr. Watt cocked his head. "I suppose so."

"Let me ask you this: If a woman breaks up with her boyfriend, is that an act that causes an extreme emotional state?"

Dr. Watt's brow furled. "It depends on the person…and any number of factors. As a general principle, ending a relationship after one date would cause a different emotional state than ending a relationship after three years. Yet there are some people who would be extremely emotionally disturbed if a relationship was ended after one date. So, basically, there are too many factors at play to properly answer your question." His tone was borderline condescending.

Ernie looked over to find Jim smirking.

"Dr. Watt, did you examine the defendant?" the DA asked, his tone growing lighter.

"No."

The DA threw his palms up. "You're a psychologist, and your job relies heavily on the interviews you conduct with people, but you didn't interview the defendant before testifying in this case?"

Dr. Watt's lips thinned. "No. That was not why I was retained. I am here for the limited purpose of discussing the time periods involved in crimes of passion. Whether I interviewed Mr. Dericardo or not is irrelevant to my opinion that crimes of passion do not occur after a two-year period."

The DA slipped both of his hands in his pockets and began to pace slowly. Perhaps he was mocking Upton, Ernie thought. "Okay, but you know nothing about the defendant, correct?"

Dr. Watt leaned back sharply, his speech pattern accelerating. "Well, I wouldn't say 'nothing.' But essentially you are correct. I am not familiar with the facts of this case except that the victim ended the relationship with Mr. Dericardo two years ago and someone murdered her recently."

Jim was openly laughing under his breath, his belly shaking. Ernie didn't think it was that bad. In fact, he noticed Upton smirking. Despite Dr. Watt's tone, the man was doing Upton's job for him with answers like that. Upton likely wouldn't need any redirect examination. *I sure as hell hope he doesn't.* The less questions, the better for Ernie.

"So your opinion is that the defendant did not commit a crime of passion?" the DA continued.

"Based on the time period involved, that's correct."

The DA launched into his next question. "Here's what I really want to know." He quickly pivoted, squaring himself to the witness. "Notwithstanding your opinion about whether this was a crime of passion, you can't say at all whether the defendant killed Mary Roletti, can you?"

"That's true." Strangely, Dr. Watt looked as if the answer changed the outcome of the case in Dericardo's favor. *Totally elitist.*

The DA pressed the man. "Let's make sure the jury understands this. So if the defendant did kill Mary Roletti, the only thing you can tell the jury is that it was not a crime of passion?"

"I'll object, Your Honor," Upton said.

"Basis?" Judge Talini asked.

"Assuming facts not in evidence," Upton responded.

Judge Talini turned to the court reporter. "Read it back please."

The court reporter grabbed at the thin slice of paper protruding from her stenograph machine and reread the question aloud.

Judge Talini sniffed.

"This witness backfired on Upton," Jim whispered in Ernie's ear, the bench creaking as the Captain leaned over.

Ernie nodded.

"It's proper expert opinion testimony, Judge" the DA threw out. "It's asked as a hypothetical."

The Judge nodded slightly. "I'll allow it as a hypothetical."

The DA grinned. "You can answer Dr. Watt."

"Please repeat it."

The DA cleared his throat. "So if the defendant did kill Mary Roletti, the only thing you can tell the jury is that it was not a crime of passion?"

After a minor pause, Dr. Watt said, "Yes."

"Will you concede that the fact that Mary Roletti ended the relationship with the defendant could have played a role in his decision to kill her?"

"Objection, Your Honor," Upton yelled. "Now he's assuming the ultimate conclusion?"

"That's sustained," the Judge said promptly. "Rephrase, Mr. Dorey."

"You will concede that the fact that the defendant was dumped by Mary Roletti two years ago could have been a motive, at least in part, for him to have committed this murder?"

Upton stood again, shaking his head. "Same objection, Judge."

"Overruled. You may answer."

Dr. Watt's eyebrows lifted. "It's possible."

"I have no more questions." The DA sat, looking pleased.

"Any redirect?" Judge Talini asked.

Ernie's heartbeat increased. *Please say no.*

"Yes, Your Honor," Upton responded.

Fuck!

Upton didn't move to the lectern, however. He simply stood at his table. "Dr. Watt, I want you to assume that a man is dumped by his girlfriend and is extremely angry about it. In your professional opinion, would that man murder his ex-girlfriend more than two years after he was dumped?"

"Objection," the DA said.

"Approach," the Judge directed.

The attorneys moved to the bench. Judge Talini leaned in and listened to both counsel before speaking at length. His head swiveled between the two attorneys, so he didn't seem to be chastising either one.

Ernie waited anxiously.

Jim was breathing heavily next to him. The noise only enhanced his anxiety.

Finally, Upton nodded before the attorneys returned to their respective tables.

"The question will be rephrased," the Judge informed the jury.

"Dr. Watt, in your professional opinion, does the fact that Mary Roletti ended her relationship with Mr. Dericardo two years prior to her murder suggest that Mr. Dericardo killed her?"

Dr. Watt shook his head. "No, it does not."

"That's all I have," Upton said as he sat.

Ernie could finally relax. He waited for the Judge to excuse the witness.

"Recross?" the Judge asked the DA.

"Briefly, Your Honor," the DA answered.

No! Ernie's frustration was starting to displace his fear. He took another deep breath.

"Just one last question," the DA led off with. He flourished a hand in the air. "If a defendant commits a murder as a crime of passion, it's not a complete defense to murder, is it? It only means the crime was not committed in the first degree; correct? The defendant is still convicted of murder, right?"

"Objection," Upton said calmly, his prior flustered tone nowhere to be found. "Asks for a legal conclusion. And compound question."

"Sustained." The Judge looked to both attorneys. "Counselors, there will be no more of that."

"Nothing further," the DA said.

"Dr. Watt," Judge Talini said, "you may step down."

Ernie sighed, much of his distress leaving his body with his breath. Another one down, he thought gratefully. Then he shook his head skeptically, his anxiety replenishing itself.

He probably wouldn't sleep a wink tonight.

Step 5.6

They milled about the hallway, waiting, bored. Chief Byron Stadmore ran his fingernails down his thick mustache, as if combing. He found the act meditative. After a number of strokes while staring at the painting on the wall depicting the swearing in of some judge from the 18th century with an awful hairdo, Byron glanced around at his officers. His own tranquility was in stark contrast to Jim Pollack, who frantically paced the hallway while regaling Ernie with some joke or story that was undoubtedly about a woman. Same old Jim, Byron thought with a mental shrug. *Damn good detective, though.* Ernie, his new homicide detective, seemed to be politely listening to Jim, but Byron could tell it was more of a necessary attentiveness than a willing one, seeing as how Jim was Ernie's direct superior. Whether he genuinely enjoyed the story or not, Ernie was working hard to stay in Jim's good graces. Ernie would make a fine detective some day. That's why Byron threw him into the homicide unit. A good detective working misdemeanors was like a star quarterback manning the water station. Curiously, the man did seem to have a little more pep in his walk the last few days. Byron didn't know what to attribute that to.

And then there was Ed, who sat isolated on a bench a good 20 feet away. He was leaning forward with hands clasped before his mouth, elbows resting on his knees, his eyes fixed on the marble floor. *Hang in there, Ed.* He wondered how Ed felt, what Ed was thinking. Byron shook his head at the pity of it all. What would this do to Ed? Byron didn't know. He simply hoped that Ed would remain on the Force.

A handful of reporters clustered a few paces further down the hall, chatting. The most brazen among them furtively snapped shots of Ed. Byron almost rose to smash the man's camera, but it occurred to him that preventing pictures of Ed from surfacing would be impossible. Ed's every expression during the trial—which was really only a singular, perpetual scowl—had likely been caught on camera multiple times, despite the Judge's ban of photography. Feeling suddenly fatherly, Byron rose to sit next to Ed, hopeful that he could give the boy some comfort.

The courtroom door swung open. "There's something from the jury," Ray said, half his body protruding from behind the door. The officers had been taking turns sitting in the courtroom, waiting for the jury's verdict, each man sitting for an hour. Ray's hour had just begun.

The hallway fell silent.

Jim turned to Byron. "How long's it been?" he asked, glancing at his watch. "Three hours?"

Byron looked to his own watch reflexively.

"If it's the verdict," Jim continued, "then it's a sure-fired guilty verdict. Only three hours of deliberation…" He flashed Ed a smile.

Ed returned that smile with watery eyes and a firm mouth. He rose and stalked into the courtroom.

Byron and the other officers followed quickly behind, his old bones popping as he moved. Many had chosen to remain in the courtroom during the deliberations. The gallery was three-quarters full, and the conjectural muttering reverberated in the cathedral-sized room.

A few minutes later, Chucky was brought in and placed at the defense table. Upton leaned over and whispered to him.

Once everyone was seated and quiet, Judge Talini looked down from his bench to the court reporter. "Let's go on the record." He waited a moment. "I have a note from the jury. It reads: 'May we review the direct examination of the police department forensic technician.'" The Judge looked up. "That would be Sergeant Burns. We will bring the jury back in and the testimony will be reread by the court reporter. Any issues, Counselors?"

"No, Your Honor," the DA responded.

"No," Upton said.

Damn, Byron thought. No verdict. What's worse, the fact that the jury was seriously considering the evidence was not a good sign. In Byron's experience, the more consideration the jury gave the evidence, the more a doubt began to grow in their collective mind. It often led to a reasonable doubt, and a reasonable doubt meant an acquittal—at least on the main criminal count.

The jury was brought in and the requested testimony reread.

Byron leaned forward to regard Ed. The young officer was glowering icily at the jury, his eyes piercing, unwavering. Ed had been a police officer long enough, had testified in court enough, to know that jury notes that did not say 'we have reached a verdict' were ominous. But, nonetheless, Ed's expression alarmed Byron. He had to do something to calm Ed down. For the moment, while the jury was present, he could do nothing. He sat, fretting slightly, glancing frequently at Ed in the hopes of seeing a softening to the boy's face. Despite the fact that it took almost 45 minutes to reread Robby's testimony, Ed's expression didn't change. Nor did his gaze falter.

Shit! The boy needs his damn father…or mother, for that matter.

"All right," Judge Talini said to the jury. "Please return to your deliberations. Remember my prior instructions."

"All rise," the bailiff called as the jury members rose and exited.

Once the jury was gone, the Judge said, "Stay close, Counselors," before moving to a back door.

Byron's officers filtered out of the courtroom with the crowd, Ray remaining to finish his watch. As they moved down the aisle, Byron patted Ed on the back a few times before resting his hand on the boy's shoulder.

Ed's only reaction was to scowl harder.

Shit! Not good.

◆ ◆ ◆

His cell rang. He listened to the familiar ring three times. "Bill Watkins," he answered before wrapping his lips around the straw of his fountain soda.

"Bill, it's Ernie," Detective Suarez said on the other end of the line.

"Yes, Detective," he said, his eyes fixed on the restaurant, his mind preoccupied. He put his cell phone on speaker, placed the phone on the dashboard, and took a bite of his sandwich, careful not to alter his gaze. Still, he could not help but examine his sandwich, his eyes pulled toward it. The bite he took was slightly larger than the last few, which marred the evenness and symmetry of his bite marks. He briefly considered spitting a portion back out and molding it on the corner of the sandwich, but decided against it. Instead, he nibbled a straight line across the sandwich before examining it again. *There, much better.* He returned his full attention to the restaurant.

"Bill?" Ernie asked, and after a brief silence, "You there? Bill?"

"I am here," Bill said flatly, his mouth full.

"Where are you? We're supposed to start working the Mitchell case. That woman's coming in in 15 minutes."

Bill swallowed his food. "I cannot make it," he said. Just then, a woman exited the restaurant. Bill leaned forward over his steering wheel and squinted. Holding the restaurant door open, the woman swiveled her head. A man and two children sauntered out of the restaurant behind her. Bill leaned back.

"What do you mean?" Ernie asked. "What are you doing? You're on the clock?"

"Yes. I am on the clock," Bill confirmed. He glanced at his sandwich, but hesitated before taking another bite. If he were to take a bite, the deformity in the appearance of the sandwich would niggle at him, and then he would be forced to take multiple bites in rapid succession, just to assuage the tick in his mind. Doing so, however, would cause him to eat too fast, which in turn could affect his digestive regularity. There was nothing worse than an irregular digestive track, he noted. On the other hand, if he did not take a bite, he would be hungry. His brow shifted as he weighed his options. *Correction, hunger is worse than irregularity.* He took a bite, chewed quickly, then took two bites of the same size across the sandwich's surface. *There, that was not so bad.* His hand precipitously moved to his belly, just in case it was to go sour.

"I guess I'm working this case by myself," Ernie said.

Bill cocked his head at Ernie's tone, which sounded different. Bill could not pinpoint it, so he remained silent. A woman exited the restaurant while removing her hairnet. Bill squinted. *Got you.*

"The Captain probably won't be ple -"

"Got to go, Ernesto," he interrupted with his mouth full.

"Hey, wait. You -"

Bill reached for the phone and ended the call. He quickly re-wrapped the sandwich and delicately placed it on the passenger seat. His gaze oscillated between the woman as she headed for her car and the sandwich resting on his passenger seat. As the woman got into her car, Bill started his own.

He pulled out of the restaurant parking lot, compelled to tail Jenny Johansson for the rest of the day…and possibly into the night. He reached over and altered the position of the sandwich ever so slightly. *There, much better.*

Step 5.7

"I have received a note from the jury," Judge Talini announced on the third day of deliberations. "It reads: we have reached a verdict." He looked up, regarded both attorneys, then said, "let's bring them in." He turned to the side door. "Bailiff," he prompted.

The tension in the courtroom was palpable, and murmurs sprang up. Reporters were poised with pen and paper or with thumbs ready on cell phones. Nervous, his heart pounding, Franklin glanced over at Chucky. Strangely, the defendant seemed completely at ease. Then again, Chucky had seemed that way throughout the whole trial. Either he knew he was guilty and was resigned to the fact that he would be convicted, was innocent and believed he would be found not guilty, or simply didn't care. If Franklin only knew…

"All rise," the bailiff announced a short time later as he reentered the courtroom. Franklin rose, his heart pounding harder. As the adrenaline coursed through his veins, he curled his fingers into fists, intent on masking the shakes in his extremities. His toes wriggled compulsively but he maintained enough control to keep the movement confined to the interior of his shoes. The jurors marched in past the bailiff, their faces grim, one and all. Franklin's heart beat faster. Wendy cleared her throat. Franklin swallowed. *Feels just like my first fucking trial…*

"Madam Foreperson," Judge Talini said to the corpulent juror sitting in seat number one, "have you reached a verdict?"

With some effort, she rose, yanking down her shirt. "Yes, Your Honor." She flashed the folded sheet of paper in her hand.

Judge Talini cued the bailiff, who took the sheet from the foreperson and handed it to the Judge. The Judge examined the sheet, his expression giving away nothing. He handed it back to the bailiff, who in turn handed it back to the foreperson.

Here goes my career…

Franklin took a deep breath. The anticipation was stronger than in any case he'd ever tried—even his very first trial. Things had come full circle, he thought.

"Madam foreperson, as to the first count against Charles Dericardo—murder in the first degree—how do you find?"

The juror looked down at her sheet, her breathing heavy. "Guilty."

Franklin sighed in relief, the shakes increasing. Gasps, cheers, and a few hoots rang up in the courtroom. He transiently pictured the frontpage headlines—his name in bold font, his face front and center.

"Quiet, please! Quiet," the Judge said, clearly perturbed. He sighed audibly, and turned to the jury box. "As to the second count—rape in the first degree—how do you find?"

"Guilty."

This time, there was only a buzz in the courtroom. Wendy gave his arm a quick squeeze. He offered her a furtive wink. He was beaming, of course, but only on the inside. It wasn't prudent for a District Attorney to gloat after winning a verdict that sends a man to jail for life, so he kept his exterior stony. He swiveled his head to the pews behind him and gave Officer Ed Roletti a sharp nod.

Surprisingly, the young officer returned it with a troubled expression and a rhythmic bob—as if in a dark trance. Franklin didn't know what to make of that, but he only gave it a momentary consideration before his own ambitions took control of his mind.

"May we poll the jury, Your Honor?" Upton asked.

The Judge nodded. "Juror number one, is this your verdict?"

The portly woman rose again. "Yes."

"Juror number two, is this your verdict?"

"Yes."

The Judge went down the line of jurors. All rose and responded in the affirmative, even number ten, the liberal. "I want to thank you, members of the jury," the Judge said, "for your service during this trial. You all conducted yourselves professionally and in accord with our justice system. Without your service, our system of justice would not function. You played a vital role during this trial. You are officially dismissed. Make sure to retrieve all of your belongings from the jury room."

As the jury filtered out, their backs to Franklin, a grin managed to escape his grasp. After a second, he stopped trying to contain it. He flashed it to Wendy who returned it in kind. My, she had a beautiful smile, Franklin thought. He quickly looked away.

Once the jury was gone, the Judge turned to the parties. "The Probation Department is ordered to conduct a pre-sentence interview of the defendant." He leaned over and conferred with his Part Clerk. "Sentencing hearing in one month from today." He stood to leave.

"All rise," the bailiff yelled.

"Great work, Franklin," Wendy said cheerily, shaking his hand after Chucky was escorted from the room. Upton scampered from the room without so much as a glance at Franklin.

He knows who the top dog is in this town... "You too," he said to Wendy. "Couldn't have done it without your help."

Things were on the up.

His mind wondered off. *Senator Franklin Dorey. Attorney General Franklin Dorey.* He still hadn't made up his mind.

Ernie exited the courtroom with his fellow officers. He felt satisfied and proud and relieved. Satisfied that justice was done and proud that he had played a part in it. Relieved that the advice given to him by the Captain and Mr. Dorey had been accurate. It was a good start to his career as a detective.

"Nice job, Ernie," the Captain said, patting Ernie on the back.

Ernie smiled. "Thanks, Cap." He thought for a moment. "What do you think will happen at the sentencing hearing?"

Jim snorted incredulously.

"The murder charge carries a possible maximum sentence of 25 to life," Bill cut in, sounding purely informative. He looked forward without saying another word.

He was like a machine, Ernie thought. Maybe he was on the spectrum.

"You want to know the sentence?" Jim said casually with a laugh directed at Bill. His eyes twinkled. "He's never getting out."

Bill didn't seem to notice, or his mind didn't grasp the sarcasm.

Just then, Robby stormed past them down the hall.

"Hey," Jim called, "where you headed?"

Robby half turned while still walking. "Big race tonight at the track. Gotta get my bets in." He began moving a little faster.

"It's a damn wonder he isn't broke yet," the Cap muttered.

As they exited the courthouse, Ernie was ready to move on to bigger and better things—well, maybe they wouldn't be bigger and better than this case, but he was ready to move on nonetheless.

STEP 6:
The Sentence

"Does the defendant care to make a statement?" Judge Talini asked, looking down at the defense table.

Upton leaned in and whispered into his client's ear.

Don't say a fucking word, Ed thought with a sneer. He wanted to run to the front of the room and strangle the life from Chucky. He supposed a life sentence would have to suffice. But if Chucky pleaded for leniency, Ed didn't know if he'd be able to stop himself from rushing the man.

Upton leaned out.

"No, Your Honor," Chucky said softly.

The Judge's lips pursed.

"Anyone else wish to make a statement on the record?" Judge Talini asked the gallery, his gaze surveying the room before seemingly settling on Ed.

Ed stared at the floor, his mind racing.

"All righ -" the Judge began before cutting himself off.

Ed looked up to find that he was moving down the center aisle. He hadn't realized he'd been moving, so consumed he was with thoughts of Chucky, with anger, with grief. What would he say? Should he turn around? Should he strangle Chucky? The questions swirled in his head. He stopped at the lectern and chewed his lip, standing uneasily, knowing that all gazes in the room were fixed on him.

"Please state your name for the record," the Judge instructed him.

"Ed Roletti," he said with a sneer.

Judge Talini's voice softened. "You may make a statement, Mr. Roletti. During the sentencing phase, I may consider factors that were not in evidence at the trial. Please, sir."

At that invitation, Ed pursed his lips, unsure what to say. His rage seemed to abate and the haze in his mind cleared. He could reveal what type of person Mary was, he could talk about how close they were, he could go on and on about their childhood, about her ambitions, and her temperament. He could talk for hours. Instead, after realizing that he'd been silent for some time, he leaned into the microphone and said, "she was all I had." He paused, wondering if he should say more, his lower lip quivering, his head lowered. "And the way he did it…" That thought he couldn't finish. It was too much, it hurt too badly. He wheeled and moved quickly back to his seat, his head still lowered. He kept it that way while he sat, scared to meet anyone's gaze, unwilling to let his emotions show through.

Ray placed a hand on his back and patted, voicing an unintelligible sound of consolation.

"Anyone else?" the Judge asked, a hint of sympathy in his tone. When no one responded, the Judge turned to the papers before him. After a brief pause, he said, "I have served as a Judge in this County for 18 years, spending 14 of those years in the criminal part. I have seen many crimes, many murders in that time, and have rendered many sentences. In that time, however, I have never seen a crime of this nature. Such brutality, such disregard for life, for basic decency. Such depravity, and callousness. The manner in which this crime was committed is disturbing, to say the least, and it will be in my mind for the rest of my days."

The Judge moved the page before him to the side, then continued. "Further, the life of a promising, young woman was taken. By all accounts, she was working hard to make the best of her life, to make a better life. She did not deserve such an end." Judge Talini shook his head.

Against his will, a single tear broke the confines of Ed's right eye. He let it stream down his cheek, fighting the tickle it caused. He didn't want anyone to see him wipe it.

"Despite all of this," Judge Talini went on, "what is most troubling to me—for the purposes of sentencing, that is—is the defendant's total lack of remorse, and his unwillingness to confess his crime even after being found guilty by a jury of his peers." He eyed Chucky before clearing his throat. "I have reviewed the pre-sentence report from the Probation Department in detail." He turned fully to Chucky. "You refused to confess during your pre-sentence interviews. And even assuming you are holding to a claim of innocence, you refused to exhibit any remorse whatsoever. The phrase used by the Probation officer was 'cold indifference.' I find such an attitude shocking to the conscious and antithetical to basic human decency." The Judge took a sip of water.

Ed sniffled softly, his head still lowered, unable to watch either Chucky or the Judge. This was all finally coming to a head. His emotions were overwhelming.

Judge Talini's voice seemed to lighten. "Of course, the District Attorney asks for the maximum sentence, and the defendant asks for the minimum. In sentencing, I am afforded a wide latitude. The main restriction I have is that the sentence must be within the range set forth by the Legislature in the Penal Code. Beyond, that, as I said, it is in my discretion.

"While I am mindful that the evidence in the case was by and large circumstantial, I nonetheless find it to be overwhelming. Taking all of the factors discussed into account, the defendant Charles Dericardo is sentenced as follows -"

Ed finally looked up, unable to fight it any longer. He cared no more that those in the courtroom could see his display of weakness. He needed to see the words pushed from the Judge's mouth, he needed to feel them, to know, at this very moment, that some justice was done.

"On count one—murder in the first degree—you are sentenced to 25 years to life. On count two—rape in the first degree—you are sentenced to 15 years to life. These two sentences are to run consecutively, amounting to 40 years to life. To that end, you will have no chance of parole. You are further fined $5,000 in accordance with the Penal Law. Any issues, Counselors?"

It is done. Ed's control over his emotions evaporated, and they came rushing to the surface. Without realizing it, he was bawling openly, his shoulders bouncing, his chest convulsing, his nose running. After a moment, he managed to rein it in.

He noticed a slight pressure from Ray's hand on his back.

"None from the People, Your Honor," the DA said.

Upton rose. "Your Honor, for the purposes of the record, the defendant objects to the sentence on the grounds that it is harsh and excessive."

Judge Talini nodded his head impassively. "Anything else?" After a brief pause without a response, he said, "we are adjourned."

"All rise," the bailiff called out.

Once Ed rose, Ray wrapped his arm around Ed's shoulder and squeezed. Drained, and unable to control himself, a torrent of tears fell from Ed's face again. He tucked his head into Ray's shoulder, wondering how he'd kept it bottled up for so long.

STEP 7:
The Appeal

"We got an appeal," Wendy said, barging into Franklin's office, waving an appellate brief in the air.

Franklin turned from his computer screen, his face darkening. Wendy could only be talking about one case. "No," he said disbelievingly. The implications of losing the appeal frightened him. There were really only two things that could happen on appeal that would be bad: a dismissal of the indictment, or a remand for a new trial. The dismissal was the worst of the two, of course, but Franklin still feared a retrial. Upton was the type of lawyer that would alter his tactics based on what happened at the first trial. He would only be better, his presentation more refined. Franklin's heart beat faster.

Wendy stopped behind the chairs opposite Franklin's desk, her face unreadable.

Franklin shook the fear out of his bones. "Well, what does he argue?" he asked, his immediate need evident from his voice.

Wendy smirked. "First of all," she said amusingly, "who is 'he'?"

Of all times to fuck around...really, Wendy?! Exasperated, Franklin threw his palms in the air. But before he let loose a tirade, something occurred to him. *Who is 'he'? she asked.* "Wait, wait, wait, wait. Are you telling me Upton didn't write the brief?"

The corners of her sweet mouth perked. "Uh...yep." Her grin widened. My, she had a beautiful smile, Franklin thought transiently before being pulled back to the game Wendy played. Anticipation and excitement began to build. This was good news. Good news, indeed.

"So Upton dropped him, huh?" he asked rhetorically, displaying a satisfied smile.

Wendy gave an excited nod.

Franklin swiveled in his chair like a child playing. "Public defender's office?"

Wendy chuckled. "Nope."

Franklin snorted. "Legal Aid?"

Wendy chortled this time. "Guess again."

"Don't tell me," he said delightedly at the only conclusion he could draw. "Come on. *Pro se*? Are you teasing me?"

"*Pro - Se*," Wendy said.

Franklin's heart beat faster, but it wasn't due to fear. It was due to the adrenaline flooding his veins from his excitement and relief. Chucky was appealing *pro se*. The idiot wrote his own brief on appeal. It was incredible, almost too good to be true. For all intents and purposes, Franklin had won the appeal before it was even argued. His laugh rose from deep in his gut.

Wendy laughed along.

"All right, all right," he began between snorts, "let me guess...he argues ineffective assistance of counsel?"

"Of course," Wendy confirmed, nodding, her grin holding strong.

Reclining in his chair, Franklin laughed again. "No way. No possible way. Upton put on three witnesses and cross-examined almost every one of my witnesses. No possible way there was ineffective assistance of counsel. Does he argue anything specific?"

"You mean anything specific that is actually coherent? No, he doesn't. The guy doesn't even have a high school diploma."

"Okay, what about a constitutional violation? Sixth amendment or fourth amendment?"

Wendy swiveled her torso back and forth, like a bored child, keeping Franklin in suspense. Her lips were pursed is amusement. It only increased her attractiveness.

Franklin would suffer the wait if it meant he could gaze upon her while he waited.

"Nope," she finally said. "Just ineffective assistance."

"Holy shit," Franklin blurted out, astounded and feeling fortunate for his good luck. *Unbelievable!*

He was confident that the conviction would've stood on appeal even if Upton had drafted the brief and argued the appeal, but the fact that Chucky drafted his own brief without an attorney made Franklin's day. The conviction would absolutely stand, especially where Chucky only argued ineffective assistance of counsel. The issue was straightforward, almost a bright-line rule, and this was certainly not a case where it applied. Besides, at best, it only meant a new trial, not a dismissal of the indictment. Franklin's political career remained in great shape.

"You want to read it?" Wendy asked, tossing the brief onto Franklin's desk.

Franklin realized he'd been gazing off at the wall. He glanced down at the brief, then back up at Wendy. "I almost don't have to." He showed her the whites of his teeth.

Wendy flashed that beautiful smile of hers.

Despite his ambitions, Franklin would miss this job…and that smile.

STEP 8:
The Exculpation

SEVEN YEARS LATER

"9-1-1, what's the emergency?" Shirley answered into her headset, her fingers ready to log the call into the computer.

"I just saw…" a man said in a whisper on the other line before trailing off.

"Hello? Sir?" She waited a second for a response. "Hello?" If she didn't receive a response, the best she could do was hope the man didn't hang up the phone. It took 80 seconds to trace a call from a cellphone.

There was some crackling and rustling on the other end of the line. Then, in a clear voice, the man said, "Hello?"

"Yes, sir. What is the emergency?"

"I just saw a man dragging a small boy into a house."

"You saw a man dragging a boy into a house?"

His breathing was heavy. "Yeah. I was driving by, and I saw an older man dragging a boy into a house. I don't know, maybe it was a kidnapping or something. The boy was squirming."

"Do you know the address of the house, sir?"

"Uh, yeah, uh, let me look." There was a pause. "It's 103 Stein Street."

"You are by the house, sir?" Shirley asked as she entered the address in her system, her voice calm. She always maintained a calm voice. She found that it helped to calm the callers, most of whom had witnessed or experienced a traumatic event, often involving someone they knew.

There was crackling and popping on the other end. "Yeah, yeah. I slowed down because it caught my eye and looked suspicious. Then I stopped outside the house." There was heavy breathing. "He might have seen me."

Just then, the address came back. The house was owned by Paul Timmone. He was registered as a Level III sex offender. *Shit!* A child's life and innocence were on the line. Shirley knew that with crimes against children, like abductions and sexual abuse, the longer it took to respond and locate the child, the greater the likelihood it would be too late. "I'll send a car over right away, sir. Can you give me your nam -"

"He's got a gun," the man yelled on the other end of the line. Tires screeched, then the call was cut off.

Shit! She looked at the tracing program. Not enough time had passed to get a trace. Looks like this tip would come in as anonymous. Still, she had the address. She quickly switched her line to dispatch. "All cars, all units. Possible kidnapping of small child. Repeat. Possible kidnapping of small child at 103 Stein Street. Repeat. That's 1 - 0 - 3 Stein. Suspect is a prior sex offender. Likely armed. Use caution." Shirley ended the dispatch call and went about checking for amber alerts or recent missing person reports in the area. Having two children of her own, these were the most difficult calls to field.

◆ ◆ ◆

The call came over dispatch. Officer Steve Simmons grabbed the CB microphone. "This is car 524. On our way."

"Roger," came the response from dispatch.

Other units responded to dispatch as Steve flipped the sirens on and slammed on the gas pedal. "Looks like we might get some action," he said to the rookie in the passenger seat.

"Finally," Tom answered, his hands moving across his holstered weapon.

Steve smiled. The boy was eager, wasn't he. *Just like I was as a rook.*

He pulled up to the house to find that two squad cars had preceded him. He and Tom popped out of the police cruiser and stood behind the opened doors, hands on weapons just in case bullets started flying from the house. The tip came in that the suspect—a Paul Timmone, who was a registered sex offender—was armed. Steve quickly surveyed the house. It was an old house, likely 80 to 90 years old, but seemed to have been well maintained. The pastel green exterior paint looked like a fresh coat, and the grey siding looked new enough to suggest it had only been installed a few years ago. An old Honda Civic sat in the carport.

Steve glanced around at the other officers, checking to see if anyone was his senior. In situations like this, where a child's innocence or life was possibly on the line, time was of the essence.

Reaching the child before any sexual abuse took place usually meant the difference between a normal childhood from here on out and a lifetime of therapy and psycho-treatment. As he grabbed the bullhorn to instruct the suspect to come out of the house, two other police cars pulled up. One was the S.W.A.T. team, who exited their car in full gear, one officer holding a battering ram. The other car was unmarked. Detective Eng emerged from the driver's seat and glanced around, assessing the scene.

Steve eyed the house, checking the windows for a weapon pointed at him, then crouched down and made his way to Detective Eng, bullhorn in hand.

"Did you give him a shout yet?" Eng asked as Steve pulled up next to him.

"Was just about to, sir."

Eng nodded and held out his hand for the bullhorn. "Ray is on his way, but we need to get this started ASAP."

Steve handed over the horn and turned to the house.

Eng raised the horn to his mouth. "Paul Timmone," he announced. "This is the police. Come out of the house slowly, with your hands above your head." He lowered the horn a bit while they all waited for movement from the front door.

Nothing happened.

Eng raised the horn again. "Paul Timmone, this is your last chance. Exit your house from the front door with your hands above your head."

There was no movement from the house.

After waiting a few more seconds, Eng motioned to the S.W.A.T. team.

The four S.W.A.T. officers moved to the front door in a tight formation, the first officer with his shield raised, two flanking officers with their machine guns trained on the house, and the last officer with the battering ram in his hands and his machine gun strapped on his back.

"We wait half a minute," Eng instructed Steve.

Steve nodded and moved back to the protection of his opened cruiser door. "30 seconds after S.W.A.T.," he yelled to the other officers. "30 seconds after." His heart began to race. He always felt the battle-lust in situations like this—although he'd only been in a few.

When S.W.A.T. reached the front door, the officer with the shield stepped aside. The officer with the battering ram wasted no time. He put his weight behind his swing and targeted the door where a bolt lock was most likely located. The door splintered and burst open with a loud bang. The officers with machine guns raced inside, one going left, one right. The officer with the shield followed with a Glock in his right hand. The last S.W.A.T. member dropped the ram, swung his machine gun off his back, and entered.

Steve counted to 30 in his head. He stood and gave the hand signal to advance. They moved forward cautiously, four officers with handguns pointed before them, up the front steps and into the house. Steve's initial thought was that the furniture was not what he expected. It was old, tattered, and stained. The juxtaposition to the facade of the house was startling. But he gave it only a momentary thought before he moved into the kitchen, his gun moving from the open areas to the concealed ones.

"Clear," a shout came from another room.

"Hands on your head," a yell came from upstairs.

The officers turned in unison and scurried up the stairs. When Steve arrived in the small bedroom, a naked man lay on the ground on his stomach, hands cuffed behind his back. The man was probably in his late 60s, bald on top with long gray hair wrapped around the sides of his head. It gave Steve the impression of Ben Franklin. *If Ben Franklin was a pedophile. A naked pedophile.*

"All clear," another officer shouted from the room down the hallway.

Steve and the other officers holstered their guns. "Let's get a thorough search, boys." He turned to Tom. "Get the Detective in here."

Tom moved down the stairs.

As officers began searching the upstairs rooms, Steve moved downstairs. He went back to the kitchen and began opening cabinet doors. You never know where a pedophile will hide a small child. All clear in the kitchen, he returned to the living room and opened a door to his right to find a closet. He pushed aside a few coats and found nothing. He opened the next door on his right to find dark stairs leading to a basement. He whistled softly to get the S.W.A.T. officer's attention, then motioned down the stairs.

The S.W.A.T. officer nodded in understanding and peered downstairs, the barrel of his machine gun preceding him. Steve checked for a light switch on the wall, but didn't see anything. After a brief pause, the S.W.A.T. officer moved down the steps fluidly, the only sign of his passing the occasional creak of the stairs.

Steve followed, his gun held before him.

Seconds later, Tom was behind him, gun drawn.

The basement was dark and dingy, with junk sitting on exposed shelves and a few boxes strewn about on the floor. In the dark, Steve couldn't make out much of anything.

"I'm clear," the S.W.A.T. officer said.

Steve holstered his weapon and managed to locate an exposed lightbulb hanging from the ceiling. He pulled the chain. The bulb lit up, causing the three officers to squint. They raised their hands to shade the sudden brightness. Once his eyes were adjusted, Steve glanced around again.

Tom moved past him.

It was junk, all right. Steve saw everything from a broken transmission to blankets that looked old enough to be dust. A boiler sat in the corner, a broken rocking chair next to it.

The S.W.A.T. officer began perusing the shelves.

Steve looked for hidden doors or cellars, but found nothing.

Tom flipped open the flaps on the box at his feet. "Porn," he announced, picking up magazines and videotapes.

"Kiddie porn, or just regular porn?" Steve asked as he moved to the second box.

"Regular," Tom responded.

Steve shrugged before unfolding the flaps on the second box to find videotapes mixed in with pictures of naked boys. "Holy shit. Kiddie porn." He looked at Tom. "This guys going away for a long time even if there's no boy in this house."

"What the fuck is this?" the S.W.A.T. officer said, bewilderment apparent in his tone.

Steve and Tom turned to see the S.W.A.T. officer standing next to a shelf, holding up a large, clear jar, twisting it in his hands to examine what was inside.

"What is that?" Tom said, moving closer with squinted eyes.

"Looks like something in like formaldehyde," the S.W.A.T. officer responded.

Steve got a closer look. "Get the detective down here," he said to Tom, his eyes still fixed on the jar.

Tom moved up the stairs as Steve threw on a pair of gloves. The S.W.A.T. officer passed him the jar and returned to examining the items on the shelves. When Steve realized what was in the jar, his breath caught. *This is fucked up.*

A few moments later, Tom returned with Detective Eng behind him. "What do you got?" Eng asked.

"This," Steve said, holding up the jar. He regarded Officer Eng with a shaken look. "Looks like…a breast." He gulped audibly. "A human breast."

"What? Let me see that," Eng said, throwing latex gloves on quickly.

"This guy is a sick fuck." Steve handed the jar over.

The S.W.A.T. officer was rummaging in the back.

Eng examined it closely for a few moments. Then, his eyes widened and his skin paled. "Holy fucking shit," he said under his breath. "Is Ray up there yet?" he asked Tom behind him.

"I'll check, sir," Tom responded.

"Get him down here immediately if he is," Eng said over his shoulder, his voice shaky, his skin pallid.

Tom moved up the stairs again.

"What is it, Detective?" Steve asked Eng.

Eng's gaze finally detached from the jar and he looked at Steve with troubled eyes. "I hope it's not what I think it is," he said with fear in his voice.

Moments later, Sergeant Lucen made his way down the creaky steps. "Did you find a kid down here?"

Eng's response was simply to hand the jar over to the Sergeant.

Ray took it and turned it in his hands. The expression on his face changed rapidly before the look of something dawning on him overcame him. "No," he breathed. He looked at Eng. "It can't be," he whispered.

Eng raised his hands forlornly and shook his head, disbelief written on his face.

What is this about? Clearly, they new something he didn't.

The Sergeant's eyes closed for a moment. When they opened, he said, "Steve, you're in charge here." He rushed up the stairs, jar in hand, Detective Eng a step behind.

Steve, Tom, and the S.W.A.T. officer exchanged a few questioning looks. Finally, Steve shrugged. He would find out eventually what the jar was about. "All right, let's get this kiddie porn marked and vouchered."

◆ ◆ ◆

"What's the verdict?" Ray asked Robby, hoping that the results were negative.

"You won't fucking believe it," Robby answered, looking up at Ray from his forensics' desk. "The DNA matches. It's hers. It's fucking *hers*. And this guy's fingerprints all over the jar."

Ray plopped down in the chair next to Robby and lowered his head into his hands. "I can't believe it," he said through the muffle of his hands.

"It's been what, seven years?" Robby asked incredulously.

Ray looked up, then nodded uneasily. *We convicted the wrong man!* It was the worst possible result. A man went to jail for seven years for a crime he didn't commit, and the killer walked free. It was the ultimate miscarriage of justice…and a colossal fuck up for the police department. "Did you tell the Chief?"

"Nope. Results just came back. You're the first to know."

Not knowing what else to do, Ray shook his head. He really couldn't believe it. Paul Timmone, convicted sex offender and pedophile, killed Ed's sister, and Chucky Dericardo went away for seven years for it on a life-without-parole sentence. He had to speak to the Chief. "I'll let him know," he said to Robby.

"Better you than me," Robby muttered before handing Ray the lab report. "I had $50 that it wasn't going to match. You can't win them all…"

Ray walked to Jim's office and knocked on the doorframe. Jim waved him in while grumbling.

"That it?" Jim asked, motioning to the lab report in Ray's hands.

Ray nodded. "It's her," he said grimly.

Jim scratched his forehead vexingly. "Shit. It's times like this that I wish Byron was still Chief. But no, of course I'm the one that has to deal with this shit. Then again, I guess it was my mess from the start, right?"

Ray chose not to answer the question asked in obvious self-pity. "So what's next?"

"I guess I got to speak to the DA about it. Shit. Once the press gets word of this…it's going national, for sure."

Wondering about Jim's intentions, Ray reasserted his position. "The guy doing the time is innocent, Boss. We got to do something."

Jim glared at him. "You think I was going to cover this up?" he asked cynically. "Whatever type of cop you take me for, I'm not the type to let a man rot in prison for a crime he didn't commit. Even when I'm the one that put him there. I'm man enough to admit my mistakes and do something to right them."

Ray tried to cover up his precipitous accusation. "I didn't mean it like that, Jim. I'm just saying…"

Jim pursed his lips. "I know what your saying, Ray. Always have, always will. Now get the fuck out of my office before you really start offending me."

"All right," Ray said resignedly. He rose and left.

Ed caught him in the hallway, halfway from the Chief's office to his own.

Shit.

"Is it true?" Ed asked heatedly. "Are the results positive?"

Ray hesitated before nodding.

"It's fucking bullshit," Ed said angrily, his eyes glazed.

"Ed," Ray said soothingly as he placing his hand on Ed's shoulder. "Listen, buddy. The lab report is conclusive. It's your sister's. I'm sorry." He licked his lips. "We sent the wrong man to jail."

Ed's eyes blazed.

Maybe I shouldn't have said that last bit. He began walking again, hoping Ed wouldn't follow.

Ed moved up next to him, his words frantic. "Ray, it doesn't make any sense. I mean, this guy is a convicted pedophile. He likes little boys, not women. It doesn't make any fucking sense."

Ray stopped and looked around, making sure no one was watching the exchange. In his opinion, this type of shit never made any sense. People committed crimes everyday without it making any sense, but he wasn't about to say that to Ed. "We found a whole box of porn in his basement. *Real* porn. The guy's fingerprints all over the stuff. What do you want me to say? I mean, maybe this guy liked women *and* little boys. It probably wouldn't be the first time." He continued walking.

This time, Ed didn't follow. "It ain't right, Ray," Ed called after him, his voice raised.

Officers in the hall turned their heads.

"Something ain't right," Ed yelled.

Ray chose not to acknowledge the comment. In truth, he didn't even know what to say. Maybe he'd become more pessimistic in his time as a cop, having seen what he'd seen, but this shit never made any sense, so there was no explaining it.

"Attorney General's office," Lorraine answered in the antechamber, the sound entering his office through the open door. "One moment please." She turned her head, addressing him. "Wendy Carter, sir, on line one for you."

District Attorney Carter...It's been a long time, Wendy. Too long. The thought of that woman's smile, her glossy lips, her bright white teeth, brought a smile to Franklin's face. "Thanks, Lorraine." He grabbed the phone. "Wendy," he said cheerily. "I'm good, thanks. So what do I owe the pleasure of this call to? It's not because you want to have dinner with me, is it?" He hoped it was, actually.

As he listened, his stomach became queasy. Exculpatory evidence was discovered exonerating Chucky Dericardo of the murder of Mary Roletti. This wasn't good. Not good at all. He had no response when Wendy stopped talking. Stammering, he managed to ask, "So...so what are you going to do?"

Wendy's response was as expected, but it still shocked Franklin to the core. "Please keep me apprised." Perspiring, his stomach in knots, he hung up the phone, unable to even exchange ending pleasantries. How would this affect his career? Would the blame be placed on him, or on the police department? These types of questions rolled around in his head. He foresaw the worst, of course—a ruining of his reputation and the end of his career. Would he have to resign? No, most likely not, but getting elected to any post after his term was up in one year would be downright impossible. He was screwed. He sat staring out the window, focusing on nothing, his eyes bleary.

As he worked through the possibilities, a disturbing thought occurred to him. "Fucking A," he muttered. If Chucky was exonerated and sued the State for damages, as Attorney General,

Franklin would have to defend the case. He raised his fingers to his lips, deep in thought now. Perhaps he was conflicted out since he represented the government at the criminal trial. Maybe he would have to recuse himself. In that case, one of his deputy attorneys general would have to defend the case. But could Franklin not be involved? He didn't think so. Yes, he was royally fucked.

Unless...he convinced Wendy to disregard the new evidence, to lock it up or destroy it and forget about it. Could he consciously do that knowing that Chucky Dericardo was innocent? Would Wendy even do that? It could get him in deep water if he even broached the issue with Wendy. Who knew how she had changed since becoming DA? Hell, she probably wouldn't have gone along even when she was just an ADA. And what about the police? Franklin didn't know who among the police department knew about the evidence. Likely everyone, he thought sourly.

He stood up to shut his door. "No more calls today, Lorraine." What would he do? What could he do?! He pondered for the rest of the afternoon and late into the night.

STEP 9:
The Vacatur

Ed sat down in the back row, his memories from seven years ago resurfacing. His anger seethed anew at the unfairness, the unjustness. If they let Chucky go, he didn't know what he'd do. Yes, he conceded, the lab report said what it said, but if Chucky wasn't the killer, the guy had a hand in it somehow. Ed knew it in his bones.

As Judge Robbins entered, those in the courtroom began to rise. "Don't get up," the Judge said as she took the bench, waving everyone to sit. She had white curly hair shaped like a fluffy helmet, a narrow nose, droopy eyes, and thick glasses. Her face was dolled up to the nines, something out of a previous era. She'd been a Legal Aid attorney for 35 years before attaining the bench, so she definitely leaned toward the defense, or at least Ed thought so. That didn't suit him at all.

The Part Clerk called the first case, a defendant in orange was shuffled into the courtroom, and the attorneys argued about whether the gun taken from the defendant was the fruit of an illegal search and seizure.

Ed was only half listening. He surveyed the room until he located the guy he wanted. Sitting near the front, his head poking above the rest of the crowd, was John Upton. Ed leered. Upton had dropped Chucky like a bad habit after the verdict, taking no part in the appeal. But now he was back. The fucker probably smelled money all over this, Ed thought. *Fucking defense attorneys!*

Jim plopped down next to him, the old bench protesting. "Did they call it yet?"

Ed shook his head.

Jim settled his big butt on the bench and rested his hands on his protruding belly.

The Judge reserved her decision on the search and seizure motion and the guards shuffled the defendant out. The attorneys from both sides moved down the aisle together, chitchatting and smiling with each other. *Fucking attorneys, all buddy, buddy!* The whole system was fucked. *I wouldn't be in this situation if it wasn't.*

"Dericardo versus the People," the Part Clerk announced.

"Ha, right on time," Jim said, giving Ed a nudge.

Ed's mouth twitched in annoyance. He pointedly ignored Jim.

The side door at the front of the courtroom opened and a guard escorted Chucky in. His sister's murderer looked largely the same, Ed thought. He hadn't seemed to age much, and those buck teeth still made him look goofy. The only difference was that the mullet was gone, replaced with a head shaved clean to the skin. Ed wondered if Chucky had joined a prison gang, like the Aryan brotherhood or something. He was probably someone's bitch. Probably had been getting fucked in the ass on a regular basis for the past seven years. The thought made Ed smile mischievously, although it was as much a sneer as it was a smile.

Upton stood and moved to the defense table where he promptly began whispering in Chucky's ear. The District Attorney moved to the other table.

Judge Robbins grabbed a folder on her bench and removed the papers within. "I have a motion by the Defendant, Charles Dericardo, to vacate his judgment of conviction pursuant to Criminal Procedure Law sections 440.10 and 440.30. Is that correct?" She looked to Mr. Upton.

"That's correct, Your Honor."

Ed knew Upton had that damn smile on his face. He wanted to bitch-slap it right off.

"And it's my understanding that the People do not oppose the application," the Judge said, making it a question.

"Yes, Your Honor," Wendy said. "Based on the newly discovered evidence implicating Paul Timmone in the murder and rape of Mary Roletti, the People are not opposing Mr. Dericardo's motion."

Ed's face pinched, his blood boiling. *I'll kill them all!* He began muttering curses.

Jim nudged him again.

Ed yanked his arm away, leering at his superior. He could do what the fuck he wanted to, especially when it came to his sister's murder.

Jim tsked, but turned back to the Judge.

Ed's leer held for a moment longer before he too gave his attention to the Judge.

"I have read the papers," Judge Robbins began, "and reviewed the lab report regarding the newly discovered evidence. Based on that and the People's acquiescence, I find that the new evidence is of such a character as to create the probability that had such evidence been received at the trial, the verdict would have been more favorable to the defendant, thereby satisfying C.P.L. section 440.10(1)(g). Further, the People concede that the essential facts of the motion are true, i.e., that the container located at the house of Paul Timmone contained the tissue of the victim Mary Roletti, that it was consistent with the crime scene and the manner in which the crime was committed, and that Mr. Timmone's fingerprints were located on the container.

"Accordingly, pursuant to C.P.L. section 440.30(3)(c), Defendant's motion to vacate the judgment of conviction is hereby granted, and the accusatory instrument is dismissed. Mr. Dericardo is to be released from prison forthwith."

Upton patted Chucky on the back, his grin wide. Chucky smiled, his buck teeth exposed.

Ed grinded his teeth and slammed his fist into his thigh. He couldn't believe they were going to release Chucky just like that. Something had to be done.

"Justice was done, Ed," Jim said, regarding him. "We got the right guy this time. Paul Timmone won't ever see the outside of a cell."

Ed snorted disdainfully. "This is bullshit," he muttered. He shot to his feet and stormed out of the courtroom. He certainly didn't think they had the right guy. Now he needed to decide what to do about it.

STEP 10:
The Civil Trial

Step 10.1

"Send him in," Franklin said into the speakerphone on his desk. He turned to the computer and tried to look busy, as if he had little time for this meeting and thought it to be of no moment. In his time as the Attorney General, he had become adept at negotiations. It was a skill set he had used often as a DA, but only in the context of plea bargains. He had never before negotiated for sums of money, which he now did on behalf of the State in circumstances where the State was both paying out and collecting. Monetary negotiations were an entirely different beast, requiring an entirely different approach.

Franklin thought that gave him the upper hand, since as far as he knew, Upton had only practiced criminal defense. Maybe John had worked on a few personal injury cases, but Franklin didn't think so. It was no shocker, though, that Upton would get involved in this civil suit—a contingency fee was at stake on a damages award that could likely reach seven figures.

The tall man entered wearing a three-button, gray, pinstriped suit with a solid maroon tie. *Power tie.* Franklin stifled a laugh. The passage of seven years did not seem to have aged the defense attorney at all. His hair had not grayed—assuming it was not dyed—and his face remained free of lines. "John," Franklin acknowledged. Franklin's own hair had grayed substantially and his face had begun to sag. *Such things come with power.*

"Franklin," Upton responded, "or should I call you The Honorable?" He smiled. "You want this open?" he asked, motioning to the door before Franklin could throw out a retort.

It was true the position of Attorney General garnered the title "The Honorable," just as a Judge did, but no one had ever called him that except at speaking engagements or award ceremonies. Franklin gave him a reticent smile and a wave. "Open is fine. Have a seat."

Upton moved to the chair, placed his briefcase down, unbuttoned his jacket, and sat.

"You mind if I finish up this thought?" Franklin asked, pointing to his computer. He really had nothing to finish, but perception went a long way in negotiations. If Upton believed Franklin didn't really care, that he had other more important matters, it would alter the manner in which Upton negotiated. It may even reduce the damages demand. An adversary that didn't care couldn't be pressured or bullied, and would defend a case at trial, rather than settle early, just for the principle of it. Most attorneys wanted to avoid a protracted and expensive trial, especially plaintiffs' attorneys, who only got paid if their client got paid. Trial expenses came off the top, after all, which reduced a plaintiff's attorney's contingency fee. As a result, knowing that the opposition didn't care, that he would fight tooth and nail to the end, changed an attorney's mentality and approach to settlement, often compelling him to lower his demand in an effort to avoid a vigorous and costly fight. Whether Franklin's tactic worked with Upton, he didn't know. It had worked in the past, so he stuck with it. He typed a few random sentences on a blank page, then grabbed the mouse and made a few clicks. "There," he said, feigning completion. He swiveled his chair.

Looking composed and relaxed, Upton crossed his legs and readjusted his jacket. "So you received the complaint?"

Franklin nodded.

"So you are not going to recuse yourself?" The tall man threw out the same smile he had given to the jury seven years ago—smug, breezy, and warm at the same time.

Franklin acted as if the question didn't rankle him. He reclined and clasped his hands behind his head. "I don't think it's necessary under these circumstances. The statute is clear as to what needs to be proven against the State. It doesn't involve my conduct or the DA Office's conduct during the trial."

John raised his eyebrows and his smile loosening. His tongue did not waggle, however.

"I prosecuted hundreds of people in my time as the DA," Franklin continued, trying not to justify himself but unable to keep silent in the face of Upton's silence. "Dericardo is just one in the crowd."

"Okay," Upton said with a head twitch. He bent his long frame down, reached into his bag, and pulled out a notepad. He flipped a page. "I want to give you my pre-trial bottom line number. Now mind you, this is my settlement number, not a number to negotiate off of, so if you come back with something less than this—well, don't. If we don't settle before the trial starts, my bottom line number is going way up."

"Shoot," Franklin said, confident the number would be outrageous. Probably something like five or six million.

"Ten million," John said matter-of-factly, his face unreadable.

Franklin laughed derisively. "Come on, John. Why don't you get serious?"

Upton smiled. "That's my bottom line. If we don't settle prior to the commencement of trial, it goes up."

Franklin leaned forward and rested his arms on his desk. "At that number, I don't think we are going to get anywhere. I mean, he served seven years, right? Even if I gave you half a mil for each year—which I think is on the high end of the spectrum—that would only be 3.5 mil. So how do you justify a number three times that amount."

"Well," Upton said, sounding like Franklin had turned the tables, "time served is not the only factor. You got the stigma of a conviction of a brutal crime with national recognition. You got humiliation, discomfort, lack of privacy…I mean, he was in maximum security. The guy is 5'8" and 140 pounds. What do you think happened to him in general population for seven years?"

Franklin waved the list away. "You should look at the caselaw, you got guys in jail for a decade or more who don't get what you're asking for?" He looked Upton dead in the eyes. "At this point, unless you come way down, we can't even start negotiating. If your bottom line is ten mil, I can't counter. I wouldn't even meet you in the middle if I was starting at zero. We'll have to let the Court of Claims decide unless you want to adjust your approach."

Upton promptly placed his notepad back in his bag and stood. "Well," he said, sounding cheery, "it was good seeing you again, Franklin." He extended his hand.

Franklin rose and shook it. "You too, John." He winked, deciding it was better than throwing up the finger accompanied by a 'get the fuck out of here, cocksucker.'

John turned and moved to leave.

"Let me know when you want to make a reasonable demand," Franklin said to John's back.

Upton stopped in the doorway and turned his head. "By the way, just a forewarning. We're going to move for summary judgment on the issue of liability after Mr. Dericardo's deposition. Like you said, the statute is clear that he meets the criteria for compensation. That only leaves a hearing on damages. So if we're not getting anywhere at this juncture, let me just give you my demand for trial." He paused, looking Franklin straight in the eyes. "It's 25 million."

Franklin threw his hands up, now beyond disbelief. "All right."

Upton gave a head bob before walking away, his lanky frame moving smoothly down the hall.

Franklin returned to his seat and contemplated the caselaw he had read regarding damages awarded under Section 8-b of the Court of Claims Act. Awards of three or four million were not common, but neither were they atypical. The only concern he had was that, at least in New York, awards of this nature were rare. Stories of exonerations in some of the southern states were prevalent in the news these days. The volume of wrongly convicted persons was so large in some states as to warrant legislation capping the amount of damages or even setting a basic scale for the damages awarded in post-exoneration civil suits against the state or municipality. That hadn't happened in New York, and based on the small number of exonerations each year, Franklin didn't think it would. That meant the damages award would turn on what was considered reasonable compensation under traditional tort principles.

He turned his thoughts back to Chucky. What was different about this case that Upton's demand was so high? Was it just Upton trying to push Franklin around, or did it have some real predicate? Maybe it was just Upton's inexperience in civil matters. Maybe the guy was just throwing it against the wall, rolling the dice. *Ten million is a nice clean, round number.* Franklin shrugged. In any case, with the number as high as it was, Franklin supposed he'd have to wait until trial to find out if such a demand was even remotely warranted. Perhaps if he waited, Upton would come down on the number.

He was, however, sure about one thing: he—on behalf of the State, that is—wouldn't pay Chucky Dericardo anything near ten million.

◆ ◆ ◆

He pulled his car over to the side of the road behind a large bush near the entrance to the neighborhood, cut the engine off, and slumped down in his seat, waiting. He'd wait all night if he had to, and the next night too. It was dark on the road and in the surrounding woods, but a streetlamp near the neighborhood's entrance provided ample light to identify the vehicle he was watching for. An hour passed while he brooded, his thinking tunneled down one path until the grumbles of his stomach interrupted. He grabbed the peanut butter and jelly sandwich next to the gearshift, unwrapped the plastic wrap, and took a bite.

Another hour or so passed with no one entering or exiting the neighborhood. Then, a car approached the main road from the neighborhood. Ed Roletti leaned forward, opening his eyes wide. It was a small two-door car, probably a Mercury Cougar or Ford Contour or some other model no longer made. *Not it.* Ed sat back.

Maybe the guy wasn't going out tonight, Ed thought impatiently, but he deemed that unlikely seeing as this was Chucky's first Friday night of freedom. He figured Chucky would be celebrating. He began brooding again, thinking of the injustice. If Chucky didn't kill his sister, then who did? Not that guy Timmone, who liked little boys. *No, it was definitely Chucky.*

Another hour passed with a few cars passing on the main road, but no one exited the neighborhood. His eyelids were starting to get heavy. He grabbed the cup of cold coffee in the armrest holder and took a sip, wincing at the cold bitterness.

Just then, headlights emerged from the neighborhood.

Quickly lowering his coffee, Ed perked. The vehicle was a truck, most likely a Ford F150. From what Ed could make out, it seemed like an older model, dark paint with silver trim. He squinted, trying to make out the driver or the license plate. The truck pulled out toward him, headlights swinging in his direction.

Ed thought his car was sufficiently hidden behind the shrubs, but he instinctively ducked.

The truck passed.

Ed shot up and turned his head, looking out his back window as the truck moved away. He spied the license plate and read it out loud, repeating it so he didn't forget. "FRH 7251, FRH 7251." He snatched the small notepad sitting on the passenger's seat and held it up to his face. It read, *FRH 7251.* A match. He smiled mischievously.

He dropped the notepad and reached to his backseat, grabbing a pair of black leather gloves. He yanked them on and raised the hood on his black sweatshirt, pulling the cords to cinch the hood around his skull. He would be hot in the outfit on this musty summer night, but stealth was paramount.

He waited, eyeballing the road in both directions. He slipped out of his car and crouched down next to a large bush. He shut the car door as quietly as possible and inched around the bush, staying low. Pausing to glance at the road, looking for the soft brightening of oncoming headlights, he set his feet into a runner's starting position. One more glance left and right before he was off, sprinting across the road, veering to the left for the shadowed safety of the forest's edge. He entered the trees huffing and turned, checking his trail. All clear.

He followed the treeline, furtively making his way to Chucky's backyard. He stepped up to the backdoor and slowly pulled the screen door open. It screeched slightly, causing Ed to freeze. Finding no movement in the surrounding houses, he continued. After a few minutes of fumbling with his metal picks, he managed to unlock the door. Where he'd learned to do that, he couldn't recall. It was certainly not the thing a cop's son was supposed to know. *Nor a cop.*

Glancing around one last time, he entered the house. If he found something connecting Chucky to the crime—no, he corrected, *when* he found something connecting Chucky to the crime—he would do something about it.

Step 10.2

"All rise," the bailiff trumpeted, "the Honorable Robert Wayne presiding. The Court of Claims is now in session." Judge Wayne sat, his back hunched in old age, his stringy white hair combed forward to tickle his eyebrows and engulf his ears, his solid, thick beard cropped short as if he had painted half his face bleach white. His eyes were slightly uneven on his thin face, one higher than the other—a borderline deformity. Franklin often wondered if the Judge had suffered a head injury as a child and had his skull reconstructed. It would have accounted for those crooked eyes that were now peering around the courtroom.

In the past two years, Franklin had become very familiar with Judge Wayne, as most of Franklin's business was litigated in the Court of Claims—the only court in New York where a claimant could sue the State. Since Franklin defended the State, he was comfortable before Judge Wayne and knew the man's propensities. The Judge loved to entertain arguments and to ponder legal theories. Perhaps he simply liked the company. It made for long appearances in court when a legal issue piqued his interest.

Chucky's case was called and Franklin and Upton stepped up to their respective tables. Upton began removing papers from his bag. As this was a preliminary conference, Franklin thought that was unusual. Something was going on, he thought suspiciously, a little worried.

The Judge looked down at the papers before him, then up at the attorneys. "This is the first pre-trial conference in this case, correct?" he asked in his deep, raspy baritone.

"That's correct, Your Honor," Upton responded.

Franklin simply nodded.

The Judge turned to Franklin. "The State has answered the pleadings?"

"Yes we have, Judge."

"And discovery is proceeding?"

"Yes," Upton answered. "We have just received Mr. Dericardo's prison records."

The Judge looked down and began notating. When he stopped, he said, "Let's set a report-back date for four weeks. Any issues that need the Court's resolution at this juncture."

"Not from the State, Your Honor."

"Just one, Your Honor," Upton said.

Franklin's brow furrowed, his mind trying to anticipate what was to come.

"We have just filed a motion to disqualify Mr. Dorey. I have a courtesy copy for Your Honor if you would like it right now?" He held up the motion papers.

Franklin shook his head in disgust, his eyes rolling.

"No, Counselor," Judge Wayne responded, waving the copy away. "I'll wait for the filed copy."

"We haven't been served with those papers," Franklin commented testily, directing it at both the Judge and at Upton, grasping for something in his favor.

"They were hand-delivered to your office this morning. You can have this copy if you wish."

Franklin frowned but took the motion papers.

"Quickly tell me the basis," Judge Wayne said, grabbing his pen.

Here we go, Franklin thought, agitated. The Judge's interest was piqued, so they would likely have arguments and the motion would be effectively decided before Franklin could even get a chance to read Upton's papers, devise the best legal argument, and submit opposition papers. He flipped through the papers frantically, trying to get the overall gist.

"Well, Your Honor," Upton began with a smile, his right hand slipping into his pants pocket, his left hand drawing tiny circles in the air. It reminded Franklin of the trial seven years ago. "As you are aware, Mr. Dericardo was wrongly convicted of a heinous murder and rape seven years ago in Schenectady County. At that time, Mr. Dorey was the Schenectady County District Attorney, and he actually personally prosecuted the case on behalf of the State. Now, today, in his capacity as Attorney General, he is defending this action on behalf of the State. But he was the one who wrongly prosecuted Mr. Dericardo in the first place. So in this case Mr. Dorey is trying to defend his own errors and misconduct. I submit that this is a clear case of personal bias that will severely prejudice Mr. Dericardo."

The Judge's eyebrows rose while Upton spoke, his eyes shifting to Franklin every few seconds. Franklin could see the Judge's mind pontificating.

"Any response, Mr. Dorey?" Judge Wayne asked.

"Well, Your Honor, I've only just glanced at the motion papers, but the evidence exonerating Mr. Dericardo was not discovered until recently. As the prosecutor, I was simply performing my job and proceeding with the evidence I had at hand." He clasped his hands behind his back, now getting into a rhythm. "Furthermore, whether I was the prosecutor is really irrelevant. Mr. Dericardo must satisfy the statute to demonstrate liability, and that has nothing to do with the conduct of the prosecutor at trial. I can and have completely separated my roles as former DA and current AG with respect to this case."

Upton threw that self-righteous grin on his face. "Even the possibility that Mr. Dorey will feel the need to defend his actions as the DA in the underlying criminal case is sufficient for disqualification. The potential bias will not only affect settlement negotiations, but will certainly bleed into the trial."

"That's ridiculous!" Franklin wanted to yell, but he didn't. Instead, he raised his voice and said, "the jury found what they found. This trial has nothing to do with the underlying criminal case agains -"

"That's enough back and forth, Counselors," the Judge interrupted with a curt hand motion. "Mr. Dorey, let me ask you this: why can't you simply turn this over to one of your deputy attorneys general? Must you be involved?"

Franklin suppressed a frown. "Well, Your Honor, it's not that I *must* be involved, it's that I am the most qualified in my office. Furthermore, the amount of money being demanded is substantial, and if the State is going to be subject to such a demand, I believe I, as the Attorney General, should be the one to handle it. This is precisely the job I was elected to do by the People of the State."

The Judge nodded, seeming to buy that argument.

"Judge," Upton followed, "I just don't understand how he can be unbiased. He clearly has a bias to make sure his name and reputation are not tarnished by Mr. Dericardo's wrongful conviction, and being directly involved in this action is one way to utilize that bias. It is highly prejudicial. Even the *potential* for bias is sufficient for disqualification under New York law."

The Judge looked down at Franklin. "The caselaw does establish, Mr. Dorey, that the potential bias or potential prejudice that may result is sufficient for disqualification. There need not be a showing of actual prejudice."

This was not going well, Franklin thought. *Best defer and give myself a chance to think about this.* "Judge, I was just handed the motion for the first time and haven't had a chance to properly review it. If you would provide me the time to brief the issue and submit responsive papers, I believe I could assuage any issues."

The Judge bought it. "Your papers must be served by the 17th, Mr. Dorey."

Franklin nodded. "Okay. And I'm operating under the assumption that Mr. Upton properly effectuated service of papers on my office today." He turned to regard the defense attorney.

Upton smiled. "I did."

The Judge cracked an unusual smile. "I'm sure you'll let me know if the motion was not properly served, Mr. Dorey."

With that, the appearance ended.

Having nothing to pack up, Franklin preceded Upton out of the courtroom, the motion tucked under his arm. He had the urge to drop it in the garbage.

"Franklin," Upton called from behind him.

Franklin turned, bristling. He should have known Upton would try to blindside him. The settlement negotiations should have tipped him off. *Damn!* He chastised himself for being preoccupied with the implications to his career. He stopped as Upton approached, putting a calm, relaxed look on his face to show Upton that he wasn't fazed.

The tall man had the nerve to lean over Franklin when he spoke. "Let me know if you have any change in posture as to settlement."

Uncharacteristically, Franklin tittered, then stormed away.

Same trailer park, same trailer, Captain Bill Watkins thought, stopping his car about 100 yards from Jenny Johansson's trailer, and settling in. He examined the mobile home, finding most of it precisely how he remembered. He did notice one anomaly. *Strange.* The paint on the left side of the trailer was faded more than the paint on the right side. He looked up at the sun, surmising that it was the only possible explanation for the discrepancy. Then he looked back at the trailer, judging its position compared to the sun. He attempted to calculate the trajectory of the sun as it related to Jenny's trailer, but it was difficult to do without an extended observation. *Insufficient information to reach a conclusion. Yet I may be here long enough to do so.* He reclined, turning his attention back to his stakeout.

He was not exactly sure why he was here. He thought he had put this suspect behind him, ruled her out seven years ago. He thought he had been meticulous in his investigation of Jenny. He had suspected her involvement from the time he first interviewed her, but his investigation had been fruitless. Why was he here? The answer was simple, really. Some switch in his brain flicked on once Dericardo was exonerated, and it compelled him to continue the investigation. He had to be thorough.

Bill was now the head of the Homicide Department, so in a way he was taking proper action. It was just so strange to be personally conducting an investigation again instead of letting one of his detectives work up the case. This case was not personal to him, but it had been investigated and closed on his watch. He could not stand for that when the tick in his brain told him to see it through. Truthfully, he admitted, with the evidence against Timmone, and the passage of time, it was unlikely he would discover anything implicating Jenny. Still, the tick in his brain told him to see it through. So he got in his car and did as his mind told him. Had he not, it would have constantly nagged him until he reached the point where he started hitting himself in the face uncontrollably, like he used to do as a child when he was prevented from completing a task. He had come a long way since that time, but the extreme urge sometimes returned.

So here he sat, seven years later, casing the same trailer, following the same person he had previously suspected. One way or the other, he would discover if Jenny had been involved. The tick in his mind left him no other option.

◆ ◆ ◆

Judge Wayne quickly took the bench. "For the record, I have read the affirmation of John Upton dated September 11, the answering affirmation of Franklin Dorey dated September 16, and the reply affirmation of John Upton dated September 18." A coughing fit took the Judge.

This wasn't good, Franklin thought. The Judge sounded like he was putting his ruling on the record, which meant he wouldn't hear further oral argument. Franklin wanted the opportunity to explain a few of his arguments, and he anticipated being able to do so.

"Excuse me," Judge Wayne commented once he got control of himself. He cleared his throat and continued. "Based on the papers before me, I am granting the motion. There is a potential for bias, whether Mr. Dorey believes there is or not. He may even act unconsciously, unknowingly, in a fashion that would more serve the interests of defending his own actions during the criminal prosecution rather than defending the state's interest. Thus, I find that the potential for bias exists to Mr. Dericardo, and even to the State."

Adrenaline flooded Franklin's body, his heart beating faster. He wanted to let out his anger. He wanted to scream and rant. Instead, he simply said, "note my exception." He thought Judge Wayne took note of his tone, but at the moment he didn't care.

"Your Honor," Upton began, a puffed-up smile on his fucking face. "I just want to confirm that Mr. Dorey will be screened on this matter, that he will not be operating behind the scenes."

Franklin almost exploded, his face crimson red, his muscles tense. He dropped his head and twisted his body to refrain from responding.

The Judge shook his head sternly. "I don't know what you're asking for. I think it is self-evident that Mr. Dorey will have no involvement from hereon out. I am not issuing a conditional order to that effect. I have granted your motion for disqualification, and Mr. Dorey will abide by it. There's no reason to even suggest that he won't."

Upton nodded.

The rebuke at least permitted Franklin to calm down—somewhat.

"Has the claimant's deposition been scheduled yet?" Judge Wayne asked.

"Yes, Judge, it's actually in three weeks from today."

Judge Wayne nodded and turned to Franklin, showing no sign that he was aware of Franklin's current state. "I trust, Mr. Dorey, that you will not have any issues assigning this case to a deputy of yours and getting him or her up to speed prior to the deposition."

Franklin grinded his teeth before responding. "We'll do our best, Judge." He tried to keep the derision from his voice. He took a deep breath and reminded himself that this was just one case of many, that he didn't want to do anything to provoke Judge Wayne or get on the man's bad side, as such action would affect his future cases. Upton, on the other hand, would likely never practice in the Court of Claims again. So he had no such restrictions.

Yet this case felt different to Franklin. It felt closer, more personal. *Maybe Upton was right*, he thought grudgingly. Perhaps he was biased. He sighed inwardly. At this point, it was irrelevant. He wasn't going to be handling the case. The only question was: who in his office should he turn it over to? He thought long and hard as he left the courtroom.

STEP 11:
The Deposition

Finally, my big break, Ron Slatern thought as he pressed the button for the third floor in the elevator. As the doors closed and the elevator shuddered into action, he took a deep breath. In his six years with the Attorney General's office, he had defended a number of slip and fall cases, prosecuted a handful of public nuisance cases, and worked on one wrongful conviction. The wrongful conviction involved a man who had been convicted of rape in 1991. The guy served a long time in jail before DNA evidence exonerated him. But Ron had been second-chair on that case behind one of the more seasoned attorneys at the AG's office. That attorney had since retired. He supposed that was why Mr. Dorey assigned him to this case. Although it wasn't much, he had more experience with defending wrongful conviction cases than any other current attorney at the AG's office. He recalled the prior case settling for something like two mil. He didn't see this case as warranting anything more. But he'd wait to see what the claimant said during the deposition.

Ron stepped out of the elevator and was met by a wall of glass. To his right sat the reception desk. Beyond the wall of glass was a small hallway and beyond that a medium-sized conference room. Ron recognized the woman sitting in the conference room as the stenographer. He had seen her before in other depositions.

"Can I help you?" the receptionist asked.

"Hi," he said, toggling his glasses, "I'm here for the deposition. The deposition of Charles Dericardo."

She smiled at him. "It's in the conference room. You can head on back."

In response, he nodded. Upon entering the conference room, he greeted the court reporter, sat, and removed his notes, perusing them silently.

A few minutes later, two men entered. Ron stood. He'd never met John Upton, but he'd heard stories. He knew right away that the tall man in the chocolate brown suit was Upton. The other guy, who unquestionably was Charles Dericardo, looked to be white trash. *My job just got a whole lot easier.*

"Hi. John Upton," the tall man offered with a bright smile, his lanky arm extended.

Ron shook his hand. "Ron Slatern."

"This is my client, Charles Dericardo."

"Hello, Mr. Dericardo," Ron said, extending his hand.

"Hi," the deponent said with an awkward nod and a weak, noncommittal handshake. That was another strike against Dericardo. A weak handshake showed a lack of self-confidence.

"So you're the replacement?" Upton asked.

Ron couldn't tell if it was simply small talk or sarcasm. Seeing as how he just met Mr. Upton, and that the tall man's smile looked genuine, he chose to believe that the question was just small talk.

"That I am," Ron responded, smiling wide.

Upton's eyebrows rose listlessly. "Let's get started," he said, gesturing for everyone to take a seat.

Feeling confident, Ron sat.

◆ ◆ ◆

"So you went to the infirmary two times during those seven years; correct?" Ron asked.

"Yep." Dericardo had that upstate New York twang to his speech. Ron pinned it on him before the man even spoke. Everything about the way he looked pointed to it—his stone-washed jeans that were likely purchased in the 1980s, his faded black T, the cut of his hair, and the simple look on his face. "Once when I got a stomach bug and then another time when I was jumped," Dericardo continued.

Ron decided he would push the limits of this deposition. If Upton didn't catch him, Dericardo would wind up saying a few things he didn't want to say. "You were jumped? You mean beaten up?"

"That's what I said—jumped." He waved away the question.

Ron laughed internally. It was exactly the perception he wanted to give to Upton and Dericardo. Straight-laced, square, unable to understand the street lingo. He wore glasses that he didn't need to enhance that perception. And just when they thought he'd never get it, that he couldn't comprehend enough to ask a sufficiently probing question, he'd spring it on them. But just one question. Then he'd go back to the ruse, as if that one question was just a mistake, a lucky stab. And after some time, he'd ask another, and eventually he'd get what he wanted from the deponent. He'd done this dozens of times, with guys just like Dericardo. "Can you tell me what happened that time you got, um,...jumped?" He said the last word awkwardly.

Upton cleared his throat oddly, suggesting he was amused.

It's totally working. Mr. Dorey said this guy was good. Ha!

"Well, I refused to, to perform my...duties, and four guys from a...a prison gang, they jumped me. Busted up my face and cracked a rib. I was in the infirmary for two weeks."

Ron was a little intrigued, so he continued on down the same line of questioning. "What do you mean 'duties'? You mean making license plates?"

Dericardo chortled. "License plates," he exclaimed, glancing at everyone in the room, even the stenographer. Getting almost no response, he became sheepish. "No, no. I mean my...duties." His head dropped, the last word but a whisper.

Ron genuinely didn't understand. "I still don't understand. What duties are you talking about?"

Dericardo looked to Upton pleadingly.

What is this? Ron immediately thought something untoward was going on. Maybe Upton was feeding his client answers. Ron eyed Upton suspiciously. Accusations of this nature couldn't be made lightly. He needed more.

Upton sat reclined in his chair, his black and gold pen flipping in his hand. "Answer it," he said to Dericardo. "Just tell him the truth. All of it. You have to be completely forthright." Gazing at the ceiling, Upton seemed to lean back farther, appearing carefree, as if this was just a lazy Sunday.

That eased some of Ron's concern about a coached witness. But still...

Dericardo cleared his throat, his fist held before his mouth. It took a few moments before he responded. "I, I mean, I refused to...suck their dicks that day."

What?! Ron was blown away.

The stenographer let out a soft gasp.

His mind reeling and his strategy all but forgotten, Ron sat there staring at the top of Dericardo's head as Dericardo stared at the table. This was entirely unexpected, and the case was turning into one unlike any other wrongful conviction case he'd heard of. He probably would've sat there another ten minutes but for movement from Upton.

Ron recovered his wits. He trudged on with his examination, not exactly sure how to proceed. His throat was suddenly dry, and his question came out in a cracked voice. "Can you, um, can you, well, elaborate?" He wiped the beads of sweat from his forehead with his bare hand, then rubbed his moist hand on his pants under the table.

Dericardo's gaze moved to the window. He spoke as if in a trance, the glaze in his eyes hiding raw emotion. "When I first got to prison, I was approached by members of a prison gang. I didn't know nobody and had no friends. These was white guys, with shaved heads. Called themselves the Aryan Brotherhood. They wasn't racist or anything, but in prison, gangs were formed by race or ethnicity. I don't know why, it was just the way it was." He sniffled and rubbed his nose.

Ron's eyes widened.

"So they told me," Dericardo continued, his voice fluctuating, "they told me I was now gonna be in their gang because the whites in prison stuck together, but they said that I was gonna be their bitch for a long time first, that I had to earn my keep."

The room was utterly silent, and Ron sat as still as a hiding prey, the anticipated horror consuming him.

"That first night -" Dericardo choked on his words, and he took a moment to recover himself. "They raped me that first night. Four of them. One after another. But first they made me suck their dicks." He swiped at his eyes, his face twisting. "I refused at first, but two punches to the face while they held me down and, and…"

Ron shuffled his papers, feeling profoundly uncomfortable, uncertain how to follow up. He looked to the window, then the table, then the ceiling, then fleetingly at Upton. He had to ask something, so he said, "And how long did this…continue?"

Dericardo's head turned slowly, his eyes meeting Ron's own. The man's mouth twisted, revealing his buck teeth. His eyes blazed. "Every fucking night, for seven fucking years," he snapped bitingly. His head dropped into his hands for a few seconds before he ran them through his light blonde hair. He seemed to recover a bit before he continued. "There was nothing I could do. They told me, if I went to the guards, they would kill me. They told me, if I tried to bite off one of their cocks, they would kill me. They told me, if I even scraped one of their cocks with my teeth, they would shiv me." He tapped at his buck teeth. "They showed me the shivs they said they would use." He sighed, but it was clear he was not done. "They told me, if I tried to fight when they fucked me, they would kill me. And it was four against one. Look at me." He motioned to his body. "I ain't no fighter. Not nothing like those guys in prison. Truth is, it didn't matter much what they told me. If it was one guy, I might'a had a chance. But four…" His gaze returned to the window. "I haven't shit right in seven years. Probably won't ever." That last bit sounded, oddly, like it was just a minor inconvenience.

Ron waited for more, but nothing came. He knew he should've moved to strike portions of the answer, but he couldn't muster the courage. He shifted in his seat, as uncomfortable as he'd ever been in a deposition. "Let's take a break," he said quickly, sweat running down the middle of his back, tickling his skin.

"Sounds good," Upton responded before stretching nonchalantly and extending to his full height. The man looked almost cheery despite Dericardo's testimony.

Ron rapidly retreated from the conference room, giving Upton's actions only a fleeting thought. He ignored the receptionist completely as he waited for the elevator. He just wanted to get the hell out of Upton's office. He felt an urge to turn around, but he fought it. As the elevator doors opened, he once again thought that this was no ordinary wrongful conviction case. If this case went to trial, the State would be in big fucking trouble.

STEP 12: The Payoff

Briefcase in hand, he stopped when his sandals hit the beach. The sunlight ricocheted off the white sand, creating blinding light that caused Chucky to blink incessantly. Scrunching his face to adjust his eyes, he threw his cupped hand on his brow and scanned the beach, watching both the water and the people. He'd never seen the ocean before in person, so he stood for a few moments, watching the waves pummel the sand, watching the waves pummel the swimmers. The dark water made him a little uneasy, and he decided that he wouldn't venture in above his knees, if he went in at all.

He turned his attention to the beach and its patrons. The plethora of umbrellas, towels and people sent his mind reeling. He followed the children running around, some building sand castles, some squealing as the tide came in and out. His childhood was never like that, he noted to himself, profoundly jealous. *Dad never took me on vacation to the beach. Hell, he never took me on vacation anywhere.* He studied the men and the women, paying particularly more attention to the women. Some were dark as could be, others golden, some reddish, some white with the sheen of half-rubbed sun block. He glanced down at his own pasty skin, comparing his tone to those in his vicinity. He was markedly pallid in comparison, and his arms were already turning pink from the edges of his tank-top down to his wrists. He'd be burnt tomorrow, he judged, but that's what always happened to him in the sun.

After a few moments of scanning left and right, he set off, waddling through the deep sand, his off-balanced canter revealing his unfamiliarity with the coastal terrain. He weaved through sunbathers, nearly stepping on a few, and stopped next to a scrawny, shirtless man on a beach chair who was somewhat removed from the rest of the crowd, the man's legs and arms splayed out, head leaned back toward the sun, eyes closed. Just then, a woman in a yellow bikini strolling the beach by the water caught Chucky's eye and he watched her as she passed, a smirk on his face, tingling in his groin.

The man in the chair didn't seem to notice his presence.

When the woman was too far away for Chucky to see anything arousing, he peered down at the man. "Don't know how you did it."

Barry—Chucky's cousin—opened his eyes and looked up, squinting against the sun's glare. He reached under his chair and grabbed a can covered in a brown bag. He gulped down what must've been half the beer before voicing his relief and smacking his lips.

"I don't think I could've done her in like that," Chucky added, glancing around to ensure no one was in earshot.

His cousin closed his eyes again and returned his head forward, then reached for his glasses and wrestled them on with eyes closed. "Well," he started, turning slightly to expose a different portion of his body to the sun, "that's why it was my plan. I do the crime, you do the time…and we both get paid."

Chucky laughed. "Speaking of that. Here it is." He placed the briefcase next to Barry's chair, lowering his voice to a whisper. "$3.1 mil. One third of the settlement. They told me it was tax-free too." He laughed again. "Shit. You should've seen me in that deposition. I may have an acting career on my hands."

Barry didn't move. "No more than I did in the courtroom, I'll bet."

"You gonna count it?" he asked, nodding toward the briefcase full of cash.

"Nope." Barry rotated again. "And especially not here."

Shrugging, Chucky plopped down in the sand and tucked his knees to his chest before glancing around. "So what'r you gonna do with your share?"

Barry sniffed and rubbed his nose. "Haven't decided yet? You?"

"Well…not much really. Buy me a new truck. House maybe." He wiped the sand from his legs. "Not sure I need anything else."

Barry opened his eyes and gave Chucky a hard look. The sun glared off his glasses. "Well," he said firmly, "don't go crazy and spend it all on crap. Put it in the bank and save it. You might need it one day, and if you waste it now it won't be there for you then."

Agitated, Chucky frowned. "I ain't no fool, Barry," he retorted. "I just said I didn't need anything, so I ain't gonna just go blow it."

Silent, Barry closed his eyes again, removed his glasses, and settled himself. "Just making sure. It took you seven years to make that money, don't forget. Seven hard years."

Chucky snorted. "Prison wasn't that bad. Not after they saw my rap sheet, anyway. Killing a girl all crazily and mutilating her and shit makes even lifers back off."

"You're welcome," Barry said wryly.

Chucky laughed under his breath. "I still can't believe we got away with it," he said, amazed.

His cousin glanced at him, eyes rolling. "Enough of this talk, man. Enjoy the beach. You're on vacation. Go have a dip." He turned back to the sun.

Chucky smiled, glancing around in search of scantily clad women. "Didn't bring a suit," he noted. "Don't even own one come to think of it."

Barry guffawed, causing beachgoers to glance in his direction. "You can march right across the boardwalk and buy one. You can afford any one you see."

"You just told me not to go crazy spending my money," Chucky exclaimed.

Barry rolled his eyes. "Do as you please."

"I will," Chucky said with as much bravado as he could muster. "And I think I'll take that dip." He rolled up his jeans defiantly and strutted to the ocean.

STEP 13:
The Suspicion

Ray strode down the hall with today's newspaper in hand, glancing at the front page every few steps to make sure it still said what it said. His solid blue tie flapped, twisting and turning as it was struck by the newspaper. He rounded the corner and entered the room housing the Property Crimes Unit. "Yo," Ray exclaimed, popping up to the side of a cubicle toward the back of the room.

Looking shocked, Ed rapidly moved his mouse and clicked, closing the screen he had up on his computer—but not before Ray caught a glance. Ed wasn't in uniform and he wasn't wearing a suit either. He sat at his desk in jeans and a gray polo shirt, collar disheveled and unbuttoned, exposing his dark, thick chest hair. His eyes looked bloodshot, as if he hadn't slept all night.

Is he even on duty today?

"Hey," Ed belatedly responded, his eyes glued to his computer screen, as if he hadn't just tried to conceal the screen he was looking at.

Ray frowned and shook his head. From his brief glance, Ray knew that Ed had been looking at Chucky Dericardo's profile in the system. Ray was seriously worried. Ed's behavior was starting to become obsessive-compulsive. Ray had to nip this in the bud, lest Ed do something rash. "Come on, Ed, really? You got to let it go," he pleaded.

"Don't tell me what to do," Ed said angrily, still not looking up at Ray.

Ray sighed. "Look at this." He dropped today's *Albany Times-Union* on Ed's desk, covering the keyboard. He crossed his arms on the top of the cubicle and rested his chin, waiting for Ed's reaction.

Ed glanced down at the front page. "So what?" he asked after a few seconds. It was a dismissal, not a question.

Frustrated, Ray rounded the cubicle. "Ed," he said heatedly, "the guy was convicted. Look!" He reached over Ed and held the newspaper up to Ed's face.

Ed swatted it away and twisted in his chair, looking up at Ray with a scowl. "Chucky played a part," he said through clenched teeth, "and not only did he get away with it, but the fucking State fucking paid him for it." He slammed his fist on the arm of his chair, his face red. "They fucking paid him to kill my sister," he yelled.

The chatter in the room ceased, all heads turning toward Ed's cubicle.

Normally, Ray would've been embarrassed at the sudden attention and would've crouched down out of site, trying to make his point discreetly. But he was fired up. He wasn't going to back down and he no longer cared who was listening. Everyone in the department knew about the situation, anyway. One way or the other, he had to get through to Ed. Maybe a public scolding was what Ed needed. "Paul Timmone did it!" He slapped his hand against the newspaper, his voice raised to match Ed's. "We got the guy, Ed. It's over. This should be closure for you. Your sister's killer is going away for life." He took a half step backwards, his arms thrown to the side, palms up. "What is your obsession with Dericardo, anyway? I mean, you didn't even follow Timmone's trial." Ray pointed to the article. "He had the fucking jar in his house. He's got a history. The evidence is overwhelming. It's a slam dunk. This—is—the guy." He slapped the newspaper one more time for good measure, pursing his lips. He rarely cursed, but Ed's behavior had gotten him so worked up that he couldn't help himself.

Ed stood and looked around the room. "Go back to work," he yelled angrily. Some officers returned to their tasks, some left the room, but some just rolled their eyes or smirked and continued to watch the show. Ed sat and turned back to his computer, then maximized the screen with Dericardo's profile, pointedly ignoring Ray. It was as strong a statement as any Ed could've made.

Ray huffed. "Ed! Listen, I'm trying to hel -"

"Just let me be," Ed interrupted coldly, his tone declaring the matter closed.

"Fine." Realizing he sounded like an angry child, he took a deep breath and relaxed his shoulders. "Just think about it, Ed." His concern suddenly overwhelmed him. He gently placed the newspaper on the side of Ed's desk and left.

If there was one man who could talk some sense into Ed, it was the Chief. He headed to Jim's office.

◆ ◆ ◆

The fucking nerve of that guy, Ed thought. He didn't need anyone to tell him what to do. It was his own family business, and he could deal with it. Chucky played a part in the murder. Ed knew it. Fuck Paul Timmone. *That sick pedophile was framed.* Ed had been involved in enough sex crimes to know that pedophiles with a penchant for young boys didn't suddenly start molesting and raping grown women. *Ray, of all people, should understand that!* The evidence must've been planted in Timmone's house. But who? And how? Chucky had been in jail, so that meant Chucky had an accomplice. *He doesn't have any family in the area. Does he even have any friends?* He'd have to look into Chucky's former coworkers at Universal Electric. Maybe it was one of them. He leaned back and stared at the ceiling absently, strategizing about the best way to investigate Chucky's U.E. coworkers. There were thousands of employees at the plant, and some that worked with Chucky may have moved on in the past seven years. Some may have retired. It was a daunting task, but it was the only thing Ed cared about. First thing to do, he thought, was to compile a list of people who where employed at the plant seven years ago, then narrow it down to the workers in Chucky's department. He began to access the census data on the system when a rookie approached his cubicle.

"Chief wants to see you, Detective," the rook announced.

Ed turned his head and gave a nod. The rook retreated.

What now, Jim? He had things to do. He almost ignored the summons, but when the Chief ask to see you, you went. He minimized the window and locked his computer screen so no one could snoop around. When he approached the Chief's office, Jim Pollack was on the phone. Ed pointed and mouthed to the Chief, silently asking whether he should come back. Jim waved him in and pointed to the chair across the desk. Ed entered and sat. As Jim finished his phone conversation, Ed regarded the man. He was still the same affable, quick-tongued guy as when Ed first met him almost a decade ago, but his hair had taken on more salt and his rounded face had begun to sag. The purple bags under his eyes were new—either a result of simple aging or the stress of the job. Ed suspected both.

The Chief ended his call and popped his chair to an upright position. "Ed," he said in greeting.

"What's up, Chief? You wanted to see me."

Jim nodded with a faint smile. "How's it going?"

"I'm good." He shrugged, wondering what the summons was about.

Jim nodded with eyebrows raised, looking at a loss for words. It was the first time Ed recalled Jim being unable to spit something out. The man usually had a quip on the tip of his tongue, ready to be flung at any moment. *What's going on?*

"You see the paper today?" Jim asked.

Not this again! Ed's lips thinned in distaste, his eyes darkened. "Yeah."

"And?" Jim reclined in his chair, the metal hinge protesting.

"And what?" Ed responded, probably with more heat than he should've. It was just that after Ray, he didn't want to be barked at twice. *Ray...of course.* "Did Ray put you up to this?" he asked suspiciously.

"Put me up to what?" Jim threw back at him. He scooted closer to his desk, rummaged through some papers and pulled out the newspaper. He tossed it in front of Ed. "Sentencing in three weeks. He's going to get life without parole. How does that make you feel?"

"*Feel?* How does it make me *feel*?" Ed's entire frame tightened. "My sister's dead," he barked. "How do you think it makes me feel?"

"Ed, come on," Jim said, an uncharacteristic compassion in his tone. "There's nothing you or anyone else can do to bring her back. All we can hope for is that justice be done. This has got to be closure for you."

Why does everyone keep saying that?! Why was this somehow closure? He'd never find closure, not even after he exposed Chucky. Never.

"Is this the end of it for you?" Jim asked, acting as if the question was off the cuff.

Ed knew better. Ray had spoken to the Chief, which is what prompted this meeting. *That little bitch.* Well, he thought, if that's how they wanted to play it, he would play along. *At least it will get them off my back.* He rubbed his face with both hands, wanting the Chief to think he was letting it all go. "Yeah," he said, nodding. "I think this is the end. After seven years, it's time to move on." He threw in a sentimental, albeit true, note. "I still don't know what to do without her around. It feels like yesterday. Do you think it will get better?"

Jim relaxed, apparently buying the act. "I'm sure it will in time, Ed. All in due time." He stood and waddled around the desk, yanking up his pants. A portion of Jim's shirt hung down outside his pants at the back, but Ed chose not to let him know. *He probably won't even be able to reach it to tuck it in...and I'm not doing it.* Ed rose, happy that he'd bought himself some time without prying eyes.

Jim held out his arm and wrapped it around Ed, moving slowly toward the door. "The boys are going out for a drink after work. Why don't you come with? Take a load off. Relax."

Ed nodded, Jim's belly fat pushing against his arm. "All right."

"Good." Jim clapped him on the back as he exited the office.

Ed returned to his desk. He returned to his task. He returned to Chucky.

"Shot of whiskey," Ed said to the bartender, forearms leaning on the bartop, a determined look on his face.

So it's going to be one of those nights, Ray thought disappointedly.

"Make that two," Jim added. He clapped Ed on the back. "Actually a double each," he called to the bartender who had already begun pouring. "You want one also," he said to Ray.

"No," Ray answered, "I'm good with a beer." He held up his bottle.

"What about you?" Jim asked Detective Nuck.

"Sure, why not," Nuck said.

Jim's smile widened. "One more."

The bartender looked up.

"One more," Jim repeated, his pudgy finger held up.

Ray glanced around. The bar was filled with officers. There were only a handful of patrons other than officers in the place, in fact. Ray hated this place and he couldn't figure out why Jim wanted to drink here all the time, rather than at *Shirley's* or *The Upstreet Grille*. At least those bars had people to look at and premium alcohol if you happened to want it. This place was a total dive. But when the Chief came out to drink—which was often—they drank where he wanted.

When the bartender returned, Jim raised his shot. Ed and Nuck followed. "Salud, boys," Jim said.

They clanked their shot glasses together and downed them. Nuck grimaced, Ed wiped his mouth with the back of his hand, and Jim gave a high-pitched hoot.

"One more," Ed said matter-of-factly. After his sister's murder, Ed had taken to drinking. It was no shock to Ray that Ed was going to get wasted tonight, but of course now was not the time for another motherly berating. *He probably already thinks I'm trying to take the place of his mother.* Ray rubbed his forehead, self-analyzing. Maybe it was best if he just backed off and let Ed sort it out alone. *Haven't made much of a difference, anyway.*

"Er, why not? One more," Jim said jovially, slapping his hand on the bartop.

"I'm out," Nuck said, his face still scrunched, his lips smacking in distaste. He moved off quickly to join another group of officers. Ray sat on the stool next to Jim, not wanting to further provoke Ed and not wanting to act like he was trying to be "buddy, buddy" or apologize. He ignored Ed, which is precisely what Ed had been doing to him.

After the next shot, Ed and Jim ordered beers, and Ed declared he was going to take a piss.

The jukebox in the back began to play. Ray turned. Royce and other officers were huddled around the old, dented music player, bobbing their heads to some *Rolling Stones* song like teenagers in the 1960s. It was always the same, Ray thought. Same bar, same drinks, same music, same act. Over and over. *Oh well, what can I do?* He glanced over his shoulder to make sure Ed was gone, then, over the volume of the music, asked, "So you really got him to drop this whole Dericardo obsession?"

Jim took a swig of the beer. "That's what he said." The Chief's eyes were starting to glaze. He'd likely be slurring his speech within the hour, yelling for *Lynyrd Skynyrd* to be played on the jukebox and singing along with "Freebird" when it came on.

Ray sighed, then swigged his own beer. "I hope you're right."

Jim nodded, seemingly not thinking much of the subject, his chubby face split into a grin, cheeks pink. No one seemed to be taking this Dericardo thing as seriously as it should be, Ray thought despondently. Ed was on the brink. Ray was surprised Ed was even able to do an adequate job at work. He wanted to ask Jim about Ed's work performance, but thought better of it. He didn't want to pry into things above his pay grade, and he didn't know how Jim would react.

Ed returned, sat, and chugged half his beer, confirming for Ray that it was going to be one of those nights. *Best that I keep out of Ed's way, then.* He hopped off the stool and joined the group of officers at the jukebox, making small talk.

Every now and then, he glanced over at the bar to find Ed and Jim in the same seats, with either shots or beers in front of them—sometimes both. After "Freebird" played for the third time, officers began to filter out, likely sick of hearing their Chief sloppily singing out of key. It would be a long day of work tomorrow for most—some more than others.

Jim sauntered over to the table Ray had moved to, swaying as if almost dancing. He leaned over into Ray's face. "Ray," he said loudly.

Ray leaned back out of the zone of Jim's breath, which smelled of soured whiskey.

"Ray," Jim slurred, "can you take Ed home?"

Ray rolled his eyes. "Yeah," he yelled back with a sweeping nod.

Jim's head dropped, as if he couldn't hold up the weight of it, his breathing labored. "Can you?" he asked after a few seconds, his head rising marginally.

"Yes," Ray yelled again. "I'll take him home."

That seemed to register with Jim, and he slowly pushed himself off the table.

"What about you?" Ray asked.

Jim pointed, his finger wiggling. "Got me a ride from…" The rest was unintelligible, but it was punctuated by a conspicuous crotch scratch.

Ray chuckled in spite of himself. He trusted that the Chief actually had a ride, and in any case, he wasn't about to start treating Jim like a baby. He looked over at the bar. Other than to take a piss a few times, Ed hadn't moved all night, and he hadn't said a word other than to Jim and the bartender. His face was in his hands, elbows propped on the bartop, eyes glued on the empty beer bottle before him.

I'm a better friend than he deserves, Ray thought as he scooted out of the booth, saying goodbye to Nuck and Officer Blume. He approached Ed. "All right, buddy. Time to go."

Ed's head crawled toward Ray. "One more drink," he mumbled sloppily, his mouth ajar. His hand came around and accidentally knocked over the beer bottle. It rolled around and stopped at the lip of the bartop. It took a few moments before Ed's gaze locked on the bottle.

"All right, that's it," Ray said, putting his hands on Ed to help him up. "Chief's orders, Ed. He said to take you home right now."

Luckily, Ed didn't protest. Ray half carried Ed to the car and plopped him in the passenger's seat. As Ray drove, Ed's head lolled, his eyes held closed as he mumbled incessantly. Ray ignored him, knowing that anything he said to Ed would be forgotten. Ten minutes of mumbling later he pulled up to Ed's house and stopped behind the cruiser in the driveway. Ed's eyes opened for a second and he began fumbling at his seatbelt. Ray exited and moved around to the passenger side, unbuckled Ed, and yanked his friend up. With Ed's arm around his shoulder, they moved up the porch. "Keys?" he asked Ed. "Ed? Hey, Ed?" He gave his friend a light slap on the cheek. "Do you have your keys?"

Ed began muttering, but Ray couldn't make anything out.

He was about to reach into Ed's front pockets when he made out the word "unlocked." He reached for the front door and twisted the knob. The door opened. The fact that Ed wasn't locking his front door was troubling, but Ray put the thought aside, focusing on his immediate task. He kicked the door shut and hauled Ed upstairs, dragging his friend down the hall before plopping Ed on the bed. "All right, buddy. You good? Get some sleep." He moved to leave but hesitated, deciding to yank off Ed's boots first. Then he left, making sure to lock the bottom lock of the front door on his way out.

Chances of Ed making it to work tomorrow, he decided as he drove away, were slim to none.

STEP 14: The Revenge

Step 14.1

A clipped police siren sounded outside her window, as if the officer had accidently switched it on and moved quickly to silence it. It was just a sliver of a sound, but in the still silence of midnight, the sound was unmistakable as it cut through her window. She cared little about the goings of the police, and in her neighborhood, they came often. Never to her house, mind you, but they had probably hit every other house on her block half a dozen times each. Pushing her stringy gray hair away from her face, she turned back to her knitting. Until, that is, she heard the soft sound of tires coasting over gravel, followed by the sharper sound of ungreased brakes being applied, suggesting that the police car had stopped directly in front of her house. That was odd, she thought, her hands frozen on her knitting needles, her head cocked.

There was nothing warranting a midnight call to her house. There was nothing, in fact, warranting a police call to her house at any time. She got into no mischief. She sat at home watching TV or knitting most of the time, tending to her cats, smoking tobacco sticks on the porch, trying to sleep when she was able, which was rarely these days. No, she decided, she must've misjudged the distance. Her hearing was getting worse, she admitted. She added it to the list of physical failings that she was no longer in denial about.

But just in case the police were coming to her house, she waited silently, head turned with her good ear pointed to the front of the house. But no knock came at her door, no doorbell, no officer burst in, no call came from outside. Maybe she was just hearing things. At her age, it was possible, but she was certain that the siren belonged to a police car.

Her curiosity was piqued enough for her to force her old bones to rise. She laid her unfinished scarf down—it was going to be violet and pink, and she had nearly finished the violet half—and pushed off her fluffy armchair with some strain. She shuffled to the window, hands rubbing at her lower back, then pushed aside the floral-patterned curtains that had treated her first-floor windows for the past 30 or so years.

"Hmm," she grunted. She was right about the siren and the car, only it hadn't stopped in front of her house so much as in front of the house across the street. *My ears are still good*, she thought triumphantly. She squinted, noticing something unusual. The police cruiser was half parked on her neighbor's lawn and half on the street.

Just then, the driver's side door opened. She scooted to the side, hiding her body from the window, only permitting half of her head to protrude into the window frame. Something was going on here, and she couldn't figure out what it was. She knew her neighbor had recently gotten out of jail, but a lone officer showing up at midnight on a Tuesday just didn't make sense. Her instinct to stay out of such affairs kicked in. Best to keep hidden, she thought, knowing how the police treated people in these parts.

The officer took a long time getting out of the car, pulling himself to his feet. All she saw was his back. He was in uniform, dark blue shirt only half tucked in to dark blue trousers, his officer's hat pulled down low. It was very, very odd. But maybe her neighbor had called the police because he had a problem. Or perhaps it was a parole officer. That made perfect sense. *But not at midnight.*

She glanced at her neighbor's house. All the lights were out and nothing seemed to be stirring or moving in the windows. She squinted, peering through her glasses, taking advantage of one of her few bodily faculties that had yet to significantly deteriorate.

The officer began walking to the house, the door to the police cruiser left wide open. Actually, she corrected, it was more stumbling than walking. *That man must be drunk.* Now she was really confused. What was a drunken officer doing at Chucky's house at midnight? The question prompted her to grab a pen and paper and take down the cruiser's license plate. She moved to a side window to get a better view and scribbled it out, squinting the whole way through, her hand shaky as she vocalized each letter or number.

By this time, the officer had reached Chucky's front door, arm extended. She returned to the other window because it gave her a direct view across the street. She made it just in time to see the door swing open and the officer move inside. Whether the door was unlocked, or the officer had picked the lock, or Chucky let him in, she didn't know. But it didn't take long for him to get inside, that was for sure. The door slowly swung back, halting slightly ajar. Maybe the officer was just confused and thought it was his own house. Doubtful, she judged. Her nerves flared. She found herself crouching down now, as if hiding from a burglar in her own home. *This isn't right.*

No lights turned on in Chucky's house.

It seemed as if minutes passed by with nothing happening.

She eased her muscles a bit. *Maybe he passed out on the couch, as drunk as he looked.*

Pop! The sound came suddenly, startling her, causing her to jump and squeal, hand held to her chest. *Oh my God!* It was the distinct sound of a gun firing—high-pitched and staccato. Three more pops followed in succession, her eyes widening in disbelief with each report. Fear coursed through her, but she couldn't move from the window, couldn't pull her gaze from Chucky's front door. Mere moments later, the officer emerged, his officer's hat pulled low, his gait markedly faster yet still wobbly.

She ducked lower, her muscles finding it difficult to maintain a squat. She shifted to her knees instead, her hands bracing herself on the windowsill. She tried to get a good look at the officer as he fumbled into his car, but his dark hat and the lack of light prevented it. He hastily shut the door.

The car horn blasted for a split second.

She yelped in response.

The drunken officer must have accidentally hit it, just as with the siren. He wasn't doing a very good job of being inconspicuous, she noted somewhat rationally in the heat of the moment, seeing as how he probably just murdered her neighbor.

The cruiser engine roared as it was revved. She suspected the man was trying to drive away, thinking the car was in drive although it was still in park.

Lights in the surrounding houses flickered on and she saw movement in windows out of the corner of her eye. But her gaze was fixed on the cruiser and the shadowed driver.

The cruiser lurched forward, driving half on the curb and half off. It swiped an electrical box before speeding away, out of sight.

She slowly stood, dumbfounded, leaning into the window, peering down the street to make sure the cruiser was gone. She couldn't believe it. She really couldn't believe what she just witnessed. After a few moments, her shock wore off and she glanced over at Chucky's house. The door stood ajar and there was no movement from inside that she could see. But of course there wouldn't be. *No one's alive in there.*

She shuddered, unsure what to do. A moment later, her shock subsided enough for her to put together a thought. She moved to the phone and began to dial 9-1-1, mouthing each number. *Wait!* She abruptly halted her finger before dialing the last number. How could she call the cops when an officer just came and shot her neighbor, she asked herself. What if all the cops were in on this? Or what if the drunken officer got the dispatch? Then he would come back for her and probably silence her. She was old, but she still wanted to live the rest of her life. Didn't everybody? Who could she call, then? She thought long and hard.

Then she dialed.

"Hello," the man answered on the other line after the phone rang a number of times, his voice sounding groggy.

"A cop just murdered my neighbor," she said straightforwardly.

After a brief pause, "Mom?"

The banging woke him up. His head throbbed, and he nearly hurled. *What the hell is going on?* The banging continued. Was someone yelling his name? Yes, he concluded. Yes. Someone was yelling his name, though it was muffled. He stretched his face muscles and blinked, exhaling deeply. With a grunt, he pushed himself to his elbows, head drooping. "Ah," he moaned, the pain in his head spiking.

"Ed," the yell came again between bangs. "Ed, open up."

Who the fuck is that? His head felt like it was going to implode.

"Ah," he groaned again, this time more in frustration at being woken up. Slowly, he moved to a sitting position. The sunlight was bright, so he closed his eyes and dug his fists in, turning his wrists. He swiped away some eye crud and rose to his feet, then sniffed hard. Blearily, he made his way down the stairs to the front door, rolling his head to loosen his neck muscles.

The banging continued. It was measured and even, like morse code or something like that. *This better be good*, he thought. What time was it, anyway? It had to be early morning.

He reached the bottom of the stairs and almost lost his feet, his body not responding as he clunked down to the wooden floorboards.

Bang, bang, bang. "Ed, open up!" *Bang, bang, bang.*

"All right," he yelled back, wincing with every word. "Coming. Hold the hell up."

He unlocked the door and yanked it open, squinting with a cupped hand on his brow to block the morning sun, eyes watery. "What?" he asked pointedly, seeing only blurry figures before him.

The closest figure coalesced into Captain Watkins, his wide forehead and narrow, beady eyes a few feet from Ed's face. Ed blinked, recoiling a half step. The Captain's face was statuesque, his eyes calculating. Behind him stood Detective Nuck, Officer Blume, and one of the rooks whose name Ed didn't know. He had stopped long ago making efforts to learn any new officer's name. What was the point?

Ed regarded them in turn through light-sensitive eyes. Upon making eye contact, Nuck dropped his head, looking ashamed. Officer Blume scratched his chin awkwardly, and the rook bit his lip.

"What?" he asked the Cap again. He dropped his hand from his brow. "What time is it, like 8 a.m. or something?"

Bill mechanically looked Ed up and down, as if appraising a piece of chattel, the algorithms probably processing in the man's brain. It was somewhat normal for Bill to react in such a fashion, but it still struck Ed as strange.

Confused, Ed glanced down. *When did I put on my uniform? Goddamn, how drunk did I get last night?*

"Ed," Bill said flatly, "you have to come with us."

"What for? My shift doesn't start until 11."

"You have to come down to the station."

Unsure what was going on, Ed decided to just comply, the conversation making his head hurt worse. "All right, let me take a shower or something. I'll meet you down there in half an hour." He began to shut the door.

"That will not suffice, Ed," Bill said, stepping forward and placing his hand on the door.

Ed's brow furrowed despite the throbbing it caused. "What's this about?" The tension of the conversation made him more alert, although the spike of pain in his head took some of his attention.

"You have to answer some questions, Ed," Bill said, eyes darting. It was the first time Ed had ever seen an expression or action from Bill that suggested the man felt awkward or uncomfortable. Men like Bill never felt awkward about anything that was said or done. The man was a machine, devoid of human emotion. *Apparently not.*

Bemused, Ed blinked, his mind starting to function. A sinking suspicious crept into his thoughts. "Just fucking tell me what this is about," he said testily. Bill was usually not someone to beat around the bush.

"Chucky is dead," Bill said evenly.

What?! His mind reeled. He almost fell, the initial shock overwhelming him. He wasn't sure what to do next. He should've been elated, he realized after sorting his jumbled thoughts. Then the detective in him took over. *But how?*

"Murdered," Bill added, as if viewing Ed's thoughts.

A moment passed.

No! he thought, finally putting two and two together. "I'm a suspect," he asked incredulously, stepping backwards. "Seriously?!"

"Just come down and answer some questions," Bill said, his mechanical nature returning.

Ed looked to his brethren, all of whom were pointedly looking anywhere but at him. *Holy fuck!* He took a deep breath. All right, he thought, best to get this over with. Maybe then he would have time to rejoice. Chucky was dead. The guy was fucking dead.

Grabbing keys on the side table, Ed exited his house and hopped in Bill's unmarked car. Nothing was said during the ride, which gave Ed time to massage his head. It did little to stop the throbbing, but it felt good otherwise. It also did nothing to stop his mind from churning. What did he remember from last night? He was drinking at the bar, and then he was home, in his bed, waking up to the sound of Bill banging on his door. *Fuck. Can't remember anything.*

When he entered the station, Bill grabbed the meat of his arm lightly. Ed looked down, then up at Bill's face. *Is this really necessary?* he thought, conveying his question through a look. Bill's head darted like a bird's, which was as much of a response as Ed would get. They moved down the hall together. The truth was, he had no idea what actually happened last night. Did he kill Chucky in a drunken stupor? No. It wasn't possible. *Or was it?*

His memory would return soon, he expected.

Heads turned as he moved down the hallway, conversations ceased, all eyes turning to him. *What the fuck is this?!* Utterly befuddled, he thought to ask Bill. Before he could, Ray stepped out into the hallway, a manila folder in his hand.

Ed smiled at Ray, happy to see a friendly face. Except Ray's eyes were wet, face registering pity. His friend quickly looked down. Ed gawked, unable to pull away from Ray's face. *What the fuck is going on?!* His feet slowed and Bill's grip on his arm tightened. His head twisted as he was pulled down the hallway, eyes fixed on Ray. His last glimpse before turning the corner was of his friend's shoulders quivering.

His stomach soured.

Step 14.2

"We've started a collection from the boys. So I guess my question is: how much would it cost?" Ray sat meekly, his face grim, his thoughts worse. He was picking at his cuticles unconsciously in his lap, heel bouncing anxiously.

The tall, lanky man sitting across from him threw him a warm smile. Ray recalled that smile from long ago.

The man clasped his fingers together on the desk. "Well," John Upton said, "the problem is not so much the money. I have a conflict of interest, you see. Mr. Dericardo was my client. I represented him in the criminal trial and in his subsequent civil trial. It would be a conflict of interest to now represent Mr. Roletti, who is accused of murdering Mr. Dericardo, my former client. So, unfortunately, the amount of money you offer me is irrelevant. You could have a million dollars and it would not change the fact that I am conflicted out of representing Mr. Roletti in this matter. I'm sorry."

Ray nodded glumly, although he expected the answer. There was nothing else to do, he supposed, but look for another lawyer. The boys had scraped together ten grand, Ray having contributed almost half of that himself. He hoped it would be enough to hire a good defense lawyer. Since the best—Upton—couldn't do it, he would have to try and get the second best. "Thanks, Mr. Upton. I appreciate you taking the time to meet with me." Ray rose and extended his hand.

Upton followed, looking down on Ray as they shook hands.

"Would you happen to know of a good defense attorney that has handled murder cases that you think would take the case?"

Upton looked pensive for a moment. He bent down and began writing on a sticky note. "Try her," he said, handing Ray the note. "She knows her way around a murder case."

Having spent almost his entire career in the sex crimes unit, Ray was not familiar with the better defense attorneys that handled murder cases. He only knew that there was a big difference between defending murder cases and other types of cases. The various crimes became subspecialties for many defense attorneys. Ray knew well the best defense attorneys for sex crimes, as he'd dealt with many of them in cases he was involved in as an arresting officer or detective. But those attorneys weren't necessarily good defense attorneys for murder cases. He couldn't take the risk of going to one of the defense attorneys from his own prior experience, and he wasn't sure he even wanted to do that. It would be awkward asking a guy who helped keep a sexual deviant out of jail to now help Ray keep a cop out of jail. So this was the best tactic he could think of—go to the best defense attorney that handles murder cases, and if he couldn't do it, go to the next best.

No one else in the department seemed to think a private defense lawyer would be worthwhile. Without saying it, they all seemed to think that it was futile based on the facts of the case, so Ed should just let the public defender handle it. Ray, however, wasn't giving up so easily.

Not for his friend.

He thought back to a few days ago, when he last saw Ed. The man was nonresponsive, as if he'd given up. Ray innately rejected such a notion, and he took it upon himself to do something about it. There was no one else that could help, anyway. He'd failed Ed in many ways over the past seven years, but he wouldn't fail him in this. He'd at least give Ed the best chance of being acquitted. It was a small part to play, but it was the best thing he could do. Hell, it was the only thing he could do. "Thanks," Ray said to Upton, acknowledging the note.

"No problem," Upton said warmly, the smile still on his face, "and good luck."

Ray left Upton's office feeling morose. He sat in his car and pulled out his cell phone. He dialed the lawyer's number. "Janet Parkerson, please."

"She is out of the country for the next month," the receptionist said on the other line. "Can I take a message?"

"No. No, that's okay." Ray exhaled, dropping his head. *What now?!* This town wasn't that big that there were many prominent defense lawyers for murder cases. Even Albany wasn't that big, for that matter. As insistent and determined as he was to place Ed in the best possible position, he knew his ingrained optimism would only take him so far, like a terminal patient who tries to convince himself that he can somehow beat the disease. Ray's optimism was starting to wane.

Only one course of action was left, he decided, after sitting in his car, silent, for a few minutes.

Sex crimes defense attorney it was.

STEP 15: The Criminal Trial

Step 15.1

Captain Bill Watkins took the stand, his bulbous head slightly cocked. He pushed his glasses up his nose with one finger and held them in place for two full seconds before lowering his hand in a measured fashion. He looked at Ed through those glasses, eyes analytical. There was something behind those eyes, Ed concluded, but it was far from emotion. The man looked at Ed like he was an equation to be solved.

Would the Captain help him out on the stand? Ed considered...but only briefly. He knew what the answer was. Such things were beyond Bill's comprehension. The man saw only in black and white, like a calculator punching out preset answers.

It took a moment before Ed realized that Bill's mouth was moving. *Damn!* He'd missed some answers due to his own daydreaming. He was having trouble focusing these days.

"We did," Bill answered the ADA.

What did he just ask? Ed glanced over at the assistant district attorney standing at the lectern in the small courtroom. Phil Duffy had an angular face, a neatly trimmed goatee and frosted hair that was buzzed. He was short, with a rhythm to his movements that compensated for his height by swaying him forward to press up on his toes. Ed had seen Phil in a few trials during the time Ed did a stint in Homicide. The ADA was a direct and businesslike lawyer. There was no embellishment, no trickery, no exhibition, no showmanship. You knew where he was going and what he was doing. As predictable as lawyers came. Yet that didn't make him ineffective, unfortunately. He bulldozed over lawyers with sheer force, never straying from course, never hesitating. There was some charm to his strategy, and Ed suspected that jurors silently thanked Phil for cutting to the chase. Ed supposed that the seasoned ADA didn't care what the defense was doing. Phil either proved his case or he didn't. It was a tactic that worked more often than not, and it worried Ed to no end.

But I'm not going to jail for a crime I didn't commit, he thought adamantly. That's why he rejected the plea bargain. Ten years was just too much to stomach, even if he had committed the crime. No, he would take his chances before a jury of his peers. *But what actually happened that night? Why can't I fucking remember?* Even after four months, none of his memories of that night had returned. He must've blacked out, although such a thing had never happened to him before, even in college when he used to seriously binge. Did he really don his uniform, drive to Chucky's, and put four bullets in his sister's killer? A part of him hoped that he did…just not the part that was currently on trial for the crime.

"Let me ask you about the projectiles," the ADA said, standing behind the lectern, his hands wrapped around the lectern's edges, his feet together as he rocked back down off his toes. "How many were found at the crime scene?"

"Four." Bill's hand shot out to touch the base of the skinny microphone sitting before him. The touch wasn't to readjust the microphone, Ed noticed, but more of a compulsive act. The man's eyes kept darting to the microphone, unable to resist its allure.

"Where were the projectiles found?"

Bill touched the base of the microphone. "All recovered from the victim's body. Three casings in the chest and one in the head." Microphone touch.

Stop fucking touching the microphone! Ed's teeth began to grind together. He quickly relaxed his jaw, realizing that if the jurors had been watching him, they would've observed anger on his face. That was the last thing he wanted them to see. He glanced at the jury box, spying a few eyes pointed in his direction. *Damn!* What was happening to him? He was on trial for murder, but he was so unfocused that his actions were damaging his own defense. *Get it together!* He straightened in his chair and carefully rested his hands on the table, trying to focus on Bill's testimony.

"Okay. So the call comes in to 9-1-1 and the tip gives you a license plate number, right?"

"Correct."

"What type of license plate number was it?"

"It was a police vehicle license plate number."

"How did you know that?"

Microphone touch. “There were two reasons.” Microphone touch. “First, the caller indicated that it was a police vehicle. Second, police vehicles have unique license plate numbers that are reserved specifically for official police use.”

“Did you run the plate number?”

“We did.”

“And what were—

Microphone touch.

“—the results?”

Bill cleared his throat, then touched the microphone, except this time it seemed like he was actually adjusting it. “The plate number, reading 3429, was registered to Detective Edward Roletti’s police cruiser.”

Ed sat back, on the verge of sulking. He felt the eyes of the jurors on him, like the sudden heat of the sun on his skin when it breaks through an extended cloud cover. *Did I actually do it?* The thought was fleeting at first, yet it crept into his anima and lingered, like a parasite attaching to a host.

Phil flipped a page in his binder on the lectern, rocking to his toes. “Okay. Let’s turn to the day after the murder. You brought Mr. Roletti in for questioning the very next morning?”

“Correct.”

“Did you notice anything about Mr. Roletti when you picked him up?”

“Yes. He was in uniform.”

“Why was that unusual?”

Bill slowly blinked. “He was not in uniform the previous day or night.”

“And what did he say when you brought him in?”

“That he could not remember anything.”

“Do you know if he had been drinking that night?”

“A number of officers went to the bar that night. Ed apparently had a lot to drink.”

“Objection, move to strike,” Ed’s lawyer said next to him, her voice firm.

“Sustained,” the Judge agreed.

Phil moved on without skipping a beat. “What happened after the interrogation?”

Bill cocked his head before fingering the microphone. “Detective Roletti’s house was searched.”

"Did you recover anything of note from his house?"

"Yes. His firearm." A microphone touch was followed by a hasty microphone touch.

Ed began chewing his lip, suddenly subsumed in the moment and extremely nervous. How could he counter this testimony? What was his lawyer going to do?

"What type of firearm was that?"

"It was a Glock. Standard police department issue."

"Your Honor," Phil said, "I'd like to mark this as People's Exhibit 4." He held up a large plastic bag with a black gun inside. "May I approach?" he asked the Judge.

"You may."

Phil moved around the lectern and handed the bag to Bill. "Is this the firearm that was recovered from the defendant's home?"

Bill examined it, flipping it in his hands. "It is."

Returning to the lectern, Phil asked, "did you examine anything else in Mr. Roletti's possession?"

Bill nodded. "Yes. We examined his police cruiser." Bill looked at Ed aslant.

Ed held Bill's inert gaze for as long as he could muster before dropping his eyes to his lap.

"Anything noteworthy regarding Mr. Roletti's cruiser?"

"Yes. There was damage to the driver's side front end consistent with the crime scene."

Phil rolled to the tip of his feet. "How so?"

"A gray electrical box on the victim's property was damaged. The cruiser had traces of gray paint on it. It correlates precisely to the manner in which the police cruiser left the scene as described by the eyewitness."

"No further questions." The ADA returned to his seat.

Bill's hand shot out to touch the microphone, almost knocking it to the ground. He looked up as if nothing had happened.

"Your witness," the Judge said to Jane.

Ed's lawyer rose. "No questions, Your Honor." She sat back down.

Ed eyed her apprehensively, biting the inside of his cheek, wondering what her strategy was…if any.

Did I do it?

His doubt blossomed.

◆ ◆ ◆

It was a big courtroom, Maxine noted while looking at the fresco on the ceiling of the New York State seal. What were those women holding in the painting? One was holding a scale and the other looked like she was holding a spear with something covering the spearhead.

"Ms. Jones?"

The question caught her by surprise and her eyes widened. "Huh?"

"Mrs. Jones," the Judge said. "Please try to remain focused. You are in the middle of testimony."

She nodded, a nicotine craving creeping up her spine.

The tiny lawyer behind the lectern looked annoyed. "Let me ask you the question again," he said. "Where is Mr. Dericardo's house in relation to yours?"

She really needed a cigarette, and her arthritis was flaring up. "It's right across the street." She winced as she bent her fingers.

"Okay, so you see this police car pull up and park in front of Mr. Dericardo's house, then an officer in uniform gets out and goes inside. What happened next?"

"I heard gun shots from the house." Her hands started shaking. *Damn nicotine. I should probably quit.*

"How did you know they were gun shots?"

She gave the lawyer a sharp look. "In my neighborhood, it happens a lot. I've heard them before."

"What happened next?"

"The officer came out of the house and left in his police car."

"What did you notice about the officer?"

"He was drunk."

"Objection," the lady lawyer called out. "Calls for expert opinion."

"See if you can lay a foundation, Counselor," the Judge said to the tiny lawyer behind the lectern.

"What was the officer doing?" he asked Maxine after acknowledging the Judge's comment.

"He was wobbling when he walked, and he accidentally hit the siren and the horn. Oh yeah, and he left the door to his car open, and he also parked halfway up the curb. When he drove off, he ran into one of those gray boxes in the yard. I think they are electrical boxes. Or maybe that's the green boxes, not the gray boxes." She shrugged.

"So you concluded he was drunk based on that behavior?" the tiny lawyer asked.

She nodded.

"Objection," the lady lawyer said again.

"I'll allow it," the Judge responded. "It's proper layperson testimony based on physical observations."

"So you determined he was drunk?" the tiny lawyer asked again.

Her nicotine craving was making her antsy. Why did she have to answer the same questions over and over. "Yes," she said hastily. She turned to the Judge. "Can we take a break?"

The Judge turned to the tiny lawyer. "How much longer do you have?"

"Only a few minutes, Judge. Maybe even less."

"Okay," Judge Reed said, turning to Maxine. "Ms. Jones, can you wait a few minutes."

She nodded reluctantly.

"Was there anything about the police cruiser that you noticed?" the tiny lawyer continued.

"You mean the license plate?" she asked.

"Ms. Jones," the Judge said. "Please do not ask questions. You are only to answer questions. If you do not understand a question or cannot answer a question, you can say just that."

"Did you see the license plate?" the tiny lawyer asked.

"Yes. The whole thing looked suspicious to me so I wrote the license plate down." Her knee began bouncing. She put the weight of her hand down on it.

"Move to strike the nonresponsive answer," the lady lawyer said, rising to her feet.

Maxine didn't know what that meant, so she looked to the Judge.

"So stricken," the Judge said before turning to the jurors. "Jurors, you are to disregard the portion of the answer that did not respond to the question."

"Ms. Jones, what was the license plate number?"

"3429," she said slowly, nodding confidently with each number.

"Are you sure it was just four numbers?"

She nodded emphatically, proud of herself for writing the numbers down. "I wrote them down."

"Nothing further," the tiny lawyer said, taking his black binder from the lectern and sitting down.

"Let's take a five minute break," the Judge said, standing and moving to leave.

"All rise," the officer in the courtroom called out.

Maxine stood as the jury exited, then she moved as fast as her arthritic legs could take her through the courtroom and down the hall. She hit the front steps of the courthouse and rummaged in her purse. She yanked out a tobacco stick and lit it up, sucking in deep. Her muscles relaxed and her tension eased. If only it could fix her arthritis, she thought in earnest. She rubbed at her fingers before returning to the courtroom.

Once she was on the stand, and the jury had entered, the Judge looked at the lady lawyer and said, "Your witness."

The lady lawyer placed a forearm on the lectern and leaned in casually. Maxine wondered if the woman was going to try and hit on her. She never did care for those types.

"This incident took place in the middle of the night, right?" The lawyer's voice was raspy and surprisingly deep for a woman. It reminded Maxine of her daughter-in-law.

"Yes."

"So it was dark outside?"

"Yes."

"How are the street lights in your neighborhood?"

"Oh, terrible. They don't do a good job at all." She shook her head. "There's not enough light on my street."

The lawyer leaned farther in. "And you testified earlier that the man had his hat pulled down low, right?"

"Yes."

"Did you see his eyes?"

"No. I just said it was dark." The nerve of this woman. Wasn't she listening.

"What about his nose? Could you see his nose?"

"No."

"What about his hair color?"

"No."

"Did you see any identifying features on the man in the uniform?"

She shook her head. "No." She glanced at the defendant. He didn't look familiar, but she never would've recognized him after seeing him that night. It was just too dark outside.

"So all you know is that it was a man in uniform, of average height, who *looked* drunk, nothing more, nothing less?"

She curled her lip. "I suppose that's right."

"Can you identify Mr. Roletti, sitting here, as the man you saw that night?"

She gave him a hard look. "No. It was just too dark."

The lady lawyer switched to her other forearm. "And…although it was dark, you were able to see the license plate perfectly. Is that your testimony?"

This lawyer woman was much meaner than Maxine's daughter-in-law…and she didn't care for her daughter-in-law much. Her lips thinned in annoyance. She knew when someone was trying to call her a liar. "I saw it. The car was still running, the headlights were still on. And, some of those lights on the back of the car were shining on the license plate." She looked up at the ceiling. "I guess some of the older cars don't have that feature, but this car had those little, tiny lights that shine on the license plate. You know, the small ones."

"You're wearing glasses today. Did you have them on at the time of the incident?"

"I put them on, yes," she answered a little snootily. "I wasn't wearing them while I was knitting, but I had them right next to the chair on the lamp stand." She smiled triumphantly, sure that she was not giving answers that helped the lady lawyer. She could play this game, too.

"Can you read this?" The lawyer held up a piece of paper.

Maxine leaned forward, her eyes narrowing.

"Objection," the tiny lawyer said, springing to his feet.

"Sustained. Ms. Jones, do not answer." The Judge gave the lady lawyer a brief glare.

Maxine leaned back and let out a, "hmphf."

Another nicotine craving began to burgeon. She really needed to quit. She turned to the Judge. "Can we take another break?"

Step 15.2

Byron Stadmore, former chief of police and recent widower, sat down tenderly, lest he inflame his hemorrhoid. Old age was a bitch. He needed a cane to walk these days, and a nurse came five days a week to help him with things like bathing and taking his medication. She also kept a close eye on his blood-sugar level. He scratched at his fluffy white mustache before resting his hands on his cane. He didn't want to think about the effort it would take to get up off the bench.

He had retired seven years ago, shortly after Ed's sister was murdered, and an officer he didn't recognize sat on the witness stand. The man looked quite young. Another reminder of Byron's age. He sighed.

"Did you conduct an initial test of those ballistics?" the ADA asked the witness.

"Yes."

An officer from the Firearms Analyst Section, Byron concluded from that question.

"What were the results of that test?" the ADA asked.

"I determined that the bullets had been fired from a Glock semi-automatic weapon."

"Officer, what type of firearm is issued to police officers in Schenectady County?"

He paused, his mouth moving. "A Glock semi-automatic." He sounded somewhat reluctant. Byron understood. It was hard testifying against a brother officer. No one wanted to be a turncoat or a snitch, even when the law compelled you to do it.

Jim Pollack, Byron's successor as chief of police in Schenectady County, plopped down next to him, throwing him a wink. Byron smiled back, suddenly self-conscious of his cane. He angled it away from Jim's line of sight. Jim always seemed chipper no matter the circumstances. Byron wondered if it was just a façade. Either way, he envied Jim for it.

"And Mr. Roletti in particular," the ADA asked the witness, "had been issued a Glock semi-automatic, correct?"

"Yes."

"After your test on the ballistics, did you have the opportunity to test Mr. Roletti's weapon?"

"Yes."

"How do you test a weapon like that?"

"It's simple, really. You fire it."

"What did you find?"

"His firearm was in working condition. It was operable."

Byron couldn't believe it. That Ed's rage would bring him to such a state as to go off the deep end like this. It just wasn't believable. He knew the kid was hotheaded, but he never believed it would lead to something like this. He felt deep regret, and a bit of shame. He had mentored Ed, after all, and when Ed's father, John, passed, Byron had taken it upon himself to look after Ed as a fatherly figure would. *What a shame.* He shook his head in sorrow and exhaled.

The Roletti family was like the Kennedys—tragedy seemed to follow them. First it was Ed's father, who was Byron's classmate at the academy. Then Alzheimer's struck Beth, Ed's mother. Last Byron heard, she was still alive, which in and of itself was unbelievable. His thoughts turned to the old age home. He fought going there as hard as he could, but with his wife no longer with him, he suspected he would eventually end up there, rotting away in some bed, unable to control his own faculties, just like Ed's mother. He cringed. His hemorrhoid began to itch, so he shifted on the bench. His thoughts turned back to the Roletti family. Then there was Mary, Ed's sister, who was raped and murdered in cold blood by a sick, twisted guy.

And now Ed...

Yes, he reaffirmed his thought, just like the Kennedys.

"And did you test to see if the ballistics taken from the victim's body were fired from Mr. Roletti's police-issued Glock?" the ADA asked.

"I did test for that," the Firearms specialist answered hurriedly. Byron suspected that the officer, resigned to the fact that he was going to help take down his brethren, just wanted to get through his testimony as soon as possible and get the hell off the stand.

'How do you do that type of testing?"

"Well, again, you fire the weapon, but you fire into a special target that preserves the ballistic. Then you compare the ballistic fired during the test to the ballistic from the crime scene."

The ADA seemed to inch a bit higher, as if he was on his tippy toes. "How can you compare those two ballistics?"

"Well, each firearm has its own unique chamber. So when you fire a ballistic, the firearm will leave markings on the ballistic that are characteristic of that firearm. It's just like a human fingerprint. Each fingerprint is unique, just as each firearm is unique. So as long as you have a ballistic from the crime scene and a weapon, you can test to see if the ballistic was fired from that weapon."

"And what were the results of that ballistic test on Mr. Roletti's firearm?"

"The ballistics that I tested matched the ballistics recovered from the crime scene."

"In your opinion as a ballistics' expert, what is the import of that finding?"

The officer made a point of not looking at Ed. Byron didn't blame him. The man was between a rock and a hard place. "It means that Mr. Roletti's police-issued firearm was used to shoot the victim."

Jim grunted next to him.

Byron lowered his head, the burning of his hemorrhoid briefly forgotten.

◆ ◆ ◆

"I am a criminologist with the police department, and I work in the Latent Print Development Unit," Charlotte said on the stand.

There was no way out, Ray thought wistfully. *No fucking way.* He sat toward the back of the courtroom, in the corner, donned in an olive suit that he rarely ever wore. He was supposed to be out investigating a recent groping incident, but here he sat, consumed by the trial, unable to leave. Or at least unwilling to leave.

But maybe I should. This seems hopeless. The case against Ed was just too damn good. The DA was piling on witness after witness, all providing damaging testimony. He supposed that the DA would take it over the top. When a cop committed a crime—especially one of this nature and publicity—the DA needed to take a hard stance, if for no other reason than to show the public that cops are not above the law, that cops suffer the same consequences as the rest of the population. In other words, the DA had to show the public that she was a woman of the public, that she didn't play favorites.

Ray eyed his friend at the defense table. Although he could only see the side of Ed's face from this vantage, he knew that Ed wore a scowl. From the look of it, the jury saw the same thing. It didn't seem like Ed was capable of helping himself. If anything, Ed was bolstering the DA's case. Ray shook his head, wondering if he should've shelled out the cash to retain a private lawyer. It was a selfish thought, but money wasn't easy to come by for a career cop. And if Ed was just going to give up, the public defender would've been sufficient.

"You tested the firearm for fingerprints?" the ADA asked.

"Yes," Charlotte answered.

"What were the results?"

"Three full prints and one partial print were located on the weapon, in a location where you would expect to find prints when someone is holding the weapon to shoot."

Ray was fed up. Fed up with Ed's attitude, fed up with being the nice guy, fed up with being taken for granted, fed up with being outright ignored. If Ed wanted to go to jail for the rest of his life, then so be it. Agitated mostly with himself, he dropped his head.

"Were you able to determine whose prints were on the firearm?"

"Yes. The prints belong to Edward Roletti." In the silence of the room, Charlotte's voice took some time to dissipate.

The only thing worse than losing a friend like this, Ray concluded, was wasting money doing so. *Time to investigate a groping.* Disgusted, he rose and left.

◆ ◆ ◆

Almost 40 and I'm still not married. What would his mother have thought? Had she been alive, she would've been nagging him about it for the last 15 years, likely. Detective Suarez smiled fondly. It was times like this that even his mother's annoying characteristics brought a smile to his face. He longed for those motherly moments again—even the pestering.

He longed for something else, too.

Ana had straightened her dark hair, which disappeared below her shoulders, framing the dark, olive oil color of her neck. Her nose was wide but attractive, her eyes almond-shaped and full of sparkle. She was the perfect Latina specimen. One to take home to his mama—had his mama still been alive.

He licked his lips, knowing that this was one of the few times where he could stare openly at Ana without anyone taking notice. He almost started drooling.

"What was the cause of death?" the ADA asked her.

Her response came in that silky alto that was sexy as hell, her speech measured and articulate. "A gunshot wound to the head with deep perforation of the brain." She moved her head slightly, causing her hair to flow out and back again.

Ernie had to find a way to ask her out. He sighed. He just had to get his nerves up, is all.

"Do you have an opinion as to how close the killer was when he shot Mr. Dericardo?"

"Objection to the characterization of 'killer,'" Ed's lawyer said, her voice the antithesis of Ana's. Ernie crinkled his brow at it.

"I'll allow it," the judge answered, almost perfunctorily.

"Yes, I have an opinion," Ana said.

"And what is that opinion?"

"All four shots were fired within 12 inches of the victim. At close range."

Ernie imagined what her voice would sound like when she was moaning beneath him. He took a deep breath, basking in that euphoric thought. Then he started, his eyes shifting, embarrassed for having such a thought in the middle of his friend's murder trial. He straightened his back, making an effort to drag his eyes from the witness stand.

"How do you know that it was at close range?" the ADA asked.

"There was evidence of stippling for each wound."

"What is stippling?"

"Minute scratches on the skin of the victim from the gunpowder. It is only present when the weapon is fired at close range because the gunpowder will not strike the skin otherwise."

Close range, Ernie thought as his eyes once again fixed on Ana. He thought about taking Ana at close range.

He crossed his legs at the sudden heat in his groin.

Step 15.3

"There is still a chance," his lawyer whispered in his ear insistently, her breath smelling of mint. She was close enough that he heard the clicking sound caused by the mint rolling around in her mouth, striking teeth.

The Judge went on speaking in the foreground, instructing the jury as to the law before sending them to deliberate.

Ed took a moment before he turned to his lawyer.

She went on, her tone more urgent. "They would probably agree to 35 years. You'd be out in 22 with good behavior. I'm sure you'd be looked after, protected by the guards." She glanced at the Judge before adding, "You'd get out and still have a life to live." She pulled away.

Biting his lip, Ed turned back to the Judge. *22 years*, he thought. It would be most of his adult life. He'd be close to 60 when he got out. What kind of life would be left to him then? The only thing he knew was police work, but he really couldn't be a cop starting over at 60, or more importantly, as a convicted felon.

"We need a decision before the jury begins deliberating," his lawyer insisted in a whisper, leaning into him again, her arm on the back of his chair. "Otherwise, any potential for a plea will be gone." She didn't add "assuming we even have a chance at one," but Ed knew that was what she was thinking. She had made that abundantly clear.

Why would the DA agree to a plea after she just prosecuted the entire case?

He thought for a few minutes. He still wasn't even sure if he'd committed the crime, but his heart told him that he hadn't. And, in any case, cutting a deal to get out of jail at the age of 60 left him very little. No, he decided, it was all or nothing. He leaned over to his lawyer slowly.

She dropped her head, turning her ear toward him.

"No," he breathed.

Jane met his eyes and gave him one stern nod. There was something in her eyes, but Ed couldn't interpret it. She clasped her hands on the table coldly and turned her attention to the Judge.

Ed retreated into his thoughts. Whether he committed the crime or not, Chucky was dead. Ed's purpose had been served, his revenge enacted. In truth, what was left? No family, maybe a friend or two, a job that now felt like just a job…

The way he saw it, he had little to lose.

"So now," the Judge said, looking up from the papers before her to smile at the jury, "I will send you back to deliberate. Remember, if you have questions, if you would like testimony read back or would like to view evidence, the foreperson should write it in a note to me. It must be in writing. The Court and the parties will determine how your question or request should be answered." She nodded, signaling that she was finished.

The jurors glanced at each other and rose.

"All rise," the bailiff called.

Ed and his lawyer rose. He watched the jurors exit the box and the courtroom. When they were gone, everyone sat, and the Judge turned to the parties.

"Stay close," she said ominously before rising and exiting at a back door.

Ed's lawyer stood, looked at him, and moved down the aisle to exit the courtroom without a word.

Ed remained seated, staring blankly, his thoughts stagnant. His life was now in the hands of 12 of his peers. He felt numb, almost listless. *How much do I really care?*

Over the next hour, people came and went in the courtroom. His lawyer sat next to him for a time and rummaged through papers. No one, however, not even his lawyer, spoke to him.

He wouldn't have had it any other way.

A buzzing sound emanated from the door cracked open that led to the room behind the courtroom. Ed knew what that meant. The jury either had a note or a verdict. *Less than two hours of deliberating. Could it be just a note?*

A hand rested on his back. He looked up.

Jane gave him an obligatory smile and sat, scooting in her chair.

The Judge entered and sat at the bench. "The jury has buzzed," she announced to the courtroom. People in the back hastily took their seats.

The bailiff entered a few minutes later and handed the Judge a folded piece of paper.

The Judge unfolded it and read it silently. She looked up at Ed, her eyes thoughtful, then moved on to look at the ADA's table.

"They have reached a verdict," she announced once the court reporter was in position. She waited a moment while regarding the parties, then said to the bailiff, "bring them down."

The bailiff exited.

What was likely only three minutes seemed to take three weeks. Ed's breathing became shallow and he began having trouble focusing his eyes. He licked his lips repeatedly. The anticipation of his fate was eating at him, but he kept his muscles tense, fighting the urge to fidget, to rock, to shake, to scream…to run. As the moment of his fate arose, he found that he was not as apathetic as he believed. He cared. He cared a lot.

The opening of the door was preceded by the jiggling of keys as the bailiff unlocked it. It was portentous, the sound of those keys, and it sent Ed's head spinning. The door cracked. Breathing evenly, he closed his eyes as the jury entered, not wanting to look at those that had been tasked with judging him. The sounds of the jurors getting settled in the box emanated from his left, but he dared not open his eyes.

"Mr. foreperson," the Judge said, "have you reached a verdict?"

"Yes," was the response, the voice sounding youthful, which belied the picture of the foreperson that Ed conjured in his head from memory.

Ed wanted to open his eyes to look at the foreperson, but he didn't.

There was a brief pause. The room was dead silent. Ed heard the beating of his heart between his ears, its rhythm steadily increasing.

"On the count of murder in the second degree," the Judge said, "how do you find?"

Ed opened his eyes.

STEP 16: The Estate

The best court appearances were the ones where he managed to say nothing, but everything still went his way. This was to be that type of appearance, John Upton concluded. Normally, he was never certain of such things, as he'd learned long ago that anything could happen in court, but today, he was as certain as he'd ever been. As his case was toward the end of today's calendar call, he sat near the back of the courtroom.

"Sit right here," he said to his client, motioning to the bench next to him.

This wasn't his usual courtroom nor his usual practice. He was used to the criminal courts, where all matters were hotly contested, where he needed to be on his feet at all times, ready to respond, ready to preempt prosecutorial strategies, ready to defend. This was different. Oh, he suspected that matters in this courtroom were often hotly contested, but more often than not a decedent's last will and testament spoke for itself. It gave him a mind to expand his practice into wills and trusts. *No. No, this is a simple exception. A very rare exception.* He held his laugh at bay, only permitting a small smile to escape his grasp.

"All rise," the bailiff announced.

The room—mostly attorneys—stood as one.

The bailiff continued. "The Honorable Ryan O'Calhan, Surrogate of the County of Schenectady presiding." Judge O'Calhan was a tall man—he looked to be almost the height of John, but it was difficult to tell from the back of the courtroom. He was young, relatively speaking as far as judges were concerned. Likely in his mid-40s. He had a face full of zeal, a full head of wavy auburn hair, and fair skin with a mild shading of auburn freckles. A distinctly Irish-looking man with a distinctly Irish-sounding name. John half-expected the man to start speaking in an Irish accent.

"Please be seated," the Judge said with a surprisingly heavy Brooklyn accent. He sounded like he was one of 'yous guys'—a contradiction to his appearance. It could've been Staten Island, not Brooklyn, John conceded, but either way, it was unusual for a

Judge in Schenectady County to have a downstate accent at all. Not many people from downstate ended up settling in Schenectady County, let alone staying here long enough to win an election as the Surrogate of the county. John wondered about the Judge's story.

As the first case was called, John mindlessly brushed at some specks of lint on his pants. He'd used the lint brush this morning, as he always did, but he must've missed a spot. He frowned as he resorted to picking at the pieces of white lint that were resistant to his brushing. The first case that was called involved a claim that the decedent's will was executed under duress. It brought John all the way back to his wills and trusts class during law school. He'd retained virtually nothing from that class once he'd taken the bar exam. Luckily, today's appearance didn't require him to bone up.

The next case involved a standard will probate. In the case after that, a person had died intestate with only a 1997 Toyota Camry to his name. Still, it looked as if six of his relatives had shown up to claim a piece. John smiled incredulously. People wanted every scrap they could get, in any way they could get it. It was the American way, after all. Hell, John was the very definition of that aphorism. He laughed under his breath.

His client eyed him skeptically, but said nothing.

The calendar call proceeded smoothly. Judge O'Calhan was succinct and competent, which impressed John. If only the same could take place in the criminal dockets. But the criminal realm was a wholly different beast, he conceded. It could never happen.

"In the Matter of the Estate of Charles E. Dericardo," the Part Clerk called out.

Finally, John's case. He rose and moved to the front, his client following behind. John took his place at the attorney's table and sat, his client taking the seat next to him.

Another lawyer quickly took his place at the table next to John's, but he wasn't John's adversary. Surrogate's Court was weird like that.

Without even bothering to hear appearances on the record, Judge O'Calhan turned to the other lawyer. "It is my understanding that the decedent Mr. Dericardo died intestate. Is that correct?"

"That is correct, Your Honor." The lawyer glanced down at his notepad. "I was appointed Administrator of the estate by the

Court approximately six weeks ago. No will has been located or proffered since that time."

John loved not having to speak. Tickled with the thought, he leaned back. The old wooden chair creaked.

"And," the Judge continued with the other lawyer, "have you been able to determine the decedent's distributees?"

The counsel nodded. "Yes, Your Honor. There is only one."

"And I suppose this is him," the Judge said with a smirk, looking to John's table.

John rose, buttoning his suit. It looked as if he'd have to say something after all. Not much, likely, but something. "John Upton, Your Honor. This is my client, Barry Higgins." He gestured with his hand.

Barry rose and nodded to the Judge, his hands clasped in front of him at the waist, his shoulders hunched inward, making him look skinnier than he actually was—and he was already in the borderline anorexic club. Barry's navy suit was dingy, faded to the point of looking gray in certain spots. He wore a burgundy shirt that he probably found at a flea market and a tie that was dark red but clashed with the hue of his shirt.

John laughed internally. The outfit was pure comedy.

The Judge quickly surveyed John and Barry. They must have looked funny, John thought, standing side by side. John—tall, refined, and well-groomed—juxtaposed to Barry—short, inelegant, and disheveled. It was something akin to Penn & Teller. Although Teller never looked inelegant or disheveled, he admitted. Just a height thing, then.

"What is his relation?" the Judge asked.

"First cousin, Your Honor," John answered. "On the maternal side. There are no living parents, siblings, or grandparents."

The Judge made some notations before asking, "What is the value of the estate?"

John looked to the Administrator, confident that his part had been played. He would probably say nothing more except "thank you."

"Slightly under three million," the Administrator answered. "Virtually all of it in cash. There is one small piece of real property."

Judge O'Calhan didn't bat an eye at the number. Even though Schenectady was not a county of means, the Surrogate dealt with estate values every day. The Judge continued notating. After a moment, he looked up and regarded both tables. “It is hereby ordered that Mr. Barry Higgins, being the only issue by representation of the estate of Mr. Charles E. Dericardo, is the sole heir to the decedent’s estate. The Administrator is directed to distribute the estate in its entirety to Mr. Higgins forthwith.”

“Thank you, Your Honor,” John said with a smile. *As predicted.* He exited the courtroom with Barry in tow, laughing in his head the entire way. He had barely said two words to get the result he wanted, and it was a damn good result considering his cut of one-third. Oh yes, it was a good appearance.

He and Barry had a thing or two to teach Penn & Teller about magic tricks.

STEP 17:
The Futile Suspicion

“Wait here,” the guard said, motioning to the spot next to him.

Ed waited, his eyes sunken and framed by puffy dark bags. He scratched his dry scalp. Since his incarceration, his hair loss had seemed to accelerate, as if his scalp knew it was the end, as if the follicles knew they no longer needed to stay fastened. What did he need hair for in prison? Indeed, there was no one to impress, nor a need to protect his scalp from the sun.

His orange jumpsuit swished as he swung his arms at his side. *472R299G4*. He had memorized his prison identification number, the same number that was blocked in black writing on his jumpsuit. He’d done so for no other reason than he had nothing else to do at the time. Now he just repeated it in his head, giving it different cadences to keep it fresh. *4…72R29…9G4*. Sometimes, he wondered if he was going mad.

The guard craned his neck, looking down the line of seats.

A light lit up above seat number seven.

“There, number seven,” the guard directed Ed, tapping him on the chest right on the prison numbers. *472…R…299G4*

Ed nodded and moved forward. It’d been nine months since he’d first stepped into the prison. Nine long months. Luckily, the prison guards had looked after him, giving him a little leeway and protecting him from danger. One attempt to shank him had already been made by some crazy guy who Ed never met, never said a word to, and never even saw before. The guy must’ve been out to kill a cop, Ed surmised. He came away unscathed, but the whole thing had scared the shit out of him. After that, paranoia had set in. Now, he was always aware of his surroundings, he routinely turned his head to glance at his flank and his backside, and he ate alone, at a table in the corner of the mess hall, seat facing outwards, always outwards. It was some fucking life, living in fear, with no friends, no freedom. Some fucking life.

This is to be my life…4…7…2R299G…4. The fact that he received a sentence of 25 years to life meant that he would likely never get out. Getting parole took jumping through hoops before the parole board, in addition to a shitload of luck. And it would be a long, long time before Ed even became eligible for review. No, he had already given up.

This is to be my life... It was only now starting to sink in, after nine months of waning denial. At first, he staunchly believed he would get out, that some mistake had been made, that they would find the right guy, that his lawyer had something up her sleeve to argue on appeal. Now he realized the truth of it. He sighed deeply. Suicide was not out of the question, he thought transiently.

He sat at number seven and clasped his hands before him, leaning forward toward the window to see down the hall on the other side. He saw nothing, so he sat back, fidgeting anxiously. This was only the second visit his mother had made. He supposed he couldn't have expected her to come every month in the condition she was in. She needed an aide to get down here, and it wasn't an easy trip. Hell, his mom probably had no idea what was going on no matter where she was, anyway. The first visit, he did most of the talking with Tracy, his mother's nurse at the home, who was nice enough to schlep mom down. Still, it was nice to talk to someone...and especially to a woman, even if Ed didn't find Tracy all that attractive. Too skinny for his liking.

I would take anything I could get in this shithole...any woman, that is. He chuckled at the thought, wondering if he was crazy. Though he supposed that he didn't really care.

Brow furrowed, he leaned in again. A wheelchair came into view. His mother sat almost lifeless, her eyes dull, her white hair severely thinned and stringy, her face blank. The only thing that had some life was the light blue blanket covering her legs. Even her shirt was a dull, lifeless tan. Ed sighed again. Her situation was worse than his, he judged. It was one thing to be locked in prison, it was an entirely different thing to be locked inside your own body.

Tracy was a welcomed sight. She wore her dirty blonde hair in a ponytail and sported a black coat over her pink scrubs. She was the only one that cared—really cared—for Ed's mother. The other nurses at the home, Ed recalled, had treated Ed's mother as just another patient, as just another part of the job. But not Tracy. Ed felt a deep gratitude. He was indebted to her. *As if I could do anything to repay that debt.* Still, it was how he felt.

Tracy smiled at him as she pushed his mother up to the window opposite Ed.

He returned her smile. It felt good. He couldn't recall the last time he smiled…even before he went to jail.

Tracy pulled up a chair next to his mother and angled it toward the wheelchair.

"Hey, Mom," Ed said.

His mother answered with a blank stare.

"Beth," Tracy said, her hand rubbing his mother's back, "Ed is here. Your son. Ed is here."

No recognition.

Tracy looked supportive.

Ed sighed and sat back. His mother hadn't spoken a word in two years. He almost wished she'd pass already. It would be a kindness at this point. He supposed he would have to make the best of this visit. "How are you, Tracy?"

She turned to him with a warm smile. "Oh, I'm fine." Her tone was bubbly, as usual.

"Any trouble getting her here this time?" he asked.

Tracy's ponytail flapped as she shook her head. "No," she said as a soothing dismissal. "You know it's no trouble."

"Any change in her condition?"

"No. She's still going strong." Tracy flashed a smile.

"Strong" was subject to debate, he thought. With little else to say, he sat back and examined his mother for a moment. There was nothing in there, he concluded despondently. He was truly alone. His eyes swelled with tears.

"I brought you something," Tracy said before reaching back behind the wheelchair.

Ed blinked incessantly to clear his eyes.

"I thought," Tracy continued, "that you'd want to see this." She pulled out a newspaper and flipped through a few pages, scanning each one quickly. "Ah. Here it is." She folded the paper and held it up to the window, article facing Ed.

Dericardo Estate Distributed To Sole Living Heir, the article was titled. Curious, he read the first two paragraphs. "Barry Higgins?" he asked, not immediately recognizing the name. Then he recalled that Chucky's cousin had testified at Chucky's trial so many years ago.

Tracy pulled down the paper. "Yeah," she answered with a hint of disbelief in her tone. "Can you believe it?"

Ed's mouth quirked. "What do you mean? You know him?"

She chuckled. "I knew him in high school."

"Oh yeah?" he said, his interest piqued. It occurred to him that Tracy was about the same age as Mary would've been.

Once her smile subsided, Tracy continued. "He was a weird guy. Like super, super smart." Her nose crinkled. "I think he went to M.I.T. or something. I heard he worked for NASA or like a government contractor." She shrugged.

Ed raised his eyebrows, his mind processing. Then something dawned on him. "Let me see that article again," he implored.

Tracy held it up.

He read, scanning the article as quickly as possible. *What the fuck?!* "Do you know if this guy knew my sister?" He pointed to the paper frantically, his heart racing.

"He must've," she stammered. "He was in high school with us."

Eyes wide, mouth gaping, Ed sat back in his chair.

"Are you done reading?" Tracy asked.

Ed barely heard her.

STEP 18: The Unintended Insurance Policy

Step 18.1

John and Barry left the restaurant and hopped into John's Mercedes. They exited the parking lot and turned down North Main Street. Both sat silently, gazes forward.

"Airport?" John asked once they were down the road, briefly turning his head.

Barry nodded. "Back to Florida…where it's warm. Away from this hell of a place."

"What's so bad about here, Barry?" John offered a smile reminiscent of the old days.

Barry tried hard to forget the old days. He shrugged listlessly, not caring to discuss such matters. After a moment, he asked, "How'd you know Chucky was going to get convicted? Seems to me like you were really defending him."

John laughed arrogantly. "I did too little to get a 'not guilty' verdict but just enough to make sure the conviction would not be overturned based on ineffective assistance of counsel. It's a delicate balance."

His friend had never lacked confidence or arrogance, Barry reflected, even in college.

They drove in silence for a few moments, nothing but the whistle of the wind for conversation as it rushed past the car.

"Let me ask you this," John said. He paused—probably to give emphasis. John was prone to such things. "How'd you conceive it? How'd you actually do it?"

Barry laughed under his breath. "That's two questions. What do they call that, Counselor? A compound question?"

"I'm serious," John retorted pryingly. "Don't you want to get it out, to tell someone?"

Barry cogitated, his thoughts turning solemn. As he gazed off into the passing woods, his memory flashed.

◆ ◆ ◆

"Do you want to pull them out or cut them off?" Barry asked Chucky, holding up the scissors in his hand. They stood crammed into the tiny, dated bathroom in Chucky's house. The linoleum floor was a faded, dirty mustard yellow, like the color of puke. The sinktop was an assortment of uneven ceramic tiles, a few of which were cracked. The grout was a grainy brown that flaked in a few spots. Barry and Chucky stood next to each other staring into the small, unframed mirror that was crookedly affixed to the wall.

"Don't you think my hair is already in there somewhere?" Chucky ran his hand through his blonde mane.

Barry sighed. "We have to make sure," he said sternly. The fact that Chucky's hair would've been in Mary's house at all galled Barry. He kept his anger inside. "Now, do you want me to cut it or pull it out?"

"Hmm," Chucky groaned. His mouth pursed in thought.

Barry was getting agitated.

"I guess cu -," Chucky began. "Ow!" he yelled as Barry yanked a few strands of hair out of his scalp, his head jerking. Chucky raised his hand and began rubbing his head. "What the fuck, man?"

"It's better this way," Barry said, holding the strands up. "It'll be more realistic. Like they just fell out." Now all he had to do was plant them in Mary's house.

Step complete, Barry thought.

...His memory shifted...

◆ ◆ ◆

He stood next to the beat-up kitchen table, wearing black spandex from head to toe, his wristwatch held up to his face. "Now," he said to Chucky.

Chucky picked up the phone and dialed, then hit the speaker-phone button. The ringing tone suddenly burst into the room. The other line picked up with a click.

"Hi, you've reached Barry," the voicemail said, the strange sound of Barry's own voice vibrating in his ears. Is that how he really sounded? "Please leave a message and I'll get back to you." A long beep followed.

Barry nodded to Chucky. "Hang up after 25 minutes. No longer." He removed his watch and placed it on the table before Chucky.

Step complete, Barry thought.

Placing the phone receiver on the table, Chucky acknowledged the instructions before displaying a befuddled expression. "Tell me again why it has to be seven years. Can't I just do two or three years?"

Not this again. Barry tried to mask his annoyance. It was fucking simple, but his cousin was an idiot. "Two or three years of imprisonment," he answered calmly, "will not be worth a lot of money." He picked up his duffle bag and moved to the front door. "It has to be a substantial amount of time or else we don't get paid. Cost-benefit analysis, my friend."

"Okay," Chucky said, sounding dejected. He belatedly added, "You won't hurt her too bad, will you? I mean, before you…"

With one hand on the door handle, Barry turned and regarded his cousin flatly. He rolled his eyes and left, deciding it was not worth a response. Besides, he *would* hurt her badly. It was what she deserved.

…His memory shifted…

He unscrewed the jar and dumped Mary's flesh into the formaldehyde. He screwed the lid back on tightly and put the jar aside. He knelt over Mary's body, the fucking slut, and trudged along, scrubbing her fingernails with a bristle pad. The bitch had scratched him just under the neckline. He thought about just cutting off her fingers, but he hadn't brought the proper tools for that—a saw, or a heavy butcher knife, or thick wire cutters. Besides, the acid would work just fine…and it was more fun this way. He liked the soft hiss of her fingers cooking.

Once satisfied with her fingernails, he meticulously checked the rest of her body for any inculpatory evidence, for any substance holding his genetic code. He went so far as to sweep the body with a blue light. He found nothing—not blood, not semen, not a strand of his dirty blonde hair. And yet why would he find hair, he thought gleefully. He'd shaved his body from head to toe, including his eyebrows. But just in case, he took a sponge and dipped it into the acid, then wiped all around the body. Only when he was certain that no one else would find anything, he slung the duffle bag over his shoulder, grabbed his bucket and jar, and slipped out the back door.

Step complete.

It took a good 20 minutes to get through the woods to the location were he had parked the used car he bought anonymously online. He threw the duffle and jar into the truck. With headlights off, he slowly drove down the old, dilapidated access road. When he reached the end, he stopped about ten feet from the paved road while still recessed in the trees, looking both ways to be absolutely positive that no cars were coming in either direction. He pulled onto the road and checked his rearview mirror. Finding only darkness in both directions, he flipped on his headlights, heading to the secluded location where he had buried his chest.

After a ten-minute drive, he pulled over and cut his lights. He checked the road again. It was clear. He hastily exited his car and grabbed the large shrub that he had previously positioned to conceal the old hunters' trail. He picked it up easily and moved it to the side. The hunters' trail was overgrown with forest, but he judged it drivable. He glanced left and right on the road again, hopped in his car and pulled onto the trail. He hopped out of his car and returned the shrub to its place at the trail's mouth. Driving slowly, he waited until he was about 200 feet from the road to turn on his headlights. Then he flipped on his high beams. He craned forward over the steering wheel to glance at the trees before him. Seeing nothing, he inched forward. The marking on the large tree to the left side of the road was where he anticipated it to be. To anyone else, it would've probably looked like an animal scratch.

He stopped the car.

From the trunk of his car he grabbed the jar, a flashlight, a compass, and a shovel, then walked into the woods, pointed 45 degrees west of his marking, counting his steps meticulously as he maintained his bearing. 300 paces later, he stopped and looked around, pointing the flashlight at the surrounding trees about 15 feet up their trunks. Last time, he'd brought a small ladder so he could make his mark high on the tree's trunk. At such a height, it couldn't be easily identified or noticed if a hiker or hunter happened to be passing by. After a few minutes, he found the mark on a tree due northeast. Thrilled, he moved to the back of the tree that bore his mark and started digging. It took mere minutes before he struck something hard. He dug to the sides, probing the ground for the edges of the chest he had buried here five months ago. When he had it cleared, he pulled the small key from his pocket, knelt, unlocked the chest, and lifted the lid.

He stood and pointed the flashlight down. The white plastic lining of the inside of the chest popped against the dark and shadowed forest floor. Inside rested a beat up brown box that contained a bunch of old porn magazines. Barry smiled, a guttural laugh escaping his lips. He placed the jar next to the box, closed the lid, and locked it. He piled the dirt back on top and padded it down. He threw some shrubs, twigs, and anything else in the area over the barren dirt. Reaching into his pocket, he tossed out some grass seeds. Hopefully they would take root and cover the area, making it look like natural cover. He needed to take all precautions in case a hunter or hiker happened by the area. He intended this chest to stay buried for a number of years.

Step complete.

...His memory shifted...

◆ ◆ ◆

"So it's 'I was angry about being dumped but it wasn't me'?" Chucky asked.

Thoroughly annoyed, Barry slapped his hands on his thighs, let out a huff, and began pacing with his back to Chucky. His cousin was a blundering idiot. *It will be a miracle if this works*. All it took was one wrong word from Chucky to fuck it up completely.

"No, Chucky," John Upton said calmly, a faint smile on his face. How John could be so calm at times like this was beyond Barry. Barry simply didn't have the patience for stupidity and incompetence. "There must be a pause. That is the critical part. 'I was angry about being dumped...*pause*...but I didn't kill her.' Got it?"

Chucky nodded. "Oh, okay. I get it. 'Was angry about being dumped...but I didn't kill 'er.'" Chucky smiled triumphantly, glancing back and forth between John and Barry.

Barry's brow eased back to a normal position, but he kept his arms crossed. He still had his worries about Chucky's ability to perform.

"That's right, Chucky," John said, patting Barry's cousin on the shoulder with his long arm.

"Again," Barry demanded. "You have to repeat it over and over until it's stuck in your head."

Chucky looked to John, who nodded his concurrence.

Step complete.

...His memory shifted...

He sat on the witness stand, maintaining a simpleton smile and dressed in the most ridiculous suit from the 1980s he could find at the thrift store in Port St. Lucie. It was actually the only one that had fit him.

"Did you speak to Chucky that day?" John asked him.

"I recollect that I did." He threw out a cheesy grin.

"What did you speak about?"

He sighed demonstrably. "Oh, I don't know. Chitchat. This and that. You know, the usual." Another cheesy smile.

"Do you recall what time that telephone conversation began?"

"Hmm. I'd say it was about 10 O'clock p.m. We usually speak to each other at night. It's just how our timing seems to work out. Maybe we're nocturnal. I don't know." He shrugged.

John smirked before asking, "And how long did that conversation last?"

Barry almost started laughing, but he managed to maintain his composure. *This is the only take I'm going to get.* "Maybe half-an-hour. I can't say for certain. Half-an-hour sounds good." Who knew, maybe he had an acting career in his future...

Step complete.

...His memory shifted...

Barry sat down and waited. After a few minutes, his cousin approached and sat down on the other side of the window. Chucky looked like he had aged very little in the past seven years. The orange jumpsuit and what it signified usually took its toll on a man. Yet Chucky looked fucking chipper.

"It took you long enough to come visit," Chucky said wryly.

Barry failed to see the humor. "You know the reason for that." Now he remembered why his cousin was such an asshole.

"So to what do I owe this pleasure?"

"It's time," Barry said matter-of-factly.

Chucky regarded him. "It's *about* time," he responded with a small hoot, his buck teeth protruding from his curved lips.

For once, something clever from his mouth. He's still an asshole, though. Without saying another word, Barry stood and left.

He returned to his hotel room and waited, flipping through the television channels aimlessly. Around midnight, he jumped into his car and headed to the spot. Hopefully, it remained unmolested. Anything could've happened in the past seven years. Weirder shit had been found buried in the middle of the woods, he was sure. He hadn't, however, seen anything on the news alluding to a strange find in the woods in Schenectady. Still, he was extra careful on the way, driving the speed limit and obeying all the traffic signs. Better safe than sorry.

It was well past 1:00 a.m. when he finally located the hunters' trail. From what he recalled, the bush looked as if it hadn't been moved. It was a good sign. On the trail, he located his markings easily and examined the spot where his chest was buried. The ground looked so homogenous that he wasn't exactly sure where to dig. It was reassuring and annoying at the same time.

It took an hour to unearth the chest. He unlocked it and pulled out the jar first. He examined it with the flashlight, turning it this way and that. The memory was still fresh. Mary's tit came off her body quite easily. Like cutting a perfectly cooked steak. Flesh was flesh, he concluded before smiling. *The bitch got what she deserved.* He pulled out the box next, paying it little heed, and returned to his car with one item under each arm. After placing both objects into the trunk, he returned to the chest and buried it once again, following the same procedure he had employed seven years ago. This time, it would stay buried for eternity. It had served its purpose.

An hour later, he was back on the paved road, heading in the direction of a neighborhood he had desperately long forgotten. No one should've lived such things, he thought, let alone a child. He didn't relish returning, but steeled himself enough to complete his task. He was, after all, righting a number of wrongs.

When he reached the neighborhood on the edge of Duanesburg—about a 30-minute drive—he slowly turned in. He took a left and drove past his old house, giving the small cottage little attention. It was the house next to his former home that he eyed keenly. The house was dark and a lone car sat in the driveway. *Good*, he thought. *He's home and asleep.*

He exited the neighborhood and pulled off onto a service road, glancing left and right to ensure his solitude. He stopped his car about fifty feet in and popped the truck. Pulling on his thin leather gloves, he checked his pocket to make sure the syringe was there. He picked up the box and jar and slowly made his way toward the back of the house. He stopped at the edge of the woods and placed the box and jar on the ground, propping them against a tree in a dark shadow. He pulled out a lock pick and crept to the back door of the house. Looking left and right, he slowly inserted the pick into the lock. It had taken him six months to train himself how to pick a lock in under 30 seconds. He was quick enough this time that he only glanced up at his surroundings once before the door was open and he was inside.

He placed the pick in his pocket and removed the syringe, leaving the door slightly ajar so he could exit easily. He stealthily made his way up the stairs, mindful of creaky floorboards. The first room was empty. He removed the cap from the syringe and held it ready before moving forward. The door to the other room was cracked. He stopped before it and simply listened, trying to filter out the sound of his heart beating. Hearing nothing, he placed his hand on the door and gently pushed it open, inch by inch.

He slipped in.

The old man was sound asleep on the bed, snoring lightly. Rays of moonlight cut the room into sections. Barry stood over the sleeping form, contemplating, his thoughts full of hate. He wanted to kill the man, he wanted to strangle him, to suffocate him…but he couldn't. It wasn't part of the plan. It didn't serve his purpose. *At least not yet…*

He stepped forward and plunged the syringe into the man's neck, administering the shot almost simultaneously. The man started for a split second, but fell unconscious just as quickly. Barry waited a full minute, watching the old man intently, before probing the limp body with a few hard shoves. Nothing, no reaction. He slapped the man hard. Nothing. *Good…and that felt good, too.*

As he moved back downstairs, he replaced the cap on the syringe and stuffed it into his pocket. He popped his head out the backdoor and glanced around furtively. Finding the coast clear, he moved to the treeline, retrieved the box and jar, and returned to the house.

He carried both items up the stairs, taking two steps at a time. Grabbing the old man's limp hand, he pressed it against the jar, making sure to get good contact with the fingertips. Then he pressed the man's fingers over a bunch of porn magazines from the box.

Back downstairs, he found the door to the basement and made his way carefully down the steep stairs. He surveyed the room. There was shelving on the right piled with crap, and more crap strewn about the floor, some piled up high in the corner.

He decided to place the jar on the shelf, making sure to rearrange the items so the jar was somewhat hidden. It would do no good for the old man to find the jar himself. Then, he placed the box in the back of the pile in the corner, stacking other boxes on top of it. Satisfied, he made his way out of the house and back to his car.

Step complete.

...His memory shifted...

He sat in his car, parked on the side of the road three houses down from his childhood home. He grabbed the prepaid cell phone he purchased at a convenience store in Florida about a year ago and dialed 9-1-1.

"What is the emergency?" the operator answered.

"I just saw a man dragging a small boy into a house." He weaved terror into his voice.

"You saw a man dragging a boy into a house?"

"Yeah," he stuttered, speaking quickly, "I was driving by, and I saw an older man dragging a boy into a house. I don't know, maybe it was a kidnapping or something. The boy was squirming."

"Do you know the address of the house, sir?"

"Uh, yeah, uh, let me look." He paused. "It's 103 Stein Street."

"You are by the house, sir?" the operator asked.

"Yeah, yeah," he said, trying to sound more frantic. "I slowed down because it caught my eye and looked suspicious. Then I stopped outside the house." He breathed heavily into the phone. "He might have seen me."

"I'll send a car over right away, sir," the operator said. "Can you give me your nam -"

"He's got a gun," Barry yelled, trying not to laugh. He threw the car in drive and slammed on the gas, peeling out. He hung up the phone abruptly before laughing raucously. *I really should give acting a go...*

Step complete.

...His memory shifted...

Today was the day, Barry decided. Ed Roletti was at the bar getting drunk. Today was definitely the day. Barry sat in his car in the bar's parking lot, staking out the place as if he was a cop trying to get the goods on a suspect. He laughed at the thought. *Role reversal, motherfucker...*

He waited, and waited, and waited.

Finally, at around 11 p.m., men—who he assumed were cops—started to filter out. It was only moments later that Ed exited, his arm wrapped around another cop. The man was almost dragging Mary's brother across the parking lot. *Good! He's shitfaced. Perfect!* Today was definitely the day!

The man plopped Ed into the passenger seat of a black Accord and moved to the driver's side. As the Accord backed up, Barry turned on his car. He tailed the Accord, making sure to maintain his distance so as not to look suspicious. Was this really what cops did? It seemed ridiculous.

He pulled over and turned the car off at the top of Ed's street. He squinted to compensate for the distance, watching as the cop pulled Ed out of the car and all but carried him into the house. *Good.*

Minutes later, the cop exited and left.

Barry turned on his car and drove past Ed's house. He stopped about 300 feet down the road, next to the woods, at the back of a row of cars that were parallel parked. He squeezed on his leather gloves, glanced around before exiting, and made his way to the back of Ed's house. He picked the lock and moved inside. Barry figured that he didn't need to be too quiet based on Ed's condition, yet he was still careful. He made his way upstairs and found Ed passed out on the bed, face down, limbs spread wide, both feet and one hand dangling off the bed. *Perfect.*

He stuck the syringe into Ed's neck and administered the shot. Ed barely even flinched. Barry snorted in amusement. He pulled the curtains closed, flipped on the lights, and rummaged through the closet. He found Ed's uniform and donned it. It was a little big, but it'd do. He rolled the pants up once at the waist and secured the belt tightly. *Now for the gun.*

Barry looked around the room, but found nothing. He pulled open drawers, but still nothing. Moving downstairs, he searched the kitchen and living room. Nothing. *Where does he keep his firearm?* He threw his hands on his hips in frustration. Moving back upstairs, he checked the bedroom again, looking in the bottom of the closet and under the bed. Nothing. He moved to the bathroom. There, hanging by a peg next to the shitter, was the firearm in its holster. Barry secured the holster belt around him, removed the gun and held it by the shaft. He took a hold of Ed's right hand and wrapped it around the gun, just to make sure his fingerprints were intact on the weapon. Once downstairs, he found the keys to the police cruiser in a bowl sitting on the table next to the front door. Hanging from a peg was Ed's police hat.

He grabbed the hat and pulled it down low on his head, obscuring his eyes and half his face. Exiting the house, he walked briskly to the cruiser, just in case anyone was outside or driving by. Once he was in the car, everything went smoothly.

He drove to Chucky's house and parked halfway up on the yard. He hit the siren, then shut if off just as quickly. *Good thing my cousin is such a heavy sleeper.* Opening the car door, he stumbled out, swaying like a drunk as he made his way to the front door. Next came one of the hard parts. He figured he might have to kick the door down or shoot it open, but he didn't want to wake Chucky. He grabbed the door handle softly. To his delight and shock, it was unlocked. *My cousin's a fucking idiot. In this day and age, who doesn't lock the front door?*

Although he has been locked up for the past seven years... Barry chuckled lightly.

He moved inside and to the back bedroom quietly. Chucky slept soundly in his bed. Barry stood over his cousin for a few seconds, breathing calmly. Then he withdrew the firearm and checked it to make sure the safety was off. He took a step closer to the bed and held the gun behind his leg to conceal it. "Chucky," he said.

His cousin didn't stir.

He raised his voice. "Chucky. Hey, Chucky."

Chucky rolled, his eyes slowly opening. He recoiled, letting out a whoop of fright.

"Chucky, it's me," Barry said, extending his right hand palm first. "It's Barry."

Chucky blinked. He clicked his tongue, clearly annoyed. "What the hell are you doing?" he asked, agitation in his tone. He looked over at the clock on his nightstand. "It's three in the morning." He examined Barry, a half befuddled and half petulant expression on his face. "What are you wearing?"

Barry smiled, but didn't answer.

"Barry," Chucky yelled in anger, "what are you doing?" He started to sit up.

"This," Barry said as he pointed the gun at his cousin's head and pulled the trigger.

Chucky's head fell back to the pillow, eyes wide and lifeless. Barry put three more bullets into his cousin's chest before holstering the weapon and hurrying out of the room.

He stopped at the front door for a split second and composed himself. Then he moved outside, careful to look like a drunk while still moving quickly. He needed to maintain the act, but it did him no good to get caught. He jumped into the cruiser, started it up, and leaned on the horn for good measure. He peeled out, heading straight for the electrical box. He turned at the last minute, clipping the box and damaging the car, but he was careful not to render the car undrivable. He headed back to Ed's house. Once inside, he took off the uniform and struggled to put it on Ed. A completely limp man was not an easy thing to move or lift, let alone dress.

Step complete.

Step 18.2

"Barry? Barry? You with me?" John asked.

"Huh?" Barry blinked.

"Are you going to answer me, or just stare blankly out of the car? I mean…obviously I know the parts I was involved in, but how'd you actually do it?" John's usual smile was gone.

Barry smirked. "Step by step," he whispered.

"What was that?"

"Nothing," he sighed.

John looked pensive. "All right," he relented, his smile restored, "so tell me this then: why? I mean, Mary I get. But your cousin…and the rest…"

The question sent Barry back to his childhood, provoking that portion of his mind he constantly fought to repress. His memory flashed.

◆ ◆ ◆

"Sit right there, Barry," Mama said, pointing to the bench. She held a tissue to her eyes as she sat.

He scrambled onto the bench and flipped his body to a sitting position. "Is Dada here?"

Mama made a noise, raising the tissue to her eyes again. "Yes, darling," she whispered.

Barry looked around but couldn't spot Dada anywhere.

"All rise," a man called out in the room.

Mama stood.

A moment later, she sat.

"Next case, please," a different man said.

"People of the State of New York versus Ralph Higgins," a woman called out.

Mama sighed.

"State your appearances."

"Franklin Dorey, Assistant District Attorney for the People."

"Eddie Smith for the Defendant."

"Mr. Higgins," one of those men said, "you are charged with criminal possession of a weapon in the second degree. Do you understand the charges against you?"

"Yes."

That voice was familiar. Smiling, Barry looked to Mama. "Dada."

Mama wept.

...His memory shifted...

◆ ◆ ◆

"Mama, Mama!" Barry whined, tugging at his mother's legs as she prepared supper. He wanted to go outside and play.

"What, Barry?" Mama responded, using her angry tone. "I'm making supper."

"Can I go play outside before supper?" He swiveled back and forth, waiting for an answer.

"Go ahead, Barry," Mama finally responded after huffing.

Barry whooped, jumping into the air before running toward the front door.

"Don't go too far," Mama yelled after him. "And be back within the hour."

Barry grabbed his baseball and glove and headed out to the front yard. He tossed the ball into the air and tried to catch it for a while, each time throwing the ball higher. He managed to catch it three times out of ten. Then he practiced pitching the ball, kicking his leg high like the professional baseball pitchers, and throwing the ball at the bushes in front of his house. He dreamed of being one of the great southpaws someday. He threw, retrieved the ball amongst the shrubs, ran back to his makeshift pitching mound—which was only a small bump in his front yard—and threw again. He repeated the process a number of times until the ball struck the trunk of a bush and ricocheted to the side, bouncing into the neighbor's yard. He ran over to get it.

"Hey there, Barry," his neighbor said, shooting out of his front door and bending down to pick up the ball at his feet.

Barry slowed to a stop before his neighbor, holding out his glove.

The man spun the ball in his hands, looking around the neighborhood. Then he smiled and bent down, resting his hands on his knees, the ball still held in one hand. "Barry. I have some candy I just bought. Would you like some?"

Barry hesitated. "Mama said I shouldn't each sweets before supper because I'd ruin my appetite."

His neighbor looked around again. He smiled wider. “What time is supper?”

“Six.” Barry started swiveling, wondering when the man would return his baseball.

His neighbor looked at his watch, then licked his lips. “Well, if you have some candy now, just a little, it won’t ruin your appetite. What do you say?”

Barry shrugged before nodding. He supposed a piece wouldn’t ruin his appetite and Mama wouldn’t notice.

“Great!” his neighbor said, moving to put his hand on Barry’s back. He dropped the ball into Barry’s glove. “Let’s go inside and get the candy.” He led Barry to the front door, glancing over both shoulders along the way. Once inside, he said, “I’ll tell you what, Barry. Let’s play a little game and the prize will be the candy.” He shut the front door and bolted the lock.

...His memory shifted...

Barry sat on a chair in a small room, swinging his feet, prancing his G.I. Joe across his lap. A few more years and his feet would touch the ground, he thought. Then he would be bigger, and maybe kids wouldn’t pick on him because of his size. His stomach growled. He was starting to get hungry.

A police officer entered the room, followed by a woman. The officer was tall, with cropped coal-colored hair, a nose with bulbous nostrils, and big eyes. The metal things attached to his belt—handcuffs, keys, a few other things—clanged together when he walked. The woman, by contrast, was short and round, with a waist twice the size of her shoulders and gray trousers pulled up high. She held a clipboard to her chest.

The officer knelt beside Barry on one knee, arched his back, and placed his forearm on his thigh. In that position, he was still taller than Barry. Barry slowed the swing of his feet and held them still.

The officer spoke in a deep voice. “Barry...there’s been an accident.”

Barry cocked his head, not sure what the officer was getting at.

The officer’s mouth twitched. “Barry, there was a car accident. A terrible car accident. And, and...your Mother, Barry, she was hurt real bad." He placed his massive hand on Barry's shoulder, squeezing gently.

"Mama?" Barry asked, worried. He started to tear. "Mama," he called out, looking past the officer. "Where's Mama?"

The round woman met his gaze. She sighed deeply, her shoulders rising with the effort, her belly jiggling.

"Barry," the officer said, "your Mama is dead."

The G.I. Joe struck the floor. Barry bawled. "Mama," he moaned, rocking in his chair. "Mama." He bawled some more. What would he do now? Who would take care of him? Where would he live? Who would love him? His Mama was gone. He cried as he thought about these things, but no answers came to him.

"I'm sorry, Barry," the officer said in a whisper, looking at the floor.

After a long time, Barry started to catch his breath, his tears finally relenting, his throat raw. He sniffled a few times, then ran his arm across his eyes and face.

The officer glanced up at the round woman and nodded. "I'm sorry, Barry," he said again, rising to his feet and removing his hand from Barry's shoulder. He moved around the woman and left the room, head downcast.

The woman stepped before Barry, bent down, and began rubbing his back—it was almost the way Mama rubbed his back when he wasn't feeling good. Almost. "Hi, Barry," she said, her voice smooth and soothing. "My name is Charlene, and I'm a social worker with Children's Services. I've spoken to your uncle. He's agreed to take you in. You'll be moving in with him in Schenectady. We should go gather your things."

Barry stood and sniffled. His head drooped as the woman guided him out. He'd only met his uncle once.

...His memory shifted...

◆ ◆ ◆

His things had been placed upstairs in Chucky's room, and Charlene had left. He tried to unpack his clothes, but he was only given one drawer and his clothes wouldn't fit. He gave up and went downstairs. In the small living room, Chucky's father—Barry's uncle—lounged in a reclining chair in dirty jeans and a wifebeater, drinking a beer and watching a Yankee's game on the small television in the corner of the room. He didn't even glance at Barry.

Chucky was sitting on the floor, cross-legged, hands under his chin, watching the game silently. He was almost a statue. Barry sat down next to Chucky and crossed his legs in a similar position. They watched the game in that fashion for a few moments.

The silence was unnerving.

Barry loved watching baseball, but now he could barely focus on the game. All he thought about was his mother. Barry's home had never been silent. Mama was always chattering, even when she was just speaking to herself. It had annoyed Barry sometimes, especially when he was watching baseball, but now he really missed it. The silence didn't feel right. His eyes started to water. *Oh, Mama...*

His uncle belched loudly. Barry turned around as his uncle crushed the beer can in his hand and tossed it casually on the lamp stand beside him before placing his hands behind his head. Barry returned to the baseball game, but not before glancing at Chucky. His cousin still hadn't moved.

"You're not my blood," his uncle said behind him, the words filled with disdain.

Barry twisted his body. His uncle was staring straight at him with glossy eyes.

"You ain't my blood," his uncle said to him.

Barry blinked, not knowing how to respond or if his uncle wanted him to. He saw Chucky out of the corner of his eye. His cousin still hadn't moved, but Chucky's muscles drew taut.

"You know that, right?" his uncle asked, raising his head from the recliner. "You ain't my blood. My dead wife and your mother were sisters. You know that, right?"

Barry nodded hesitantly.

His uncle's head dropped back to the chair.

Barry turned around and returned his focus to the television, not sure what was going on. The Yankee's batter didn't reach base, and the inning ended. Barry sighed.

"I never liked your mother," Barry's uncle said, his voice still heavy with scorn.

Barry turned again, but jerked when Chucky abruptly got up and moved swiftly upstairs. Watching Chucky dash out of the room, Barry became frightened.

"You ain't my blood, so I ain't gonna treat you like it. You understand?" His uncle peered down at him.

Barry nodded slowly, not sure what his uncle meant.

"You're gonna do what I say, or you get the belt. You're gonna work here. I ain't your Daddy. You're gonna work. Give me any trouble, and I'll lock you up in the basement in a dog cage. Understand?"

With wide eyes, Barry nodded, his jaw quivering, eyes beginning to water.

His uncle nodded once before dropping his head again to the recliner. "Now go get me a fucking beer, and when you're done, get started on the dishes in the sink. Those dishes better be spotless clean, you hear." His uncle's gaze returned to the baseball game.

Terrified, his eyes bleary, Barry rose to comply.

...His memory shifted...

He dropped his backpack in the corner and headed straight for the fridge. Finding very little inside, Barry grabbed a few pieces of bread and the peanut butter. He slathered the bread and began shoving the sandwich into his mouth, watching the wall clock closely. It was a miracle the old clock still worked. Barry hoped it was accurate. Otherwise, it could spell trouble. Still, even if it was accurate, his uncle would be coming home soon, and Barry had to eat as much as possible before that happened. Chances were he wouldn't get to eat dinner. Oh, he'd be cooking it, and he could probably sneak in a few bites here and there, but his uncle wouldn't let him have a proper dinner. Chucky got one, but not Barry. His uncle said it was because they didn't want to waste food and money on someone that shouldn't have been living there in the first place. Barry ate the last bite of his sandwich and filled a glass with water from the sink faucet. He chugged it, then looked to the clock. He had time for one more sandwich, he judged, which he hastily made. Halfway through it, he heard the front door open, followed by a deep grumble and the stomp of heavy boots. Barry knew what that meant, and his eyes widened in fear, his mouth still stuffed. He shoved the bread and peanut butter jar back into the fridge and tippy-toed through the small dining room to evade his uncle who usually went through the living room to get to the fridge for a beer. Last time Barry was caught eating like this, his uncle gave him ten whips of the belt—from the end with the buckle. Barry hadn't walked right for two weeks after that.

He glanced around the corner as his uncle stomped the other direction. Waiting a few seconds, he sprinted for the stairs.

"Forgot my -" his uncle said, turning back to the entryway, his hands on his shirt pockets. "Hey!" he yelled.

Barry froze three steps up the stairs.

"What the hell are you doing?" his uncle asked angrily.

With his back to his uncle, Barry chewed as fast as he could, managing to swallow the bite in his mouth. But he still held half a sandwich in his hand.

"Get down here!" his uncle yelled.

His head down, Barry turned slowly, trying his best to conceal the sandwich. He held it at his side and shifted it to his back as he turned, then plodded down the steps. He thought about dropping the sandwich, but that would've been too obvious. When he reached the bottom, he looked up into his uncle's angry eyes.

"What do you got?" his uncle asked deviously. His tone indicated that he probably wanted to find something, that he was eager to punish Barry. His eye twinkled below the arrow of his brow.

Barry gulped, but otherwise didn't move.

His uncle stepped forward and roughly grabbed at Barry's arms, pulling both forward, palms up. His jaw visible tightened as he eyed the sandwich scrunched in Barry's fist. He looked into Barry's eyes once, holding the gaze for a split second before ripping the sandwich from Barry's hands. "You little shit! What did I tell you?!"

Although he had just started high school—a man for all intents and purposes—Barry began to whimper like a child, knowing what was coming.

His uncle crushed the sandwich in his hand and threw it on the floor, his face a mask of fury. Next came his belt, which made a soft flapping sound as it was pulled free of the pant loops. The fire in his uncle's eyes intensified.

Barry cried harder.

Once the whipping was done, Barry hobbled to his backpack, sniffling the entire way, grabbed it and slowly headed upstairs, step by painful step. He ignored Chucky and tenderly sat on his bed, wincing at the pain. Probably sensing the mood, Chucky left the room.

Barry had had enough. Something had to be done. In the past seven years, the memory of the love that his mother had given him had slowly faded, becoming distant, intangible, and the home that he knew had been a loving and warm one was now only a hazy image in his head, undefined and unfocused. It was something he grasped at, that former love and warmth, but was simply unable to reach.

"Barry," his uncle yelled from downstairs, "get your ass down here and bring me a fucking beer."

Oh yes, Barry decided, something had to be done…and today he was going to do it. He reached into a pocket of his backpack and removed the liquid dropper. Stealing the dropper from his chemistry class was easy. Getting the liquid it now contained was much more difficult. It took him a number of weeks researching on the internet at the school library what liquid he needed and in what proportions, and more than double that time to actually acquire each element he needed to mix. Those hours he wasn't home earned him the belt from his uncle…but it was worth it.

He concealed the dropper up his sleeve and headed downstairs, hobbling down the steps from the pain of his fresh whipping. His face, however, was a cool mask. He entered the living room to find his uncle in the usual spot and Chucky lying on the floor. Chucky had not been asked to get a beer, despite that he was a mere steps from the kitchen. Chucky never was asked. But no matter, that was all about to end.

"Hurry up," his uncle chastised him. "I'm thirsty."

Barry didn't even acknowledge his uncle. He moved to the kitchen, grabbed a beer from the fridge and popped the tab open. He glanced over his shoulder. As usual, his uncle's gaze was fixed on the television. Barry squeezed the dropper, releasing the liquid into the beer. He concealed the dropper back up his sleeve and took the beer to his uncle. He stood intently as his uncle took a sip and sighed.

His uncle noticed him. "Get the fuck out of here."

Barry turned immediately and headed back upstairs. He was no idiot. He knew the consequences. This meant foster care for him and Chucky. But anything was better than his uncle. Besides, 18 and adulthood wasn't too far off. Now he had to dispose of the dropper so no one would ever find it.

…His memory shifted…

◆ ◆ ◆

This class was ridiculously boring, he thought for the third time in the last 15 minutes. Derivatives, convergences, series, absolutes, exponentials, quotients, harmonics. Calculus was so rudimentary that Barry had taught it to himself at age 11. He mostly sat through the class twiddling his thumbs. Sometimes he thought about physics and mechanical engineering, trying to solve problems in his head, but today he was tired, so he sat with his head in his hands, simply trying to stay awake. He would ace the final exam and the class, but if Mr. Hatman caught him sleeping in class, it could affect his grade.

That, Barry couldn't permit.

As Mr. Hatman was rambling about differential quotients—a concept that was beyond half of the class—Barry slowly ripped off a small piece of paper from his notebook, taking precautions not to rip it too loudly. He picked up his pencil and placed it on the paper, about to write. Yet he couldn't move. Fear gripped him. Was he really about to do this?! It wasn't the first time he'd asked himself such a question. Hell, it wasn't the first time this week he'd asked himself such a question.

He glanced over his shoulder furtively, eyeing her out of the corner of his eye while pretending to look out the window.

She sat at her desk, chewing gum, twirling a lock of her molasses hair with a finger that sported a long nail colored cherry red. She was utterly ravishing—the airiness of her skin, the slope of her nose, the deep tint of her eyes, the vibrant hue of her lips, the brightness of her perfect teeth, the shine of her hair. And that was only her head. The mere glimpse of her started to harden Barry's cock. He wanted to turn farther and get a look at her tits, but he knew it would be too overt a move. He settled for picturing them in his mind, recalling the look of them he got when he first entered the classroom.

That settled it.

He began to write. It was a typical high school love letter…or what he expected a typical love letter to be. He read it five times, sighing after each one to slow the beat of his chest. Should he rip it up, like he'd done many times in the past, or should he fold it up and pass it along?

He pondered the decision for a few minutes while Mr. Hatman tried to pry out of dumbass Martin an answer to the problem on the board.

Fuck it! He pushed his glasses up his nose, signed his name at the bottom of the note, folded it in half, and wrote *MARY* on the front. He tucked it into his hand and waited for Mr. Hatman to turn to the chalkboard.

When his moment came, he tapped Beth—sitting next to him, two chairs in front of Mary—on the shoulder and displayed the note, motioning with his head for Beth to take it. She looked to Mr. Hatman with lips thinned, then reluctantly grabbed the note from Barry's hand.

Mr. Hatman turned around, causing both Barry and Beth to straighten. When he returned his attention to the board, Beth looked down at the note. Barry gestured with a finger to Mary. Getting the point, Beth passed the note to Jay behind her.

Jay looked at it for a long time, the name on the front not seeming to register. Barry hoped to God that Jay didn't open it and start reading. Glancing at Mr. Hatman, Barry hissed at Jay, motioning for him to pass it back to Mary behind him. Finally, Jay nodded and passed it back.

There. It was in Mary's hands. One way or the other, it was done, out in the open. Barry couldn't bear to look, so he faced forward, pretending to focus on the lecture. His mind raced. How would she react? Was it a mistake?

Before he knew it, the bell rang. Unsure what to do, he ran from the room and headed to the cafeteria for lunch. He sat with Chucky as he ate his peanut butter and jelly sandwich, trying to ignore what he just did. Maybe Mary threw the note away. Maybe she was coming to the cafeteria right now to find him and confess her own love.

He hoped.

Toward the end of the lunch period, a ruckus developed at the other side of the cafeteria, and students began racing out of the room. Barry and Chucky gave each other confused looks, but ultimately decided to follow. They followed the press of bodies to the courtyard, where students were huddled around the corkboard. Barry's brow creased.

When he approached, faces turned to regard him; only a few at first, then in a torrent. Shortly, everyone was looking at him, laughing, pointing. His eyes widened and his face turned beet red. He didn't even need to see his love note posted on the corkboard to know that it was there, displayed for all to see, for all to read. His eyes lost focus.

"She dates bad boys, not dorks," a female voice yelled at Barry from the side. The crowd erupted with laughter. Barry looked to the speaker. One of Mary's friends.

"And older guys, too," another girl yelled.

The crowd—which by now seemed like the whole school—laughed harder.

Humiliated, he turned and ran, pressing hard through the crowd before the tears started to stream down his face.

It was far worse a feeling than any beating his uncle had ever given him.

...His memory shifted...

The phone was ringing. Barry dropped his backpack, shoved his hand in his pocket and yanked out his keys. Three rings. He hastily shoved the key in the lock and twisted. Four rings. Throwing the door open, he lunged for the phone. It could've been Amy returning his call. It was the first girl he had attempted to flirt with in a long time, and although he slipped her his phone number unprompted, he thought she liked him. "Hello," he said, breathing hard.

"What's up, Bro?" Chucky said.

Barry huffed. "Hey," he responded disappointedly.

"What's new in Boston?"

The door to his dorm room was propped open by his backpack. He picked up the phone base and inched toward the door. Preoccupied, he said, "Not Boston." He reached down and took hold of the backpack with his fingertips, pulling it inside. The door swung shut with a heavy bang. "It's Cambridge. M.I.T. is in Cambridge, just like Harvard." He was getting tired of explaining it to Chucky. He was graduating in two months, meaning this same conversation had been going on for almost three years. Sometimes, he thought Chucky did it just to provoke him.

"Whatever. It ain't New York."

It sure as hell isn't Schenectady. Slightly agitated—both at Chucky's sheer stupidity and at the fact that Amy hadn't called—

he barked, "What do you want? I'm busy. I have finals coming up." His scholarship didn't pay for itself, he thought. Well, he corrected, it actually did. He just had to maintain his grades, which was easy enough.

The tone didn't seem to register with Chucky. "Just calling to see what's going on, is all."

Immediately regretting his outburst, Barry softened his tone. "Not much, really. Same old stuff."

There was a brief pause. "Well, I got something to tell you."

Barry began removing his books from his backpack. "What?"

"Remember that girl Mary from high school?"

Barry froze, his hand shoved inside his backpack. His eyes widened, the flood of emotions from that dreadful day returning. The ridicule he received over the next two years reanimated in his mind, the pain seemingly fresh. He swayed on his feet, his skin flushed. "Yeah," he finally managed to croak. *How could Chucky possibly think I wouldn't remember her!* Was the question deliberate, he wondered.

"Well, I just started dating her," Chucky said.

Barry dropped into the chair at his desk. His head was spinning. How could this be possible?! How could Mary be dating Chucky, of all people?! What did she see in him?! In the back of his mind, a disturbing thought occurred to him. Mary was doing it out of spite. She was doing it to fuck with Barry's head. She knew Chucky was his cousin. She knew they were close. It wasn't over, this whole ordeal. Mary wasn't done with him, wasn't done tormenting him.

And Chucky! He must have known that Mary was just dating him to fuck with Barry, but Chucky still dated her. His own fucking cousin betrayed him for a piece of pussy.

Something internally snapped, a tether loosened and popped.

"Barry?" Chucky asked.

He dropped the phone, his eyes staring intently at the veneer backing of his standard-issue dormitory desk, his pupils vacillating rapidly as his mind began to calculate, to plan step after step.

He didn't move for hours.

Step 18.3

"Hey, what is with you today?" John asked, exiting the highway for the airport.

Barry blinked hard and gave his head a shake before regarding John.

"So you're not going to tell me why either?" John asked, sounding astonished at the slight. His smile was even more restrained.

Barry placed his elbow on the car door and propped his head on his hand. "What do you care, anyway?" he asked. "You got your contingency fee…Two contingency fees, actually," he added a little more heatedly.

John raised his eyebrows. "Just curious, is all. Wondering what it took to set you off."

Barry eyed his friend, now slightly apprehensive. "Just remember…I go down, you go down," he commented coldly.

John's laugh was shallow. "No need for threats, Barry. I know the consequences as well as anyone." He glanced at Barry for a second before returning his gaze to the road. "But while we're on the subject…" He paused.

Now it was Barry's turn to eye his college friend.

"Should I happen to wind up like your cousin, or Mr. Timmone, or Mary…well, should that happened, word will get to the authorities fairly quickly about all of this." John glanced out the driver's side window. "It's been arranged."

Barry was silent for a moment. "So, is that a threat?" he asked, somewhat amused.

"I'm just saying," John responded with a shrug. "With you tying up loose ends and all. I have to ensure I'm not one of the ends being tied up, you see." He flourished a hand in the air. "An insurance policy, if you will."

Barry turned to look forward again. "Not a bad idea," he commented genuinely. "But unnecessary. You never did me wrong. You were my friend."

"And still am."

"And still am," Barry repeated, nodding his head once.

They drove in silence for a few minutes.

John's laugh, which was infused with wonder, brought Barry's head around. "Boy, I'd not like to be your enemy," he commented earnestly.

Barry was silent for a long moment. "Ain't none left," he muttered.

ACKNOWLEDGEMENTS

I'd like to thank the following people who performed autopsies on this book:

Ross Dymond

Bobbi Dymond

Jisha Dymond

Hilary Kamins

Your autopsy results revealed much that made this book a better one.

I'd also like to thank the composite artist, Darcie Saleh, who helped me apprehend *you*, the reader, with a book cover that was so spot on, you walked into my literary custody without even knowing it.

And, of course, I'd like to thank the team at Chunky Pops Publishing.

www.ingramcontent.com/pod-product-compliance
Lightning Source LLC
Chambersburg PA
CBHW021621030826
48979CB00035B/1266/J
* 9 7 8 0 9 9 6 9 6 7 7 2 3 *